BLACK MARKS

PETE ALDIN

Cover art by Chuck Regan

Edited by Jason Nahrung

CHAPTER ONE

It coils, cramped within this man It hates, the man It wears like skin, like camouflage … like shackles.

So long. So long since It ran free. So long since It fed.

Somewhere far above, the song is building, gaining strength, calling. And through the man's senses, It glimpses the singer, Its pale skybound lover, and burns to rise toward it and run together in the night. The singer grows larger, grows nearer, grows stronger, and in the days and nights ahead, the song will gain the power to pull It from the confines of this man, this puny thing.

And It will be happy.

Unless the man uses the powder.

It coils and shifts and strains for a way out. The man cannot keep It down every month. He has failed before. He will fail again. There will be a time, one of these months. There will be a night…

The skinny buyer was taking too long. Jake chewed a nail, blinked away sweat and wished she'd get her goddamn business over with so he could do the same.

The market roof where he was hiding was saw-toothed, a series of wood-and-steel waves headed south. Jake lay pressed into the strip of shade along the base of one wave, tracking the conversation in the service alley below, picturing the movements of the players. The woman, scratching at bare arms, gabbling about the hot day and the pressures of life and how much she needed the dope and what she could offer in exchange for a discount. The dealer, chuckling as he ran through a list of perversions and the woman gave him her yes and her no and her maybe. Her begging turned Jake's stomach, but she wasn't bad and neither was she a victim; she was just a woman doing what she could to get through the days, get through the nights.

prey, the Animal rumbled in the back of his head and Jake dug his fingers into his thighs to move his thoughts on. But he grudgingly agreed: the woman was an easy mark for predators of all sorts.

This time of the month, he could hear everything she said, crystal clear even at this distance and even though she was mumbling. He could smell her too, her and the dealer.

And she was taking too damned long.

Five minutes she'd been down there now, arriving right when Jake had been bracing to jump the dealer. He'd never heard any of Zee's crew's names. This one he thought of as Jarhead because of the guy's crewcut and the AK47 tattoos on his forearms. Last time Jake had seen him - exactly one month ago - Jarhead had threatened to cut Jake's balls off if he showed up without money again: "Strictly business, you unnerstand?"

Jake understood all right. He also understood he didn't want the seething, churning *thing* inside him to erupt in a few nights' time. The Animal had done enough damage. And there was only way to keep it subdued.

Strictly business, you unnerstand? he told It.

This area north of Fisher Freeway was always quiet; the market itself looked and smelled like it went bust years ago, a husk of its former self. A mile or so in the distance, he could make out one of Comerica Park's lighting towers. He'd been over there earlier, the area alive with cars and foot traffic, people on their way to the baseball game. The couple hours he'd spent asking for work at food vans and merchandise stalls and makeshift parking lots had been wasted time: no one was hiring smelly white trash with dreadlocks to serve clean, well-dressed families. Nice people. Normal people. If he wanted money and H in time for the Big Moon, this was the way he was getting it.

A shift in the odors rising from the alley below, a shift in conversation from words to grunts, and it didn't take Jake's enhanced senses to figure out the pair had reached an agreement on her discount.

He squinted into the white-hot clouds above him, let the sounds wash over him and chewed over the actions he was planning here. Robbery. Assault. These were crimes; these were *sins*.

"No choice, Momma," he whispered to the sky. "Worse if I don't do it."

He thought of what she'd once said. *Don't you turn out like your papa, y'hear? Just you don't.* At that time, he couldn't imagine how he would, how he could. *Don't you turn out like your papa ...* He'd been in the bath, he remembered that clearly - a small boy with nothing on his mind but the cool water and the faucet's gentle music and how good it felt to have his momma right there with him, right there making everything safe, making the world a good place—

It was quiet below. He turned over onto hands and knees. Senses straining, he picked her up, the skinny buyer - a scratch of hurried footsteps out the south end of the alley as she made off with her purchase. He heard little else, nothing but traffic noise from the freeway and a huff of breath from Jarhead.

Jake swung himself over the side and dropped fifteen feet to land in a crouch behind the dealer. Jarhead swung toward him, mouth open, hand on his zipper.

"Strictly business," Jake said and punched him in the jaw.

Jarhead's knees sagged as he spun with the impact. A couple of bills fluttered away on the warm summer wind. For a half-second Jake considered going after them, but that would leave Jarhead free to recover. Jake caught him by the back of his muscle shirt, kept him upright. Arm around the shorter man's throat, he put enough pressure on the windpipe to prevent him crying out and murmured, "One word, you go down for good." The asshole's buddy was still out there in the parking lot.

He shoved Jarhead against a battered dumpster, nose wrinkling at the stark odors of ancient garbage and fresh cat piss.

"You f—" Jarhead managed before Jake tightened his grip, long enough for the air to stick in Jarhead's throat.

He eased off the pressure and the dealer coughed. Jake murmured, "Warnin ya."

He used his free hand to pull at the lump of steel in the back of the dealer's jeans. A glance revealed a snub-nosed .357. He pressed Jarhead's cheek a little harder against the dumpster, drawing a gasp, then risked a peek around it at the lone car in the weed-peppered lot on the far side of the market. The Camaro had its hood raised, a dealer's ploy in hopes that nosy cops would think the owners cooling it off, getting water for the radiator. He pressed the gun behind Jarhead's right ear and let go of his throat, felt the guy's pockets front and back. Nothing. Shit. He'd timed it wrong, should've stepped in before the woman took her package, but he hadn't wanted to scare her. It wasn't right to do that. He glanced back: perhaps he could catch her, find some way to pay her for half…

He snorted, watching as the bills blew down the alley toward the parking lot. Pay? That was a joke. That was the whole reason he was doing it this way.

"Where's your blow?" he growled. It had taken a couple of months to get used to Detroit people calling heroin that. Down south, blow was coke.

Jarhead hissed a laugh, raising a cautious hand to feel his jaw. "Dunno what you're talking about, officer."

The little foils of heroin Jake needed would be buried nearby or tucked in hidey-holes. He shook the dealer hard. "Get me some."

"Not doing it," Jarhead said, voice warped by a jaw that wouldn't work properly.

Anger flashed through Jake. And beneath it, the craving, an itch along his soul. Within him, *It* whispered,

kill. feed. let me.

Jake looked up at the thing he hated most in life: the moon, out in the daytime and mocking him, a fingernail clipping low in the afternoon sky. A few more nights and it'd be too strong for him. A few more nights and it'd turn him inside out, unless he got what he wanted here. He passed his free hand across his sweaty brow and wiped it on his pants. There had to be a way to get this prick to—

"'Sup?" someone called from the other end of the alley.

Jake sneaked a look and immediately cursed himself for the mistake. He jerked his head back, but one glimpse had been enough. And enough for the other guy, the fat dealer he called Piggy. In that split second of locking eyes, understanding had passed. Piggy had already been reaching for his gun before Jake withdrew.

"Shit."

Jarhead tensed, bracing himself against the dumpster, ready to strike. Jake felt it coming, stepped back and kidney-punched the guy as hard as he could. Jarhead gasped, then slid onto all fours. Jake stepped back. A gunshot. A bullet clanged off metal. Jarhead, moaning, shuffled into the meeting of dumpster and wall and made himself smaller.

"Let him go!" Piggy fired again.

Jake took the pistol in his left hand, fired blind around the dumpster, grimacing at the kick. Commotion told him Piggy was either hit or getting his fat ass down on the ground.

He shifted the gun toward Jarhead. "A gee. All I want. Where is it?"

One hand rubbing his back, Jarhead used his free one to flip Jake the bird good and slow. A bullet chipped brick above them. Jarhead shouted at Piggy that he was there too.

Jake sidled closer. Jarhead pressed harder against the wall, one hand up to defend himself though murder darkened his eyes.

"Where is it?" Jake repeated.

"Never find it before he gets you. I was you, I'd run. I'd run far away from here. *Jake*. Oh, yeah, I remember you, bitch. I know you. Believe it, you better run far."

Jake roared in frustration, fired two rounds into the air: he'd been so damn *close*. He ran, head down, keeping the dumpster between him and Piggy.

"You're dead, Jake!" Jarhead yelled. "Dead!"

Piggy fired again. Jake didn't hear where the bullet went. A couple seconds later, he was around the corner and *moving* fast. Ten more seconds and he was off the market property and neither dealer was going to catch him. The junkie was nowhere in sight.

He forced the gun into his waistband, the barrel hot against his belly. He tugged his shirt over the top, and kept on sprinting toward where he'd hidden his backpack. The moon kept pace with him.

He had no dope to suppress the Animal already scratching to be freed, and no money to buy more. What was he going to do? What the hell was he going to do this far up shit creek?

Not so deep within him, he felt Its pleasure.

CHAPTER TWO

One look at the four-year-old's body and Gwen's heart contracted as if squeezed by a fist. The child's breath rattled. Spasms wracked his shattered arms. The man in the bed on the other side of the curtain coughed wetly and groaned, while four nurses rushed about like ants from a kicked-over nest attending to both.

Lucky me, Gwen thought and swept her hair back into a scrunchy. She slowed her breathing. Two crisis cases coming in at once wouldn't normally be a problem, but Emergency were short-staffed today. Her supervisor Pam was handling two concurrent code blues at the other end of the ER. The new intern, Dennis or Danny or something, had gone out into the waiting area where an elderly patient needed assessment.

This little boy and his attacker were all hers.

"Dammit," she whispered as she leaned over the child.

Little kids always looked so thin and helpless. This boy was worse than most, his skin pale, muscle tone limp and skinny little arms clouding with contusions. Blood from a head wound had smeared across his swollen face and bare chest. His nose and mouth were hidden beneath a breathing mask and a nurse squeezed the bag, counting off twenty-five breaths a minute.

"Intubating," an older nurse - Gabby - announced while Gwen shuffled around the trolley to tease the dressing from the side of the boy's head. A shallow depression and laceration ran along the skull above the ear; blood welled to obscure it. She turned to bark an order, but a second nurse, Jan, had anticipated it, leaning past her with sterile gauze soaked in saline to replace the soiled one.

Though the two patients had arrived in separate ambulances, a single paramedic lingered at the edge of the curtained cubicles, reeling off the same facts that would no doubt make their way onto tonight's Channel 7 news: "...kid intervened in a domestic violence situation between mother and step-father. Intra-cranial trauma, possibly TBI, multiple fractures to arms and ribs. Step-father's a biker. Took to the boy with a chain." One ambulance had phoned ahead, so she'd been expecting the last detail; still, she winced at the sight of it.

Beside her, the nurses babbled vital sign figures in support of the paramedic's bleak narrative: BP, O2 levels, heart rates. None of them encouraging for either patient.

"Child is Willie Anderson, four years of age," the paramedic continued. "Step-dad's Michael Ormond, mid-thirties. Mother stabbed Ormond in the chest with a screwdriver before calling 911. Mom's with the cops currently."

Gabby sidled out of Gwen's way as she moved from Curtain 4 to Curtain 5, from the child to the man who'd beaten him to within an inch of his precious little life. Like Willie, Ormond had been stripped to the waist. His muscular chest, shoulders and arms sported a catalog of tattoos, smeared with blood. The screwdriver's handle jutted from the pressure bandages holding it in place. Ormond was looking wildly about and one hand kept darting up to push at a nurse.

"Restrain his hands," Gwen snapped. She checked the catheter inserted by the paramedics to relieve pressure from fluid building up around the lung.

The paramedic's narrative continued while helping strap Ormond's wrists to the bed. "His vitals improved a little when we put the catheter in to relieve the tension pneumothorax - much to the displeasure of the badges who followed us in," he added with a glance over his shoulder.

She noticed the uniform then, lingering across the walkway, keeping an eye on proceedings. She'd seen this same cop a few times around the hospital, hitting on nurses - a man with Eddie Murphy's looks but without the charm. His nametag said *Holland* but she'd always thought of him as Officer Creep. He caught her eye and called, "Leave this piece of shit, Doc. See to the kid."

As if she could make that choice.

She stuck a stethoscope to Ormond's chest, listened to the straining heart and lungs for a moment, consulted his blood pressure then told a nurse: "Get him to OR."

As the nurse began wrestling the bed from the cubicle, the heart monitor in Curtain 4 shifted to a flat tone and Gwen's heart leapt.

"Code blue!" Gabby and Jan shouted together.

Shit.

Gwen pushed her way back to Willie Anderson's bedside while Jan scrambled for the crashcart. Gabby pumped up and down on the boy's already bruised ribs. If they were fractured as the paramedics had suggested, this'd make them worse, but it might also save his life. Gwen got in a position to watch both the monitors and Gabby. Officer Creep was a brooding presence nearby, glaring at Ormond as the biker's bed passed him by. The crashcart arrived and Gabby lifted her hands to allow the placement of pediatric pads on the patient's chest. She resumed CPR the moment they were fixed.

Gwen barked, "Charge to sixty. One milligram of epinephrine in." The two assisting nurses complied while Gabby pumped away. Gwen consulted the monitor. "We have a shockable rhythm now!"

"Clear," Jan called, finger on the button, and Gabby stepped back. Willie's body arced then fell back. Gabby immediately resumed compressions while Jan looked to Gwen.

The monitor showed nothing encouraging so Gwen ordered another shock. Thirty seconds later, she ordered another. And then another. This time Gabby didn't return to her CPR. Gwen slid in, taking over compressions, aware of Gabby's hard gaze. A waft of urine-stink hit Gwen's nostrils and she noticed the stain spreading along the sheets beside the boy. "Goddamnit!"

"*Doctor*," Gabby snapped.

"Shit." Gwen stepped back. Her fists clenched. Like she could punch the Universe in the mouth for this.

Jan sighed and slowly peeled the pads off the boy's chest. The third nurse hurried off with the crashcart.

"Clean him up," Gwen said.

Gabby - older, seasoned, used to dealing with abruptness from doctors and unwilling to concede to it - continued to eyeball her. She reached for a clipboard instead. "Time of death?"

"I said clean him up," Gwen said, louder.

"You're the attending physician. You need to call time of death."

Gwen unfurled her fists and wiped her palms on her scrubs. Willie's eyes perfectly captured the grotesquery of death, bulging slightly beneath parted lids. She wanted to touch them, make them see again. She wanted to stroke that fine blond hair. She wanted to wash the blood from his chest.

She wanted him to take a breath.

"You do it," she said and stormed off.

By the time she was out of Emergency and into the hospital reception area, she was moving like an Olympic power-walker, headed for the elevator. Up in the locker room, there'd be cool metal surfaces to press her throbbing head against and at least one trash can to kick. She stabbed the elevator button repeatedly, her forehead against the wall above it - and jumped when a hand touched her shoulder. Expecting Pam, she jumped again when she found Officer Creep's bovine eyes close to hers.

"Think you need a drink, Doc," he said.

She jerked away, gaping at him.

"You know, debrief?" he added.

Was he for real? Was he actually trying to pick her up? This was not how professionals behaved. Professionals - decent human beings! - didn't pick up exhausted doctors immediately after they'd lost a small child. And professionals didn't run away from their work just because it didn't go well. Like Gabby, they switched off their feelings, turned on their cold-hard-bitch-at-work selves and moved on to the next patient. Only, Gwen could no longer find and sustain that self. But she did have patients. She did have duties.

This life - the job - had her trapped. That was her story. Willie Anderson's story needed an ending.

Abandoning all thought of the locker room, she shoulder-charged Officer Creep, forcing him to duck aside. She glanced off his arm, hard enough to hurt him if the sudden jolt of pain in her own shoulder was any indication. Marching back the way she'd come, the words *assault on a police officer* swam up into her forebrain.

They made her feel a little better.

"Gwen!"

She had almost made it out the main entrance at the end of her shift when Pam's fingers curled around her bicep, or at least the flab where she used to have one.

"You okay, hon?"

People die who shouldn't. While people live who shouldn't...

"I'm fine, Pam." She turned her face from the older doctor's scrutiny, wriggling her arm free and adjusting her bag on her shoulder. She looked wistfully toward the doors. *So close. So close.* "Just another day at the office."

"Mm. Right. You been down a lot lately. Even before this happened today. When's the last time you debriefed?"

She ignored the question. The last thing she wanted to do was talk about how she felt, about how screwed-up life had become. Halfway through her residency, there was still so far to go. She'd worked her ass off for a decade and her dream job had turned about to be a really bad fit.

Oh, yeah, and a kid died.

She dug her finger nails into her palm. "I'm just tired. Really need a good night's sleep." That much was true.

Pam scrutinized her for a moment longer then gave it up. "Subject change. You hear what I heard about him?"

"Him? Him who?"

"Him-him, stupid."

"Okay. And what *rumor* would that be?"

Pam gathered her thin cardigan around her plump middle.

Gwen wondered if she would look like that in ten years' time.

"Apparently Doctor Barry's been trying it on with Denali."

"In Radiology?"

"Mmh-hm." Pam's jowls bounced as she nodded. "Denali told Gabby. Gabby told me." She put a hand back on Gwen's arm. "That sumbitch needs a hard kick where the sun don't shine, you ask me."

"It's okay, Pam." Gwen forced a smile. It *was* ok, wasn't it? "We're not together. Haven't been for weeks."

"For good this time? You're better off without that sack of crap, you ask me. You can do a whole lot better."

Then why don't I? Oh, that's right: I've got a flabby tummy, my hair's terrible, I work double-shifts so no time for a social life, I'm as grumpy as hell…

"So what did Denali do?" she asked. "I hope she said yes. I'd like Barry to move on. Actually I'd like Barry to swallow a scalpel. Oh, did I say that out loud?"

Pam drew herself up, dragged Gwen through the doors into the driveway for privacy even though it was busier out here than within. The thick August air was a shock after the hospital's crisp air conditioning. "He bothering you? If he's bothering you and you don't want him to-"

"Pam. Look at me. I mean *look* at me. I've put on twenty pounds in the last two years. I'm addicted to coffee-"

"There's worse things-"

"And I hate my job!"

Heads turned. She quieted down, returned to the safer subject. "Barry's not bothering me, he just won't let it go. I'm past believing he cares; he just thinks I'm an easy lay. Especially when people like Denali have too much class to give in to him. He keeps looking for ways to talk to me. To keep the contact alive." Pam was giving her that look. "Ok, so that adds up to bothering me. Ya got me."

"Well, if there's anything I can do about that, you let me know." Pam wiped a fresh sheen of sweat from her brow, slipped out of her cardigan, jaw working. Gwen waited her out. "So you hate your job? You're looking for a new one? That'd be a shame, because you're a solid emergency physician and we need you. Find a way to see your residency through. Please."

Gwen saw blood smeared across the bruised and battered ribs of a child and tried to blink it away but couldn't. Willie Anderson would join the honor role of dead that often played like a slide show before her eyes when she travelled home, when she tried to sleep, when she raised a glass, when she raised a bottle. "I've an application in for Quality Control."

"Okay. That's good. I guess."

Good was relative. Quality Control would be a temporary fix at best. She couldn't see how moving to an administrative role was going to improve her life other than get her away from the deluge of brain-damaged children, beaten spouses, violent meth-addicts and teenage stab victims.

Besides…

"Guess who's on the selection panel?" Gwen said.

"Barry?"

"Uh huh."

"Shit."

"Uh *huh*."

"So has he actually said to you 'Sleep with me one last time and I'll get you the job'? Because we could nail his ass for that."

They paused while two paramedics wheeled past a gurney. The old man on the trolley flashed panicked eyes above his O2 mask. Gwen turned her back.

"No," she said. "He's too cunning for that. Shrewd. And I don't wanna give him the chance. Far as I'm concerned, Denali is welcome to him." She smiled and pulled back the sleeve of her scrubs, but she'd left her watch in her locker. "Listen, we'll do coffee tomorrow." She leaned in for a peck on the cheek and took to her heels with Pam's disgruntled expression seared into her memory.

Better that than Willie Anderson's dead bug eyes.

She turned right along Saint Antoine Street. People were every-where, lingering over conversation in the balmy evening or hurrying from one place to another, just like her. She was always hurrying. She'd hurried through her childhood, desperate to be an adult. She'd hurried out of Carrington the second she'd finished high school, hurried to college and med school, hurried toward a "better life" saving the world. Hurried into the relationship with Barry. Now she was hurrying home. And it wasn't like there was much *there* to look forward to. Not even Sam anymore: Barry had taken him when she ended the relationship, which was probably for the best since she really had no business looking after a cat. But there was wine at home. And probably a *CSI* or *Bones* marathon, something banal enough to help her sleep.

Barry had taken the car too, which was fine since it was technically his. And it forced her into a small amount of exercise a day: home-to-work, work-to-home. Detroit was awash with cheap second-hand cars. She'd buy one soon. She would. When she had time. When she had energy. Besides, the walk wasn't all that bad on a warm afternoon. Her street was tucked into the maze behind the hospital and around the university precinct; it wasn't that far and it wasn't dangerous. Unlike much of the city, the area was busy, middle class and as friendly as any other American suburb.

Walking, too, was shown to be a great stress management technique.

Yeah, that's been working real well for me so far.

At the corner of Mack, she turned right and fell into introspection, body operating on autopilot. She had several unkind thoughts about Barry, about Pam for stopping her at the door and many more violent thoughts about what she'd like to do to the vile slime who'd beaten Willie Anderson.

What's that little oath you made about doing no harm?

But it was so fricking unfair, so *wrong*. She knew she should have developed the thicker skin of other emergency professionals, and it had been there for a time, maybe the first year of residency when she'd joined in with the black humor and hadn't woken up every night thinking work thoughts. But the constant horrors, the injustices, had worn through that carapace, and begun eating at her soul.

Near the corner of South Thomas Ave, she snapped out of it and cut through the Gimmler Apartments parking lot. Home was less than ten minutes away. She'd shopped recently and her pantry was stocked with all the things she needed: cheese, bread, chocolate, booze.

Gwen's four food groups.

A service alley ran off South Thomas along the back of the apartments and a white delivery van was tucked inside it, engine idling. A man in a baseball cap stood by the driver's door and she hurried past, not wanting to make eye contact. She was just past the alleyway when shoes scuffed the pavement behind her. Something - *an arm!* - snaked over her right shoulder and across her left breast. Her bag slipped from her shoulder. Jerked from her feet, clamped against her attacker's torso, she slid backwards, heels scraping against cement. She scratched at the arm, but her stubby nails failed to penetrate the man's sleeve. Her hand stretched for his face, but he pulled his head out of reach. She smelled beer and sweat and halitosis.

It was only when he dragged her back into the alley that she truly realized the danger she was in. The van's engine rumbled ominously, a lion in waiting. Someone else - a second man? - slid open the side door.

It was then Gwen screamed.

CHAPTER THREE

Radio chatter announced a patrol car coming up behind him and it was all Jake could do to keep from bolting. He kicked himself for keeping the gun, now wrapped in his spare t-shirt within his back pack. If they stopped him, if they searched him...

He gave them a glance over his shoulder, nodded politely and walked on, being cool, being innocent. The car shadowed him the half block to the corner, then sped away, leaving him to turn into the narrower side street.

A couple of kids tossing a football moved to the other side of the street to let him pass, doing what Normals did: distrusting strangers, distrusting freaks. They were smart to do so. Their parents watched him with wary eyes and he picked up his pace so the kids could get on with their game. Moments later, one of the kids congratulated the other on a great throw. Jake wondered why folks called it a football when he never saw anyone kicking one.

Sweat coated his scalp like a cap beneath his dreads, running in rivulets down the gully of his spine to soak his shirt. All he wanted was to curl up somewhere dark and cool - maybe load his veins with sweet relief just for the hell of it this once. But what would that make him if he started using for the same reasons as other people? A junkie. And junkies didn't go to Heaven; he felt sure Momma would've agreed if she was here.

To continue doing this one wrong thing, it had to be for the right reason.

And with four days to score, he had to keep trying the decent way to get money: by earning it. The shame of it was, in the past he'd occasionally resorted to burglary and even muggings, but most of the time he'd been able to get a little work. A day here, a day there. Just enough money for three nights of oblivion each month while the moon was largest. Other towns and cities had places a guy could work for a day and not get asked for a social security number, places like Huntsville, Jackson, Topeka, De Moines—

Rockford.

He didn't want to think about Rockford.

Detroit had been a mistake, but leaving wasn't easy. Without even the bucks for a bus fare, he was stuck here. But Detroit had no work, not even for educated people, clean people, Normals. And winters were colder than in Illinois, he'd heard, though he couldn't imagine anything colder than that. He'd almost died there.

Jake didn't want to die. Not until he knew for certain he'd be joining Momma. Not until he turned it all around, did enough good things to rub out all the bad...

Hunger pangs tightened his gut as he neared the corner of Mack and South Thomas. He had protein bars in his pack that he'd been saving. No point keeping them now, he figured. The zipper was between his thumb and forefinger when a woman screamed. Probably someone arguing with her boyfriend - that kind of bullshit happened all the time. Better to stay out of it. But a flash of movement at the edge of an alleyway down South Thomas made him pause. Had he really seen that? A woman's shoes kicking and jerking around, disappearing backwards? Someone was dragging her into the lane!

He broke into a run. He dropped his pack by a handbag where it lay outside the alley, its contents bleeding onto the sidewalk. A young guy was coming around from the front of the apartments and he shouted a question at Jake. Jake ignored it as he swung into the alley.

A man dressed in sweats and a hoodie was grappling with a woman in the loose-fitting clothes of hospital staff. He had her next to a van, grunting curses and trying to get a leg up behind him so he could pull her inside. She shrieked again; her shoes scratched against the cement as she tried to get purchase. A second man began climbing from the van just as Jake arrived.

Jake's shoulder hit the driver's door, smashing it into the driver's face. He skidded to a stop by the woman and launched a flurry of punches at her startled attacker, striking arm, ribs, and ear. The woman fell, connecting hard with the road. The guy also toppled back, swearing, legs flailing as he disappeared into the van. As Jake reached to pull the woman up, the second man barreled into him. Arms wrapped around Jake's shoulders, the driver rode Jake into the ground. They landed hard and rolled free of each other. Spitting and cussing, the guy rose to his feet, nose gushing blood, and pulled a short, nasty blade from the back of his shorts.

Jake put a little more distance between them, moving across to guard the woman's retreat as she scuttled away. The punk danced sideways and waved the blade as he sized Jake up, pressing his other sleeve against his nose. He jerked his head as if asking Jake to step aside, but the next instant he was moving, blade whipping toward Jake's gut.

Gwen scurried away from the van. After a few yards she got to her feet, hands stinging where her fall had scraped flesh from her palms. A young guy was standing at the corner where she'd come from, his cell phone out, videoing. She moved backwards until she stood by him.

The man who'd rescued her was dressed in a button-down shirt and grimy denims, his long hair wild, his shoulders hunched and tight with aggression. His opponent was half his size, dressed in thin hoodie-shirt and cargo shorts; a blade appeared in his fist.

"Call the cops," she snapped at the guy with the phone.

Light flashed from the knife as it lashed out. Gwen gasped. With reflexes just short of miraculous, the stranger caught his attacker's wrist and wrenched it sideways. Gwen heard a pop.

Dorsal radiocarpal ligament, she thought automatically.

Yanked forward, the scrawny guy stumbled into the stranger's chest, bounced back and swayed on his feet. He stared wide-eyed at his hand.

Pain's yet to register. She hoped when it did, it would be the most excruciating thing the brutal little shit had ever felt.

Then the stranger drove his fist into the driver's gut, folding him like a cheap tent. The blade clattered to the sidewalk. The stranger took a couple of steps backward, his focus on the downed man. Gwen felt a ridiculous urge to cheer. Instead she gasped in shock when the man who'd grabbed her appeared at the wheel of the van and started it. She and the cell phone guy had just enough time to scramble out of its way as it careened out of the alley and down South Thomas.

The van had roared away and the fight was over, but Jake stood above the moaning driver curled-up on the ground, vision tunneling, heart thundering in his ears. The little bastard's blood smelled sweet. The Animal howled for a taste while Jake sucked in air, reached for control. He shouldn't have let himself get this angry.

He shouldn't have tried to cut *me!*

It was all he could do to take a step back, to *not* reach down and wrap his hands around that puny throat. He took a step back and then another.

The nurse or doctor or whatever she was had retreated out the end of the alley, standing with the guy who'd come to investigate with Jake. He shouted something jubilant, waving a cell phone in the air. Someone came out of the building behind Jake. He spared them a glance: just a kid and his girlfriend, edging around him toward the nurse. He wondered if anyone had called the cops. A car pulled over on the opposite side of the street beyond the laneway, but it was just people. No police. Not yet.

The weedy punk on the ground tried to get up, groaning like an old door being scraped open. He cursed Jake as he cradled his injured arm.

"You tried to take her!" The Animal roaring in his chest, Jake threw himself onto the man and pinned his cheek to the ground with a hand on his neck. He paused, teeth only inches from the punk's pulsing carotid. The man's eyes were white around the iris, nostrils flared. He whimpered like an injured puppy. *Submission*, Jake's instincts told him, though the thought was more concept than word; the man was signaling submission.

But he was also injured, weak, unable to defend himself. The Animal - the thing he hated, the thing that wanted to own him - it wanted nothing more than to rip the bastard's throat out, to cherish the rush of salty blood, to make him suffer—

Jake sprang away, chest heaving, shoulders and hands trembling. His opponent crawled in the other direction.

And then the lady was talking to him, her words muted by the rush of blood in his ears. She clutched her bag to her belly. She looked wary, chest heaving, but her chin was up as if in defiance of the men who'd try to take her. Her gaze was direct, her irises gray. An ironic half-smile creased one cheek, even after an ordeal such as she'd just suffered.

He dropped his head as shame settled over him like a clinging mist. He was bad, as bad in his own way as these kidnappers were in theirs. And she would see it if she looked too long at him. His peripheral vision tracked the would-be kidnapper slinking down the alley away from the gathering crowd, breaking into a shuffling run. With the woman close, Jake wanted to leave too.

With the bloodrush fading, the sounds of the street became clearer, as if earmuffs had come off his head.

"That was awesome, man," said the phone guy. He'd ventured closer, his focus on his screen. Jake turned his shoulder to him, hair swinging across his face as he searched around for his pack. The guy kept on prattling as people climbed from their cars, and as the teenage couple came closer, asking over and over, "Did you see that?"

Sure they'd seen that. But none of them had helped. Jake would have liked to maybe shove that cell into his throat, or somewhere even tighter.

"I didn't see them coming," the nurse said.

Gwen drew a deep, juddering breath and continued, "They blindsided me. Holy shit, if you hadn't ..." She swallowed and glanced back at the teenage couple picking up her belongings; she found she could care less if they made off with them. She had nearly been raped and probably murdered.

Yep, if he hadn't...

She considered him, the stranger who'd come to her aid from out of nowhere. The shiver that raced along her spine and shoulders had more to do with the prospect of her vanishing forever than with the stranger's sour odor. She'd smelt far worse in the ER. She forced herself not to wrinkle her nose, to touch his arm by way of thanks. His head was down, and he startled at the contact. The response was odd, out of sync. Socially awkward? Or a homeless man not used to middle class people acknowledging him, let alone touching him?

"Thank you," she offered, catching his eyes beneath their veil of dreadlocks. They were nice eyes, she realized, almost caramel in color, the kind of eyes that had overloaded on pain and turned that pain into strength, into compassion, rather than hate and bitterness. On impulse she raised herself up on her tiptoes, moved some hair aside and brushed her lips against his cheek above his stubble where the skin was clean and smooth.

The teenage boy wolf-whistled. His girlfriend clapped, calling, "You go, girl!"

Suddenly self-conscious, she let go of his arm and stepped back. He shot their audience an angry look and made to move past her, to escape, as if it were he who'd assaulted her.

"Wait," she said, reaching out a hand but well short of grabbing him this time.

He paused, half turned. His posture was guarded, as if she posed further danger to him. His eyes - his startling eyes - flashed.

Gwen realized she didn't actually have anything in mind to say. It just seemed wrong to let him go with a kiss on the cheek and a polite thank you. "Let me buy you food." She winced and hurried on. "Dinner. I'll buy you dinner."

A ghost of a smile flickered across his face before his expression sobered. He shrugged and studied the car parked opposite them, the gawkers leaning against it. "That's okay."

His voice had a pleasant resonance, comfortably deep like a radio announcer's but with a mild Southern burr. What might it be like to listen to him talk about his life, his struggles, his pain? She realized with a start she'd prejudged him, thought him a bum. For all she knew, he had a job, a family, a normal life.

He just had thick dreads, stank like a laundry basket, and fought like an animal in defense of complete strangers.

The injured kidnapper had vanished. The camera guy was playing his footage to the young couple. They made appreciative noises as if watching ice-hockey.

Vultures.

The stranger continued, "Restaurant wouldn't let me in, lookin' like this." He brushed his knuckles across his grimy jeans. "Better ask those folk over there to drive you home."

And with that piece of sage advice, he was gone, jogging back in the direction of the hospital. While a woman came over to see if she needed anything, Gwen hugged her bag to her chest and tried not to replay the last three minutes of her life over and over in her mind.

The woman and her daughter drove Gwen home. Numb, she heard little of what they said during the five-minute trip, except their insistence that she call the cops and see a doctor. She nodded as she climbed out— "I will" — and stumbled to her front door. When she closed it behind her, chaining and dead-bolting it, and sliding her back down it to sit hunched on the floor, Gwen kept thinking that she should at least have learned that good man's name.

CHAPTER FOUR

Jake lies curled in a nest of pine needles, surrounded by young trees, freezing his nuts off, butt-naked, a metallic taste in his mouth. Beneath the sheen of dew, stickiness mats his beard and chest hair. He rises, off balance, swaying and shivering in the dawn air. The sun chooses that moment to peek above the horizon, coating him in an orange light and revealing the tackiness on his beard and chest and belly as dried blood and mucosa.

Hands race across his chin, his throat, his chest, feeling for a wound. But understanding hits him a moment before the sunlight touches the lump on the far side of the clearing, resolving it into a pile of human remains: torn-up limbs, intestines spilling like ruined groceries from a broken bag, the slaughterhouse stench wafting his way on the breeze.

He Changed last night. And with the Change, a bad thing happened. Finally happened. He killed a man. Without even knowing he was doing it.

He awoke, curled on his side and leaking tears. Even in sleep, he couldn't escape it.

Even in goddamn sleep…

He'd kicked off the painter's drop sheet he'd been using as a blanket. The night air seeping through the cracked walls of his squat was cool; maybe that had prompted the dream.

Dream, hell, he thought and turned onto his back. He pulled the sheet up to his chest. *Memory.*

The mattress beneath him stank of mold and rodent piss despite the old tarp he'd found to cover it. The paint spots on the drop sheet smelled much better, and up until a few nights ago they'd mostly covered the mattress stink — but this close to Big Moon, scents and odors became clearer, separating into distinguishable units.

Jake lay that way for many minutes, tracking the drone of a searching mosquito, slowing his breathing and heart rate, his gut rumbling. The peeling wallpaper of the squat's living room showed in the ambient nighttime light as flayed skin. His hand reached from beneath the sheet, fingers brushing dusty bare floorboards until they reached his pack. There was no reason for it *not* to be there, but he checked it anyway. Old habits.

Habits.

His fingers roamed farther out to touch his rig — finger pricking on the needle. The spoon and square of folded foil beside it were cool, the disposable lighter a smooth plastic lump. Just objects, useless without the heroin. Inside him, It smiled. He *felt* It smile, hating Its smugness.

The mosquito's whine drew closer as if attracted to the tiny wound on his fingertip. He put the finger to his lips, sucked at the salty dot.

The Animal's smile vanished, stirred by the taste of blood.

Jake pulled the finger from his mouth. The hand lashed out, caught the mosquito from the dark and squished it. He kicked off the drop sheet, sending dust into the air and setting his nose itching. He emptied his backpack into the bright square made by the street's solitary working streetlamp, spreading his things in a neat circle around him. Again, it was an old habit, formed during many nights in shared squats when it was sensible to check and recheck things weren't missing.

A little clothing and food, enough to get by. He'd survived with less.

His gear intact and waiting for H to fuel it. A reminder he had mere days to score, or his dream of the torn-up body in the woods might repeat itself.

The plastic sleeve containing three clippings torn from stolen newspapers. He hesitated over it, then pulled out the oldest and angled it toward the light. It had faded as badly as his own memories of that event but the married couple still stared back at him with accusation in their eyes. As if he'd been on the other side of that camera.

Jane and Alec Armstrong, he knew the caption read, *speak out about the darker side of foster care.*

The darker side. It hadn't been Jake that assaulted Alec, not really. Later, Jake had realized it was the first time the Animal had tried surfacing, the Big Moon immediately after his thirteenth birthday. He had read the article before tearing out the picture to keep. Apart from the facts of the assault, it had been bullshit: the Armstrongs were heroic carers for an orphan boy, a boy thankless and troubled. Jane and Alec were ordinary people, not heroes. And though they'd never physically abused him, they hadn't genuinely cared for him. Jake had never been a true part of their lives, or their world.

He put their photograph away and resisted looking at the two articles. The one about werewolf "myths". And the recent one, the one from Rockford…

Why did he do this to himself? He wanted never to think of Rockford again, of that kind woman and what had happened to her. Why in hell keep a newspaper article? He needed no reminder of his own crime, *any* of his crimes, least of all this one! So why? As proof it happened? Proof he wasn't crazy? It would be better to be crazy!

What am I?

He slid the plastic pocket back into the backpack and turned to his momma's brooch, fingers tracing its embellishments, summoning up her voice, her homey scent, the caress of her fingers against his cheek. He needed her here; he needed her with him, though she'd been taken so long ago.

He squeezed his eyes shut, pressed the brooch to his lips, tried to remember.

He was back in a bare-boarded room not so different from this one, the air dusty, gaps around window frames where sunlight shone through even with the thin shades were drawn. Momma was kneading dough as he stood at her side, him clutching the frayed edge of her apron.

"Is Papa *good?*" he asked her.

She glanced toward the closed cellar door, squinted as if trying to hear past it. He was down there, Jake knew it. The chains across it said so. As did the bread she was making for their regular three-day journey into the woods where they'd wait out Big Moon.

"No, my beautiful boy, no, he's not," she replied in a whisper. "That's why you gotta be careful round him, specially this time-a month."

"Am I bad too?"

She dropped the dough on the board, crouched and faced him. "You are not! You are good, good to the bone." Her finger pressed his breastbone as if to locate that goodness, to glue it down. Her touch left flour on his shirt. "You remember all the things I been tellin you. Remember God, remember Heaven and Hell, remember the way to both so as you choose the right one. Remember to care for folks the way I been carin for you."

Jake's turn to glance at the chained door. "You care for Papa too."

"Sure I do." She brushed hair off her face with the side of one hand. "Somewhere in the good book, it says to love them as don't love us."

"Why, Momma? Why don't Papa love us?"

She had no answer for that, no response except to return to her frantic kneading.

Back in his derelict Detroit house, Jake sucked in a lungful of cool night air and opened his eyes. He didn't know how much of the remembered conversation was actual and how much he'd added over the years like the fine patterns around the brooch had been added by its maker. But the heart of the conversation, his momma's truth, remained.

hate you, whispered the Animal.

Jake didn't know if It meant him or Momma, but he told it, "Right back atcha."

He carefully wrapped and put the brooch behind him on the bed and picked up his single EpiPen, a reminder that danger was always close by. A single touch from silver and he could start swelling and choking.

Silver, he thought and rubbed his tired eyes. *What am I, Momma? What am I, God? A monster? A man? Which is it?*

Most times after a change, he was a mess, a man waking from one nightmare to another, blood and dirt on him, occasionally injured though it always healed quickly. But sometimes after a Change, he had come to himself, naked all right, but *clean*, and standing upright. He'd wondered about it: did that mean his human side was somehow awake and aware before his actual mind switched back on? Did that mean his human side worked *with* the Animal?

When he picked up the spare shirt, Jarhead's pistol fell out with a thump on the floor that made him wince. He wrapped his fingers around the grip, turned it this way and that. Its weight was seductive. In the streetlight, it glinted. This was power. This could end a life. This could earn a man respect. He popped the chamber open and emptied the shells and spent casings onto the floor. Three bullets left. Plenty enough to march up to Zee, blow his head off and steal *all* his blow.

No. That was the Animal speaking, not Jake. The Animal might kill someone, but Jake never would.

Reloading it, he wondered about hiding it in the drywall. But this was something he could pawn. It might make him some serious dollars. It went into his pack.

Jake swept the small pile of belongings in with the gun, burying it at the bottom. He rocked back on his heels and rubbed his palms together, felt the Animal shifting within him, straining toward the moon outside. The night before full moon, the night of, the night after — those three nights Jake had no hope of resistance in and of himself.

What am I? A monster? A man? How can I be both?

The few churches he'd been into all taught that humans could be saved, while monsters burned eternally, unforgiven and unforgiveable. In the side pocket of the pack, he had three coins. He took one out and turned it one way, then the other, flipped it and watched it clatter across the floor until it stopped outside the rectangle of streetlight.

One side always faces up. Right now, I'm man. And the hell if I won't stay that way.

not for long, It told him.

His drug gear went back inside the cavity in the drywall, safe and ready for the night before full moon.

Stretching on the bed, he took up the brooch and kissed it. He needed work tomorrow. He needed money. He turned the brooch over and over, called up Momma's voice in his mind. She said, *It will be okay, my beautiful boy. You'll see: it'll turn out fine.*

"I hope so, Momma," he whispered and crossed himself the way he'd seen her do. Tears stung his eyes. "I sure hope so."

CHAPTER FIVE

The courtroom reminded Carter Moffat of church. The pine paneling. The hushed environment. The insiders playing by unspoken rules which kept tripping him up. He suddenly had a new empathy for non-believers visiting a church for the first time, for the sense of otherness and confusion they must experience.

There'd been no sign of Elijah and there wouldn't be. The case worker from the Illinois Department of Children and Family Services had told him his son remained with the foster parents to spare "the little boy" the stress of the hearing.

What about my *stress?* he'd wanted to scream. *What about Elijah's stress over losing contact with his father so soon after his mother's murder?*

But he'd kept it in, bottled it up while the case worker and her agency lawyer began arguing facts with *his* lawyer, and the judge watched with the keenness of a cat waiting for a bird to slip up. Not one of them seemed to care about what he was going through, about what he'd been through. A wife eviscerated. The assailant never brought to justice. His son removed because he was "unfit to care for him".

He'd done his best, damnit. He'd fed the boy, clothed the boy, got him to school on time - most days. It was his prick of a boss: if he had cut Carter a little more slack, understood what he was going through.

"Mr Moffat."

Getting fired would have hurt him a year ago, would have hurt him bad. After the hell of the past five months, it had felt like nothing. He'd received the news in a dull haze of grief.

"Mr *Moffat.*"

He blinked himself into the present and offered the judge an apologetic smile. "Yes, Ma'am."

Geez, if she didn't remind him of the actress off that old TV show, the one Beth had loved: he saw her, his darling wife, his soulmate, legs tucked beneath her on the sofa, a steaming mug of peppermint tea resting on one thigh, eyes glued to the screen. He fought a sudden constriction in his throat.

Really shouldn't think about her. Really shouldn't think about old times.

"...sympathy for your loss," the judge was saying, "and can't imagine the grief you're going through, but we need to examine facts in this hearing. First, we have the police forensic statement concluding that your wife's death was due to a wolf attack. While the incidence of wolves in northern Illinois is certainly unlikely, and attacks on humans are rare in the United States, wolf DNA on Beth Moffat's remains indicates this to be the case. Your assertion that she was in fact killed by a *were*wolf-" here she paused to read the word from a sheet as if it were new to her, pulling her head back in a *Did I read that right?* pose.

Her play-acting raised Carter's blood pressure more than a little. "I no longer believe that, Your Honor. I was traumatized by finding my wife's mutilated corpse and didn't know what I was saying."

"That is all on record. Please refrain from speaking while I'm speaking."

"Sure, your Honor, sorry."

"Your assertion that she was killed by a werewolf was the first in a long list of behaviors that cause concern about your fitness to retain custody of Elijah. And despite your claim that this belief was some form of temporary insanity, you have on two occasions traveled to other cities chasing werewolf sightings.

"Second, your recent loss of income has made it difficult for you to provide the necessities of life for Elijah."

"I'm-" He was about to explain that he was looking for work. That he had savings. But he bit his tongue and bowed his head in contrition. He wouldn't get the boy back by pissing off the judge. Besides, after the funeral, and after missing so many weeks of work, there wasn't enough left in his savings to impress anybody.

"Third," she continued, "we have the court-ordered psychiatric report indicating you are in need of therapy. Which you have repeatedly declined."

That damn shrink had it in for me the moment he met me. He was crazier than I am.

"Based on these three reasons, the court has decided not to release Elijah into your custody at this time."

He clasped his hands beneath the table, curled them around each other. His head stayed down. If he looked at her, if she saw the rage in his eyes....

"Your repeated erratic behaviors represent an unsafe environment for the child to live in. And your trips elsewhere not only wasted money you don't have, on both occasions your nine-year-old son was discovered having to fend for himself for days at a time. For the time being, Elijah Moffat will remain in foster care with the relevant DCFS agency. There is an application for custody currently being lodged by the child's maternal grandparents."

Carter's head shot up at this. What the hell were Tom and June playing at? Elijah was his boy. *His* boy, dammit.

"The court orders you to undergo a weekly course of grief counseling with your church and then further psychiatric examination at a time not more than three months from today. Pending the results of that examination, the next hearing will examine both your claims to custody and those of the child's maternal grandparents. Until then, this disposition hearing is adjourned."

Carter was halfway home when his cell rang. He answered it without checking the caller ID.

"Yeah?"

"Carter?" The voice was nasal, taut.

Ah, crap. "Hello, Pastor."

"Carter, how was the hearing?"

You'll be getting a letter soon, letting you know all about it. "Pretty much as I expected. I'm a lunatic. An unfit father."

"Carter..."

"I need psychiatric help."

"Carter…"

"You'll get a letter telling you I need to see you for counseling. So I guess we'll have plenty of time to talk about it then." They certainly wouldn't be talking about it on Sunday. Even if Pastor Gillis had the time to talk then, there was no way Carter was setting foot in a service there again, not with the way people looked at him.

That was another thing that should have pissed him off: the way these godly folk treated him like a leper for what he'd said about werewolves rather than offering tea and sympathy and helping him track down a great evil loose in the world.

"…werewolves," Pastor Gillis was saying. "That's my greatest concern: that you no longer believe that."

Carter changed hands on the wheel, shifting the cell to his other one. "*That's* your greatest concern? Not that my son's been taken away? Not that I've lost my stinking job? Not that my wife had her insides ripped out?"

"You're misinterpreting me, Carter."

Suddenly the prissy voice was too much. The whole damn shooting match was too much. Suddenly he couldn't be bothered with pastors, with judges, with lawyers. Suddenly nothing at all mattered, least of all pretending to be calm and rational and polite. "I don't think I'm misinterpreting anything. And you didn't see what I saw!"

"What you saw has been warped by psychological trauma, Carter. It's okay-"

"It's not okay! How is it okay? And it's not trauma. Beth was doing another one of her volunteer days with *your* social welfare arm, where you should be keeping her safe, meeting this bum Jake-"

"They're not bums, Carter."

"This *homeless* man, this Jake Brennan. Doing her good deed for the day. Going the extra mile - dragging me with her. Looking for him in the middle of the night. Dragging me to that bastard's squat, worried he OD'd or something. Telling me to stay in the car. God knows why I let her go." *Why in hell did I let her go?* "You didn't hear the screams from that backyard. You didn't run to help."

He'd grabbed his .32 out of the glove box before chasing after her around the back of the rundown home.

His vision blurred with the terror of what had followed and he slowed, pulled over to the curb. Someone honked him and he flipped the bird.

"Carter, we'll—"

"No! *I* saw it. I shot it, scared it off." But it had been too late for Beth. "It wasn't a wolf. Something bigger. Something bigger than me. Something a hell of a lot like a *werewolf's* meant to look!"

Gillis spoke over the top of him. "Come in and see me at three o'clock. I have an opening."

"Yeah, I have an opening too. It's called the huge hole in my life where my wife should be. Screw you, Pastor. Screw all of you."

He didn't bother disconnecting the call, just dropped the cell on the passenger seat. Gillis remonstrated for about a minute and finally hung up.

Carter didn't know what to do. For the first time in his life, he didn't know what to do. It had all fallen apart. It was all gone. The .32 was still in his glovebox, its four remaining rounds unfired even after two interstate trips chasing monster sightings. What if he was crazy? What if he hadn't really seen what his eyes and memory told him he had? What if he hadn't scared off a werewolf but a man, a big-shouldered man named Jake Brennan, a man with long dreadlocks and thick beard, who looked wild because he lived on the streets? The cops hadn't found Brennan, though they insisted they'd tried. They no longer suspected him anyway, since their verdict of animal attack.

But there was the one sliver of science that Carter could cling to: that forensics said a wolf had killed her. The "wolf" he had seen reared back on two legs, though it ran off on four when he shot it.

Maybe I just saw a wolf and tried to make it worse than what it really was. Maybe I'm nuts. Maybe they're right and I'm not a fit father. Maybe Elijah would be better off without me. Maybe the whole world would be.

It was 9:55 in the morning and his life was over. How could his life be over and he hadn't even had lunch yet? The handgun was in the glove box. There was a park not far from here - even better, there was a police station. It'd save time and taxpayer money if they found his body in their own parking lot. That was one last mercy he could offer the good folk who used to be his friends and family: not having to deal with finding his ravaged body the way he'd had to with Beth. And if he went to hell, so be it. What had God ever done for him anyway?

He headed back toward the police station, a great peace settling over him.

A block later, the cell rang again.

What now? My guardian angel trying to talk me out of suicide?

He chuckled at that.

After four rings, the cell went quiet.

"Thanks a bunch, guardian angel. My life's not worth persisting with a little longer?"

It was probably the phone company, chasing money. They'd cut off the home phone. The cell couldn't be far behind. Someone else's problem soon.

He made a right. The police station was halfway down the road. He realized his seatbelt was off and decided to put it on, rather than risk being pulled over. That'd be ironic, a cop delaying his suicide by giving him a ticket, then the same cop finding him in the parking lot dead. Maybe they would blame themselves. He couldn't have that.

The cell rang again.

Seriously?

He reached over and flipped it face up. The caller ID read *Dungeon*.

Now, that was interesting.

He swung into the curb again, brakes squealing, and pushed the button. "Yeah?"

"It's Doug. From Dungeon Ink Comics."

"I know where you're from, Doug. I have caller ID."

"Oh. So you seen the news today?"

If Doug was ringing him, there was only one thing this could be about. Butterflies launched themselves into Carter's stomach. "Been busy," he said.

"Well, you better come on over, man. Right now. If you're still looking for that homeless guy, there's something you should see."

CHAPTER SIX

Gwen wasn't going to work today. She sat in her beige box of a living room, picking at the plasters on her scraped palms and staring at the phone.

She had a helluva headache and she'd barely slept despite polishing off most of a bottle of cabernet last night. Her mind had a mind of its own, replaying the events of the previous day over and over, needling her, tormenting her. She'd saved a woman-beating, child-beating prick and watched an innocent child die. She'd been attacked, rescued within a hair's breadth of kidnap, rape, murder. Right now, she could be tied up and bleeding in someone's concrete cellar. Or covered in loose soil in a shallow grave.

She shivered. The wine bottle sat on the coffee table just out of arm's reach. She left it there, though she wanted nothing better than to dull her thoughts. Maybe later she would. Maybe sooner, rather than later...

She'd been threatened before, a dozen times, more, in the ER. Junkies, angry parents, people sick of waiting. Policy said you needed regular formal debriefs. Stress counseling and personal leave were available for the most traumatic experiences, but no one made use of them. Threats and abuse were part of the job, and people who couldn't handle it were seen as weak. But to be physically attacked like this. Immediately after losing Willie Anderson.

And to not feel shock. To not be shaking like crazy, or weeping. Even the numbness had passed quickly.

What's wrong with me?

Maybe it was all the practice she'd gotten in her job, but she didn't feel traumatized. Hell, she just felt *angry*. She'd even started wishing *she'd* been the one to tear that punk with the knife a new one. She'd started seeing it in her head: Dr Gwen Cheevey kicking the hell out of both those … animals!

The numbness had faded the moment she'd called the police last night, replaced quickly by the anger. The longer the cops' questions had gone on, the angrier she'd gotten. One seemed concerned, the female officer, but the male acted like Gwen was wasting their time. She'd been about to tell him she didn't appreciate his apathy, when the woman officer placed a hand on her arm and calmly told her they'd try their best to find the men who assaulted her.

"Try?" she had responded.

"Got more on our plate than just y—" the male officer had started to say, but the woman had gestured him into silence. He had left the house then.

The female cop had then said, "*When* we find them, we'll need you to ID them. You'll have to come in and do that. All right?"

Teeth clamped together, Gwen had said yes and seen her out of the house. Then she'd thrown a plate, kicked a door and opened the cabernet.

Gwen stopped picking at her plasters. *To hell with going to work today. To hell with everything.* She picked up the phone to call in and heard the pips indicating she had messages. She'd check them later. Maybe after lunch. She punched the hospital's number.

"Emergency," said a nurse when the connection went through.

She lowered her voice and made it husky to mask her identity, asking for Pam.

The senior doctor sounded harried when she finally came to the phone a full three minutes later.

"Gwen! Where you been? I made five calls to you. Your phone broken? I thought maybe you'd left town, gone to your sister's. Or worse, gone over to Barry's—"

"Wait - why were *you* calling *me*?"

"The news this morning. It's on YouTube too if you want to check it." Someone in the background was crying. Another voice remonstrated with a staff member. Someone else asked Pam if that was Dr Cheevey on the phone.

"What's on YouTube?" she asked, then remembered the dude with the cell phone. "Oh, no. Seriously?"

"You okay? I mean you looked okay. Especially when you gave that big lug a kiss. Like that moment from that *Spider-Man* movie, only not so ... upside down."

"Pam. Stop it." *That dickhead put me on YouTube.* "Listen, I'm not coming in today."

"Don't blame you."

"I mean, I know that leaves you short-staffed..." She took the phone into the kitchen, headed for the coffee pot.

"Gwen. Someone tried to abduct you. You're entitled to a day off! We got this. Rest up. Talk to someone."

"So. It's been on the *news*?"

"Damn straight it's been on the news. Couldn't believe my eyes when I saw it this morning. The anchors going on about the Good Samaritan who stepped in to kung fu a couple of kidnappers. They love that stuff. God, you were lucky he was there."

Am I ever.

The way he'd charged in, planting himself in harm's way to save her life, the sheer physicality of it, the courage. Barry could never have measured up to that.

"What else are they saying?" She hated news - and now that she *was* news, Gwen couldn't think of anything worse than watching herself on it.

"They're saying it's another example of brazen street crime in broad daylight, that our police can't protect us, that our police *won't* protect us..."

Gwen had to admit to surprise that the cops actually came to see her and so quickly. She'd once heard a talkback radio caller describe Detroit as being like Mogadishu only worse, a wild zone. If the hospitals were harried and overwhelmed, the cops must be too. Maybe it was the media attention that had prompted their response. She wondered what would have happened if she had not been white, middle-class, wearing hospital clothing...

God I hate living here.

She poured coffee. "So, they know who I am? The reporters, I mean."

Pam made a noise, moved the handset away from her mouth to shout abuse at the member of the public making the ruckus. Gwen went to the fridge for cream.

Pam said, "A couple came by, asked about the scrubs. We told 'em we didn't know you. You weren't clear enough on the video. I think they went up to Human Resources."

"Crap." She poured the cream and stirred in sugar while Pam took an enquiry from a nurse. Gwen finished most of the cup before Pam came back on.

"Sorry, honey. I'd better go."

"Yeah. Listen, the cops been there? About my case, I mean."

Pam's laughter was answer enough. Of course they hadn't. They had more to do than go the extra mile on a case like this. More than half the murders in Detroit went unsolved. For the first time, it hit Gwen that as much as she hated her job, the cops' must be worse in its way.

"Did you tell them you knew the attackers from the hospital? No? Well, they got no reason to come here then. They'll look for the car, girl. That's all they'll do." Pam sighed theatrically and told someone she'd be right there.

Gwen said, "I'll see you tomorrow."

"All right. Look after yourself. And buy yourself a damn car."

"Smartass," Gwen told a dead line.

Yeah, she'd talk to someone this time, debrief. After she had another coffee. And maybe went back to bed for a while.

Jake backed out of the store with his hands raised and stumbled down the step. The shotgun barrels followed him as far as the doorway. The door swung shut to pin the gun against the plinth, the impact hard enough to make Jake flinch.

The old lady's face appeared in the gap, eyes enormous behind horn-rimmed glasses.

"Keep going," she said.

A moment before, she'd been swearing at him, language he'd never heard an old woman use before - at least an old woman who didn't live on the streets and whose mind wasn't fried.

"I'm sorry," he repeated. "I was just askin for work."

"Don't care. Just keep going!"

Against his instincts, he turned his back on the Mom-and-Pop corner store and stepped to the curb. He could still feel the gun aimed at his back, sensed the moment the door would close half a second before it banged shut and made him safe. A kid skateboarded past on the other side of the street, eying him speculatively.

He'd offered to do a day's work for forty bucks, half a day for twenty. Whatever she wanted: cleaning, putting stuff away, lifting heavy things.

He knew the reason for her rejection, of course. It was the same thing he'd experienced around the ballpark yestereday, the same thing he'd often faced since fleeing the Armstrongs' place at thirteen to live on the streets. He wore the mark of homelessness. Maybe it was his clothes and smell. Maybe it was something in his eyes. Maybe his hair and beard. Maybe it wasn't something *on* him at all, but something missing, something Normal folk all had and he didn't.

Perhaps they saw through his human form to his problem. Perhaps he really was an animal and they knew it, sensed it. The way he sensed things he couldn't see especially this close to a Big Moon, like that door closing.

In the end, everyone was an animal of some kind; he'd learned that long ago. Like in the wilderness, there were predators and prey - the dealer and the user, the kidnappers and the nurse. All his life it seemed he'd tried not to be like the predators, but he hadn't always been successful. He sure as hell hadn't.

Right now, he had needs to attend to: keep looking for work; find some food to settle his growling stomach; find another way to score H. Three days now until Big Moon started; Jake didn't need a calendar, he could *feel* it. He plunged his hand in his pocket and felt the brooch. Not far from here there was a row of small stores, two of them pawnbrokers.

The kid on the skateboard was coming back. He had something like admiration in his eyes. Which was really weird. "Ain't you the guy who took out those rapists?" he asked, using the curb to brake.

Jake flashed him a look that knocked the reverence off the kid's face. He'd been stooping to pick up his board, but he straightened and flicked it onto the road with his foot, ready to flee.

"What you talkin about?"

"That lady doctor. You saved her from those perverts." The kid looked less sure. "Didn't you?"

That guy with the cell phone. He must've got it onto the news or something.

Shit.

There were people out there who wanted him dead, people who'd wanted him dead long before he got in deep with Zee and his guard dogs. Strange bastards who wore black trenchcoats marked with strange symbols, who'd chased him all over Birmingham and again in Jackson. Worse, there would be police on his ass in no time if they made him - there was the little matter of a murder in Rockford they no doubt wanted him for.

He fingered his clothes. His hand moved to the thick bristles on his chin and then up into his hair. The clothes and the beard were easy to lose. But his dreads? He'd come to rely on them. They stopped people looking in his eyes, seeing who he was.

The kid was rolling slowly down the road now, but twisted around, watching. Jake turned away and picked up his pace. He had to score and score big. He needed new clothes, food, and a shave.

Then he had to get the hell out of Detroit.

Lunch was early and it was bad - a bologna sandwich on white bread with corn chips and mayo as a side salad - and she was halfway through it when she remembered she hadn't called the hospital's counseling service yet. Angry, she might be. Dealing with it, she might be. But there was no denying she was a mess and maybe if she just talked to someone, about the attack, about her job…

She was reaching for the phone when it rang, startling her.

"Hawoh?" she said around the mush in her mouth.

There was a pause, then an aristocratic voice, the voice of the quintessential elderly gentleman. "Gwen? Is that you?"

Oh, Christ. Great timing.

"Ait a ninnit!" She dropped the phone, raced into the kitchen and spat the mouthful of sandwich into the sink. She grabbed her glass of Sunkist and swished it in her mouth. "Sorry, Uncle Richard. Had my mouth full." She sat, folding her legs beneath her.

"Oh," he said, dubiously. "And you're all right? I saw it on the news this morning. Have you told your sister, your Mom about what happened to you?"

She let out a shaky laugh. "One question at a time, please. Yes, I'm ok. And no, I haven't called them."

"Don't you think you better?"

Nope. I've had enough pain and suffering for one week. "Uncle Richard, did Mom ask you to offer a guilt trip on her behalf or are you ringing me because you care?" She took another pull on the Sunkist.

A pause, then a light chuckle. "The latter, I assure you. Quite a to-do. The press loved it, but they don't seem to know your identity yet. Or his."

"Let's hope it stays that way. I can live without reporters parked outside my house, treating me like some damsel in distress."

Although, if she wanted to find that guy and thank him properly, the publicity might help.

Nah. Screw that. He did his good deed. He moved on. Karma will do the thanking for me, surely.

"That's the Gwen I know. Tough as nails, eh?"

Suddenly she found herself in tears. She didn't know how it happened; she hadn't cried in years. She felt ashamed even as words gushed from her mouth, garbled by her childish sobs. "Oh, Uncle Richard, I hate it here. This freaking city. The gun violence. The stabbings. The *people!*"

"Gwen."

"Yesterday in the ER … I can't even tell you what happened. It was bad. A kid. It was bad."

"Gwen, calm down, it's all right."

"Then those frickin' rapists. And that guy came outta nowhere." She took a shuddering breath. "He saved me. But he was ... just wild, you know?"

"Okay, Gwen. All right. Listen to me. Catch your breath and listen to me." The old man waited a moment while Gwen drew another breath and another, then wiped her nose on her sleeve. A string of snot stretched away from her as she moved her arm and she had to break it with the other sleeve. She was glad the old man was not there to see it.

"Gwen, it might be time I made a suggestion. It sounds like you're ready for it. I'm getting older. And your father's not around to help here anymore. You're fresh out of residency and have some highly valuable experience under your belt."

Oh, golly. He's not going to say...?

"I'd like you to join me in my practice down here. Learn the business and take it over when I'm gone."

"Uncle Richard."

"And no more calling me Uncle. I think we can dispense with that now." He was her father's oldest friend. A good man in all regards. A great mentor, or at least he'd tried to be until Barry had come along and usurped that position.

Barry. Two years ahead of her in med school and she'd let him take Richard's place. She'd made a lot of stupid choices in her life, usually because she didn't think them through first. This could be another bad one if she hurried it.

"It's a great offer."

"But you think returning to Carrington makes you a failure."

"I didn't say that."

"But you were thinking it. It'd be admitting to your mother that Detroit was a mistake. I can see how that'd eat you up."

"It's not just that. I have a shot at a job in Quality Control."

"Huh. That's great." He didn't sound impressed. She'd disappointed him. He'd hoped for her company, her assistance. She was letting him down. "I'm sure you'll get it. And Barry? How are you two?"

"I broke it off a couple months ago."

"You did?" Was that barely restrained jubilation in his voice? If so, she could understand it.

Out of nowhere, an image of Willie Anderson's battered flesh sprang into her mind. Her heart jolted and a moment later she felt an arm snake over her shoulder to grab her...

She lurched to her feet, chest constricting, pulse hammering. She fought to get a solid breath. "Listen, I have to go. Police want to speak to me at the station."

...and when we find them, you'll need to come down and ID them, ma'am...

Her brow was cold, but clammy with sweat.

"Yes, of course," Richard was saying. "As long as you're all right. And listen, remember my offer. Please. It'd be great to have you back."

She forced some cheer into her voice. "I appreciate it. I'll think about it."

"And Gwen. Look after yourself."

She rubbed the receiver against her cheek after he hung up, watching the wall clock count off a full minute. She replaced it and wiped a sweaty hand on her top.

There. She'd now spoken to someone. She'd debriefed. And her heart rate was slowing, so she'd survived her first panic attack. She didn't need to do anything now except look after herself. She returned to the kitchen for the last quarter of her sandwich. The bread was dry as toast.

Sixty bucks.

The notes were scrunched in Jake's fist as he stepped out of the pawn store.

Fifty for Zee's .357 was fair enough, but ten for the brooch? Sonofabitch had conned him. It wasn't enough to get him a bus fare *and* smack, but it would get him through the next moon cycle if he stayed in town. And he would have to stay around if only to get enough cash to buy back Momma's brooch. Ten bucks. Yeah, that guy had conned him all right.

go back! kill—

He shook it off. The immediate problem was supply. There was another dealer - a guy who kept a low profile, trying to keep out of Zee's way - but talk was his stuff was poor quality. Jake couldn't be sure it would be strong enough to prevent a Change. So he'd have to buy twice as much, have extra as a backup.

All the way to the park, he ran his fingers over the notes in his pocket. Aloud he said, "Momma, I needed this. I'm sorry. I'll get the brooch back before they sell it to someone. I just need to get through this Moon."

The park was a small one, the kind of skuzzy playground a child would be crazy to play on and a parent criminal to let them. A banana skin lay in the exact center of the single worn picnic table, splayed out like the limbs of a starfish. The dealer had been here, and not long ago judging by the freshness of the empty peel. Jake had missed him by minutes. The skin was the code Tiny Bob had told him about: *Back here at 1 p.m.*

It had been a little after twelve on the pawnshop clock. He moved off to the side of the park, into the sliver of shade along an aluminum fence. Someone had sprayed their tag above where he sat in fluoro purple: *Quoth the Raven.* He wondered who'd be crazy or stoned enough to call themselves Quoth? Or was it a new street word for something? Kill the Raven, or Screw the Raven? Maybe Raven was a new word for dope or meth.

He dropped into a heat-haze dream. Something about snapping off a needle in his arm and getting dragged into a van full of banana peels. He blinked and the sun had shifted position slightly. It was still hot. He smacked dry gums and thought about dinner at the nearest mission.

Movement drew his attention to the picnic table. The dude was sitting there, a skinny mutt pretending to play a game on his cell phone but watching him. Jake sucked in thick summer air and wandered over. Tiny Bob had said this guy's dope was cheap. Jake could only hope it was also clean.

CHAPTER SEVEN

The pervasive odor of dead mice threatened a similar fate to all who entered the comic store. Lazy Seventies rock - a melody Carter vaguely recognized - hung in the air like smoke. Tiny lamps perched above the racks of comics, DVDs and erotic magazines, their narrow beams leaving the boundaries of the store in perpetual shadow. Black walls were smattered with obscene and murderous art. Dungeon Ink Comics was a dive by any definition and Carter always had trouble deciding if this was by design or whether its tacky nature was a logical extension of the proprietor.

Summoned by his thoughts, Doug's voice rose from the gloom to greet him.

"Hey, man!"

Carter blinked rapidly to catch his night vision. He took the barely carpeted step down into the store carefully, hand on the rail. His palm came away unclean. He headed toward the voice and a moment later, a tan blur resolved itself into Doug's features: pince-nez glasses clamped on a brawler's nose, mutton-chops framing a fleshy face, long hair brushed back into a ponytail. Doug shifted the dusting cloth to his left hand and held out his right. Carter shook it briefly and looked around.

There were two customers down toward the back: a young Goth girl flicking through comics so fast he was surprised she could read the titles, and a Suit whose attention was split between a shelf of porn DVDs and the Goth's miniskirt and fishnets.

"News?" Carter prompted.

"Yeah," said Doug, tapping his nose. "Let's go out back where we can talk." The way Doug said *talk* made it sound like the most important business in the world.

To Carter, it was.

Out back was a tiny office at the end of a tunnel-like stock room. The lighting was better in here - a table lamp plus a 60-watt globe swinging from the ceiling - indicating that Doug wasn't as photosensitive as Carter had once assumed. Even when he'd first met the comic aficionado at a horror convention where Carter had hoped werewolf experts would gather, Doug's stall sat in an alcove without lighting. He'd wondered how the guy had hoped to sell things when people couldn't see his goods. Judging by the two customers out in the store, there were always those more attracted to darkness than to light.

Doug threw himself into a leather office chair behind his desk, one with a dangerous lean. He waved Carter into the folding chair on the opposite side and studied the bank of CCTV monitors set beside his laserjet. Carter was always interested to note that one of the cameras used thermal imaging, but it made sense in the shop's murky light.

"Perverted freak," Doug muttered at the male customer's image. "Never comes in here to buy anything, just to ogle chicks. Watch him try to pick her up in a minute. Ain't you never heard of a nightclub, asswipe?" he asked the monitor.

"So. You have something."

"Oh, yeah, man. I got something." Doug leaned forward and angled his computer monitor around so they could both see it. A YouTube clip was loaded and ready to go, its freeze-frame showing a tilted image of a suburban alley between a brick building and iron fence. Two men were captured, apparently in mid-altercation near a green van. "Guy took this with an iPhone. Though there's better models out there with better resolution—"

"Not really needing an infomercial right now, Doug."

"Yeah, sorry, man. Just brings out the technogeek in me." The mouse scraped on bare wood as Doug positioned the arrow over the play button. "You ready for this?"

Forcing a patience he hadn't felt for months, Carter grunted.

Doug's eyebrows waggled before his finger clicked the left button and the video lurched into life.

The image jolted and jiggled as the cameraman moved to capture the action. A skinny guy lashed out with a short blade but a big guy in work shirt and jeans caught the arm and yanked it, somehow avoiding being stabbed as he bounced the smaller guy off his chest. He followed it up with a punch to the gut and watched his opponent hit the pavement.

The cameraman swore and laughed, the volume and proximity of his voice inappropriate and jarring. The camera lost sight of the men for a moment as the van sped away, forcing the cameraman and a woman near him to dodge out of the way.

"How about that?" Doug said.

Carter let a gasp escape.

The camera tracked the van for a few seconds as it raced up the street past the spires of a large Catholic church before swinging around and reentering the alley. The large man had the smaller one on the ground. The cameraman stepped closer. Teeth were visible beneath the bigger man's dreadlocks. Then he flung himself up and away, while a teenage couple slipped past him from a rear door of the building. The beaten man began to crawl away, an injured hand pressed to his chest.

"Two guys tried to take this lady," the cameraman told someone off camera. The too-loud narration was irritating. He sounded out of breath, though he'd done nothing but film. "Drag her into the van. That dude saved her. Good Samaritan."

Doug added unnecessarily, "Woman being abducted. Big guy comes to the rescue. Hell of a story."

The woman, dressed in hospital clothes, stepped up to her rescuer. She was young, late twenties maybe. She looked rattled, engaging the Samaritan in conversation the camera didn't pick up. She leaned in for a kiss. Someone whistled and clapped.

The cameraman breathed, "That was awesome, man." The video jerked and stopped.

"That Jacob Brennan?" Doug said and started the video again, speaker muted. "I swear it's the guy you showed me. Look at the dreads."

Carter's hand went to his wallet in the front pocket of his chinos, but he left it there. The photo he'd slipped inside the license pane was imprinted in his memory after long hours staring at it: a group shot, it showed Beth, two other shelter volunteers and a small group of indigent men gathered around a meal table. Brennan was to the right approaching the group from the back with a bowl of stew in his hands. His expression was one of surprise, as if caught doing something he shouldn't. In the months since the murder, Carter figured Jake Brennan didn't like getting his photo taken. Given that the cops said he'd dropped off the radar at age thirteen, that made sense. Yet here he was, caught on camera again - Doug had paused the video on a good shot of Brennan's face beneath his tubular bangs.

Twice in twelve months, Brennan. Getting sloppy.

The room felt airless. The light too bright. Carter's voice came out strained. "I'm going to Detroit."

Doug's eyes were wide above his pince-nez. "Cool, man." He fished a pen from a squeaky drawer, slipped a piece of paper from the printer, then clicked on his email contacts. "I printed off a map of the location. That church you saw is the Dearest Heart of Mary. Shouldn't be hard to find someone around there who saw something."

"That's great, Doug. That's perfect." He held out his hand for the print-off.

"Wait." Doug skipped screens. "Let me get you a number of a contact there. Or at least the Michigan chapter-"

"No." Carter grabbed Doug's mouse hand, squeezed it once to still it, then leaned back. "No more of those guys."

"What? What d'ya mean? The Hunters are—"

"The man you put me touch with last time was a waste of space."

Doug looked hurt. "He's a good guy. He's a little spacey, but, hey - he hunts *things*. That's gotta do something to ya, man." He twiddled his fingers near one ear, then dropped his hand abruptly. "Oh. Sorry, man, I didn't mean you."

Carter stood. "Look, I don't need help. You've got me in the ballpark. I can take it from there."

"You can't take one of them on alone. Take this number, man. Or let me call the Hunters for ya. You need back up."

Carter remembered the stink of murder, gunpowder and wet animal. He remembered the size of the monster he'd shot at. "All right. Give me the number."

A huge grin shifted Doug's mutton chops further apart as he wrote down a number. Carter shoved the paper in his wallet without looking at it.

"Appreciate the help, Doug."

"You'll let me know what happens, won't you? I mean, don't leave me hanging, man. I gotta know how the story ends."

Carter moved to the door. "When I get back, you'll be the first person I tell." He was halfway along the stockroom when Doug called out again.

"You still think he's a …? I mean, I believe in them, I been out with that Hunter a couple times, but I never *seen* one."

Blood and fur. A nightmare monster large as life and standing over his wife's corpse. Terror and grief. Gore. The disintegration of his peaceful little life, his family, his faith.

"Believe me, Doug," he said. "You never want to."

To a guy like Doug, this was a trip, a thrill ride, better than drugs or any extreme sport. It was entertainment. As he plunged back into the murk of the store, Carter decided that the man had served his purpose. He never wanted to speak to Doug again.

CHAPTER EIGHT

"Not too shabby, friend."

Angelo, the Listening Ear Mission's director, crossed his beefy arms and smiled as Jake emerged from the shower block behind the main mission building. In Jake's experience, there were smiles that hid dark intentions, smiles that mocked, smiles that were come-ons - and he'd had them from women *and* men - but this guy's smile was okay. It was friendly, a fella trying to put him at ease, do a good deed. Jake wanted to be just like him.

Freshly shaved, freshly showered and wearing a new pair of army pants and a long-sleeve tee, he had to admit he felt better, a tiny bit safer. He'd eaten lunch in this mission a few times over the past few months - he'd always felt good here.

Jake gestured his thanks and held up the workshirt and jeans he'd been wearing the last few weeks, dripping on the concrete yard. He'd washed them while he showered. "Got a plastic bag? I'll dry these at home."

"I can throw them in the dryer. Or on the washing line there. No? Okay, then I'll find a bag." He gestured for Jake to follow him. "Sorry that was the only pair of pants I could find in your size."

Jake followed Angelo across the yard. The shower block nestled alongside a couple of construction site toilets in one back corner of the property. Angelo was headed for a shipping container in the other corner.

The main building had been converted from a suburban house, any lawn long since concreted over. A single strip of weedy garden bed traversed one edge of the driveway. The fences along both sides were the chain link variety common around Detroit, but the rear one was all wood, about seven feet high. The main building was where meals and food parcels were handled. A woman stood by the back doorway smoking and picking at pustules on her arms, thick purple veins prominent along her bloated legs. Earlier he'd seen someone heading away on crutches, food parcel in a shopping bag hooked over his neck. Jake had his problem, but he didn't have theirs. At least he could work when given the chance. At least he never got sick and healed quick.

At the container, Angelo unlocked two padlocks on separate chains and eased one of the doors open. Jake stopped outside, unwilling to follow Angelo inside. It wasn't just the hot air rolling from within; it was the idea of being trapped in a confined space with only one means of escape.

Angelo emerged with a plastic shopping bag.

Jake shoved the wet clothing into the bag then dropped the bag inside his backpack, almost filling it. The pack was maybe big enough to carry a full change of clothes - if Jake had owned one. All he had inside were an unopened bottle of cola, a five-dollar bill, two protein bars, a crumpled gray tee - long-sleeve to hide the track marks the Animal seemed unable or unwilling to heal for him - plus a change of underwear. And the EpiPen - by far the most valuable thing he owned. These items represented the sum of Jake's entire wealth - not counting his rig, securely hidden back in his squat. It'd be stupid - real stupid - to carry that around.

"So where *is* home, friend?" Angelo asked. "You staying close by?"

Jake figured he could trust Angelo. The guy worked with street people for a living and was hardly going to track down Jake's squat to rob him. And he wasn't one of Zee's goons.

"Not too far," he answered. "Empty house."

"Plenty of them about." Angelo disappeared inside the container once more while Jake put the plastic bag inside the backpack. A few seconds later, he returned holding a pair of khaki shorts, a gray tee, a rolled-up pair of black work socks and two pairs of new Y-fronts still plastic-clipped to their cardboard packaging. "I'm sure these will come in handy. You need a toothbrush, toothpaste?"

"Sure. Could use some food too. If you got it."

"Okay. You missed lunch, but the kitchen'll have some leftovers. I can put them in another plastic bag for you. Won't be too heavy?"

Jake frowned. Was the guy jerking him round?

"Just kidding, friend. Just kidding."

Jake waited in the container's shade while Angelo locked it, then vanished into the house. The smoker waddled in after him. The building was bleeding people out the front and onto the side driveway: folk who'd eaten their fill and didn't want to help clean up. He'd done the same plenty of times. Eat and move on. You hung around, people wanted to talk. You talked, people got to know you, remembered you. Or wanted something from you.

Snatches of conversation drifted through the open door: women joking; Angelo's booming laugh; someone scolding him for getting in the way, him, the guy who ran the place. People had no respect. This was a guy doing good with his life.

Maybe I should help out in a place like this, he thought.

He could do it without having to talk to people. Play stupid. Pretend he couldn't talk. Yeah, in the next town. He could start again, find one of these places where no one knew him and help out sometimes. It would go a long way in making him a better man. Erasing the marks against his name.

A rail-thin woman appeared in the driveway with two girls in tow. They held shopping bags full of groceries and chattered like birds at sun up. The little girl was skipping and she looked back at him. She waved. He couldn't help himself - he smiled and waved back. She grinned, then crashed into her mother, who'd stopped to wait. The mother swore, caught Jake looking and blushed at his attention. She shoved the girl ahead of her and dropped her voice, but kept up the reprimands until they disappeared from view.

"Food, glorious food!" Angelo lumbered down the back step. He held out a bag for Jake to inspect: a disposable plastic container of still-warm lasagna, apples, and toothbrush and paste. Jake's mouth watered at the sight of the pasta.

"You don't mind me asking," Angelo started, then stopped at something in Jake's eyes. "Okay. Fair enough. Well, I better help clean up in there. No rest for the wicked. Stay safe. You need anything, you drop in. Even if it's just to talk. Don't think you do much of that though, do ya?"

Jake was already at the corner of the house. "Thanks," he said over his shoulder. He wasn't sure if he meant it for the food and clothes or the offer of conversation.

Coming on to the street, he realized the mission was by far the best-maintained property in this neighborhood of broken sidewalks and abandoned houses. Some properties were little more than piles of rubble with waist-high weed-clusters as thick as Jake's arm. One lot sported the front wall and stairs of a house with little behind them but the charcoal trash of a past fire.

He was halfway through the vacant lot beside the burnout house when a woman started screaming.

More screamin.

"Help! Someone oh god help *help* she's dyin! Oh god!"

Feeling like he'd gone back in time to the day before to the attack on the nurse, he clamped the pack and shopping bag to his chest as he broke into a jog. But when he emerged onto the new street, the scene was very different. It was the family who'd left the mission ahead of him - the mom and two girls. The younger girl who'd smiled at him lay on the busted up pavement, her legs twitching and writhing. The mom crouched over her so he couldn't see exactly what was going on. The older girl bobbed up and down nearby, her arms and hands moving like pistons.

"Oh baby," the mother moaned again, then gasped as Jake stooped down beside them.

The kid was in bad shape. Real bad. Her face looked like someone had taken to her mouth and eyes with bare knuckles. Bumps and spots were appearing wherever her skin was visible and her fingers were swelling.

"Allergic?" he asked the mom. "What to?"

The woman lost her voice at that moment, shaking her head frantically.

"Never happened before," said the older girl in a tight voice.

It was a fast reaction for a first time. The only reaction he'd seen happen this bad this fast was his own. He glanced at a wrapper fluttering nearby in the slight breeze: a Snickers. Maybe the peanuts.

"That hers?" he asked the other girl. She nodded.

The sick kid's breath wheezed in and out, in and out. Her eyes were swollen shut now. She wasn't gonna make it. Not this bad.

"Do something," the mom said, the words whispered like air escaping a punctured tire.

A car was cruising down the road, slowing as the driver took in the entertainment on the sidewalk.

"Tell em to stop," he told the older girl while he dumped his pack.

"Yes, yes, stop them, Melly," the woman told her.

Jake stuck a hand into the front pocket of the backpack. His fingers closed around the EpiPen and squeezed hard as he fought the decision. It was his last one. And she might be too small to use it on anyway. Would it kill her if the dose was too big? He'd never had to think about that before, but he vaguely remembered there was a smaller one for small kids. If the car stopped, maybe he wouldn't need to.

Melly stepped into the gutter and waved her hands over her head. Jake didn't see the driver's face, but there was no indication of him even considering stopping.

Shit. It was save the girl's life now and risk his own later. Or…

There was no *or.*

"Goddamn sonofabitch!" the mom screamed at the departing vehicle. "Son-of-a-bitch bastard!" The cry turned half sob.

Jake took out the EpiPen and pulled off the cap. The skin on her ears was turning blue. He grabbed the little girl's leg tight. Jake shoved the end of the device against her thigh muscle and held it there. At the click of the needle inserting, the girl's leg jerked from the sting though she showed no reaction in her face. He kept a firm grip and counted to ten before he pulled the injector away.

"Hospital," Jake said. "Gotta get her there right now." He picked her up. She felt as light as his pack. What if the dose had been too strong? She coughed and he anticipated the convulsion with enough time to turn her sideways so she threw up on the ground and not his shirt. When she'd finished, her breathing sounded stronger, and she called for her mommy.

Jake righted her in his arms while the mom stepped up close enough to brush shoulders with him, stroking the girl's hair and reassuring her. The woman smelled like mildew and stale marijuana.

"Hospital," he repeated, searching the street. There were no other cars, but a few of these homes were occupied. A guy had stepped out onto his porch a few doors down to watch the ruckus, hand over his eyes to block the glare. Jake started towards him at a run, the girl bobbing and whimpering in his arms.

"Get my bags!" he shouted over his shoulder, but didn't stop to check if they did.

When he was a few yards away from the guy's property boundary, the guy reached for the wire door.

"Don't you move!" Jake bellowed. He huffed to a stop on the smattering of grass and dirt that passed for a front lawn and jerked his head at a car parked in the driveway. "Hospital. You get your keys and drive us."

The man pushed his glasses back up his nose. The hand continued upwards to smooth his sparse gray hair. He glanced at the old Capris uncertainly.

"Do it!"

The man flinched, then disappeared inside his house. Jake swore to himself that if the guy stayed indoors, locked the door on them, he'd rip him apart.

"Gotcha bags, mister," said Melly holding them out to him.

"You just hang onto that for me 'til your sister's okay. What's her name?"

"Sophie," said the mom. "What the hell's wrong with her?"

"Peanut allergy. Maybe. She'll be fine if we can get her to a doctor." She was breathing better and the blue had disappeared from her ears, though her face and fingers were still badly swollen. Jake didn't know much, but he knew about anaphylaxis; with a reaction this bad, she could well get all the symptoms back again without help.

Visions of digging silver from his leg with a pocket knife swamped him. That had hurt like a bitch - two bitches even - but getting it out of him had prevented the reaction coming back; it had only cost him one EpiPen. The scar on his calf itched as if responding to his thoughts.

The man resurfaced, jangling keys. He pivoted at the step and locked his door, then shuffled as fast as he could to the car. He still hadn't said a word.

Jake laid Sophie on the back seat and stepped aside for the mom to squeeze in beside her. He indicated for Melly to jump in the front bench seat, holding the door for her. She cast furtive glances at the driver who was pumping the accelerator and trying to start the car.

"He wont hurt ya," Jake assured her. She smiled up at him with what he thought a girl might look at her dad with: trust, reassurance. Things people rarely offered him. That was twice in a few days now people had trusted him.

He held out his hand for the backpack and Melly passed it up to him. The shopping bag was on the ground by the front wheel. He picked it up. The engine started with a cough and splutter, toxic plumes billowing into the yard. He should shut the door, he told himself. He'd done something good. Time to move on, take his clothes home and dry them, make ready for the Moon.

But that had been his only EpiPen. Where the hell was he gonna get another?

"Scoot over," he told Melly and squeezed in beside her.

CHAPTER NINE

Carter knew he shouldn't have brought the photo album on his train trip. Next to it, in the side pocket of his sports bag, he had the old legal novel that first inspired Beth to help "the marginalized" - as she preferred to call them - and a pocket New Testament. They were much better choices to flip through. He had resisted looking at the photos the whole bus trip from Rockford to Chicago. He'd resisted pulling it out while he hung around Union Station, marching around the platforms and tunnels, burning off adrenaline while awaiting his connection. And he'd forced his eyes to track the words in the novel for the first hour of the train journey to Detroit, occasionally fantasizing about suing the author over his wife's death.

When he realized he was reading a line about a Miata sports car for the fourth time, he dog-eared the page and laid the book on the empty seat beside him.

The lure of the photo album was relentless. He slipped it from the bag, ran his hands across the soft, glossy surface, and admired the way that photos poked out the sides haphazardly. This was his private album, the one he'd constructed from Beth's more clinical books with their perfect lines and trimmed edges and anally retentive chronological order.

He shouldn't open it. He knew he shouldn't. But he did.

The disjointed timeline of images chronicled a fifteen-year period, designed to rebreak an already broken heart: Beth nursing a dark pink blob in the maternity wing; Elijah on his first swing set, his fourth birthday present; Beth twenty-one years old and graduating from Bible College, first in her class. In this last one, her hair was beautifully sculpted, her collared dress dated but somehow regal. Was that really only a month after they'd first met? Had they already been so in love that he knew to take a picture of his own, that it would mean something, the picture and the girl both keepers?

He was sinking again, the gravity well of depression dragging at him. The six coffees he'd had merely added an accelerated heart rate beneath the melancholy, and burned his throat with nervous reflux. The album wasn't helping. He should get up and move around. He should read his New Testament and pray like he used to, seek peace for his soul.

Peace.

Sure.

It wasn't peace he needed. The Bible might say that vengeance belonged to the Lord, but the Lord hadn't lost His wife to a werewolf. The hope of vengeance was the only thing keeping Carter going.

In a flash he realized something. He could let go of the whole thing, actually let it go. He could abandon this mad crusade and forgive - forgive a monster. He could work toward getting Elijah back. He could honor Beth's memory by living the way she had lived. For a moment, he actually felt it: the release that would come from letting go of the hatred, the anger, the outrage. He wondered if this were the type of thing that qualified as a religious experience. He'd never had one before. A warmth touched him at the core, as if hot fingers were unraveling bitter tendrils from around his gut, his heart.

That thing killed my Beth.

The thought snapped him out of it, clamped those tendrils back in place. He'd be damned before he ever forgave a werewolf.

Like a whisper on the wind a new thought came to him: *Perhaps you will be, Carter. Perhaps you will be.*

The note sat in Gwen's pigeonhole like a not-so-well-disguised booby trap. The pink paper was turned faced down, but she could see the reverse impression of handwriting pressed through from the other side. Barry's writing.

She slipped the other paperwork from beneath it, turned her back and leafed through the documents. She tossed the ones she didn't need back on top of the pink note and got on with her day. A message from Barry was nothing she couldn't deal with later, when she was really tired and grumpy, grumpy enough to screw it up without reading it and without feeling any guilt.

Her palms stung, the left one still covered in plasters. Other bruises from the scuffle made her walk stiffly and she wished she was allowed to drink on the job. The thought stopped her in her tracks, halfway down the hallway from the locker room to the lift. That was a dumb thought. A real dumb thought. It scared her that it had come from *her* brain.

She shook it off and continued to the elevator.

Another doctor patted her shoulder as he passed. "Glad you're still with us."

She made a friendly noise and stabbed the button. People had been sending her intense stares since she'd walked in a half hour ago. The staffers who actually knew her asked after her: Was she okay? Had the cops caught the men who assaulted her? Who was the guy who'd stepped in to help? She'd dodged the questions the way she'd dodge the two reporters staking out the main entrance, keeping her head down, keeping moving, saved by normal hospital busyness, the constant stream of need that flowed through the doors to clog the hallways and exam rooms. People were busy themselves and let her pass without stopping her; the reporters had been too interested in their cell phones and their own reflections in their compact mirrors.

On the way down to the ground floor, she thought about the pink note: what Barry wanted was obvious. A conversation dripping with concern for her welfare—

Then why didn't he stop by to check on me? Or phone?

—followed by a couple of dinners, a concert and a quickie or two. Then it'd be back to him being too busy to talk except for *Gwen, I wish you'd let me buy you a better blouse than that* and *I'd like to see you try a little harder with my friends.*

She didn't need him. She never had. Amidst all the insanity in her life, that was one thing she'd been able to fix, to *excise*. And no way was she going back there. If only he could get that through his thick skull.

ER craziness swallowed her the second she stepped out of the lift so that she immediately forgot the pink note. And the terrors of the day before.

Twenty minutes into her shift, she was attending to an older woman with a scalded hand when an orderly and an agency nurse she didn't know wheeled a new bed to the other side of the partition wall. A little girl lay on it, the lower half of her face hidden beneath an oxygen mask; her mom and older sister hovered. The agency nurse called to her that the girl was in anaphylactic shock and Gabby scurried into Gwen's cubicle to take over bandaging the old man's hand, freeing Gwen for the greater emergency.

The sniffling mom fussed over her supine daughter, so that Gwen had to dodge her to get to the bed. The orderly backpedaled out of there, replaced by a male nurse. Gwen felt the girl's hands and throat. Her skin was cool, blood pressure probably low.

"She's had a shot of epinephrine ten minutes ago via EpiPen," said the agency nurse, all business. She already had saline going and now applied a blood pressure cuff. "They think it's a reaction to peanuts. Never had one before."

"Please help her," said the mom.

"That's the idea, ma'am," Gwen said, somewhat gruffly, as she bumped into the shaking woman for the third time. There was still evidence of urticaria, though the hives seemed to be fading. The girl's breath wheezed loudly beneath the mask and Gwen ordered the first nurse to check O2 saturation while the male nurse took her temperature.

"We'll look after her," he told the mom, more gently than Gwen had. "If you could just take a seat there, it'd make it easier for us."

The mom sank into a nearby arm chair.

With nurses barking numbers, Gwen checked the girl's eyes. She was awake, pupils shrunk to pinheads with anxiety more than allergy. "Fifty milligrams Benadryl and one ampule Albuterol via nebulizer."

The male nurse jumped to it immediately.

"Intubate?" the other asked.

Gwen shook her head. "Give her another shot of epi. See how she goes with the medication. What's her name?" she asked the mom.

The woman was rocking in the chair, one arm scratching her skinny ribs, the other hand playing with her stringy hair. She whispered something Gwen couldn't catch.

"Pardon?"

"Sophie," said the girl's sister.

Gwen had all but forgotten she was there. She craned her neck around and smiled reassuringly. "Maybe you could go stand by your mom, sweetheart. Looks like she could use a hug." She turned her smile on the patient. "Sophie, honey. You're gonna be fine. We're gonna make you all better."

Sophie blinked back at her and murmured "Okay" into her mask.

Gwen moved away to let the male nurse administer the medication. She moved around to the older girl who was trying to rub her mom's shoulder. The woman had folded in on herself, hands clamped between her knees as if her daughter's ministrations weren't welcome.

Gwen squatted to look the mother in the eyes. "We'll get her comfortable again, keep her under observation. All going well, you should be able to take her home later tonight."

"She'll be okay?" the mom asked, eyes widening. Had she expected the worst? In a life awash with tragedy, had the prospect of a new heartbreak filled the woman with expectation? Something she could play on for sympathy and charity?

"Code Blue!" someone called from the epicenter of a commotion breaking out across the ward. The female nurse with Gwen scrambled to respond.

The male caught Gwen's attention. "I got this, Doc."

She winked at Sophie, then raced across the ward, feeling spent. She wondered that she had ever enjoyed the adrenaline rush of this job when now all it did was piss her off.

As Carter buried the photo album deep as he could in his bag, his knuckles brushed the cold steel of the .32. He almost laughed at the fact he was carrying it in a train across state lines. No one had asked to screen his single carry-on bag. None of the cops wandering around the station had hassled him, not even the one with a sniffer dog. He hadn't seen a single law enforcement person on the train. What was to stop him going postal right here right now, plugging that teenager over there who kept trying to look up that lady's skirt? Or that cocky musclebound guy talking loudly? It was scary how easy it was for people to kill other people if they really wanted to. Post-9/11, you couldn't bring a water pistol through LAX without a strip search, but you could travel the country by rail and coach packing as much heat as you could conceal inside your duffel bag.

He checked his watch. The train would pull into Michigan Central in just under two hours. What the hell was he going to do when he got there? He slid the novel in beside the album and pulled out the tacky little tourist map he'd picked up at Union Station. The various panels bragged about stunning historical and cultural sights to see; everyone but the Detroit tourist industry and its mayor knew Detroit had been five steps away from the apocalypse for decades. It was nothing but a great location for rap videos and zombie movies, and he could think of no more appropriate place to hunt a monster.

But where to begin? That was the question. The cops would be no help, given they had never suspected Brennan in the first place. He had a location for the assault Brennan had intervened in. He could go door knocking. He could search the shelters and soup kitchens. They were reasonable plans. And they might be a complete waste of time.

Carter had little in his wallet but the one-way ticket and a couple hundred bucks. It wouldn't see him through an extended stay, especially with taxi fares or car hire. He hated to admit it, but he'd need help.

He yanked out his wallet and unfolded the scrap of paper with Doug's chicken scratchings on it. Ten digits. No name. Perhaps he'd hurried Doug so much, the comic book seller had forgotten to write it. Perhaps Doug had been instructed not to give out names. And perhaps Carter should stop stalling and just call the damn number.

With a grunt of frustration, he slipped out his cell phone.

When the code blue was over, the elderly patient's heart beating on its own again, Gwen looked up to find Pam's head poking around the half-curtained doorway. "I need you for a moment, Doctor. You ain't gonna believe this."

"*Aren't*, Pam. The word is *aren't*." She issued instructions to the nursing staff and stepped over to the curtain. "Whassup? Kinda busy here."

Pam shook her head, a curious smile fixed to her face. "You have to see it. That is, if you *aren't* too busy for something truly interesting."

Returning to work had been a mistake. *Home* had her bed. *Home* had food and TV and wine. *Work* had more to do than Gwen could keep up with. *Work* had people almost dying, and people actually dying, people who'd hurt themselves because no one but a hospital would give them any personal attention, and people who'd come to hospital with minor complaints they could have seen their family doctor about, people whose addictions had caused them harm, and people harmed by others' addictions. *Work* was something Gwen could never complete, never look back on with a sense of achievement. The stream of misery never ended, the pressure never abated. And now that she was here, she couldn't leave, because there was always something else to do.

Grumbling and cussing, hungry and tired and headachey, Gwen followed Pam. She stopped short when it became clear just what - or rather who - Pam wanted to show her.

He leaned against the wall like a side of beef in cheap clothing. His head was down, dreadlocks hanging over his face. It was that pose she recognized more than anything else. Who else could it be, but him?

"That the guy?" Pam stage-whispered, drawing quizzical looks from a passing paramedic.

Gwen lifted her chin in acknowledgment. "Can you take over?"

"That's why I'm here," she said with a pat on the bottom. "Make sure you get his number. But don't take too long."

Butterflies figure-skating along her intestinal wall, Gwen straightened her scrubs and waded through the people in the corridor. He raised his head when she was a couple of yards away to stare straight at her, almost as if he'd sensed her coming. She was struck again by the strangeness of his eyes; in the neon light of the hallway the caramel of his irises was flecked with gold or yellow. Unique eyes. Wary eyes.

"Hi," she said, brushing a stray strand from her face and wishing he'd do the same with his own curtain of hair. "Didn't expect to see you again."

"I'm here with the girl," he said. His voice was deep, gruff, and a little raspy as if his vocal cords were rusty. His gaze lifted off her, scanned the corridor.

"Which girl?"

"Had a reaction. Almost died."

"Wait, you're with Sophie Wallace? I treated her. That's weird, right? That our paths would cross twice in the same week like this."

He nodded. "She okay?"

"She will be. How do you know her? She your daughter?"

He snorted, dropped his head, the curtains closing on his face.

Okay. Not your daughter then.

"Listen," she glanced around, self-conscious. A couple nurses were huddled with Pam at the main desk, peeking at them through the shifting mass of people. Pam gave her a little thumbs up. Gwen turned her shoulder and cleared her throat. "You left so quickly the other day. I didn't get a chance to thank you."

"Yeah, you did." His gaze shifted back, catching her with a jolt.

She recalled the feel of his dreads on her ear, his beard on her lips as she'd given him that peck on the cheek. Her skin warmed. He didn't smell so bad today. In fact, he didn't smell at all. He was wearing different clothes and they were clean, if old. The same tarnished backpack sat between his feet on the ground along with a plastic shopping bag. He had one foot clamped on a pack-strap as if preventing it crawling off. This hyper-vigilance reminded her he was probably homeless.

"Well, I did kinda - I *said* thanks. I just feel like I owe you something. What you did was…"

His honey-colored eyes softened. "It was no bother."

"You saved my life and I don't even know your name. I'm Gwen." She stuck out her hand, kept it there until his engulfed it briefly. His palm was warm, the skin soft, with few callouses.

He glanced up and down the hall, as if making sure no one was listening. "Jake."

"Well, Jake, it's good to meet you." A pause. "So you have the day off work or something?"

"Still trying to find it."

She felt stupid. It had been a clumsy attempt. "It's hard out there, I hear. What kind of work you looking for?"

He shrugged. "I don't mind. Was gonna try the docks tonight, but depends what happens with—" He jerked his chin toward Sophie's ward again. "Maybe tomorrow."

"Doc's?"

"Docks. Port of Detroit. You know, ships?"

"Oh."

Back behind one of the curtains, someone swore. A patient bumped her shoulder, moving past her without apology; Gwen's heart rate spiked. She flashed back to another bump from behind, a hand reaching over that same shoulder.

"Dr Cheevey?"

She turned to face the nurse, suppressing a yelp.

Gabby jerked her head back toward the triage counter, where an obese man in gym shorts and way-too-small t-shirt remonstrated with the registrar. "Got a family member demanding to speak with a doctor." Her gaze flicked to Jake and back.

"Okay, I'll be there in a sec."

Gabby made a sure-you-will face and trotted away.

Gwen brushed the errant hair from her forehead again. "Listen, Sophie will be in for a while. I'd like to get you a coffee later, maybe an early dinner? Cafeteria's right upstairs."

He studied his backpack. Was he thinking of leaving? He wasn't Sophie's father. But couldn't he be hooked up with her mom, that emaciated shrew in there? Could he?

"I'll buy for your wife too ..."

He recoiled. "I'm not with her."

"Sorry. I just thought ... So, you were out doing good deeds again?"

"I need EpiPens," he said.

She blinked. "Pardon?"

"If you wanna gimme somethin', I need some EpiPens. As many as you can get me. Gave my last one to the kid."

"Oh. Okay. Wow, that was kind." Kind? No, it was normal. Who could possibly stand by and watch a child die when they had the means to save them right there in their pocket. Was she that citified now that she thought ordinary decency an act of heroism? "Sure, I can prescribe a couple. What are you allergic to?"

"That's my business." At her expression, he softened again. "They're not only for me; they're so I can help people like Sophie."

"That's good of you, but you can't just use them on anyone. Little kids need a smaller dose. Sophie was only just big enough to take the dose you gave her. Not that it was the wrong thing to do. You did the only thing you could. But … well, you can't just give them out. People need their own prescription."

"Hard for some folk to get a prescription. Even when they need it."

She cocked her head. Folk? He meant the homeless, the poor. His use of the word *folk* made her wonder at his accent again with its touch of the South.

"Okay then," he said, misinterpreting her pause as reluctance. "Just for me then. Two would be great."

"Dr. Cheevey!" the registrar called from her desk.

Gwen lifted a hand. "Well, what are you allergic to, Jake?"

He shifted uncomfortably, mumbled, "You wouldn't believe me if I told ya."

She frowned. It wasn't like he was asking for methadone or amphetamines - someone using epinephrine for recreational use was going to feel a little energetic for a few minutes then get a nasty headache straight after. But it was illegal. And if he had an allergy, she wanted to help. Help properly. "I can't just give them to you. I'm sorry, there are rules."

Jake's face clouded, then he stiffened as a pair of cops shouldered their way down the corridor, headed for the reception desk. He ducked down for his backpack and shopping bag and said, "Gave my last one to the girl. How'm I gonna replace it?" He straightened and kept his gaze on the pack, hair covering most of his face.

God. This wasn't going well. All she wanted to do was repay his kindness?

Out the corner of her eye, she could see Gabby wandering past making *WTF* signals at her. The fat family member was still making a pest of himself at triage.

"Look. I'll help you. Really. But epinephrine's a prescription medication. I'll need to run tests. Or contact your last family doctor, get them to fax your file over. And I'll need your social security number."

He jostled the pack, tugged one of the zips closed and flashed a look toward the cops at the desk. Most people distrusted police, Gwen knew, the homeless most of all.

Great timing, guys.

"Don't worry about it," Jake said. "Tell Sophie's mom I'll be outside waitin'."

He turned on his heel and shuffled down the hallway. Whereas the two police officers had had to push their way through, people got out of Jake's way. Hopefully, she thought, the two reporters outside had grown bored or been called away to the next flavor-of-the-moment story; hopefully the big lug wouldn't get cornered by them. She didn't think he'd cope well with that attention.

Gwen caught Pam giving her a slow shake of the head. She shoved her errant lock of hair into her scrunchy and headed for the triage counter. She needed a coffee. She needed a minute to herself. But she was only half way through her shift and she had a troublemaker to contend with. And then there'd be something else after that…

I didn't do anything wrong. I can't just give Jake medication.

The oath she'd taken had been to *Do no harm.*

Increasingly Gwen felt like she was doing no good.

CHAPTER TEN

Carter's contact was easy to pick out on the narrow Amtrak platform. Several people scanned the stream of passengers with varying levels of anxiety and excitement, but only one had a flat-top haircut, a handlebar mustache as thick as an index finger, black-and-gray camouflage pants, army boots and a dark brown leather jacket over a Pink Floyd tee.

Carter nodded when they made eye contact and the guy looked momentarily nonplussed.

What, I'm not urban guerilla enough for you?

But he shook hands amicably enough, yellow teeth showing beneath the huge mustache.

"Carter Moffat?"

Carter straightened the gym bag strap on his shoulder. "That's me."

"Good. Come with me."

His contact set a fast pace along the platform. Carter only caught up with him when the Hunter reached the top of the ramp down to the parking garage and had to stop while a young couple wrestled a stroller past.

"I didn't catch your name," he puffed.

The man gave him a sideways look. "Not here." He started down the ramp.

Seriously?

At the bottom of the ramp, Carter suddenly wondered if he should be following this guy anywhere. What if it was a set-up? Detroit had a hell of a reputation: fifth highest murder rate in the US. He'd checked that before leaving home. The sun had almost set, so it seemed the right time for the criminals to surface and commence the night's nefarious work.

He chuckled bleakly at the irony: *Brennan gives himself away by taking out a couple of rapists; I come to Detroit and get assaulted myself.*

Shifting the bag around against his stomach so he could get at his pistol quicker if needed, he leaned against the railing and stretched a cramp out of his back. The Hunter made it a dozen yards before realizing he was no longer being followed. His beady eyes squinted back at Carter.

"What's the problem?"

"Not going any further until you tell me where we're headed."

The man scratched at one ear, frowning. "Gonna get in my car. Gonna get you kitted out." He waited while a man jogged past Carter headed for the street, then came closer. "Gonna find a theryon."

"Theryon?"

The man put two straight fingers to each side of his head in imitation of dog ears and bared his teeth.

Carter allowed himself a small shake of his head. But really, what choice did he have but to trust this weirdo? Still, there was one more thing to settle before he'd pick up his bag and follow.

"Your *name?*"

The man raised his hands in mock surrender. "Call me Darkrider. Now come the frack on." He started off again, waving for Carter to catch up.

Frack? Darkrider? What planet did this guy live on? Then again, what normal person hunted werewolves in modern America?

Carter watched a father hugging his little boy on the platform above. The son started babbling about all the things that had happened since his father had been gone. A woman looked on proudly. A couple of years ago, this could have been Carter's family. He hugged his bag tighter and lugged it after his guide.

Darkrider was waiting by a 1970 Chevelle, black with twin white stripes along roof and hood. For a guy who didn't want to be known by his real name, he wasn't very good at keeping a low profile. Carter refused to dropp his bag inside the open trunk, clutching it under one arm and shutting the lid while the Hunter got in the car. He dropped himself onto the passenger seat and slammed the door, kept a hand on the zipper of his bag. Darkrider was checking something on his cell and Carter took a moment to identify the heady mix of odors mingling in the car's small ecosphere: moldering fast food, stale cigarette smoke, unwashed armpits. He was stuck with this tool for the moment, he needed him, but when he tried to make nice the best he could manage was mild sarcasm.

"So, do I call you Dark or Rider for short?"

The Hunter gave him a frustrated look for the longest moment and finally growled, "Tim."

"Ok, Tim. I like that name better anyway." He smiled and hoped it looked reassuring. "Never met a Tim I didn't like."

'Til now.

"Tim, I'm going to raise this subject up front. The last 'Hunter' I worked with wanted money. Got a little pissed when I wouldn't give him any. I'm being straight up here: I'm down to my last hundred bucks." *Well, almost straight up.* "I'll probably be hitching home to Illinois. So if you're expecting a tip…"

Tim was already shaking his head, face screwed up like he was swallowing lemon juice. "That guy shouldn't've asked for money. We pay you. We pay a bounty. And we look after expenses. If—" Tim raised a finger "—your lead is bona fide."

"Why didn't Doug tell me that?"

"Who's Doug? That Hunter? Don't know a Doug."

"The guy who gave me your number. Owns a comic book store."

"Maybe he's not a member."

Member? Bounty? Who the hell are these guys?

"Anyway," Tim continued. "Don't worry about money. Money's not an issue."

"Really?" Carter said, scanning his guide's outfit.

Tim retrieved a backpack from the back seat. "Not an issue at all. You bring ordnance?"

"Ord…? Oh. Yeah, a .32."

"Thirty-two? That's, like, a girl's gun. It holds, what, five rounds? It's packing silver, though. Right? Silver bullets?"

Carter fought the urge to roll his eyes. "WalMart didn't have any."

Tim made a noise like Carter had just farted in his car. "Lucky you got me, pal." He pulled a larger handgun from his backpack and held it up between them. "This is a Glock 17. Single stack of ten nine-millimeter rounds in the clip - less than the standard seventeen but still double what your pussy little piece carries." He handed the weapon to Carter. "You may as well sell your pop gun for loose change if you're that hard up for cash. You'll be glad of the extra rounds, believe me."

Carter pressed his lips into a straight line, accepting the rebuke as graciously as he could, and hefted the Glock. He had to admit it *felt* more powerful than his little revolver. Even just the weight of it was reassuring.

Tim grinned. "Nice, huh? We'll go practice with a standard clip somewhere if we get time, but it's basically point and shoot. Bullets are silver, handmade by our smiths. One clip loaded, one spare." He reached into the bag and produced the spare magazine, which Carter tried to slide into his jeans pocket. It refused to fit. "Leave them in the bag for now. We'll get you dressed for the job later. "

"So, before we start, can I ask, what's your interest in this? I mean, why help me out? Neither Doug nor the last Hunter were too clear on what you guys are in this for."

"Isn't it obvious? Hell, you're kinda one of us now. We just don't want these things loose in our world. Evil sons-of-*bitches*."

"That's it? You'll risk your life and pay me for the privilege of risking mine with you? Just because you don't like them?"

Tim wrestled with his shirt. For a frightening moment, Carter thought he was going for another gun and wondered whether he should slug him in the jaw. Then Tim got his shirt untucked and lifted it up above his hairy nipples. Carter couldn't help but gasp. Tim's chest and stomach were a patchwork of angry scars, as if someone had dipped him belly first into a woodchipper. A whole chunk of muscle on one side of his abdomen beneath his ribs was missing - like he'd had a bite taken out of him. Carter didn't need any further explanation but Tim gave him one anyway.

"Twenty-oh-five. I'm camping. Thing comes outta nowhere and jumps me. Bastard's clawing the hell out of me, but my buddy Gus shoots him. Bastard turns on Gus and drags him screaming into the woods. Never saw him again. Lucky there was some other campers around. They get me to a hospital, while I'm holding my guts in with my hands. Kinda made an impact on me, you know." He dropped the shirt. "No one believed what I saw, what I said did it. Apparently you've had something of the same experience. But I saw it. Just like you did. The Hunters found me when I was in rehab. Recruited me. Offered to pay my medical bills. I said yes before they'd finished their pitch."

Carter's face was hot, his hands trembling. "Brennan killed my wife. Right in front of me."

Tim extended his hand for the second time that day. "We both owe these theryon bastards some payback, brother. Together we're gonna make this right, if we can trust each other and work together."

With more enthusiasm than he had the first time, Carter gripped Tim's hand.

CHAPTER ELEVEN

Around nine o'clock - as the daylight was turning orange - Sophie's Mom came out of the hospital. Jake was lurking in the shade of the public entrance, hoping to catch them on the way out. He'd eaten all the food Angelo had given him, but he needed a replacement injector and the mom was his best bet. She walked over and offered him a smoke he didn't take. The chemical stench enveloped him as she lit one up.

"You did good by my girl."

"Couldn't let her die."

"Wish I could repay you or something, but ..." She showed her hands as if to say that the cigarette packet and lighter was all she had, then flashed a broken-toothed grin. "Might be another way I can thank you."

He took a breath to reply, but she pressed on.

"They're letting Soph out soon. You wanna come in and see her?"

"Sure, I guess." He waited for her to finish her cigarette, then followed her inside.

Sophie sat upright in bed, in her own clothes and propped up by a pillow, her sister at her elbow. She looked normal again, her skin pink and healthy, a big smile on her face. Neither girl noticed him as he took up a position against the wall in the walkway opposite them. They had eyes only for Gwen - who didn't notice him either. A young nurse stood by while the doctor scribbled on a clipboard. Sophie's Mom took up a position by the pushed back-curtain, shifting from foot to foot.

"No more Snickers, young lady," Gwen said in a mock stern voice, which made both girls giggle. "No more PBJs, no more nut bars, no more satay sauce." Gwen slapped the clipboard against her thigh.

"Sounds terrible doesn't it? Like I'm leaving you nothing yummy to eat. But just remember, you can still eat lots of awesome things - just not nuts. "

"Fries?"

"Sure! As long as you share them with me." Gwen ruffled Sophie's hair, then helped her down from the bed. "How much do you hate big needles?"

"A lot," Sophie replied.

"Then if you want to avoid them, you have to do what I say, okay?"

"All right."

"Or else I'm gonna come after you with a real big needle."

Sophie giggled and Jake found himself smiling too. He wondered if Gwen had kids of her own.

She looked tired, dark circles under her eyes, her face paler than he remembered it from the street. Well, she'd had a hard time of it yesterday; it was impressive that she was here helping people after something like that.

Gwen noticed the mother then, checked her name from a form. "Gail. Sophie's okay to go. I've requested allergy tests from a pediatric allergy specialist here at the hospital. You'll get a letter to notify you of a date soon. In the meantime, as I say, no nuts of any kind."

"Okay," Gail said.

"Check all packaging carefully before she eats anything, especially cereal, food bars, stuff like that. Make sure there's no warnings on them like 'May contain nuts'."

Gail's head bobbed as if in contrition and hugged Sophie to her. "Sure."

"We're giving you some prednisone tablets for Sophie to take for the next three days, plus an EpiPen." Gwen tore a paper from the clipboard and handed it to her. "This is a prescription for a spare EpiPen. You can fill this at any pharmacy. You might want to think about getting her a medicalert bracelet too, in case this happens at school or somewhere you're not around."

Gail stared down at the prescription as if it were something poisonous. Jake wondered fleetingly if she could read, but he was more interested in the clear plastic bag full of medication the waiting nurse handed over.

"This is the tablets the doctor mentioned plus an EpiPen Jnr," she said, then indicated Jake. "It's just like your friend used on Sophie, only a lower dose. Instructions for it are on the plan. But he can show you how."

At the nurse's mention of "friend", Gwen noticed him for the first time. Her cheeks reddened but she offered him a smile. He returned it briefly, but his gaze slipped to the meds. When it returned to her, she was already headed for the next curtained cubicle. He felt a pang of loss and shrugged it off as quickly as it came. He had no business with feelings like that.

"You're a good man," a voice said at his shoulder. The nurse. She patted his arm and moved on to another bed.

Three sets of eyes now stared back at him - Sophie, Melly, Gail - as if the next move was his. As if he would tell them what they should do now. As if he had any idea.

It turned out Sophie, Melly and Gail lived pretty close to him. The trailer park was a fifteen-minute walk from his squat. After what had happened to Gwen the other night, Jake insisted on walking them home. He carried Sophie; she felt as light as the pack on his back.

No one said much. The streets were dark, the sidewalks broken in patches. A few groups of men looked them over as they passed, but no one ventured closer. Melly lagged, pulling on her mom's arm. Jake's mind was on the injector in Gail's worn shoulderbag. It seemed kind of rude to ask for it. But then, he had saved the girl's life. It'd be pretty fair to give him theirs and fill the prescription they had sometime soon - plus they had those pills.

Problem was, EpiPens cost about forty bucks. And Gail had been picking up her food at a charity earlier, not a supermarket.

She walked beside him, her hand twined in her Sophie's hair and occasionally brushing his chest. More times than could be a coincidence.

"You work?" Jake asked. It seemed right to check if she had enough money to buy another before he asked for the injector and got away from them.

She dropped her hand to her pocket. "Cleaning. Afternoons at a school, a Korean restaurant up by Claude Street on Wednesday nights. Why?"

The weight of the girl prevented him from shrugging properly. It was weird that he could carry a kid all this way and not get tired, even one this light. Other people complained of aches and pains and weaknesses all the time.

"Just askin," he said.

They finished the journey in silence.

The family's trailer was a shit heap in a park full of shit heaps. Ivy grew up the side and it had a lean like one corner had sunk into the soil.

She ran a hand along his arm. "You could stay."

He could stay just one night, of course. A man did have needs. The kiss from Gwen had reminded him of that. The Animal stirred him low down as if in approval, adding Its fuel to the fire.

take her.

He pulled his arm away from Gail. "Where do I put her?"

Gail scowled and pointed to a small room at the end of the hall running off the small living area. Melly led him through.

He put Sophie - already asleep - on her bed and bid Gail good night, avoiding her sullen gaze, and headed out into the night before the Animal could change his mind.

He was lonely, he was a man, but he didn't need the complications.

He was home and on his bed before he realized he'd forgotten to ask for the injector.

CHAPTER TWELVE

"Christ Jesus," Tim muttered from the driver's seat. "You know, this whole street was families when I was a kid. It was nice."

The V8 purred as it cruised in low gear. Carter's pistol rattled among the cassettes cases in the glove box. He had one arm out the open passenger window, catching a breeze as warm and thick as treacle, eyes scanning the decaying buildings and diseased lots for a man with dreadlocks. His wallet lay open in his lap, exposing the image of Beth at her soup kitchen; he stroked the plastic panel covering her face and winced as Tim continued his seemingly unending discourse.

"I had friends who lived here. Look at it now: nothing but crack houses and perverts." The Hunter wound down his window, slowed as he neared a corner, hawked and spat outside.

What would Elijah be doing now, Carter wondered. Was he thinking about his Dad?

Will he know me when I come back?

Will I know myself?

"Crack houses and perverts," Tim repeated. He took the corner and gave it a little gas. "Perfect place for a theryon."

Carter closed the wallet. No more looking at that photograph or the album in his bag. No more pining for his wife or his son. Not until this thing was done. When it was done, then he could rebuild, his boy with him. Then he could grieve in peace.

"Why theryon?" he asked and shoved his wallet in his back pocket.

"Huh?"

"Why do you call them that?"

"It's an ancient word, Carter, for an ancient threat. The whole 'wer' prefix started in the Middle Ages in Europe, but these creatures have been the whole human race's enemies for a lot longer than that. A lot longer than that. And they weren't always wolves neither."

"Not always wolves? You mean there's people who turn into other kinds of animals?"

"Not these days. Don't think so anyways. Wolves are all I know about. But the Org calls 'em theryons, so I call 'em theryons."

Tim turned down the cassette player, muting Steely Dan as the Chevy turned from one pockmarked street into another. "This is promising." He slowed to a crawl, beetle brow wrinkling as they passed a cluster of homeless gathered around a shopping trolley on the pavement. Carter saw no dreadlocks among them, just varying degrees of oily or wiry hair. The faces returned his gaze, sullen, guarded. Hands disappeared behind backs. Someone had been dealing something. Or maybe they were afraid he'd take whatever it was they had. Maybe they had weapons shoved in their pants.

He rubbed one tired eye as Tim headed toward a larger crowd up the street.

After he'd slept poorly on Tim's couch last night, the Hunter had taken him to a rail yard at six a.m. and three homeless shelters and a derelict library in the four hours since. "The homeless - they hear things," he'd explained as they'd picked their way between rusting tracks toward the small community piled up against the embankments. "They see *everything*. You and I cruise past them - unfamiliar on their turf - they notice. Maybe they'll discuss it with each other. You get a big burly white guy with a Jamaican hairstyle at the shelter or the clinic - a guy who wasn't around a year ago - you better believe one of them saw him, one of them remembers him. This shouldn't be difficult at all."

But it had been difficult. No one knew him - or said they did. Offering money for information only made them angry. Or made them laugh. As if they would turn in one of their own, Carter figured.

"Someone will," Tim had told Carter more than once. "Someone will."

They pulled into the curb a hundred feet from where a crowd milled around a clinic. Balloons and streamers festooned the two-story building. A trio of security guards watched the crowd while a young female clown sat on a stool by the front door, face-painting children. A sign half-attached to a light pole said *Family Day*.

"This is bullshit," Carter said. Tim's pistol was under his seat. The proximity of two loaded weapons around so many women and children...

Tim slammed his door and rested his butt on the hood of the car, facing the clinic. "Bullshit, how?"

Carter rounded the car. A reluctant breeze carried with it the tangs of a barbecue and his stomach tightened with hunger. The food would be free for the poor, but maybe he could give them a couple of bucks for a burger. "Hunting someone we're intending to kill, hunting in amongst families, kids. I dunno. Just feels ... bad."

Tim peered at Carter over the top of his mirror shades. "Bad?"

Carter buried his hands in his pockets, squinting briefly at the sky. The August sun was hot even mid-morning; it was only going to get hotter. A foretaste of hell? he wondered. A down-payment?

He waited until a couple of teenage gangbangers scarfing hotdogs passed before asking, "Do you ever wonder if this is right? I mean, hunting people and killing them?"

"You're doing it, aren't ya?"

"But I have a reason. Okay, you do too. But if we didn't stop to question it, we'd be no better than the peop—the *things* we're hunting." Tim maintained his stare. Carter added, "I keep wondering whether Brennan knew what he was doing. Whether he remembers it."

Tim took off his glasses and squeezed the top of his nose with thumb and forefinger. "This is the whole *can-they-really-help-it* debate. Look, serial killers have some loose wires in their skulls, but it doesn't sanction what they do. Law enforcement hunts them down and deals with them. Kiddy fiddlers have something wrong with them - they say they can't help it - but we keep them away from our kids. Whether they want their theryonism or not, whether they can help it or not, it makes no difference: werewolves are a significant danger to society. We've always hunted and killed that which threatens us. It's natural. It's right."

It made sense. Certainly. But then so had the Final Solution to the Nazis. So had crucifying Christ to the Sanhedrin. You could justify anything if you tried hard enough.

He summoned up the image. His wife eviscerated and cooling in front of him. Carter too scared to touch her. Dialling 911, blundering through the call. Wondering what he'd just shot. Knowing what it was. Wishing to God he and his wife had never come here. Where was the divine purpose in his wife's brutal death?

"Okay," Carter said.

"We good?"

"We're good."

Tim replaced the glasses and retrieved a folded square of paper from a pocket. The screen shot he'd printed from the YouTube video. He held it out. "You go in. I'll wait out here."

"What? Why me?"

"It's a nice day. I need the rays. Vitamin D."

"I don't know what to say."

"You've seen me do it five times today. Your turn."

He waggled the photo. Carter didn't take it.

"What if something happens? What if he's in there?"

"He won't be. Not at a family day." Tim gave him a hard look. "He didn't have a family, did he?"

"Not that I know of. Look, just come as far as the door. You can grab a hot dog while I'm asking around."

"Time for you to spread your wings, little chick." He proffered the photo again. "In you go if you wanna find Jake Brennan."

Carter snatched the photo and trudged toward the clinic.

He spent twenty minutes flashing the photo while avoiding staff and security guards who might ask him questions he couldn't answer convincingly. The poor and homeless, it seemed, were used to people asking questions; none of them asked any back, just shook their heads or muttered variations on "I dunno him".

He paid five bucks for two hotdogs with mustard and onions. "Donation," he told the woman, guilty he couldn't spare more. A day among "the poor" was beginning to explain why Beth had sympathized so much. Frequently the people he passed swore inappropriately in front of children - who often swore back - they argued over nothing, many smelled bad. But not a one of them wanted this life. Of that he was sure. And they also shared generously with each other from meager possessions, they watched each other's backs against the outsider, they found humor in the blackest of situations.

He went back to the car and handed Tim his snack. "Same as the other places. Nothing."

Tim took the photo from him and bit off a chunk of hotdog. Onions hung from his lips like entrails and Carter had to look away.

Carter followed his gaze and pursed his lips. His hastily devoured hotdog roiled in his guts. The experience at the rail yard had been more than a little frightening, most of the residents preferring to stare wordlessly at them; it was as if he and Tim had wandered into an animal enclosure. If these guys on the corner were dealing…

"They could be trouble."

Tim cleared his mouth in a couple of hard swallows. He put his hot dog on the hood. "I have this." He lifted his shirt to show he'd moved his handgun into the waistband of his pants. He took the twenty dollar bill he'd been using all day from his shirt pocket and handed it to Carter. "But this is better."

"That'll stop them knifing me?"

"Courage, brother. We're not gonna find Brennan sipping high tea at the Marriott. These are the guys we need to be talking to."

Carter ran his fingers over the bill. This whole routine was already getting old. "You don't have any other methods of finding theryons? I mean, I just thought you'd, you know, find them some other way."

"What, like a psycho-kinetic energy meter or ecto goggles? This isn't *Ghostbusters*. Ninety-nine per cent of what we do is good old-fashioned detective work. C'mon, Nancy. I'll do the talking."

The five men regarded them with a familiar weary hostility as they approached.

"Gentlemen," Tim beamed, holding the photo of Brennan up before them. "Need to find a buddy of ours. His poor ol' Gramps just passed away and we gotta get him to the funeral tomorrow." He raised the twenty and held it beside the photo, stepping closer. "You know him? Anyone?"

"No," said one of the men.

"Nope," another agreed, turning his back.

Two more just stared, but the fifth man, his pot belly straining against his t-shirt, leaned in for a better look. His buddies scowled and mumbled but didn't move to stop him.

The man ran a hand over salt-and-pepper stubble. "Yep," he said. "Sure."

His buddies muttered swearwords and stepped onto the street, giving Tim and Carter a wide berth as they headed for the clinic.

Carter tracked them as they left, hope accelerating his heartbeat.

"You do?" Tim asked, pulling the money away while pushing the photo closer.

The man met his gaze evenly. "Yep. I seen him at a mission gettin' handouts. And hangin' round a park tryin' to get served."

"Served?" Carter asked.

"Score drugs," Tim explained, then asked their informant, "Help us find him, brother?"

"Yeah. Yeah. I can show ya both places. Course, you'll pay me, right?" His hand sneaked towards the twenty, a cat advancing on a bird.

Tim stepped back again, the hand with the money behind his back. "You'll get it when we see our guy. That's fair."

"Fair!" the man blustered, face turning purple. Carter flinched at the speed with which the man went from idle to full rage. "I don't trust you, you sonofabitch!" He stepped toward Tim but the Hunter lifted his shirt to flash the gun. The man stopped, jaw working, nostrils flaring.

Carter sighed. He whipped the money from between Tim's fingers and ripped it in half.

"What the?" Tim snapped.

Carter held out half the note to the man. "Half now."

The man reached out and snatched it, his rage going off the boil. "What good's half?"

"The rest when we find him. I'm sure the mission has tape you can use." Carter indicated the Chevelle. "Shall we?"

Tim scowled at him, but led the way back to the car.

"All right," the man muttered, falling in step behind the Hunter as he studied the mutilated money in his fist. "All right."

Carter pocketed the other half. Hope hammered at the inside of his ribs and pinched his gut. This was real. This was really happening. They were just a step away from finding Brennan.

This thing was almost done.

CHAPTER THIRTEEN

Her paperwork forming an effective model of the Leaning Tower of Pisa on the counter, Gwen tried to focus on the pen in front of her and shut out everything else. Apart from the vagrant in Curtain 12 yelling for his trolley, the ER was pretty quiet today.

"Who's gonna protect my stuff?" the man snarled at a passing orderly. "You tell me that. You *tell* me that!"

The constant noise was giving her a headache. How long until a bed upstairs became available, she wondered. Maybe she could trank him to shut him up.

Real nice, Doctor, she scolded herself.

The man had stab wounds to his thigh, his shoulder and his neck. He was lucky a cop car had been nearby to intervene in his fight, lucky the paramedics had been as quick as they were. The last thing he should be worried about was a pile of crap wrapped in old shopping bags.

She ground her teeth at her lack of charity. Whatever his "stuff" was, it represented everything he owned in the world. How would she feel if the contents of her house had been strewn across the street shortly before she'd been forced into an ambulance and driven away?

Disemfrickingpowered, that's for sure.

Where was Jake today, she wondered. What did the homeless do on days like today when the August sun broiled the joy from life and piqued tempers? Where did they go? If she hated her life with its spoiled-for-choice moments at the supermarket, its cable television and health insurance, what must they think of theirs? And where did she get off thinking of "them" as one homogeneous group, a collective mass with identical psychological profiles and thought patterns?

"I want my fuckin' trolley!" shouted the hyper-vigilant man in Curtain 12. "All you assholes be gettin' me my trolley!"

This patient was a person and not a "homeless", she told herself, an individual. Jake was an individual. He'd saved two lives that she knew of. If he needed an Epi because he'd given his only one to help a little girl, then he should damn-well have one. It wasn't crystal meth, for Christ's sake. Did she get into doctoring to help people or not? She owed him. There was so little kindness in this world. She owed him not just for helping her, but for making a difference.

Jake had mentioned looking for work at the Port of Detroit. That was a big place to go looking, but what other choice did she have if she wanted to find him?

And she wanted to find him.

"My stuff," the man in Curtain 12 wailed. "Oh, how'm I gonna get my stuff?"

The day she graduated, her father had said to her, *You can't save everyone, Gwenny-bear, you remember that. But you do your best. Always your best.*

Her best seemed to be achieving less and less around here.

But there was Jake. Was anyone out there trying to help *him*? Was a hospital the only place where Gwen Cheevey could help people? And did it always have to be by following rules?

Gwen would prescribe and pay for two EpiPens from the hospital pharmacy herself. That part was easy. Without a car, getting someone to drive her around the docks after her shift - that was the hard part. This was one significant consequence of not making many friends. Pam *might* help her, but Pam had been complaining about having a string of family commitments this week - playing taxi driver for her kids, accompanying her lawyer hubby to a work meet-and-greet, and so on. Taxis were unreliable and could get expensive, plus their drivers loved talking conspiracy theories and politics.

Gwen suspected there'd only be one person who'd be willing to help her out.

The last person in the world she wanted to spend an evening with.

In Gwen's mind, a city's docks were long wharves she could drive a car along and park right beside a huge container ship. And maybe they *were* like that - beyond all that security fencing and razor wire. Or maybe she'd got that idea from one of her Dad's *Tintin* comics.

What she and Barry found was a maze of dark streets lined with chainlink fences allowing tantalizing glimpses of shipping containers, ship bows, lights reflecting off water. Shifting shapes in the distance might have been men and would have been easier to discern without the glare of giant overhead lights blazing from unseeable gantries while the streets they cruised along were cast in almost perfect black.

After he'd reached the same dead end for the third time, Barry U-turned, hands cranking the wheel of his green Lexus as if hauling a huge pirate ship about in a gale.

"Gwen…" he began.

"He's here somewhere. He said there was work. We just have to find a manned gatehouse where I can ask after him, see if he can come out and talk for a minute."

"And if he can't? If this *Jake's* shift ends at six a.m.? Are you going to stand out here all night waiting for him? Because I'm sure as hell not sitting here in my car all night."

"My hero."

Barry's sigh was like the hiss of a bus's airbrakes. "Gwen."

She caught the flash of something off to her right and leaned toward the glass, squinting. "Hey."

A man was crossing a vacant block between the streets. He had big shoulders and the outline of his head was a woolly mass against the distant lights of the next suburb.

She hit the window control and stuck her head out into air sticky with humidity. "Hey!"

"Gwen, for God's sake…"

"That's him. Pull over. Pull over now."

Gravel crunched and popped as they skidded to a halt. The man in the wasteland started running.

"Crap, he's bolting." She threw open the door, half climbed out. "Jake! Jake, don't run, it's me, Gwen!" She dropped back into the seat, slammed the door. "Dammit! Drive, Barry!"

"Make up your mind."

"Catch him!"

By the time the Lexus made it into the next side street, the fleeing figure was already crossing the street at the far side of the lot and headed for more wasteland.

God, he's fast!

"Hurry up."

How can he run so fast across the debris? He'll turn an ankle!

"I'm trying," Barry snapped back, tacking into a cross-street Jake had passed over twenty seconds earlier. "How do you even know it's him?"

"I'd know that hair anywhere."

She stuck half her body out the window and yelled again as they rounded another corner. The runner was headed toward a ribbon of darkness where an overpass blocked out the city lights.

"Jake! Jake, it's Gwen! From the hospital!"

The figure was gone. Vanished into the black. She slumped in her seat and ran a hand through her wind-tossed hair.

Barry pulled up and yanked on the handbrake. His pout was clear even in the low light of the dashboard. "Yes. Well. That was an evening well spent."

"He's so frigging fast," she said.

"And I'm so frigging hungry. If you're ready to accept that our wild goose chase is over, perhaps we can go get some take-out."

"How can he run over all that building debris and not get hurt?"

"Take-out? Food? Heard of it?"

Gwen pushed her head back in the headrest. "Just take me home. I'll make a grilled cheese."

"I hate grilled cheese."

"I wasn't offering it to you."

"Oh. Ok. So it's fine for me to do a favor for you. A long favor lasting—" He checked the dashboard clock. "—one hour fifty-two minutes so far."

"You're keeping track?"

"But a little dinner is impossible for you to contemplate in return?"

"Wait. Are you …? Did you expect *Dinner* with a capital D after this?"

Barry massaged a crick in his neck and studied the lights back near the docks. "I expect *something* for my troubles."

"Something?"

"Just … contact. Conversation. Conviviality."

"Good God, you're incredible."

"You used to think so."

"I used to think you were *passable*. Until I found out you were screwing every intern you could get your slimy hands on."

"One, Gwen. It was one woman, one night, one mistake—"

"One mistake's all it takes, bub. Geez, one mistake's exactly what I made thinking you'd do this for me out of kindness."

"You were appealing to my kindness? Or to my guilt?" He put his hands up in a Time Out signal. "Okay. I get it. I owed you. Well, consider my debt repaid."

"Repaid. With a little taxi driving? A decade of my life, Barry. I don't get that back. That debt's never repaid."

"You had someone else to be with in those years?"

She was trying to decide between slapping him and calling him every name from every Schwarzenegger movie she'd ever watched when someone spoke from the darkness outside her open window.

"What are you doing here?"

In unison, they both jumped and swore.

Barry disengaged the handbrake. Gwen put her hand over his to stop him shifting into Drive.

"Jake. How did you—? You came back?"

"I heard your voice. Sneaked back to check."

Sneaked?

He'd covered a hell of a lot of ground fast, both running away and running back. She could see him now, silhouetted against the city glow. His chest swelled with deep breaths, but those breaths came easily and she couldn't even smell sweat on him. His mind might be screwed but his body certainly wasn't. Who the hell was he? An athlete who'd had a breakdown?

Barry's hand shifted, a finger curling up and between two of hers. She pulled away and pushed the door open. Jake backed up to give her space.

"You're looking for me?" he asked.

"Ye-es," she said, and cringed at her own inanity. "So did you get work here?"

He shook his head. "Why are you looking for me?" He peered into the car. "Who's that?"

"He's no one."

"Thanks a lot," Barry muttered.

She stepped away from the car. "Listen. I wanted to thank you. I didn't do it properly at the hospital. Here."

She held out the two hundred dollars and though it was all she had, it felt like a pittance.

"I don't want your money."

But she had seen a brief flash of hunger in his eyes, belying his claim. How could he not need cash, without a steady job, bumming around the Port of Detroit for a hard night's work, living like …

Like what? How does he live? What do you even know about him?

"Please," she insisted. "It's the least I can do."

He sniffed, shuffled his feet and mumbled, "A hundred then." And more quietly when she separated the bills and placed the c-note in his grimy hand, "Thanks."

"Wait a sec." She opened the back door and fished out her bag. Hiding it with her body, she pulled out the two-pack of EpiPens. He took it, a smile spreading across his face. She grabbed a t-shirt, bunched it into a ball and held it out. "This is almost new. Worn once. I washed it." She felt embarrassed. What if he thought she was making a veiled statement about the fact that his clothes weren't washed? He was back in the long-sleeved work shirt and worn denims he'd had the day he intervened in her abduction.

But he took it, shaking it out and holding it up to the headlights. "It's nice. Thanks."

Barry stirred within the Lexus. "Hey, is that—?"

"I have more," she said.

"—my John Lennon tee?"

"Shut up, Barry," she growled over her shoulder and pasted a sweet smile on her face for Jake. He was stuffing the tee into a jacket pocket. "More clothes that is. Jeans. Shirts. A sweater. Gloves. If you'd like them."

"Gwen, you didn't say anything about giving away my—"

She thumped the car with her heel and Barry's complaints fell away to a dull burble of expletives.

"I'll come see you at the hospital if I need them," said Jake. "But don't come back here, don't look for me on the streets. You know it's not safe." He dipped his head and smiled again. "Well. Thanks. This is … Thanks. Be safe."

With that ragged farewell, he took to his heels, jogging out into the black wash of vacant land. She watched him until he was a blur, and then nothing.

It's not safe. There it was again. The pauper watching out for the relatively affluent doctor, instead of the other way around. She was so lost in thought, she didn't remember climbing into the car and closing the door.

Barry glowered at her, arms folded.

"What?"

He took a moment to answer. "That's your rescuer? Your hero?"

"What about it?"

He put the car into gear and rolled forward.

"Spit it out," she said.

"There's rebounds and then there's rebounds, Gwen."

"Are you kidding me?"

"I care for you. You know that. I don't want to see you hurt."

"Are you kidding me!"

He had the decency to at least squirm a little. And to shut up. The silence lasted the entire trip to her place, for which she was grateful. Her mood seesawed between fury at Barry and a gnawing emptiness that she had unfinished business with Jake.

Leave it, girl, came Pam's voice in her head. *You've repaid him. Forget about him.*

She sighed as the car pulled over out front of her home.

Yes, I should. I will.

He probably represented a distraction for her, something to take her mind off her work woes, her general unhappiness. And it had felt good to do something for him. Such a simple act - and at so little cost to her, compared to what he'd risked for her - and yet it had meant so much to him.

"Listen, Gwen," Barry said as he turned off the engine. "I'm sorry. I shouldn't have said those things. I have no right."

Tired, she waved it away as she unbuckled the seatbelt.

"It's just … I miss you." He leaned across and she jerked away, shoulder pressing into the door.

"Get off."

She shoved him awkwardly and he retreated, lips peeling back from his teeth.

"You ungrateful … After all I've done for you! One little indiscretion—"

"Most of what you did for me was cart me around like a fifth wheel while you sucked up to your friends. Pardon me - your associates."

"You dumb bitch. You wouldn't have even passed your finals if I wasn't there to help you."

The insult landed like a physical blow. She gaped at him. Did he really believe that?

She fumbled the door open and hoisted herself out, wrenched open the back door and ducked in for her bag. But Barry flipped it past her into the gutter.

"Prick," she spat.

"Frigid cow," he snarled.

She flung the door shut. "Get—"

But he was already laying rubber, the passenger door slamming shut as he sped off.

Dumb bitch, was she?

"The only dumb thing I ever did was hooking up with you!" she screamed at his tail lights. A chain reaction of dogs barked along the street. "Goddamnit."

She grabbed at her bag and felt in the gutter, making sure nothing had tipped out.

She wiped grit onto her pants and waited until the Lexus slewed around a corner. The jerking motion of the vehicle put her instantly in mind of the green van racing away from her attempted abduction and she pinched her thigh to jolt herself from a flash of panic. The pinch hurt: she'd done this a few times now and a bruise was developing there. She turned toward her door, walking steady, refusing to hurry no matter who might be out here waiting for her. And made it halfway before breaking into a jog. It took three attempts to get the key into the hole.

"Goddamnit," she said again, when she had the door closed and locked behind her. She sunk to her haunches and put her head in her hands. "Goddamnit, I hate my life."

CHAPTER FOURTEEN

"Do you know any way I could get some money?" Jake shoved his hands deep in his pockets to keep them still. He spread his feet wide in Angelo's doorway, keeping balanced, keeping cool. The smells coming from the mission kitchen were making it hard to forget how hungry he was. And the Animal was growing stronger inside as the Big Moon grew closer, nagging for attention like a junkie's itch.

He added, "I'll work for it. I don't want no hand out."

From behind his messy desk, Angelo eyed him hard. The mission director put down his pen, turned the document face-down and came around the desk. The office was as small as the bathroom in Jake's squat, made tighter with filing cabinets and a couple of folding chairs. There was just enough room for a desk and a man to squeeze behind it.

He stepped back into the hallway as Angelo came to lean in the doorway.

"Not really a recruitment agency, Jake. But maybe I can do something." His eyes glazed for a moment while he retreated into thought, then he blinked his way back again. "I'm a good reader of character. Have to be. There's something about you, dunno what it is. You seem like a good man at heart. Trustworthy."

Jake tried to force the vague and cloudy memories - of blood, of need, of screaming and pain, of violence and horror - to coalesce into something real, something he could understand, but they slipped through the fingers of his mind like so much slimy water.

A good man? If Angelo only knew...

"You look me in the eye and tell me it's not for drugs."

"Need the money to get my Momma's brooch back from a pawn shop. And sumthin to live with. Not drugs." It was true, he thought: he already had the blow he needed for this Moon. But bus fare out of town, and money enough to set him up in a new town for a new month—that would make life a lot easier.

Angelo glanced up and down the hallway. There were people banging things around in the kitchen and a few early lingerers roaming the yards before lunch. But no one was within earshot. "You tell anyone this, you won't be welcome back here. I don't usually find work for people. But there's a buddy of mine remodels homes. Needs someone from time to time, cash only. I'll call him."

He waited a beat longer as if giving Jake one more chance to come clean. Jake returned his stare, squashing down a desire to snap at this challenge: *It* didn't like people staring him down. Angelo grunted, then went to his desk and punched numbers into an old-looking phone. Jake listened distractedly while he made the arrangements. Being eyeballed like that had stirred the Animal up. Tonight, the night when the moon was almost completely full, he would lose control to it. No: tonight, he'd be holed up, sleeping heroin dreams instead of tearing people's chests open. The crack of Angelo's phone hitting the receiver snapped him out of such thoughts.

"Okay, you got four days' work. He's tearing down some inner walls and putting up new drywall."

"Sure. Great. I've done that before."

"Maybe a little painting. Sixty bucks a day. Not much, but it's all they can offer."

"No, no, that's good, real good." It was all he'd need to set up somewhere new, maybe Alabama where winter wasn't as cold. For years he'd been drifting north with the original idea of slipping across into Canada - the movies he'd seen at elementary school always made it look like a haven and the woods might be the perfect place for him. But then he'd tried to live off the land once and that had been a disaster: birds and animals seemed to survive out there just fine but he hadn't been able to find anything to eat at all and wound up stealing from farms.

Maybe he should've taken the whole two hundred bucks from Gwen. But he couldn't keep taking all the time. If he did that, he'd never do enough good things to outweigh the evil he'd done. He'd never get to be with Momma. Still, Gwen had offered clothes. And if they were as nice as the t-shirt, they'd be a helluva lot better than the crap he normally scored from thrift stores and missions like Angelo's. The clothes had to go to someone; it wasn't like Gwen was going to wear them. It could be nice to turn up to this job in good clothes, different clothes, each day. Look like he was deserving of the work.

It would be nice to see her again.

"You go to this address, not tomorrow, but the following day. Eight a.m. sharp."

Angelo scribbled on a pad and Jake thought, *Day after tomorrow. Day after full moon. I can do that. I can.*

"This isn't charity, pal," Angelo said. "The work's hard. But you're fit and Carl's a fair man. You do good by him and he'll also provide lunch those days." He tore off the sheet and handed it to Jake.

"That's great. I'll work hard, promise. Thanks, man." He frowned at the note. The address was easy to read, but Jake had no idea where it was.

Angelo seemed to read his thoughts. "I'll show you." He pressed past him and signaled him to follow. In the large dining room, a map of the city took up half of one wall. Angelo pointed to two spots with different hands. "*This* is where we are. *This* is where Carl is."

Jake nodded. It was easy enough to remember. "Yeah, I can walk there."

"That'll take you a couple of hours. Eight a.m. start, remember."

"That's okay, I'll start early." He would come awake at dawn; that's usually how it worked. Just enough time.

Angelo's hands dropped to his hips and Jake noticed the guy's arms flexing, wondered what he might have done in a previous life to get so big. Weightlifter? Boxer? Yeah, the guy looked like he could handle himself. That was good. In this life, in the city, that was very good.

"You hungry, Jake?"

meat! the Animal growled.

The scents of grilled onion, sauces and frying fat were playing kickball with Jake's guts. "Yes, I am, sir."

"Tell you what, lunch isn't for another hour, but you help me tidy one of the storerooms out back, you can eat early with me. First pick of whatever's on offer."

"That's fair."

They spent fifteen minutes shifting bags of donated clothes and toys from a pickup parked out back into the container. Jake turned, expecting another to get tossed to him but Angelo was dusting his hands on his pants, regarding him thoughtfully.

"When you say you won't use my buddy's money for drugs, I believe you. I guess you got another way of getting supplied." He rubbed a bare forearm across his brow, wiped it dry on his shirt. It was a hot day, hotter in the shipping container.

Jake folded his arms across his chest. "I ain't an addict."

Angelo smiled. "Takes one to know one. Sometimes takes an ex-one to help another one get free."

Free? This guy had no idea what he was talking about. Normals got addicted. Normals got the taste and then hurt and itched when trying to stop. With Jake's problem, none of that affected him; it wasn't the drugs that imprisoned him.

"I use sometimes, but I'm not an addict."

"You use, you're a user. Addict, user, not much difference. You wanna get free of it, you come see me."

Jake found a place to lean amongst the crap in the storeroom, wishing he was outside in the fresh air, but Angelo's bulk blocked the door. He had no doubt he could get past him, boxer or no boxer. He could break one arm over his knee, sink his fingers in to his throat, squeeze, squeeze and tear—

Damnit!

The guy meant no harm. It didn't hurt to talk once in a while, did it? It wasn't like they had to be friends. He'd talked to that lady doctor and gotten an EpiPen and some cash, a new shirt. There were good people in this world, people like Momma, people like he was trying to be. Maybe it would actually help his cause to let them be as nice as they wanted to be.

"I got an illness." He tapped his forehead with a finger. "Up here. Gets aholda me a few nights - days - a month. I use a little those days just to get me through. The ... illness ... leaves and I stop usin again."

"'Til next time."

Jake looked away.

Angelo studied a bag of VHS videos and cassette tapes, then tossed it outside into the sun. "I know a guy drinks once a year. The anniversary of the day he killed his wife in a car wreck. Takes a week of his annual leave and drinks himself stupid then goes back to work the following Monday as if nothing's happened. He doesn't think there's anything wrong either. Only thing he says when I bring it up is 'This is my way, Ange. I'm handling it.'"

"Sounds like he is."

Angelo clasped his hands behind his neck and stretched. "'It filled him with a great unrest and strange desires. It caused him to feel a vague, sweet gladness, and he was aware of wild yearnings and stirrings for he knew not what.'"

Jake frowned. "Bible?"

"*Call of the Wild*. My favorite book." Angelo smiled. "My friend only goes on a bender once a year, but he's an alcoholic."

"I ain't an addict."

"If you can't stop using, you're an addict."

"I'm not."

"Buddy, we're all addicts in some sense. It's a human predisposition. These days I'm addicted to helping people, to my gym and to bad coffee. Better than what I used to be addicted to, though."

Jake tugged at his collar, willing air to dry the trickle of sweat running down his neck. "I don't think your problem was as bad as mine."

"That's what everyone thinks. Listen, I said you're a good guy. I meant it. It's written all over you. Maybe you don't want help right now. I get that. I won't mention it again, unless you bring it up. Just want you to know that people here can help you. And there may be people here who need your help too."

Jake struggled for something to say. What would his foster parents have said to someone being nice to them? "I sure do appreciate your thoughtfulness," he said. "I'll keep it in mind."

Angelo seemed satisfied with his answer, and poked another bag with the toe of his shoe.

Jake hoped the talking might be done. He'd eaten his last protein bar that morning and his stomach was tight with hunger. "The universe might just have a great plan for a guy like you. There's a lot you can achieve in this world."

A plan? People with homes and families and money - Normal people - always thought in terms of plans. He'd heard them discussing their plans on buses, on trains, in malls, on the sidewalk as they passed, pretending he wasn't there.

What plans had Momma made? Not for the first time he wondered if she'd lit the fire, if that had been her plan, to save his life at the cost of hers?

"C'mon." Angelo stepped into the sun. "Time for lunch. Got a checkers board I haven't used in a while. We can play while we eat."

"Sure," Jake said. One last meal here. Eating and smiling and playing a game like he was really among friends, part of a group. It'd be a nice change.

And straight after that, he'd leave and never come back here. It wasn't just the possibility that Hunters and cops might be out looking for him, now he'd been made kind of famous by that jerk with the iPhone; he had to leave because anywhere people cared about each other, anywhere he could hurt someone good and kind as this man Angelo, anywhere people made plans - that was a place Jake Brennan shouldn't be.

CHAPTER FIFTEEN

The park had been quiet all day apart from a mother and her two kids playing on the teeter-totter while their pit bull watched from its sentry position, leashed to a post. Carter thought the park reflected everything he had quickly come to pity and despise about Detroit: the weeds, the post-apocalyptic emptiness of estate after estate, the snowdrifts of garbage piled against fences and gutters. It put him mind of a Wild West ghost town, the empty shell of a once booming community now rotting in the aftermath once the boom moves on.

A skinny guy in a jacket too thick for August had passed through the playground a couple of times. He was back now and this time, he noticed the Chevelle. He put his hands in his pockets and slipped away toward the far side of the park.

"Thinks we're narcs," Tim laughed. "If only you knew, *compadre*."

Carter's wristwatch read 4:18. The optimism he had felt the day before had evaporated like sweat in the hot summer breeze. The homeless man named Varley - their would-be snitch - had been less than helpful, leading them on what amounted to a wild-goosechase. "Brennan hasn't been here. Or the mission," he said.

"Gee. Really? I did not realize that. For I have been up on the International Space Station. Thank you for the update."

"Sarcasm. That's a great response there, Tim. You know, I'm going to come right out and ask this. Do you actually know what you're doing?"

"You're angry. I get that. Newbies are always keen to—"

"Newbies? It's not a game, Tim."

Tim untucked his Black Sabbath t-shirt. "You have to tell me that?"

Carter turned away from the scars. Once had been enough. "There must be more we can do besides sitting around waiting."

"When you're hunting an animal, you find its most frequented pathways and you leave traps. We *are* the trap because we can't leave actual traps - not unless we find a lair, *then* we can have fun, lemme tell you."

Carter shoved his door open and lurched out. He marched up and down, twenty paces this way, twenty that, counting them off, burning off frustration and getting some air. It was hot in the car. Hot and smelly. The homeless man's odor yesterday had permeated every atom, coming back to haunt them. And Tim's preferred diet of eggs, burritos and cheese sticks wasn't helping.

Tim eventually got out too and leaned his elbows on the roof, then pulled them hurriedly away from the hot metal. He rubbed at the scalded flesh. "Patience, grasshopper. We'll get our shot at the guy. Trust me, I've done this before."

"Oh, yeah?" Carter came up to the other side and mimicked Tim's pose. "How many times? How many actual theryons have you killed?"

"Shh-shh." Tim waved his arms. "Not so loud."

The street was empty. Even the traffic noise was blocks away. "No one's hearing us. So, what's your score so far?"

"The score? The score is Werewolves 1 - counting my friend on that camping trip - and Darkrider 2."

Carter straightened. "Including the one that got you?"

"Who knows? Maybe. Got one in Minnesota. One in Toronto. Maybe the Toronto one was."

"So, you hunt these things. You shoot them with silver bullets. Don't the authorities ever, you know, stop you afterwards and ask what the hell you were doing? Who's that dead guy with the big teeth and bullet holes? Where do the bodies go?"

Tim winked. "That's what the Org is for."

"Org?"

"Organisation."

"You're called The Organisation?"

"No, there's no name. That's just what me and a couple of others call it between ourselves. The Org." He appeared proud of the idea.

"So the *Org*, what, they clean up after you?"

Tim winked again. "Now you got it. I just call it in. If I'm the one who ends the theryon. Toronto was different: we had a big team there, nine of us in the end. Clean-up crew were part of it from the start."

Carter shook his head. Secret societies hunting werewolves and leaving no trace. That night at Brennan's squat in Rockford had torn open the curtain to a world Carter never knew existed and it seemed like there was plenty more curtain left.

"Then get that big team down here."

Tim studied something on the car roof. "We're good. Just you and me."

"Brennan could be anywhere - headed anywhere - while you and I sit here with our heads up our asses admiring drug pushers and pit bulls. Let's get some more heads and legs on this case, find this sonofabitch."

Tim rubbed his face, covering a sudden flush Carter realized wasn't from the heat. "We're good. Let's get back in the car and just wait this out."

"There's more, isn't there? Why can't you get a bigger team down here?"

Tim turned his back, faced the park.

Carter rounded the car. "Are you even a Hunter? I mean, are you even in the 'Org'?"

Tim swore, hawked and spat. He stayed staring at the park with his teeth grinding for a full minute before Carter had had enough. He yanked open the back door and reached for his bag.

"What're you doing?" Tim asked.

Carter maneuvered the bag over one shoulder. "What's it look like? Anyone can go ask around homeless shelters. I'll do it alone."

Tim put out a hand. "No. Wait."

Carter met his gaze, waiting him out.

Finally, Tim slumped. "All right. Okay. I'll level with you. I *am* part of the Org. Or at least, I was."

"Was?"

"You asked how many I've killed. Well, the answer's actually four. Only..." He ran a hand through his hair and blew out a breath. His voice when he spoke again was like that of a kid caught stealing from the teacher's desk. All the swagger had gone out of him, deflating him. "Last two guys I killed weren't theryons."

Carter gaped at him. *Holy...*

"You got the wrong guys."

"Wrong guys. Yeah."

"But, how did you know they weren't real theryons?"

"Kidding me? Theryons blow up real big when you touch 'em with silver, let alone shoot 'em. Neither of those bastards were the real deal. I mean, they were punks, criminals, to be sure. They'd killed people, so I don't feel all that bad about popping 'em. World's better off and all that. But, it was still a mess to clean up, right? And the Organisation - the main guys - they don't forgive easily."

Carter dropped his bag onto the street. "So, how come Doug called you?"

Tim shrugged. "Your guy called one of my buddies. Someone who knows what I do on the side. Guess I was lucky that way."

"Lucky?"

"Carter, I need a way back in. A scalp. A real one. A *good* one." He turned to face him, eyes imploring. "You know Brennan. I've only seen him on a video, but you *know him.*"

They stayed that way a few moments, facing off. Carter almost laughed, it was so ironic. He needed Tim, and Tim needed him right back.

"Look," he finally said. "I'm frustrated. That's why I was going to take off. You know how important this is to me."

Tim's expression lightened. "Of course. It is to me too."

Carter tossed his bag back on the rear seat.

"Be patient, grasshopper," said Tim. "Trust the process. We know roughly where his territory lies, so it's just a matter of time. Let's go get an early dinner and catch some zees, get up around eleven o'clock ready for the show. He'll probably go to ground, but if something happens, we need to be alert."

Carter frowned. "Catch what show? Tomorrow's full moon, not tonight."

"Yeah, it's waxing moon tonight, du—Wait, seriously? Man, that other Hunter you worked with was a real prick, not explaining this to you. Okay, hear this. They get active not just the night of the full moon, but the night before and the night after. Waxing moon, full moon, waning moon: the three nights each month when the moon's most chunky. That's the way it works."

"He didn't say anything about that."

"All I can do is apologize on behalf of the Org. But this time, you're with a pro."

Carter took one last look into the park and got back in the car.

It rocked with Tim's weight as he settled behind the wheel. "Sorry I was a little loose with the sarcasm earlier. I guess I'm hot and flustered too. We good?"

"We're good."

"Awesome." Tim turned the key. "Let's go for some burritos."

CHAPTER SIXTEEN

Using only his hearing, Jake tracked the fly's trajectory and swatted it into the ground the moment it strayed within reach. That made twelve so far in the hour since he'd come to lie behind the hedge down the road from Gwen's house. Summer storm clouds bruised the sky to the west, but they continued to pass by. That was good. Turning up at her door drenched would hardly make a good impression.

There'd been a White Pages in the mission's dining area. Jake had the opportunity to study it while Angelo got called away midway through their second checkers game. It felt like a trick finding out where Gwen Cheevey - the name on her hospital badge - lived, but he guessed Normals did it all the time when looking for friends.

or prey.

He grit his teeth. The moon really was at him today, like someone was pulling on the skin on the back of his head. It was all he could do to keep his thoughts straight. On the way here, he'd walked like a drunk man acting sober, putting his feet in front of him carefully, concentrating on everything at once.

Her street was full of nice homes and a couple of low apartment blocks. He'd walked it several times, working up the courage to knock, and scoping out exits in case he needed them. Finally, he'd knocked, but there'd been no movement within. Finding somewhere to sit and wait without drawing the attention of cops and neighbors had presented a problem. This hedged garden lay just around the corner from her small house, but it seemed a safe place to wait her out; also it had a view along her street so he'd see her coming. The cool earth and tall hedge provided welcome relief and he'd dozed on and off, waking for cars and pedestrians.

He'd started tracking a thirteenth fly when a taxi came zooming up the road - taking the corner to Gwen's street too fast - and there she was, visible through the back window and looking pissed at the guy's driving. He slid from cover and jogged to the corner lamp post, peeked around as Gwen got out of the cab and headed into her home. No one else was visible on the street. He tinkered with one shoelace until the cab had passed him, then walked fast toward the yard she'd entered. Those clothes she'd offered - he needed them to keep his new boss happy after his job started tomorrow: Normals didn't like it when you wore the same clothes day after day. Angelo had given him some, but the more he had, the more he could wear. The more Normal he could appear.

Gwen's house was narrow, set on a narrow block, with peeling paint and grass in the gutters. Her small garden beds were nests of weeds. As he approached, It stirred again, the way it had around Gail. He was meeting a female - would be alone with her.

"You ain't gettin her," he muttered, but a memory of Gwen's face pressed against his consciousness, so forcefully he couldn't ignore it. Her button nose, her dimpled smile, her eyes…

She had eyes the color of sunwashed asphalt. They should have been dead eyes. And he'd seen a kind of death in them when she'd appeared in that ER hallway, her exhaustion, a wariness that might be caused by that street attack. Yet she'd found the strength to care, to joke … yes, she was funny. She had made Sophie smile. Hell, she'd made *him* smile.

take her, It whispered.

Jake shook his head. In. Out. Be back in his squat with plenty of time to load up his veins just before midnight. That was the plan.

I'm gonna make it through this Big Moon. No one's getting hurt.

He halted on the stoop, raised one hand to knock, dropped it again. What should he say when she opened the door? What did Normals say when they greeted each other in public?

Hello, you.

Great to see you.

You look great.

Hey, hey!

Yo!

How ya doin?

It was all too confusing. Pick the wrong one and she might slam the door in his face. Or chase him off with a shotgun like the old woman from the store.

No, he was better off keeping it simple.

"I was wonderin' about them clothes."

Gwen stared back, uncertain. Questions bubbled up into her mind. Where in hell had he come from? How had he found her?

Was he dangerous?

Her screen door was locked, so there was a barrier between them. But did she really have anything to fear from a man who'd defended her life at risk to his own?

Jake looked toward the street. Nervous about witnesses? No, he always did that, struggling to maintain eye contact for more than a second or two.

Gwen managed to say, "Uh. Yeah, sure. Wait a sec?" She turned away to fetch the garbage bag of Barry's clothes, intending to hand it to him out there on the stoop - keep him at a distance, keep him from invading her world. More than he already had. But she stopped a few steps down the hall, and punched herself in the thigh, right in the bruise she'd given herself. She took a deep breath, let it out slow.

He's a good guy. He's a good guy. He helped Sophie and her family. He helped me. It'll be okay.

She stomped back and unsnibbed the door, shutting out the news report playing in her head about a murdered ER doctor.

It'll be okay.

"Come in. And hi, by the way." She let him pass, then pulled the wire door shut without locking it, and left the front door wide open.

Just in case.

He stood in the middle of her hall, head down, looking lost. Lost and hot.

Sweaty, she corrected herself. The air in the hall rippled with his body odor. *He looks sweaty.*

"I have Seven-Up. And Kool-Aid, I think. Would you like some?"

He looked uncertain, but said, "Kool-Aid. Thanks."

Man of many words. As usual.

Two could play at that game. She pointed down the hall. "That door. Couch. Go sit."

He complied, backpack sliding off his shoulder into his hand before he disappeared through the doorway.

Probably getting his knives and plastic sheeting ready.

She shook her head and went into the kitchen to make drinks. Spying the bottle of ouzo, she was tempted to add a little to her Seven-Up. But that wouldn't do. Not at all.

He was perched on the edge of the couch, backpack on the cushion behind him. He accepted the glass with a grateful - and shy - half-smile, gaze quickly scanning her up and down before fixing on the floor. She took the arm chair and sipped her soda; many single women would wish those caramel eyes would do a little more scanning. Gwen didn't know what to think.

He looked at her and she looked back.

Damned if I'm gonna make all the conversation here. Your turn, sir.

He dropped his gaze and sipped his drink. She waited him out, watching the second hand move around the clock. Jake made little sipping and clicking noises as he drank.

He'd shaved, showing off the squareness of his jaw, the superhero chin. His thick chest heaved with each breath. Her own chest was pounding, and not with fear. After what she'd been through on that street, the last things on her mind should be his chest and shoulders and the color of his eyes and how he was right here in her home... *This ain't good.*

She had to change the subject in her head, so she concentrated on her hands. They'd healed enough for her to remove the plasters but the scabs rubbed against her glass. The bruise on her wrist had faded to yellow and no longer hurt.

When the clock had counted off sixty-one seconds, she marched back into the kitchen. *Screw it.* She tipped two fingers of ouzo into her soda. It warmed her pleasantly when she took a gulp, that warmth spreading through her belly and sternum. Then, ready to try again, returned to the living room.

"So," she said, taking her seat. "You were saying?"

He blinked. "Uh. You offered some clothes, ma'am. I just... I wondered if..."

Her giggling stopped him cold. "Ma'am? Really? Who are you, John Wayne?"

"John Wayne?"

She frowned at him. "You're kidding me. You're not kidding me? You don't know John Wayne?" *Oops. A little indelicate. Maybe the poor guy never had a TV in his life.* "Doesn't matter. You wanted Ba—those clothes. I'll get them for you in a sec." She sucked down more cocktail. Medicinal purposes only.

So what the hell do men like to talk about? Sport, jobs...

"Did you get work?"

He brightened. "Yeah. I start tomorrow."

"That's *great*. Where at?"

"House refit. Near Hamtramck."

"I'm glad to hear that. Will you be painting? Putting up walls?"

"Won't know 'til I get there."

"They're keeping you guessing, huh? Well, a little mystery is a good thing. So, is that ongoing? Fulltime?"

He made a face, suddenly nervy again, and swallowed the last third of his drink. "Four days is all."

"Oh. That's a shame. You deserve a ..." She nearly said *real job.* "... better chance than that."

He shrugged. "It's perfect. Really. I'm heading out after that."

"Heading out? What do you mean?"

"Leaving Detroit."

"Oh." The clock ticked. A dog barked in the neighbor's yard and someone yelled for it to shut up. Jake's throat clicked as he swallowed his own spit. She took a long pull of her drink. "I ... maybe I could get you work at the hospital. In the kitchens or laundry."

He took a deep breath, let it out slow, placed his glass carefully on the carpet so it didn't topple. There was a perfectly good coffee table right in front of him, but the idea of putting the glass there didn't seem to occur to him. "You've been real kind to me, ma'am."

He wants to go.

And you should let him.

"Stop with the ma'am thing. I'm Gwen."

"Gwen. Those clothes…"

"Yeah, yeah, in a sec. Listen, don't you want a steady job? I'm sure there's work at the hospital. I could always have someone killed, create a vacancy." She laughed. He didn't.

"I need to leave Detroit. I'll do the four days' work, then… go."

She grunted, swished her drink. "Four days. You'll end up with a few hundred dollars in your pocket. Hardly seems enough to set up elsewhere."

"I've made do on less."

I'll bet you have, you poor guy.

"Why are you leaving? Visiting family? Is your Mom sick or something?"

He winced. "She's dead."

"Oh. I'm sorry—"

"Died when I was eight." He ran a hand across his face.

Way to go: finally get him talking and uncover a wound.

She softened her tone. "So. What's the hurry then?" When he didn't answer, she added, "If I can get you a few weeks' work at the hospital, you could save up some more cash. Make it easier to start fresh."

And why in hell are you so keen to have him hang around, missy? Assuaging your middle class guilt? Got a thing for the socially awkward and marginalized?

"There's people after me," he said. "I can't stay longer."

People after…?

He swept his dreads over his head, off his face. "And I'd like to pay you for the clothes and pay you back the hundred dollars you gave me, but I just can't at the moment."

"What people, Jake?"

"Bad people."

She watched expressions flit across his face like cloud shadows until he noticed and dropped his head, his bangs slipping back across his face.

You poor bastard.

He had no one. That much was obvious. And she wasn't going to let him into her life any further than she already had. But she did owe him: she would always owe a guy who'd saved her from the worst death imaginable. Always.

He was starting a new job tomorrow. For the first time, she noticed the soil on the knees of his khakis and the heels of his hands, as if he'd been playing on the ground. And that sweaty smell was hardly doing him any favors.

"Okay, I'm sorry. The interrogation is over. Listen, you have work tomorrow and - I'm not trying to be rude - but if you don't have a working shower at your home, you can use mine now. I'll leave the bag of clothes by the bathroom door and you can try them on rather than take them if they're too ..." those shoulders "... small."

He seemed about to decline then reconsidered. "Sure. Okay. Thanks. I don't have my towel with me though."

She placed her glass on the coffee table. "I've got towels, Jake, it's fine. Bathroom's at the end of the hall. I'll drop the clothes outside. You take your time." She checked the clock. Just after six. "I can make dinner, too, if you'd like. You can eat it here or I can make it to go."

"Thanks."

"I'm not much of a cook. My specialties are grilled cheese, grilled cheese and bacon, or microwaved potatoes with cheese and bacon. I splash a mean ketchup too."

He actually smiled at that. "Grilled cheese is cool, thanks. I can maybe wash your dishes for you."

She followed his gaze through the open kitchen door to the stack of dirty cereal bowls, coffee mugs and bread plates. For the first time since coming home, she noticed the turned milk smell coming from the bowls.

Looks like he's not the only one making an odor, Little Ms Prim and Judgmental.

"Two grilled cheese sandwiches on wholemeal in exchange for you washing my dishes. You have yourself a deal, mister."

She stood - glad she'd hadn't had more ouzo - and stuck out a hand. After a moment he stood and gripped it briefly, returning her smile. His palm was like warm leather. Something crept into his eyes, something—

She shivered and let go, made off for the closet where she'd kept Barry's things. A few seconds later, the bathroom door closed with a gentle click.

CHAPTER SEVENTEEN

Gwen waited until the water in the bathroom stopped running before she slipped the sandwiches under the grill. She wondered if Jake was schizophrenic with the whole people-after-him thing.

Has schizophrenia, she reminded herself. *Not is schizophrenic. See the person, Doctor, not the condition.*

The aroma of toasting bread crept from beneath the grill to overpower the sour smell of her dirty dishes. She'd added some oregano and coriander, sprinkling it on the cheese - yep, she was a *cordon bleu* chef all right.

The bathroom was quiet. Would Barry's clothes fit Jake properly? If they didn't, she would toss them in the trash. The nerve of that douche-bag, trying to cop a feel, thinking he could worm his way back in. No, his clothes would fit Jake and they'd look a damn sight better on him than on Barry. Dr Play-the-Field had the shoulders and height, but the skinny arms and paunch had always spoiled it for him.

Like I can talk. She grabbed a half-handful of flesh beneath her navel and jiggled it.

"These fit good."

She gave a little cry. Jake filled the hall entrance, the Humor Maali dress shirt open to the waist and the lowrider jeans living up to their name on his narrow hips. Gwen soaked up the gestalt, the sharp lines of his pecs and abs beneath a jungle of blond body hair, the border of his underwear showing above the denim.

Sheesh, Doctor, get a grip, for crying out loud. You've seen anatomy before.

No, she was not going to shame herself. This way she was feeling, it was a simple desire for pleasure, no more surprising than emotional eating or reaching for a wine bottle the night after the attack. There was nothing wrong with looking. This showed her strength, surely: putting a trauma behind her, along with a bad relationship.

There's rebounds and then there's rebounds, Gwen, Barry had said.

Damnit. I was just looking. Nothing more.

Apparently oblivious to her attention, Jake fumbled with the odd zipper arrangement of the dress shirt - an eclectic purchase Barry had worn only once. "I also wanted to say thanks for the EpiPens. Is there any chance you could write me a prescription for one more?"

She flicked the griller off and took her time shifting the sandwiches from tray to plates. With his gaping shirt and his wet dreads swept back from his face, he could have passed as a model. Now *there* was an idea for him if he was seeking work...

"What's your allergy, Jake?" she asked without turning back. He was still a couple of yards away back in the doorway, but it felt close.

How's a street bum get so damned cut?

He murmured, "Silver," as if he were confessing a sin.

She spun around, unable to keep the frown from her face. "Silver!" He still hadn't managed to get the zipper lined up properly and looked about to give up on it. *Damnit. Keep trying.* "A silver allergy won't kill you. Certainly won't trigger anaphylaxis. I don't know who told you it would, but all you'll get is some skin irritation. When's the last time you had a reaction?"

"Long time ago," he said.

"And you had a bad reaction?"

He took a long slow breath. "Real bad."

"Okay, so there's *something* you're allergic to. But it can't be silver. Let's get you in to see a specialist, run some tests and determine the real culprit before you accidentally come in contact with it again. I'll work it so you don't have to pay."

"I know what the problem is." For the first time since he'd come barreling into her life, he held her gaze, gently staring her down.

What was the harm in prescribing another dose of epinephrine? It wouldn't kill him, not unless he was regularly taking high doses, which could cause arrhythmias. But even that would be unusual. Did the benefit outweigh the risk? If only he'd submit to testing.

"Okay, mister. Come by here tomorrow night, same time. I'll have a prescription you can fill anywhere in the country."

He grunted a thank-you, now ogling the sandwiches. But she'd be damned before she sat down to eat with him with that shirt open.

"Listen, if you want this, you have to learn how to do it up. It can't be that hard." She darted forward and reached for the two halves of the shirt at the bottom, tried to jiggle the pin into the pull tab. It wasn't as easy as it should have been; no wonder lazy-ass Barry had only worn it once. Faint pale lines along Jake's chest stretched from the sternum along his left pec to vanish under his shirt. Now she looked carefully there was a star-shaped scar that could have been an old bullet wound high on the pec. What looked like the scar of a stab wound marred the otherwise flawless skin above his navel. She lifted one hand to the bullet wound.

"Were you a Marine?"

The blond hairs were thick but soft, like fur; his skin warm beneath.

She raised her face to his, intending to ask again. But he kissed her, hard. She made to take a step back but a hand in the small of her back pressed her to him and the next instant she found herself pushing him back into the hall and against the wall. Her tongue brushed his teeth and she was pleased to find them clean. An instant later, she had his shirt off his shoulders, pesky zipper and all. The buttoned sleeves snagged at his wrists and she disengaged to help him unbutton them.

And saw more scars along his forearm, inside his elbow. Old scars. Needle tracks.

She pushed away, her elbow catching the door frame on the way through. A junkie! God, what had he stolen while her back was turned?

She retreated further into the kitchen until her hips pressed into the bench by the stove. *A goddamn paranoid schizophrenic junkie!*

"Gwen, please. You don't get it." Barry's expensive shirt hung from his outstretched arms like the membrane of a bat's wings.

"Get what? I know tracks when I see them." She folded her arms about herself, aware suddenly of the nearness of the cheese knife. Jake stood beyond the door, his mouth tight, animal hunger smoldering in his eyes. But he made no move toward her. She felt smaller, deflated, embarrassed. She'd been so stupid. Substance abuse was rife among the homeless. What had she expected? "Please, just leave."

"Gwen."

"Stop." Thoughts raced through her mind like expressway traffic, part of her mind kicking her ass for trusting a vagrant, part scanning what she could see of the living room for things that might be missing, another part worried that he might flip. He already thought he had a life-threatening allergy to silver, that men were after him. And with the lifestyle of a junkie, maybe they were. Maybe he owed money. She had to keep the situation safe, controlled.

"Look, you want a prescription? I'll get it for you. Drop by the ER tomorrow after two, and it'll be waiting at the desk. But we're done."

"Done?"

She could see it in his eyes. He wanted her. His jaw worked as he struggled for control. With a flurry, he ripped off the shirt. A button from the sleeve flew her way. She flinched and shifted in front of the knife, one hand slipping behind her.

"Okay then," he said, and his voice was abruptly softer. He lurched out of view along the hallway, then flashed past the living room door on his way out, backpack in hand. The bang of the front door slamming was like a gunshot and she jumped.

He's gone, she assured herself when she finally worked up the nerve to move. She held the knife before her as she peeked into the hallway, making sure. Empty. Her bedroom was empty. She peeped through the front window before opening the front door to lock the security door.

He's gone. It's okay. He's gone.

He'd left the rest of the clothes. The garbage bag was shoved up against the trash bin in the bathroom and she dropped the zipper shirt on top.

She splashed water on her face, rinsed her mouth and headed for the ouzo bottle.

Kidnappers, junkies and arrogant rat-bastards, she thought as she took her first chug. *Gwen always attracts the best.*

He hadn't slowed down long enough to put on another shirt and passers-by stared at him as he stalked toward his squat.

They should look the other way! Why aren't they staring at all the other guys without shirts?

i'll rip their eyelids off. i'll drink their—

"Damnit!"

His thoughts were beginning to mix with the Animal's. He was losing track of who was who. The moon was out there, growing larger, ready to rise on him and draw the beast to the surface.

"God*dammit!*"

He'd been so close to her. Every other wound had faded - why not his *tracks?*

A simple answer to that, he suspected: It hated him for using, knowing dope suppressed It. Needle scabs were the price It made him pay for control.

control? go back, control her!

He'd wanted her, right there, right then—or was that the Animal? How much was him and how much was It?

She'd started it, after all. The aroma of lust, of sex, so quickly turning to fear.

go back, take her!

No, you evil bastard!

That was rape. The very thing he'd saved her from only days ago. Gwen was a nice woman, a *good* woman. He'd never ever hurt a woman.

Memories of Rockford flooded over him. He kicked a trash can, spraying garbage across the strip of weeds between pavement and gutter. He bent over the mess, chest heaving.

What the hell had happened back in Rockford? He had woken up fully clothed in the same tool shed he'd shot up in. Fully clothed meant he couldn't have Changed. He couldn't have killed her. Could he? Could the Animal have had enough brains and enough control in the morning to clean him up, dress him? The idea was enough to make him shiver despite the heat. The killing had been the only topic of conversation at the shelter that morning, people saying it was a stray dog or pack of them. But it hadn't been dogs. From the description,

Jake knew to the core of his being that only one thing could have done that. *Would* have done that.

That same Animal rumbled in his chest, indicating it would like to do it all over again if he'd let it. As if he didn't have enough marks against his name. He kicked at some of the trash and stomped off.

"Sonofabitch."

As he walked, It kept scratching at his awareness, like a dog at the door. It took him several seconds to realize It was telling him something wasn't right. He slowed, finally realizing a guy was keeping pace on the other side of the street, walking parallel to him. He studied the man from beneath his hair: not one of those trenchcoat freaks from Birmingham, and not a cop. That left one possibility. Just as Jake thought he better make a run for it, another man stepped out from behind a wall onto the pavement ahead of him.

A purple bruise covered Jarhead's forehead where Jake had smacked it into the dumpster. He carried a baseball bat in one hand and wore a glove on the other. As if he was off to the park.

The guy across the street made a beeline for him. Jake reversed and almost crashed into a third man. Piggy. Holding something square and glossy like a movie ray gun. Wires shot out. They hit Jake in the chest. Pain smashed through his torso like he'd been hit with a giant hammer. A fist clamped around his lungs. The sidewalk jumped up into him. He struck his head and his vision faded round the edges. He smelled hot plastic and burnt hair. He made it onto his knees, got one foot beneath him before the bat hit him on the meat of his right shoulder and the guy from across the street kicked him in the head.

Face down, vision swimming, he couldn't resist as strong hands pulled his arms behind him and adhesive tape wrapped his wrists tightly.

"No gun," one of them said. "Musta dumped it."

The world wiggled and pulsated, light appearing and disappearing in swirls and flashes. One moment he was on the concrete, the next he was being carried. He tried to kick; his hands strained against the tape. No good.

For an instant, he was not himself. He was It, It was him.

It snapped at them, teeth clacking.

They laughed and dumped him in a trunk reeking of gas, blood and urine. The Animal scrabbled inside his chest, spooked by the stench of danger. He tried to sit, to prevent the lid from closing. Piggy grabbed his hair and pushed him down. Jarhead jabbed something into his bruised shoulder. Jake cried out. Warmth seeped through him, soft and moist like custard flowing out and up, into his his arms, into his mind. He slumped, cheek pressing against sticky carpet.

"No. No…"

"You really should be more cooperative," Piggy said and slammed the trunk.

Soft light.

Slowing thoughts.

just wait 'til they let me out

Blackness.

CHAPTER EIGHTEEN

Crisp dawn air sucking the heat from his naked body, Jake stands above his victim, but he can't look at the mangled heap of flesh. Not directly. Peripheral vision takes in the flak jacket and camo pants of a deer hunter. A hat hangs nearby, hooked in a bush. The stench drives him away to retch into a thicket bordering the dusty clearing. When his gut finishes heaving, he sees the glint of the rifle on the other side of the bushes and the hunter's hide set into the forest ten feet beyond it. He stumbles back through the clearing, drops on his knees in the small stream bisecting it, scrubs at his skin until not a speck of blood remains. He runs his hands through his short hair, again and again, until it feels clean. The water is even colder than the air, his skin pebbled with gooseflesh; his knees sting from the stones in the creek bed, but his numbness equals his pain.

I killed a man.

The man is a hunter. Was a hunter. Maybe he hadn't been hunting deer. Maybe he'd been hunting Jake.

I killed a man.

It might've been self-defense. The hide. The rifle. Jake hasn't seen any deer up here. There'd been those dark-coated maniacs with the pistols back in Birmingham, shouting gibberish about "theryons" and silver bullets and a true mission as they lost Jake in a maze of alleys. Maybe this guy was after him too. Maybe there was a whole mess of them.

Maybe they'd been after his dad.

How they know he is a wolf, he has no idea. Has he given himself away somehow?

There is one way to check if the man was after him. Unload his rifle and check the bullets. He knows what bullets should look like, and he knows silver since it almost killed him once when he handled old coins.

Even at eighteen, Jake knows what he is. He's watched a couple of werewolf movies, feeling sick every time the creatures appear. Feeling excited, aroused. He hates himself. He hates the Animal, as he's begun calling the thing inside him. He wants to die. But suicide's a sin. It was on the list Momma used to recite to him and he remembers it clearly because he's always wondered why she'd tell him that, him just a little boy at the time. He doesn't want to die in sin; he wants to be good when he dies, so he can see Momma again. He wants an eternity without suffering, without feeling the way he does right now.

Without the misery in his heart and the pain in his cheek—

Jake snapped awake. Someone had just slapped him, hard. He was in a camping chair, his wrists taped to the arms, his ankles to the legs.

"—especially with my own gun, bitch!" a man shouted at him.

Though he was cold, sweat poured down his face, sheeted his shoulders, his ribs. Not in the woods then. Not back ten years ago with blood on his hands.

"What time is it?" he croaked. His vision was cloudy, the room swimming, colors washing into one another.

Piggy stood three feet away, right in front of him, legs spread in a fighter's stance, eyes narrowed. "Zee says 'hey'. He's sorry he won't be able to make it tonight, but he's looking forward to the video." He pointed at something indistinct on a benchtop. A camcorder? "Oh, and thanks for the cash and the other crap." He hefted Jake's backpack, shook it to show it was empty and tossed it onto a black stain on the concrete floor.

Concrete.

He squeezed his eyes shut and opened them again. A garage. They had him in a mechanic's workshop, the air oily with machine smells. Between Piggy and the closed roller door sat a partially deconstructed car without plates.

"Awake, Jake?" Jarhead said from somewhere behind him. "Pleasant dreams, I hope. Electric dreams were they?"

This was bad. Real bad. He didn't know of any garages near his squat, but he had to hope he was in the vicinity. How long had he been out? If he could get out now, sprint home as fast as possible, he might make it. He could—

Too late. A low thrumming was building beneath his skin, beneath the throb of his injuries. The thrumming called to him, the moon's love song playing his blood. He heard more than that: the heartbeats of the two men pulsed a counterpoint to his own. He smelled their blood lust, and a sour taste rose from his gorge, so pungent he had to cough to avoid puking. It had been so long, so very long since he last Changed. But there was no mistaking how close it was.

It seethed, hungry for blood. Jake strained against the tape. "Let me go!" It might be too late for that. And as bad as these two *sonsofbitches* were - as much as he suddenly wanted to *rip* out their *throats* and dip his face into their *hot pumping fuel* - he couldn't let it happen. Because after he'd killed them he'd be free to kill someone else, someone who mattered, someone it would be a sin to murder. His only chance was to get to his squat and lock himself away. "You've got to let me go!"

Piggy laughed, jowls shaking. "I don't think so, dickwad."

Jake pulled one wrist back through the tape toward himself and succeeded only in tearing hairs from his arm.

Piggy chortled.

"Lock me up then. Put me somewhere safe. Somewhere I can't get out."

Jarhead made a sympathetic noise. "Boy needs a taste. Pity he didn't pay us for some. Pity he shot at us. Sucker-punched me. Just look at him sweat."

Jake pulled his head away but the skinny prick reefed him back by the hair and ran a finger along his brow. Jarhead waved his glistening finger tip in front of Jake's eyes. "Sweatin like a junkie pig."

Jake almost snapped at the finger, wished he could bite it off. His skin was hot; his breath scalded his throat and chest.

"Needing the needle?" Jarhead said with a laugh. "Or just plain scared? Don't get too scared yet, Jakey. We've only just begun." He minced away from him, humming an old song Jake remembered his Momma playing.

Piggy watched him closely.

"You need ... to leave," Jake said. Words were becoming hard to form, and it wasn't just from the blow to the head. He was growing bigger, the tape cutting into his forearms, pulling tighter around his ankles.

Piggy socked him in the jaw. His skull rang with the impact. He whipped his head back toward his attacker, teeth bared.

kill you - i'll kill you!

Jarhead crooned from the far end of the shop.

Jake's fingers curled around the arms of the chair. Claws scraped beneath the surface of his skin, *wanting* to emerge, craving release.

"Get ... *out!*"

Jarhead turned on a blowtorch above a workbench. "You're going nowhere, Jakey-snakey." He played the blue-white flame along a length of metal that might have been a file or chisel. "You're not going to like this. But we will."

"I love the smell of burnt flesh in the morning," Piggy drawled, before bursting into a cackle. A fleck of spittle hit Jake on the lip.

Jake licked it.

"It's night-time, asshole," Jarhead snapped.

"I know that, *asshole.*" Piggy sounded hurt. "What, are you stupid? You never seen *Apocalypse Now?*"

No. No! Can't let...

Jake tried to speak, to make one last attempt to get the men out, but his throat betrayed him, constricting, widening, constricting again. The words came out as grunts and growls. The camp chair was rocking beneath him, but he no longer knew whether it was him or the Animal trying to escape its clutches.

"Dumbass junkie." Piggy cuffed him round back of the head before he moved aside to allow Jarhead in close. The chisel shone yellow-red at the tip like a kid's glowstick.

"Get ready for Mr Pain," Jarhead said.

pain?

Jake was already in pain.

Pain like hot wires running through his joints, his spine, his fingertips, his skull, his jaw. Pain like the Taser twanging the muscles along his legs, his arms. His nails *were* claws now, fingers swelling beneath and around them.

i'll show you pain

Jarhead stopped just out of reach, the hot metal forgotten, eyes growing round.

The chair's cloth back groaned; the fabric split along the line of Jake's spine. The tape around his wrists burst open like paper.

Jake heard Piggy say, "Fuck—", and then the gray-yellow haze enveloped him.

CHAPTER NINETEEN

Gas. Blood. Urine. Old sweat and stale farts. Paint and thinners.

The odors were disorienting. Familiar. For a moment Jake wondered if he was still in Zee's trunk. But that wasn't right. It was too bright.

Morning light slanted in through the tiny back windows of the van he lay in.

Van?

He sat up quickly and regretted it. Pain lanced like a bullet through each eye and out both temples, blinding him temporarily. The muscles along his limbs and spine felt bruised and twisted. When the world stopped spinning and the silver sparkles disappeared from his vision, Jake opened his eyes again. He was naked, covered by a cotton blanket. Patches of his skin were sticky - with blood, he discovered with dismay, and not his own blood - but they were only patches: it felt as if he'd been partially washed or wiped down. He could still smell and feel the chemical residue now that he concentrated on it.

The van was furnished with shallow cupboards along each wall and the mattress he lay on. A partition separated him from the driver's compartment. He squinted toward the doors. A mound of clothing lay at the foot of his mattress. He tossed aside the blanket and slid down, carefully testing his sore muscles. The bundle consisted of a pair of new Calvin Kleins, generic track pants and a Lakers shirt, all with price tags still on. Had someone left them for him? Had someone picked him up and brought him here - wherever here was?

He tugged off the labels and slipped on the undies and pants, then glanced out the dirty window. The van was in a parking lot, the faded lines interspersed with hip-high weeds. Thick woodlands rose like a wall around the lot. The hum of distant traffic was the only noise. He pulled on the shirt and turned the handle gingerly. The door creaked as he eased it open a crack.

"To hell with it."

He kicked it the rest of the way and leapt out. Dizziness hit him and he lurched back against the van, fighting for balance.

"Re-entry's a bitch, ain't it?"

Jake whirled toward the voice, his teeth bared.

The man was sitting in front of a low gas barbecue. Middle-aged and lean, he wore denims and a thin red hoodie with the sleeves pushed up to the elbows, revealing powerful forearms. Shaggy, graying hair and salt-and-pepper stubble. He took a handful of bacon rashers from a plastic tub beside his camp chair and tossed them on the hotplate.

"Was beginning to wonder if you'd ever wake up. I won't offer you eggs. Too hard to clean up after. And besides—" he turned his dark eyes on Jake's for the first time "—carnivores prefer meat."

The whiff of frying meat made Jake's guts bubble. He rubbed a hand across his belly and was dismayed to find it distended. He'd eaten already. And that meant…

He picked at something stuck in his teeth. Something pink and soft.

Flesh.

He fell onto hands and knees and retched until nothing came up. Spasms rocked his body and he crawled away from the mess with his eyes screwed shut.

He realized belatedly he was helpless - if the guy making breakfast wanted to hurt him, he could have done anything right then. Instead, the man made a *tsk*-ing noise and murmured, "Good thing I brought you breakfast."

The man shifted the cooler around the other side of the hotplate with one foot and then waved Jake to take the chair. His smile was friendly enough. "Sit down 'til you've eaten. Get your strength back. I've already had something." He sat on the cooler and shifted bacon around the hotplate with a spatula.

Jake sniffed a string of snot back up his nose, spat bile from his mouth, got to his feet and shuffled closer. "Who are you?"

"Name's Eddie, Jake." He put the spatula down. "I'm your cousin."

CHAPTER TWENTY

Jake rinsed his mouth with the water Eddie offered him, then took a long pull.

Eddie shoveled more bacon into his mouth and wiped grease from his chin. "God, it's taken me a long time to find you. Well, actually, I found you in Rockford but you disappeared before I could be sure it was you."

"How'd you find me *here*?"

Jake knew the answer as soon as he'd asked it.

"Saw your video on a breakfast news show. You were famous for a couple of days there, man, until they found some other flavor-of-the-hour. A real hero."

That was just great. It was a wonder he didn't have a dozen cops on his ass by now.

"Who was the girl? Hope she found a good way to say thanks?" He grinned.

Jake shook his head. He considered sitting in the foldout chair, but it reminded him too much of the one in the workshop. So he squatted beside it and sipped water. Who was "the girl" he'd helped? Just a woman. She was no one to him. No one.

Eddie watched him for a moment, then shrugged. "Anyway, once I knew where you were, it was just a matter of hanging around 'til the next fat moon."

"Why then?"

Eddie laid his fork on his plate with a clatter that hurt Jake's ears. "Easier to sniff you out while you're lupine. We can smell each other at any time, but it's a hell of a lot easier when we've both shifted."

Jake choked on his water.

Eddie waited until the coughing had ended before asking, "You didn't know there were more of us? Figures. Your daddy wasn't exactly the communicative type, from what I remember. And you disappeared into state custody before any of us could get to you."

"Us?"

"Family."

"Family? You mean…?"

"Well. Not any more. You and I are the last. Of our *branch*, anyway."

"You're a—You're like me?"

Eddie offered a double thumbs-up.

"So you found me in the workshop. While I'd Changed or after?"

"After. But I stayed outside 'til dawn. Better that way. Besides, the sentries were plenty enough to keep me busy."

"So you couldn't have come in and helped me."

"No, not a good idea to get two wolves in the same room when they don't know each other. Just ask Uncle Mike. Oh, that's right, you can't, coz his daddy had to kill him the first time he had his full *metamorfoz?*."

"He killed his own son?" That was what Momma sometimes told him his own father had wanted for him. "Does that happen often?"

"Sometimes. Not often, thank Christ." Eddie jabbed a fork in the last rasher of bacon and held it out, but Jake, his gut turning, waved it away. Eddie shrugged and stuffed it in his mouth. He chewed noisily, then said, "I'm sorry, bud. I woulda been there for you after your daddy died. But A, none of us knew where you went, and B, I was doing a stretch in Attica."

Jake jerked in alarm. "Prison? What for?"

"For being myself, Jakey boy. Just for being myself."

"How long for?"

"When your daddy died, I'd just started my nine years."

"Nine years! How'd you … how'd you stop from …?"

"It's good I finally found you." He mopped up some grease with a finger and sucked it clean. "Your dad never got control, so he couldn't teach you. But I can."

Control! Jake had only dreamed of such a thing. If he could stop himself changing, without drugs—

He had taken a serious backward step last night, even though the two guys were scum. But now he wondered if perhaps his Momma was getting God to help him by sending Eddie. Maybe life was finally looking up.

"Where are we? I need to go to my squat. Get my stuff."

"I'll get you in the area of that hospital your girlfriend works at. You can find it from there?"

"She ain't my girlfriend," Jake said.

Eddie chuckled, then pointed to a pack of baby wipes by the chair. "I'll pack up. You go wipe yourself down. Maybe behind those trees over there. When you were still out, I cleaned off your face, your arms, your legs, but I wasn't going anywhere near your man bits. That's your job, buddy."

Jake had to admit the new clothes felt less new with the cloth sticking to him. He picked up the wipes. "The garage. The bodies. The cops will find our ..." What the hell was that stuff called?

"I torched it. They won't find nothing they can use. And if the overworked Detroit cops actually care enough about four dead drug bunnies to go sifting through that mess for our DNA, good luck to them. We'll be long gone by then."

"But you have a record."

"Yeah, I do. But like I say, they won't care that much. To regular upstanding citizens and law enforcement officers, criminals don't matter. That's to our advantage."

"Wait. My pack. My backpack. Did you get it?" He started toward the van.

"Sorry, Jake. Didn't see a backpack. Maybe they ditched it."

Jake swore. The pack had clothes, EpiPens, toothbrush, cash - hell, everything that mattered except his rig and his H.

"They probably had it melting in a barrel of acid. Which is where you woulda been if you hadn't shifted." Eddie dumped his plate and fork into a garbage bag. "You have to admit, cousin, your true nature is a real blessing when it saves your life like that."

Saves my life. And if Jarhead had been an hour earlier with the blow torch or they'd stuffed him in the trunk *before* he'd gone to Gwen's … Had Eddie already been sneaking around in the background watching them, waiting, making sure? Would he have intervened if things hadn't gone in Jake's favor?

Busy cleaning down the hotplate, Eddie said, "Timing is everything, buddy," making Jake wonder if werewolves could read each other's minds, too.

Clutching the packet of wipes, he trudged out to the treeline, aware of Eddie's eyes on him the whole way.

run, the Animal said. *get away!*

Jake told it to shut the hell up. As bizarre as this was, if this stranger could really control his problem, then he had brought Jake his first real chance at salvation.

They drove south toward Hamtramck, silent apart from Eddie's violent cussing when a motorcycle cut him off. Jake tried to keep it sneaky as he studied him, but he could tell Eddie knew. The guy didn't seem to care; he didn't seem to have a worry in the world, apart from motorcyclists.

Eddie had a round raised scar on his right forearm. Jake had one just like it on his chest, left there by a bullet. Gwen had touched it - was that really only last night? So much had happened since then. He didn't remember receiving his own scar; it had been there the morning after a Change, the misshapen lead slug lying on the ground nearby, the wound already closed over.

Eddie's camp had been a long way north of Forest Park where Jake had his squat. They'd been driving for about thirty minutes when Jake's appetite surfaced.

"You got anything to eat?"

"Ah, America, the land of plenty."

Eddie pulled into a Burger King.

They ate parked in front of the playground while squealing whooping toddlers buzzed around the equipment like flies on bacon. A child cried and the noise jolted loose a memory. When Jake had been newly placed with his foster parents, Alec Armstrong tried to lead him onto a plastic playground like this. Jake had hated the feel of the things, the static electricity, the smell. He'd cried and resisted, pulling out of Alec's grip and running to press himself against the fence. Sharp words had followed before a silent car trip home, just the two of them, Alec Armstrong a brooding hulking presence in the driver's seat, Jake curled in on himself against the passenger door.

"So, this is what I know," Eddie said, spraying burger. "Your dad married your mom and fled to Alabama. Distanced himself from the rest of us. By rest of us, I mean my dad, my other uncle, my brother and me. All that were left of our branch. Your dad changed his name, too." He swallowed and rinsed his mouth with Coke, then elbowed Jake playfully in the ribs. "Your name's not Brennan, it's Barrow. But that was changed, too, way back when our forefathers moved here from Europe."

"Europe?"

"Originally we were called Bukovec. It's Romanian."

"Romanian. Huh." He didn't know where that was, so he took another bite of burger. It would be full moon tonight and things always tasted better, *richer* around now. Flavors exploded into his mouth, so solid he could almost touch them. Meat like a warm bed. Onion like a sunrise.

"I know your folks died in a fire, Jake. You were, what, seven, eight? I'm guessing your dad tried to kill all three of you. He never liked what he was, never came to terms with it. And I just don't get that."

Jake knew the truth of the fire, but he wasn't telling Eddie. He wasn't telling a near-stranger that he agreed that his Dad had started the fire on purpose, dragging Momma and little Jake down to the cellar to wait it out together. How could he explain what it felt like that your dad tried to kill you, that your momma had to fight him to give you time to run, that you never stopped feeling guilty for leaving her there to die?

He wasn't telling his cousin any of that until he knew him a lot better than he did now.

Eddie shook his head and took another bite. Flecks of bread flew from his mouth as he talked. "I know the state put you in foster care. Is it true you ran away just before your thirteen birthday, after you'd assaulted your foster father? Yeah? Well, that would have been your first *metamorfoz?*, your first shift: no fur, no teeth, no claws, but you would been mad as a burning snake and twice as mean. It woulda been building up all day until around midnight you couldn't contain it anymore. Sound about right?" He snickered. "That dumb dogooder had no idea what hit him, did he?"

Jake had never thought of the Armstrongs as dogooders. Jane, maybe, but Alec Armstrong had been a dour, miserly sonofabitch. He hadn't felt too guilty about hurting him, just scared by what he'd done - scared of the rage that engulfed him on the following two nights also - and scared of what the Armstrongs would do to him if he ever went back there. Where did you go from foster care when things went bad? Juvey?

Eddie crumpled his wrapper and flicked it out his window, then slurped down the rest of his soda.

Jake, overwhelmed, said nothing. His dad a wolf? Jake had never known for sure. Deep down Jake had always believed his curse was a punishment from God for failing to save his momma. But he must have caught his problem like a disease from his violent bastard of a father. Those nights the man locked himself in the cellar while Jake and his momma fled into the woods made a whole lot more sense now.

The soda cup went the way of the burger wrapper and Eddie shoveled fries into his mouth. "You want a shake? Yeah, I feel like a shake, fill up all the empty spaces in here." He patted his stomach.

"Sure." The burger was doing nothing to assuage his hunger. "Uh, vanilla, thanks."

"Two large vanilla shakes. And then I'll tell you the story of where we came from." Eddie backed out without checking his mirrors. A horn blared and he flipped the bird, chucked the shifter into D and heading for the drive-through.

The night had been as uneventful as the day before. As the Chevelle pulled up outside the Listening Ear Mission, Carter could only hope the werewolf would return here today. That moment in Doug's office, watching Brennan on the computer tussling with the kidnapper, watching him receive that kiss on the cheek, Carter had believed the end was close, resolution was coming. So far, Detroit had produced a whole lot of nothing.

No sooner had Tim ratcheted his handbrake on than a hand lanced in through the open driver's window, palm up. "I want the rest of my money," a voice snarled.

Tim grabbed the hand and shoved it outside, cranking the window-handle fast before the arm could snake back through. Carter relaxed a notch, recognizing the owner as Varley.

"You'll get it when our friend appears," Tim said. Invective and threats spewed against the glass and Tim giggled. "Faced scarier beasts than you, pisspants!"

Carter climbed out and opened his wallet. "Here, buddy." Varley's head popped up above the car, meerkat-like. The stream of abuse cut off. Carter held out the other half of the bill he'd torn in two the day before as the man shuffled around the car. "He shows up, my friend here will give you another ten."

The guy plucked the money from his fingers and shuffled away, pressing the two halves of the twenty together as if expecting them to magically heal. He turned once on his path to the mission and swore long and loud in Tim's direction.

"There's gratitude for ya," Tim muttered as Carter returned to his seat. "Never give these guys a break. They won't thank you for it and they don't deserve it, most of 'em."

"My wife thought they deserved it."

Tim stayed silent, and Carter thought the choice was a good one.

He checked his watch: 11.12 a.m. The sun was up above the houses along the street and he wound his window down to try to catch some of the intermittent breeze. A number of people were already hanging around the front of the mission.

"What time's lunch?" Carter asked.

"What am I, their website?"

"Grumpy bastard."

"That's my money you're giving away there."

"I thought money wasn't an issue for you."

"It's the principle of the thing."

"I'm serious about lunch time," Carter said. "I want to know how long we'll be waiting here."

"We wait here until something happens. We have a lead."

"How do we know Varley actually saw Brennan at all?"

"Great question, Einstein. After nothing panned out yesterday, that's why I wasn't paying him until it did."

"You have a lot of friends, Darkrider? Get invited to a lot of parties? I'm only asking because your people skills are outstanding."

Tim pressed his lips shut and hid his eyes behind his shades.

Carter did some deep breathing to get his frustration under control. "I shouldn't have said that."

"Whatever. I don't care."

"Yeah, but I shouldn't have said that."

"Whatever."

Carter tried another tack. "So, you guys fight vampires too?"

"Huh. You watch too many movies." Tim caught Carter's ironic smile and acknowledged the lame joke with a thin smile of his own. "Then again, there are more things in heaven and earth, eh? Who knows what else is out there?" He chuckled.

"Heaven." Carter's smile soured. "Yeah."

He lay his head against the rest and for the first time in a long time, he prayed - he really prayed.

God, if you do exist, and you do care, and if evil is meant to be opposed in this world, then send him to me. Send Brennan to me soon.

They'd parked in much the same spot, facing the playground. It seemed like there were more kids in there than before and Jake wished they could park the other side of the lot, get away from the noise, find some shade. Before he could ask, Eddie started talking again, so Jake just stuck the straw in his mouth, sucked on shake and tried to focus on his cousin and not the noise of the children and the heat of the morning sun.

"Eastern Europe in the Thirteenth Century was a messed-up place," Eddie told him. "Religious conflict, territorial conflict, social conflict. And into this mess, the Spaniards sent a handful of missionaries. One of these assholes was named Dominados Alegis. Good ol' Dominados got himself a large 'parish' out in the boondocks of Moldavia. He wasn't a real good priest. In fact, man was a badass. Shacked up with a witch. Loved his food and his drink. Loved the young ladies. Loved hunting. Loved anything with a thrill attached. More than anything, Dominados loved power. The Church gave him political power. But he wanted more. And he didn't give a shit where that power came from: potions, books, magic charms, God, the Devil, *other* gods.

"Because it was a dangerous world back then, Dominados had himself a small army of mercenaries. One day he started thinking what if they weren't enough? He knew the kind of power his missus the witch owned. He'd tasted it himself. What if some upstart warlords came onto his turf with their own witches at their side who had even greater power? So he dug into the local lore until him and his missus came up with the idea of werewolves. They discovered an ancient 'curse'. They cut the throat of one of their soldiers, used his blood to seal the curse and laid it on the dead man's twin sons: Boian and Patrascu Bukovec. And what d'ya know, the curse worked. The boys were fourteen at the time, men in those days. Dominados now had himself a pair of bona fide shapeshifters. It would be tough for anyone opposing him to face that kind of power. And the best thing was, the curse they used included this kind of ongoing clause — the Bukovec boys would one day have sons and those sons would carry the line onwards, so that all of Dominados's descendents would have their own superhuman protectors."

Eddie wiped his hands on a napkin and flipped it outside, checked Jake was listening. "You need to memorize this. It's what makes us who we are."

Jake nodded dumbly. The squeals of children in the playground were giving him a headache.

"Here's where the story gets real interesting," Eddie continued. "You know how people say 'Never work with children or animals'? Well, Dominados worked with both, ha. And of course, things didn't go to plan. He didn't know what the hell he'd released. Because those two boys, those two *wolves*, they turned on him. Chomp chomp. Yum yum. No more Father Dominados Alegis. No more witchy wife. Just two strong young shapeshifters who now had their own merc army and their own patch of earth to run the way they saw fit."

Jake allowed the strange words to process, his head pounding harder.

"Cool, huh?" Eddie said.

Jake turned to the window, desperate for fresh air. In the playground, two small boys had a bigger boy baled up against the fence, their fists curled into guns and aimed at his head.

"So it's passed to all the kids?" Jake asked.

"Only the males. No daughters ever transform."

"Why?"

"Just the way of it. Probably 'cause they only wanted male soldiers back then."

"So ... how do we, like, cure it?"

Eddie roared with laughter. "Why would we do that?" He slugged Jake playfully in the thigh. "Listen, you've been adrift your whole life, pal. No one to show you what's what, teach you what a gift Dominados gave us. That and the fact you can't control it isn't great. You've attracted attention, quite a few times. We can't let the world know we're out here. It's hard enough with these douchebag Hunters after us."

"Hunters?" He thought of the two guys in trenchcoats who'd stalked him in Birmingham and Jackson. The shit kept getting deeper.

Eddie said, "What if we had the Feds and every armed militia in the country out gunning for us too? Homeland Security armed with silver bullets? Someone has to take you under their wing. Someone has to look out for you. And that, cousin, will be me."

"What about the others? Your dad, *his* dad?"

"Our grandaddy died in a car accident about thirty, thirty-five years back. Then my dad disappeared about twelve years ago. I figure the Hunters got him. My other uncle - not your daddy - he got shot up after a bar fight. And my brother Matt, a true wolf that guy, well, he drowned." He raised his brows at Jake's expression. "Oh, you think we live forever, huh? Can't be killed? It's not just silver that does it. Rip an arm off and you'll bleed out, super-healing or no super-healing. A million ways you can die. Lose an organ to a shotgun blast. Drown. Course, silver-poisoning's the worse. You ever experienced it?"

Jake winced, pressing down hard on the memories, the pain, the terror.

"Sure. We all have. Touch a vase, a necklace, an old coin. We're just lucky silver's not that popular these days. Unless you're some old lady with a tea set. So there you have it, a family blessing. We're the best of the best. And your sons will be the same."

Sons?

Jake closed his eyes on the boys in the playground. His head felt like someone was trying to crack it open with a pry bar. "And the Hunters?"

"That's another story for some other time." Eddie spat out his window. "Maybe we'll catch us one. Get them to tell their side of the story, though it's sure to be a bunch of entertaining bullshit. Yeah, another time I'll explain them, Jake. For now, what's important is who you are. You got all that? Making sense?"

Jake stumbled from the van. "I need to take a dump." He weaved between cars and lurched into the restaurant. The air in the dining area felt like syrup, but he tried to hold himself steady, press through it without looking drunk or stoned. No one paid him much mind. No one wrinkled up their nose, despite the filth he felt sticking to his skin, the filth that stuck to his soul. No staff members tried to stop him. No mothers glared at him when he passed their kids. He crashed through the outer and inner mens room doors and stumbled into a cubicle. He twisted the lock so hard he felt a screw on the catch loosen. He flicked the lid down and sat, head in his hands.

It was too much. A cousin tracking him down, a family cursed for hundreds of years. He had no idea where Moldavia was. It sounded as exotic as the other names Eddie had rattled off: Dominados, Boian, Patrascu, Bukovec.

He jolted as a new realization hit him. "The job. No!"

It was meant to start this morning. Maybe he could get through tonight and try again tomorrow. He could see Angelo, make sure it was still okay, apologize.

He sucked in air. The walls pressed in and he pushed against them with both arms. He felt strong. He could push them over, could smash them, could rip the room to pieces...

The outer door banged open. He tensed, ready to catch the cubicle door if it got kicked in.

Try me. Try me!

Someone whistling *Jingle Bells* opened their zipper and started pissing in the urinal. *Jingle Bells*. In summer.

What a tool.

He sucked in a deep breath, held it a long time, let it out slow. Repeated it. His heart rate slowed. The pisser had a bladder the size of a hot water tank. He took forever to finish and when he had, he took his time washing and drying his hands, whistling the same damn tune the whole time. By the time he left, Jake felt he had his emotions under control. He washed his face and arms, and only when he was certain there was no residue left from the night before did he return to the van.

"Thought you'd drowned in there, buddy," Eddie muttered as Jake slipped back inside.

"You can really help me get control of this ... thing?" Jake asked.

Eddie clapped him on the shoulder. "Of course. What's family for?"

"I need my stuff. We gotta go back to where I'm stayin."

"I saw you in Rockford, at a distance. Didn't look like you had much 'stuff.'"

"Well, I do," he said.

"All right, all right, don't get tetchy. Not good, two wolves getting tetchy round full moon. I'm just saying. Cousin Eddie here can buy you a whole lot better stuff. New stuff. Next town we go to, you can paint houses with me, make some money and buy your own crap. But if you wanna go get your gear, that's peachy with me. I'm your taxi driver, your chauffeur. So, where to, sir?"

Jake realized again he didn't know where he was. Detroit was a big city. He could ask Eddie to take him near the hospital, but instinct made him keep Gwen out of the conversation. "Can you get me near the Eastern Market?"

"That near where your girlfriend works? Already told you I could."

Jake fought a scowl. "I can get you to my place once I see somethin I know."

"As I said, your chauffeur, at your service." Eddie started the motor. "There's nothing in the whole wide world as beautiful as a family reunion."

CHAPTER TWENTY-ONE

Jake smelled smoke two blocks before he saw the gray smudge against the blue sky. He rubbed at his jaw while an anxious pressure built in his chest.

Eddie gave him a couple of sideways glances. "Your place, you thinking?"

Jake said nothing until they reached his street. "Slow down, stop around the corner."

Eddie took the corner harder than necessary and pulled up with a screech of brakes that set Jake's teeth on edge. There were no fire engines. And no rubberneckers. No sign of Zee's goons watching the neighborhood. A green hatchback sat way down the other end of the street, but pushers wouldn't be seen dead in a car like that.

"Drive down there *slowly*," he said.

"Please," Eddie muttered, but he complied, progressing at a speed Jake was far happier with.

The house had been reduced to blackened rubble with only part of the frame intact at the back. No police tape. He couldn't tell if the fire department had been here or whether the flames had burned themselves out. With empty lots on either side, no other houses would have been threatened. Hardly anyone lived in the street anyway. Fires were pretty common around Detroit; unless whoever owned the pile of crap filed an insurance claim or complained to the cops, there'd be no investigation.

"Musta found their friends or what was left of them this morning," Eddie said.

Jake didn't need anyone to explain this. This was a message to one person and one person only: *I know you killed my boys and I'll find you.*

He squinted at the hatchback. From forty or fifty yards away, and with sun glare on the windshield, he couldn't tell if anyone was inside. Zee might have someone watching from the house across the street, but Jake wasn't about to trawl through the ruins. His rig had been hidden in the dry wall - along with the pawn ticket for his Momma's brooch! He swore loudly and punched the door.

"Easy, tiger," Eddie said. "I told you I'd buy you more clothes."

"That's not all," he mumbled. "Let's get outta here."

Eddie sped off. They passed the hatchback at a speed Jake thought of as stupid. At the next corner, Eddie seemed to get his energy under control, slowing. "Where we going now, chief? I'm about ready to leave Detroit, unless you're spoiling for a fight with those guys. I didn't ask you who they were, but I'm guessing they're not members of your soccer team." He checked his mirrors, grunted in satisfaction and pulled into a side street. "Drug dealers, weren't they? You've been using to stop yourself from shifting? Not a bad way to keep the wolf inside - if you don't know how to control him. But you don't need dope to do that any more. You've got me, now."

"You can teach me to control it tonight, by midnight?"

"Risky. It's only a few hours' drive to a forest. Let's try it. We'll find some deerhunter's shack or lake house or something and I'll chain you up for the next two nights while I teach you how to embrace your nature. Without you tearing my throat out." Eddie seemed to find something funny in what he'd said.

Jake couldn't see anything amusing. How was he gonna get the brooch back? How could he let Momma down this way? How could he lose the one real thing of hers he had left? Without it, he might forget her completely; he might lose touch with the good in him, the good she'd put there. And without *that*, he'd be without hope, without a chance. A chance in hell.

"There's a pawn shop near here," he said. "I need to borrow some money from you. Please."

Eddie scratched his cheek as he considered. "All right."

"And I got a couple people I gotta apologize to before we leave."

"You don't gotta do that. People should be apologizing to you. Look at you: the world let you down. Your folks let you down." His eyes narrowed, searching Jake's. "You don't owe that little doctor a thing, if that's who you're thinking of. None of my business what happened between you two, but you saved her life, for Chrissake. Let her go. We'll find more women somewhere else. Listen, I got money, I got my paint business, so we'll get you set up in a new town with a new identity and you can do what you like when you're there - as long as you don't get caught. Yeah, that's the trick. Not getting caught. But you're good at staying under the radar. Mostly." Eddie straightened in his seat, abruptly all business. "So. What's this about a pawn shop?"

"Before we go anywhere else, I wanna know more about control. I wanna know how."

Eddie turned off the motor. "We can *start*, I guess. Neither one of us can fully shift during the day. But around full moon, we can get close." He bared his teeth in what Jake thought at first was a smile, except it kept growing.

Eddie's teeth *stretched* - the lower half of his face inflating, bulging, mouth widening to accommodate the fangs and molars of a larger creature. Muscles expanded at Eddie's shoulders, straining at his shirt. A seam popped. His hair stood out on his head and his eyes turned from green to a shiny gray. He raised one hand, palm up, and the hand broadened, the fingers stretching, the nails growing, thickening…

Jake swore.

A moment later, Eddie was Eddie. And Jake - pressed up against his door, his hands braced on seatback and dashboard - wondered if he'd really seen what he'd just seen.

"Holy shit," Jake said.

"Pity we can't go crash a frat party, huh? That trick would definitely impress the ladies."

"That's how I look?"

"You like it?"

Jake didn't. But he didn't dare say it. "You mean I'll be able to do that?" If he could shift at will, Jake might learn to *not* shift, or at least to hold it back without resorting to drugs.

Eddie fussed at the shoulder of his shirt, grimacing at the split seam. "To control it, you have to *be* it."

A doggy smell filled the cab: Eddie's wolf-scent. Jake found it both repulsive and energizing, as if the smell called to him, activated something in his veins.

fight!

No!

then run!

"Let me try," he said to Eddie.

"Let you? The question is *can* you?" Eddie shoved open his door and jerked a thumb over his shoulder. "Let's go in the back. You lose it, I want somewhere I can hold you down, okay?"

Jake hesitated before following him. What if this was a trap? What if Eddie saw Jake as prey?

run, the Animal insisted. It was usually correct about danger, but...

No, that made no sense. Why wouldn't Eddie have hurt him already if that was his plan? He followed the man who called himself *cousin* into the back of the van and closed the door behind him. He crouched, one hand on the handle. "What now?"

Eddie squatted at the other end. "Now you try."

"Try what?"

"Let the song take you."

"Huh?"

"You know it, boy. You must hear it singing in your blood. The song of the moon. The song of the wolf. Sing along, boy, sing along."

The song? Did he mean that vibration he always felt, that pull to look upwards, to burst out of his skin, to ... to be more. Only last night, it had overpowered him. He'd resisted, he'd fought, but it had won. He could recall it - just. Pain as if he were being pulled apart.

But behind and beneath that pain, there was something ... something robust. Something *alive*. It hummed in his anger, howled in his hunger. Power fired in his legs, his shoulders as the Animal surged. His blood thickened. Something new and hot roared in his ears. The light filtering through the van's window became yellower. And something at the other end of the van burned red: prey! The red-lit burning heart of prey!

yes, kill, eat!

Jake yanked down on the handle and tumbled out onto the road. The searing heat of sunbaked asphalt shocked him back fully into his body. He wrenched himself to his knees and felt his face, relieved to find teeth, not fangs; fingers, not claws..

A crunch came from behind him - Eddie leaving the van - but Jake refused to turn to him. The urge to rip and tear was relentless as gravity.

"Never mind, chief. You'll get the hang of it." A heavy hand clasped him on the shoulder and it was all he could do not to bite it. "Maybe it's time to visit that pawn shop. Then we can get the hell out of this shit hole."

CHAPTER TWENTY-TWO

Jake slipped the chain over his head and pushed the brooch down beneath his shirt. It looked weird there, judging by the pawnbroker's raised eyebrows; Jake couldn't give a rat's ass what the guy thought. He turned his back, pretending to be interested in the guitars lining the wall.

He'd solved one problem, with Eddie's help, but Eddie himself was a problem. It was time to return to his cousin's van, head out of town and start a new life. But was that a smart move? Did Jake really want to live with another werewolf? Did he want to learn "control" when control meant giving in to the Animal?

How would being *more* wolf-like help him get into Heaven?

The experience in the van had frightened him. What if he had turned fully wolf? What if he'd been injured or he'd hurt Eddie?

And why did *It* keep trying to tell him that something was wrong?

"You buying or wasting my time?"

Jake shot the pawn broker a look that drained the color from the smartass's face. "I'm thinkin. That okay with you?"

The man got busy dusting the inside of the display case.

Jake touched the brooch through his shirt and felt relief. And then a new worry. Outside, he could just make out Eddie behind the wheel, watching the skirts on a couple of passing teenagers and playing drums on the dash. The guy had been making Jake's neck hairs prickle ever since he'd offered him breakfast. Would hooking up with an ex-con make Jake a better man, or send him tumbling backwards? The way he'd sneered when he'd mentioned Gwen, the way he was looking at those girls right now...

There'd been an old man named Sticks on the streets of Birmingham. A good guy, kind to the young ones, teaching them survival skills. He'd kept a couple of bucks in his underwear, calling it *insurance*. Jake slipped a fifty out of Eddie's wallet and shoved it down his y-fronts.

Back at the van, he tossed the wallet in the glovebox and pulled up his shirt to show the brooch. "My Mom's. Thanks for getting it back for me."

Eddie fired up the van and pulled out without looking. A horn blared and Eddie ignored it. "So now you got your bling back," he said, "I recommend we head west. Maybe pick up a hitchhiker or two. Get through tonight in the forest and hook up again in the morning to let your lessons begin."

"Wait. Hitchhikers?"

"I hear that tone in your voice, Jakey. It worries me. I know you never got initiated into the joys, but I would've thought it'd come naturally. I mean, it *should* come naturally. You're a wolf, for Chrissakes."

"I'm a *man*."

"You're more than that. You've killed people. You know the rush. You must do."

Rush? Jake turned to the window. There'd been the one in the forest. A guy who tried to mug him. The woman in Rockford. Probably more he didn't know about, in the early days before he found a way to treat his problem with booze or drugs. Jake remembered no rush, nothing but horror and fear and guilt.

"It's in your nature, Jake. It's natural."

They passed a man and a woman having an argument. The man had the woman pressed against a chain-link fence with a meaty finger in her breastbone. She was screaming abuse. Jake turned away from them. "I want to be better than that. I am better than that."

Eddie laughed. "*Better?* Better'n what? What kinda life is this, shooting up, holing up? You'd be *better* embracing the wolf than staying a junkie the rest of your life. You were born to be free, not sleeping through each moon under bridges, hiding in shit-holes! I'm gonna keep saying this 'til you get it through your dumb head: we've been blessed.

As long as we're wily about it, we can do what we like and no one's ever gonna catch us."

But Eddie *had* been caught. He'd done time. And now the mad sonofabitch was planning to kidnap some hitchhiker and murder them, blaming it on his condition. He had slowed the car, head angled to watch the fighting couple in Jake's side mirror as if he wanted to join in.

Jake said, "Killing innocent people…"

Eddie's gaze snapped to Jake; his lips curled back from clenched teeth. "You think any one of those 'innocent' people wouldn't try'n kill *you*? If they saw you as you really are? If they had a gun in their hands while you were shifting?"

"I'm not gonna kill people," Jake growled, fingers tightening around the arm rest.

"You did it last night. You killed two people."

"A couple of drug dealers is one thing," Jake started, but Eddie kept on talking.

"And you didn't tear them apart because they deserved it. You didn't do it in self-defense. That's what a man might do. You did it because they were in front of you." Eddie swerved, narrowly missing a cyclist and throwing Jake against the door. "You did it coz you were hungry."

Stomach acid scorched Jake's throat. He tasted pickles. "Shut up about that."

"I was watching you in Rockford, Jake: you're soft. You didn't shift the first night the moon was strong and I thought maybe I had the wrong guy. But the scent was unmistakable. And the family resemblance. Yeah, you look just like Daddy. So I figured you were using something to suppress it. I was gonna make contact, take you under my wing, but you just vanished. Left town without leaving a clue. Cops looked for you over that woman, but even they gave up." Jake's heart lurched at that news. "Lucky for me you *are* soft though, coz saving that doctor's ass got your face in the papers. It let me know where you were."

"I'm not soft. I'm…"

What was he going to say? *Good?* No, he wasn't that; not yet anyway. But he had to try. He had to.

"Yeah, you're soft all right. That's why we have to release the beast, get you in touch with your lupine side. Coz you sure weren't soft last night."

Jake slammed the dash with his palm. "I didn't *want* to kill them! I couldn't help it!"

Eddie's smile was more of a grimace. "Of course you couldn't. Taken off the street like that. No drugs to bomb you out. The timing couldn't have been better."

Eddie's smug expression made something click for Jake. He'd been so careful ensuring no one knew where he lived, least of all Zee. "You led them to me."

Eddie pulled the van to a screeching halt on top of an overpass. Jake was thrown against the dashboard, but in his anger he didn't feel it. Horns and abuse assailed them as drivers veered around them.

"Had to see what you were made of, cousin. Had to bring you out."

"You sonofabitch!"

Eddie scanned the road, apparently unconcerned by Jake's outburst. "How do I get onto that freeway?"

But Jake knew exactly where he was. And he knew where he didn't want to be - not now or ever.

He clambered out and sprinted back along and off the bridge until he came to a house. He paused to check behind him, but the van still sat in the middle of the overpass, driver's door shut and brake lights on. Jake didn't wait to see if Eddie would get out. He ducked into the yard and vaulted a side gate. He landed in a kid's wading pool, slipped and fell heavily on his side. A chihuahua clambered out from under the back stoop, machinegun-yapping at him. Jake rolled onto hands and knees and roared obscenities at the dog, who skidded to a halt, then fled, yelping, for the shelter of the porch.

He scrambled from the pool, sloshing water, and scaled the back fence with care as bruised muscles protested. Clothes dangled from a washing line stretched from fence to back door in the yard and Jake whipped a thin hoodie from it as he counted all the ways he was in trouble.

If Eddie was right, there might be men with silver bullets after him - "Hunters" - and he had no EpiPen. He had no heroin to see him through the next two nights. He had nowhere to lock himself up. He had an insane relative on a mission to convert him to his insanity.

Trouble indeed. And there were only two people who could get him out of it.

CHAPTER TWENTY-THREE

Gwen came to a stop in the middle of the corridor and swore beneath her breath. He was here? After the incident at her house only yesterday?

Seriously!

She took a breath, stuck her pen in her mouth and carried her clipboard to the triage desk. She had hoped never to see him again. But there he was, beyond the ropes and stanchions, trying to blend into the crowd. A mountain of a man squished in between an obese woman with a specimen jar and a skinny old man in overalls nursing one arm in the other. His hood was pulled over his unruly shock of hair - as if that would disguise him.

Gwen busied herself with forms she wasn't reading while she considered calling security or the cops. Maybe she could keep away from the waiting area until he left.

She had hoped to put this personal idiocy behind her - she corrected herself: this *latest* personal idiocy behind her. She saw it now, the myriad ways her impulsiveness had gotten her into situations she regretted: at the death of her grandfather, she had decided to be a doctor; at Barry's confident advances, she had jumped into his arms and followed him to University of Michigan rather that her father's choice, Johns Hopkins; at a comment from a lecturer that only the strongest medicos need apply for ER work, she had decided her residency and a career track that had brought her to the end of her tether. And based on a single kind act and Jake's good looks, she had risked contracting hepatitis and God knew what else - she had trusted a man who couldn't possibly be worthy of it. Again.

Why was he here? The prescription?

Gwen scanned the pigeon holes behind the desk and found the script still where Pam had left it. She heaved a sigh that felt theatrical even for her. She didn't want to make a scene. She didn't want to hurt the guy by calling security. It was better to defuse this - or at least give him a chance before she involved the guards. Hell, maybe he'd come to apologize.

"Yeah, right." She snatched out the script, marched into the waiting area and stopped in front of Jake. "You. Follow me, now."

Gwen stomped out through the front doors without waiting. One of the security guys - Art - was lounging against a pillar near the ambulance bay. She caught his eye and indicated the door. Art returned her nod and stood straight. She stopped far enough away to have a private conversation but close enough for Art to intervene if necessary. A moment later, Jake emerged.

"Take that ridiculous hood off," she said. "What do you want?"

He refused to meet her gaze; for some reason this gave her satisfaction. "Epi," he mumbled and set his dreadlocks free.

She held out the script and when he took it, folded her arms and turned up her glare a notch. "There's your prescription. Pharmacy's that way. Away you go."

He mumbled something, head down, as he shoved the script into his pocket.

"What's that?" she snapped.

"Don't have enough money," he said louder. He patted the pocket. "For this."

"You don't...?" Her arms uncrossed and her hands found her hips. "The other night, I gave you two injectors *gratis*. That means free."

"Yeah, but—"

"Last night, you told me you were off to work where you'd be making money. So I really don't see the problem."

Art started their way. She waved him back.

Jake plunged his hands into his pockets. "I had some trouble."

"Trouble?" She softened her tone. "I get the feeling you're always having trouble."

He checked Art's position, said nothing.

"Keep the damn prescription. You stay right there. I'll go get one more injector and I'll give it to Art there to bring out to you." She made a wide berth around him then stopped. Without turning, she said, "You helped me. I helped you. We're even. Whether you leave Detroit or not, I never want to see you again. Never. Do you understand me?"

Jake started to say something.

"Stow it," she said, and jerked her head for Art to follow her inside.

Never.

"That him?"

Carter jolted awake, glued to the seat by his sweaty shirt, his mind clinging to the remnants of a meaningless dream. He moved a swollen tongue about his mouth, trying to prompt some moisture. The sun had moved a long way across the sky; he'd been out for a while. He felt nauseous and...

Beside him, Tim had said something.

"What?" he asked and sat up straighter.

"There," Tim said and pointed.

Seventy yards away and jogging closer was a well-proportioned runner. Square-shouldered. Narrow hips. Long legs. His mismatched sweat suit incongruous in the August heat, the runner had his hood up, bearing down fast on the mission.

"Whatcha think, dude? That your theryon?"

Vision fuzzy with sleep, Carter caught a glimpse of dreadlocks beneath the hood before the runner turned into the mission. Carter had only seen Jake Brennan once in the flesh, and he'd shaved and changed his clothes since he'd been filmed in the street brawl. But...

"The hair's the same," he said and reached for the door.

Tim stopped him. "Let's not spook him. And let's be sure too, huh?"

Carter's blood pressure rose a little. His diner breakfast churned in his gut. He was sure. The moment was here. The guy was here. The murdering *thing* who'd taken Beth, destroyed his life.

The people milling outside the mission had parted to let Brennan through, as if they sensed what he was. Or did they *know*? Was there some pact amongst them? Were some of them theryons too? And how would anyone know until they'd turned into monsters?

He dropped the glove box open and slid the Glock out, its handle warm against his palm.

Tim waved at him to put it away. "Not yet, man."

"It's him!"

"You wanna march in there and shoot the place up, gangster-style? Huh? Didn't seem so keen on that at the Family Day yesterday. Look, we don't do collateral damage. Not our M.O. Just chill. He has to come out sometime." Tim settled back in his chair, pushed his sunglasses higher. "We're in the home strait now."

The last thing Carter wanted to do now was wait. This search - this *hunt* - had cost him almost everything and now the end was in sight - right over there inside that building. He imagined it: a crowded soup kitchen, a man with dreadlocks bent low over a plastic picnic table and slurping from a bowl, Carter pulling the handgun out of his jeans and firing again and again and again, Brennan tossed onto his face with blood spurting from his back.

The fantasy turned belly-up then: a woman beside Brennan at the table falling sideways with a hole in her hip, another bullet passing straight through Brennan and into the child seated opposite him, arterial blood arcing from its neck...

Jaw grinding, Carter pressed the metal slide of the Glock against his cheek for a moment.

Patience is a virtue, he thought, then slid the gun back in the glove box. *Patience is a pain in the ass.*

The volunteers were putting the last dishes away and mopping the floors when Jake got to the mission. They gave him blank or surly looks as he slipped through the dining area.

"You missed lunch," called a teenage girl.

She had the yellowing remains of a black eye and he wondered how she got that, who would do that to a kid.

My cousin, he answered himself. *Guys like him.*

She added, "Nothing left."

She seemed cheerful enough so he offered her a smile. "I ate already."

"What'd you eat?"

"Burger and a shake." And a couple of drug dealers.

"I wish I had a burger and a shake," she said wistfully and vanished into the kitchen.

Angelo wasn't in his office, but Jake followed the sound of his voice into the backyard. He was packing second-hand clothes into a shopping bag for a woman who looked a lot like Sophie's mom. When he noticed Jake headed his way, his features clouded. He turned a shoulder and took his time completing the conversation: something about parking tickets and the car she was staying in.

"Great," Jake muttered to himself. Another person pissed at him. He seemed to be getting a lot of that lately.

When the woman finally thanked Angelo and left the yard, Angelo turned to Jake and simply raised his eyebrows.

"Look, some dudes jumped me. Tased me." Jake lifted the hoodie and shirt to show off the marks.

Angelo didn't seem impressed. "If they're Taser marks, they're old ones. Nothing happened to you last night, except—" he pointed to the inside of Jake's elbow, though it was covered by a sleeve "—except maybe you used. Maybe you got nervous." He rubbed his palms on his pants. "It happens. But like I told you, if you got a problem, you gotta deal with it. Me, I'm not putting in another good word for you until I know you're straight, until you've earned my trust." He took a few steps toward the main building, but Jake blocked his path.

"I need to stay somewhere, somewhere you can lock up."

Angelo took a step back, putting space between them. His pose looked relaxed, but Jake recognized a fighter's stance when he saw one. "Lock you up?"

"I'm ... This time of month, I'm bad to be around. I ... screw up."

"Time of the month. Huh. So either you have a bad dose of PMS or you're a werewolf." His tone softened. "Either way, my friend, you have to admit it sounds a little wrong."

"I just need somewhere overnight. Somewhere I can be locked in and not hurt anyone."

"Listen, Jake, you want to get into the psych ward for a few days, I'll get you in. You want to go to rehab, I'll call in some favors and fast-track it. But you don't need to be locked up for full moon. And where would I lock you up anyway?"

Over his shoulder, the door of the big clothing container swung lazily in the breeze, open and shut, open and shut, as if beckoning Jake. Yes, he thought, that could work.

While he was distracted, Angelo slipped by him. "Think it over, Jake. You want me to start the process, I'll be in my office. But I'm leaving at six o'clock sharp. Dinner with my in-laws. Can't be late to that."

Six o'clock sharp. All Jake had to do was hide himself in the container before it was locked for the night. But not so early he was discovered by people rummaging around in it. He wiped a thin sheen of sweat from his forehead. It was going to be hot in there - probably would stay that way all night. He just had to hope no one was around to hear the ruckus he was sure to make. As long as no one opened that container, everything would be fine.

Before he left, he poked his head into the kitchen and gave the teenage girl his safest smile. "Do you think I could get a bottle of water?"

"Sure," she said, fetching one from the fridge. "I'm Jenny. Who are you?"

"Jake. Thanks, Jenny. I owe you one."

"Damn right," she said and patted his hand.

He felt her eyes on him as he returned to the yard and scaled the back fence to drop into the factory lot behind. It was a simple matter to wait out the next few hours until people started closing things up for the night. His back to the fence, he took stock of his stuff: one EpiPen, a prescription, fifty bucks and the clothes he wore. Also his momma's brooch, a warm presence against his chest. He'd strip to his y-fronts when it came time to enter the container, roll his stuff up in a bundle and shove it where no one would find it.

And where it wouldn't get torn to shreds.

With the sinking sun sucking the dregs from Carter's patience, he grabbed the pistol. Ignoring Tim's remonstrations, he climbed out of the car, peeled his sweaty shirt from his back and shoved the pistol under it.

"All right, all right," said Tim as he heaved himself out. "We do this carefully, we do it right."

Carter marched toward the mission. "We do it now."

Tim struggled to keep in step. "Yeah, yeah, that's okay. Pretty sure the last staff member left an hour ago anyway. So if he's there, he's probably on his own. But just in case..." He put an arm across Carter's chest to slow him. "We're not shooting him in front of civilians."

Carter stopped and glared. "Tim. You want back into the Org. And I want this over with." He wanted his son too, but he could never face Elijah again if he didn't go through with this. And as much as he hated Beth's parents for going behind his back, the boy would be safe with them. He said, "If I go to jail, I go to jail."

"I don't wanna go to jail."

"If your friends are as powerful as they say, they can probably get us out."

Tim pursed his lips. "They'd be pretty grateful for the scalp." He stared toward the mission, then squared his shoulders and adjusted the pistol in the waistband of his trousers. "Let's do this."

The adrenaline rush pumping through Carter's blood began fading about five minutes later. There was no sign of anyone about the mission property, least of all Brennan. They peered in windows, searched behind the shipping container and shower block, checked over the fence.

"Nothing," Tim said. "He musta ducked over the fence. Probably went to ground for the night."

Carter swore, scooped a concrete chip from the driveway and flung it at the back fence.

Tim clapped a hand to his shoulder, but Carter pulled away from him. The Hunter said, "All hope is not lost, my friend. We know he's been here. He'll be here again. Next time, we'll try a different approach."

"Different how?"

Tim winked and produced a tiny bag from his pocket, leather, the kind jewelry was kept in. The drawstring was pulled tight. "Got this little bag of ground-up silver here. Silver dust. One of the tricks of my trade. He comes back here, I get close enough to tip it down his neck or lace his drink with it - bam! No more werewolf."

Carter sucked in a deep breath, trying to relax. He leaned against the shipping container, still warm from a day in the sun, and cursed until he was calmer. He had to trust Tim's process, believe that eventually this would pay off.

He threw another concrete chip, this time at the container. They were so close.

So damn close.

CHAPTER TWENTY-FOUR

The first thing Jake was aware of in the morning was that he had one hell of a headache.

The second was the stink of old steel and fresh dog-piss.

He unfurled himself from the nest of torn fabric in the corner of the container and stretched his stiff, sore muscles. There was a dull burning in his chest. He felt like he'd been tased all over again. Just one of the things he didn't miss when he was able to avoid a Change. With heroin, he never experienced anything worse than a dry mouth and maybe a sore back if he'd slept in a funny position. This was like being squeezed into an unnatural shape by giant unseen hands.

But I made it. I made it. The sun wasn't long up, but light already sliced inside through a dozen rust wounds and rivet holes in the walls. He was cold, all the heat from yesterday having fled through the steel walls in the early hours.

The inside of the container looked like someone had taken to it with a wood chipper.

Worst of all, in his wolf-state he'd taken a dump in front of the big doors and urinated just about everywhere else. He'd be putting up with this stench for a couple more hours probably. Naked, he tied a couple of rags around his nose and mouth and began rummaging for something to wear. He soon found his water bottle, still one third full. He sipped at plastic-flavored water. After another ten minutes, the only clothing he'd found was a couple pairs of packaged underwear way too small for him, several packs of socks, a beanie, a bra, and a purple dress. His sneakers were amongst the strips of urine-soaked fabric in one corner and there were no other shoes anywhere to be found.

"Sonofa*bitch*."

He put his head in his hands. If he didn't want to hit the yard naked, his choices were few. He could wear the underpants and give himself the kind of pain no man wanted to feel. He could put a sock over his weenie.

Or he could wear that huge purple dress.

He kept rummaging.

After what must have been close to a half hour - long after it was obvious there was nothing else for him to wear - he kicked his drink bottle from one side of the container to the other and picked up the dress. It would only be until he grabbed his bundle of clothing. No sweat.

Time fused into one long moment, punctuated by breathing and the pulse of his headache while he squatted in one of the clean patches, waiting for someone to open up. It might have been an hour, it might have been three, but eventually he heard voices outside, none of them Angelo's. He was gonna look a real sight: a big man in a purple dress with a cotton-gasmask wrapped around his face.

It could have been worse.

It took them longer than expected to open up. Just when he was losing patience there came the rattling of keys at the doors. He steeled himself for the fright he was going to give whoever opened them.

One door creaked open, flooding the container with harsh light. A woman gasped. Blinking his eyes into focus, he saw she had backed away, one hand over her own mouth and nose.

"Holy shit," she kept saying.

She hadn't seen him. Could he really be that lucky?

"Raelene!" she called as she headed for the main building.

Jake bounded out of the container with one hand bunching the dress over his groin. He retrieved his knotted bundle from where he'd hidden it - covered in ants but otherwise intact. He had to find somewhere to get changed and reassess his next moves. He didn't fancy climbing the wooden fence to the factory in bare feet and a dress, so he pounded down the driveway while goggle-eyed faces pressed up against the kitchen window. If he'd wanted to get away without being noticed, he'd gone exactly the wrong way about it. A flicker at the window's far end: the young girl Jenny waving at him. He barely had time to raise a hand before he was past the building and out on the pavement.

He paused. Where to? *Idiot.* He'd had hours to think about his next steps but last evening he'd been focused on getting through the night and this morning all he could think about was—

Two pale faces were visible behind the windshield of a black and white Chevelle nestled against the curb a hundred yards to his left. Twenty yards beyond it, a white van. Eddie.

Jake turned right and sprinted as hard as his bare feet would let him while a motor started up behind him.

When the man in a dress came to a halt out front of the mission, Tim hunched over the wheel, eyeballs bulging. "Oh. My. God."

Carter lifted his sunglasses to get a better look. "Can't be." There was no mistaking the dreadlocks, but this was hardly the way he'd expected Brennan to appear.

Tim turned the key and Carter winced at the amount of time it took the motor to start; Brennan was headed away from them fast.

"That's our transvestite theryon all right!" Tim laughed. He dropped the clutch and left rubber on the road as he gave pursuit. He whooped, one arm frantically working the window winder. He swapped hands on the wheel, shifted into second and gestured. "Gimme your pistol!"

They were closing fast, but Carter stared at him. "In broad daylight?"

Tim's gaze flicked to a man sipping from a paper bag by a fence ahead. "Good point. I'll run him down, then."

Before Carter could respond, they were mounting the sidewalk and Brennan was a purple target in the center of the hood.

Jake darted into a vacant lot as the roar of the car came up behind him. The vehicle missed him by inches. The wind of its passage nearly buffeted him from his feet. He careened off a corrugated iron fence, regained his balance and pelted across debris and gravel toward the rear fence. Pain lanced through his bare feet. Gaps in the fence were large enough that he didn't break stride to leap through into the high grass of someone's backyard. He knew the area - had checked it out the first day he'd come to Angelo's. Across the next street was a patch of wasteland and beyond that a disused railway track: lots of scrub there, ditches, culverts, places to hide. The sedan - it hadn't been Eddie's van as he'd expected - was growing fainter but that didn't mean he was safe. They'd be circling the block, and they would be in the street within seconds.

Three teenage boys lounged on the back porch, passing a joint. "Hey!" one yelled at him as he passed. He hurdled the low brick fence onto the sidewalk. The motor noise leveled out then grew louder as he crossed the street. The Chevy appeared at the crossroads to his left, slewing around to face him with another screech of tires on asphalt. He plunged into the wasteland and tried to dodge bricks and other detritus hidden like landmines beneath the sedge grass and thistles. Up ahead the silvery line of the railway's chain-link fence announced refuge. Thirty yards.

The Chevy growled in protest as the driver mounted yet another curb. Gears crunched. Jake glanced over his shoulder. The car bounced and drifted, struggling to find traction on the fallow ground. Who the hell were they? More of Zee's crew?

And what had happened to Eddie? That was definitely his van back there.

His foot turned on a piece of wood and he stumbled. Almost fell. Numbness spread around his ankle, but there was no pain. Not yet. The Animal complained within him, surging. On four legs, a wolf could cover this ground twice as fast and more sure-footed. Would Eddie have been able to Change?

He tucked the bundle of clothes under one arm like a wide receiver and pushed on as hard as he could. Soil and stone crunched as the car slid to a halt twenty or thirty yards back. They couldn't crash through a fence, not if they had any brains; they weren't going to catch him.

He leapt and landed high enough up the fence to avoid using his toes, grabbed the top and swung a leg over. The cold metal bar at the top of the fence pressed painfully against his inner thigh and he narrowly avoided tearing his ballsack on a wire-end. The dress snagged. He tugged at it, bent double, and something pinged off the bar below his gut. The next moment he was on his back, flattening a patch of thistle, with what felt like a heavy weight on his hip. He touched it; his fingers came away bloody.

Hit me!

He had to get up. Now, while the car's transmission complained as someone hurriedly put it in gear. Now, while their aim was off.

Get up.

Pain pinned him to the ground, a white-hot wire above his right hip.

Get up*!*

He turned over. Somehow. Got on hands and knees before the pain in his gut sucked him back onto the earth. He sobbed and cursed himself for a sissy.

The car crawled closer and someone fired. He heard the shot this time. The bullet whined past to his left. Down amongst the weeds like this, they maybe couldn't see him. He pressed his right hand over the bullet wound, hot blood slicking it like treacle, while he looked for his clothes. He scrabbled towards his bundle.

A squeal of brakes and a car door groaned open. Another shot and someone snarled, "Don't waste them!" A voice he didn't know. Not a pusher. Not a gangbanger.

Hunters. Had to be.

He felt it then, just as his hand closed on the parcel of clothing. A creeping, prickling malignancy, spreading deep inside from the epicenter of the bullet wound, bubble wrap inside him inflating and popping, sending poison through his system.

"Where is he?" the Hunter whispered.

"Shut up!" another replied.

He moved his right hand from his abdomen to his back. No exit wound. The slug was still inside.

That meant no time. He needed the injector. Running would be useless unless he did. Unraveling his clothes, he dug his fingers between the knots, jaws clenched against the pain.

"Climb the fence, I'll cover ya," one of the Hunters said.

The fence chinked with someone's weight.

Jake had one chance. Get the epinephrine in and hope to hit his attacker hard before the bastard could aim. His fingers nudged the injector, pushing it deeper into the bundle. He got a firmer grip on the knot and tore it as hard as he could. He grabbed the injector as a thump announced the arrival of a Hunter on his side of the fence. He jabbed the EpiPen hard against his thigh, started counting, got his other hand and leg ready to propel him at whoever was coming.

Thuds and a revving engine provoked shouts.

A gunshot. A scream.

The crunch and scrape of braking tires on earth, the whine and crash of metal on metal.

The man near Jake fired. Fired again. The whine of a vehicle reversing provoked a string of frightened curses from the gunman, who fired again.

Jake raised his head. A white van was weaving backwards across the vacant lot, fast disappearing from his view. The Hunter close to him - so damned close to him - had his back turned and was steadying his pistol in two hands to get better aim at the van. He fired and fired again until the hammer came down on an empty chamber. Jake lurched to his feet and took off in the opposite direction. With one hand pressed on his hip, he stumbled toward the railway line.

He made it to the embankment without tripping, but snagged a foot on something at the top and rolled down. At the base, he found his feet again, swearing at himself to keep moving. He only had one thing to do: get away, get safe. A hundred yards down the tracks, he risked a look back. No one was coming. That was good, real good.

His initial reconnaissance of this whole area when he'd moved here had revealed some kind of science lab at the end of the tracks. If he could get to that, he could ask someone to call him an ambulance.

Even with the medicine loosening the clamping sensation from about his throat and dulling the painful swelling inside him, the perspiration creeping over him was not the warm sweat of exertion, but the cold sweat of impending death. The medicine had given him a short reprieve, nothing more. There was only so much an EpiPen could do when there was silver inside of him.

CHAPTER TWENTY-FIVE

What am I doing? Carter wondered, even as he squeezed the trigger over and over.

The van reversed away, its windshield starred in the top right hand corner and another bullet hole making a false nose above the bumper. And Carter was standing there firing an empty gun at it, the hammer clicking over and over while his forearm started to cramp. The van pulled a j-turn and took off down the street.

What am I doing?

It didn't matter who that had been. It didn't matter that Tim lay sprawled and broken and bleeding in the dirt. It didn't matter that Carter had only escaped because of the fence between them. And it didn't matter whether he'd hit the driver or not.

What mattered was that Carter was on the same side of the fence as an injured werewolf, something that didn't need a car to kill him. And Carter's magazine was empty.

He fumbled for the spare clip in his pocket. But Brennan was running, one hand clamped over his gut, that absurd purple dress torn and flapping in his wake, white buttocks flashing like a deer's behind. Carter tried to find the button that ejected the spent mag, dropped the spare, had to bend and feel around the grass to find it again. By the time he'd reloaded, Brennan was too far away to shoot at. Carter caught a final flash of white butt before Brennan vanished down an embankment.

He should give chase.

There were no sirens, but even the thinly stretched Detroit P.D. couldn't be too far off.

Damnit.

What was he going to do?

Brennan was out of sight, But he would be dead soon - he *would* be. Carter had hit him, judging by the way he was moving. And … yes! There was blood on the ground. He'd done his job. He'd avenged his wife.

"Eat silver, Brennan," he murmured.

He put the gun away and climbed the fence. Tim was a crumpled mess. Fighting back vomit, Carter felt for a pulse. Nothing. And he wasn't surprised. He turned away, wiped his bloody fingers in the grass.

The Chevelle's motor was still running. Carter got back inside and drove it away to find somewhere he could torch it. He tried not to think about Tim's body. He tried not to think about what he was going to do with his life now that his crusade was finally at an end. He made a list in his head of all the things he had to do to cover his tracks and get back home. And as he did, he wondered who the hell had been protecting Brennan? Who killed Tim? A friend? A lover? Maybe. If there were people who hunted them, then maybe there were people who loved them too.

Stranger things in heaven and earth, he told Tim's ghost and hoped his friend was in a better place.

Gwen met the paramedics at the ambulance doors, Gabby beside her.

"Male gunshot wound plus anaphylactic shock," the paramedic pushing the trolley said. His female partner headed off for the main desk to log it.

"Geez, this guy got a raw deal," Gabby said.

As Gwen went for the anaphylaxis tray, she had the impression of a tall man lying naked beneath the blue medical blanket. Hurrying back to the trolley, her breath caught when she noticed the long dreadlocks.

No way.

She shouldered Gabby aside, causing her to swear and scoot to the opposite side to continue checking vitals. Lifting the oxygen mask long enough to confirm Jake's identity, Gwen murmured a swearword of her own. His eye lids were puffy, but they eased open a little, the irises clearly visible as the pupils tried to focus on her. She leaned over him while the paramedic shoved the trolley ahead.

"Hey," she said. "You'll be okay."

Jake's eyes closed again.

"What's the story?" she asked as they raced along the corridor.

"He's had epinephrine and Benadryl. He self-administered one EpiPen and we gave another dose on-route—" the paramedic checked his watch. "—seven minutes ago. Bleeding's controlled. No sign of internal bleeding. Bullet may be lodged in the abdominal muscles."

Gwen was already teasing the dressing up to examine this for herself. The wound above Jake's hip was small, either a .22 bullet or a fragment of a larger caliber. A little blood welled up and she pressed the dressing back down and held her hand to it. His skin was blue in places, his breath a little labored. One of his hands clamped on her wrist, then fell back almost immediately. She let his sheet drop and fell back behind the others.

A gunshot wound and allergic shock. *What the hell have you been doing now, Jake?*

"BP is 88/55," said Gabby.

Shit.

"Start him on saline. What triggered the anaphylaxis?" she asked the paramedic.

The man shrugged. "Wouldn't say. He stumbled into a company's reception area. Wearing a dress."

An orderly had arrived, ready to take over the trolley. He and Gabby looked askance at that last piece of information. The paramedic winked at Gabby. "Weirder things than that happen around here, babe, right?"

"Call me babe again, you'll be digging my shoe out of your ass," she replied, but she was smiling.

Gwen pushed it from her mind. She had a job to do. This was a patient on the dolly.

Yeah. A patient. Not a friend.

"Okay. Doesn't appear to have lost much blood," she confirmed. "Let's get him stabilized before theater. Maybe the bullet passed through something he's allergic to before hitting him."

As the orderly took the cart and steered it into Curtain 6, Gwen handed Gabby the EpiPen from the tray. "Give him another shot plus fifty milligrams of Benadryl."

As the nurse took over, Gwen leaned close to the paramedic and whispered, "A *dress?*"

He chuckled and started away. "Weird, huh?"

Weird wasn't the half of it. Jake Brennan and weird went together like Thanksgiving and turkey.

CHAPTER TWENTY-SIX

Gwen's first break came late in her double-shift, around two in the morning. She chose to spend it completing paperwork at the nurse's station, scarfing bad coffee and even badder donuts, her eyes blurring with fatigue, a nasty headache squeezing her temples. And yet, completing paperwork she could only half-read and eating crappy food was way better than sneaking up to Jake's ward room to check on him. She had questions - boy, did she have questions - but they could damn-well go unanswered. He'd done the Good Samaritan thing, she had repaid him with money and clothes, and that was that. Story over. While in the hospital, Jake Brennan was a patient who'd passed through her care and into the hands of other specialists in the system. In particular, an allergy specialist who could run some skin tests.

But why had he been wearing a dress, for God's sake? Had he had a dissociative episode? Did he now identify as transgender?

She growled at herself and changed the subject. She had enough crap of her own to deal with without diving back into the cesspool that was Jake Brennan.

She was holding a shoulder x-ray up to the light and forcing her tired eyes to focus when Pam appeared.

"Mr Brennan got out of surgery a full eight hours ago, you know."

Gwen leaned toward the x-ray and made a noise of assent.

"Right, like you're not interested." Pam put her hand over Gwen's. "Well, this should interest you. The bullet fragment they pulled from him was silver."

The x-ray film crackled as Gwen's fist spasmed. "Silver?"

"Made of silver. Just when you think you seen it all." She took the x-ray from Gwen and straightened it on the bench, while Gwen gaped at her.

After this, Gwen continued the next two hours of her shift on autopilot, unable to get Jake's case out of her mind. She was a half hour off leaving when Gabby hustled into the nurses' station. "Dr Cheevey, I thought you should know. Your ... friend ... with the bullet wound?"

"What about him?" Gwen's tone sounded abrupt even to her own ears, but the way the nurse said *friend* made it sound like Jake was her crack dealer.

"He took off," Gabby said, turning on her heel and heading back to her patients.

Gwen darted after her. "Wait!" Gabby turned, eyebrows raised in mock patience. Gwen took a breath. "Sorry. It's been a long shift. Little grumpy. You said Jake Brennan took off?"

Gabby rubbed her nose, glanced at her watch. Gwen pressed her lips together and waited her out. "Can't find him anywhere. Just vanished."

"How long ago?"

"Last time they checked his vitals was twenty minutes ago."

Gwen put a hand to her sternum. Walking out of hospital straight after surgery like that was dangerous. "No one saw him leave?"

Gabby shook her head. "Security's still searching, but not hard. Another patient's clothes disappeared from his bathroom, so they figure Brennan got dressed and—" she waggled two fingers in a walking motion "—skedaddled."

Gwen returned to the nurses' station to bury herself in work. The poor guy was nuts. But he didn't deserve to open up his wound and catch an infection.

Hopefully the cops would look for him. Or he'd collapsed somewhere in the hospital's vicinity and would be found soon and brought back to his ward. He didn't need her help. And there wasn't anything she could do for him anymore.

There wasn't.

She'd sat in the lounge for the better part of an hour after her shift had ended. When she noticed the new cup of coffee in her hands, it was stone cold; she couldn't remember making it.

A silver bullet. A silver frigging bullet.

He'd had an allergic reaction to it. He'd nearly died. He'd been telling the truth about that.

But ... a silver bullet? Someone else agreed with Jake's werewolf delusion - perhaps based on his bizarre allergy - and they had shot him. *Really?*

"The world is full of stupid people," she said to herself, quoting her favorite song. And it was full of weird ones too. There were kids who filed their teeth, drank blood and slept in coffins. There were would-be superheroes like the thirteen year-old last year who'd tried to stop a bus and stopped living. There was that New York drug-user who splattered herself over the sidewalk when she tried to fly from her apartment.

There were people who thought they were werewolves.

And now it seemed there were people who believed *them* and set out to hunt them. These same headcases were after Jake. They'd fed his psychosis, entrenched his delusion.

But a silver allergy? A life-threatening silver allergy? Unheard of. More than bizarre. It made no sense whatsoever. And it was in a real sense making his life hell.

That poor guy.

Jake was a good man; she'd been a beneficiary of his selflessness, and the girl Sophie had too. Jake was good man and she had lost her way as a doctor. She had seen his goodness, she had seen him as a human being she could help, and then lost sight of all of it because of her prejudice and her self-disgust. It wasn't his fault that he'd somehow come to believe he was a monster. Hunted by psychopaths and with a gut wound, he needed help.

Do no harm, Doctor Cheevey.

But what *good* could she do? Where would he be?

The lounge door banged open, Pam bursting in with an "Oh, there you are!"

Gwen tapped her disposable cup with a ragged fingernail. "Shift's over. Needed caffeine."

Pam paused halfway across the room. "You heard then?"

"Heard?" Gwen straightened. "They found him?"

"Found who? Oh, the Jake Brennan matter. I don't think they did, but I'm not talking about that."

"About what, then?"

"Weng *thought* you were still around. He's been looking for you all over."

She checked the clock. "At five-thirty?"

"In early, and said you were his first ... *task* of the day. The asshole."

Weng? Her transfer! She began to rise, intending to head straight to the administrator's office. Then Pam's body language came into focus; the concern in her eyes made sense. Gwen sank into the chair, deflated.

"I didn't get it?"

Pam shook her head ruefully. "Sorry, baby."

How could they not give it to her? She had some great experience and she was the only internal applicant, someone who knew the hospital.

Barry! He was golfing buddies with Weng. But was he really that poisonous, that malicious? Hell, why was she even asking that question?

"I'm stuck in the ER." She would spend the rest of her career propping up the corpse of this city, *Weekend-at-Bernies*-style: *Detroit is a zombie. Downtown is the brain that doesn't realize it's dead while the rest of us just drag ourselves around.*

"It's not as bad as that, baby doll." Pam came over and put an arm about her shoulders. "There'll be another chance. And we do need you down there. You do good work."

"Good work," she repeated. She saw a dead child, the latest in a long line. She saw an injured man calling for his trolley - *my stuff!* - a man who would no doubt end up in another knife fight one of these day. She thought of a wounded mentally ill homeless man in real danger out there. She felt hollow.

"I hate this job," she whispered.

Pam gave her another squeeze and headed for the fridge, fished out a can of cola. "Maybe you take another sick day, huh? After what you've been through… And now this… No one will blame you. Maybe take two days. Or three. I'll get a replacement somewhere. Come back when you're ready." One final smile and Pam was gone.

Ready? she thought as the door clacked shut. Gwen realized then that she'd already made her decision. She'd made it the very day she'd met Jake Brennan.

She had become a doctor to make a difference, a phrase that had never been concrete and clear in its meaning, until now. She couldn't make a difference to the thousands of people who streamed into Emergency every year, but she could make a difference to Jake. And she was going to.

Then she'd find another job.

She sneaked into an office were no one would bother her, logged on and accessed patient files. Jake Brennan had no address. Of course he didn't - duh. But Sophie Wallace did. Jake had been friendly with the family. Maybe they'd know him. The Wallaces lived in a trailer park over in Near East Side. Gwen wrote down the address and on a whim, looked up internet news to see if there was mention of what had happened to Jake. She found a story about shots fired and cars chasing a man along the footpath near the Listening Ear Mission. One of the cars had run down the driver of the other when he'd gotten out of his car - whether this was an accident wasn't clear. Crazy happ'nins near a mission, including shots fired? That had to be the incident involving Jake. The street name was there in the article. It was on the way to the Wallaces' home. She'd try there first.

Again the choice to pay a taxi to chauffeur her all over town, or Barry's car. She needed her own freedom for the afternoon. Barry was at work already; she'd seen him right after Gabby told her about Jake's disappearance, had ducked down a hallway to avoid him. After grabbing a paramedic medbag, she took the Lexus keys from his locker.

When she found the car, she made sure she only slightly scratched the paint around the lock as she opened the door.

CHAPTER TWENTY-SEVEN

A drive-through coffee-and-muffin later, Gwen pulled in to the street near The Listening Ear Mission.

Quaint name!

The mission took up an average suburban lot in a street typical of this part of Detroit, where vacant lots sat interspersed among old properties like missing teeth. Gwen took a good gander as she cruised past to park next door. The mission consisted of a converted house with a ramp out front and in the yard behind a shipping container and commercial fridge or freezer. She caught a glimpse of another cinder-block building to the side. A minivan and a motorbike were parked out front.

She got out of Barry's car, and was suddenly the focus of attention of a group of disheveled men, smoking what looked like joints in a semicircle around the mission's mailbox. She wondered if she should leave, but there was nothing menacing in their body language. Instead they seemed vacant - like the house she'd parked in front of. She was simply new, odd in their territory. And surely bad people weren't out this early in the morning, she joked to herself.

The men coughed in unison as she passed them, phlegm rattling in their throats and chests, but otherwise made no noise. The air smelled sweetly of cannabis.

There was a sign above the corner of the building pointing along the driveway, stating "Toilet Block" in thick red spray paint. It was a neat job. It was a cheap job. A smaller, manufactured sign told her the "Office" was through the main entry.

She entered up the wooden ramp, nearly stumbled where a board sagged. Why the hell didn't they keep the thing maintained?

Immediately inside the door, a large room had been converted into a dining room crowded with tables. Double plastic doors opened into the kitchen beyond it where there was much banging and chatter. The tables were set with cereal spoons; the air curdled with the odors of burning toast, urine, mildew and smoker's breath. An obese woman with varicose veins like vines along her legs sat in a corner, sighing with every second breath, eyes on nothing. A couple of school-age kids sat at a table at the back, crayons poised above coloring books. They regarded Gwen as if she were a dangerous predator entering their clearing.

She smiled and gave them a little wave. "Hi."

The woman heaved a particularly loud sigh. No response from the kids.

Why weren't they in school anyway? *Oh, it's Saturday,* she realized. With her lifestyle, all the days blended into one. And whose kids were they? The sighing woman looked too old.

A head poked around the kitchen doorway. A teenage girl. "Hello."

"Hi," Gwen repeated.

The young woman marched into the room, skirting tables with the grace and style of a ballroom dancer. She offered her hand after wiping it on her skirt. "I'm Jenny. Who are you?"

"Gwen." She shook Jenny's hand. "Can you point me at someone in charge? A manager?"

Jenny studied Gwen's scrubs with a hand on her chin. "You a nurse?"

"Doctor, actually."

"Cool. Fix him up good, we need him."

"Sorry?"

Jenny moved her hand to cup her mouth and hollered, "Angeloooooo!"

Gwen flinched, then forced the smile back onto her face.

Jenny turned and danced toward the kitchen, still yelling, "Your doctor's here!" She patted both kids on the shoulders as she passed and they returned to their coloring as if she'd found their on-switch. The woman in the corner wheezed an imprecation that the children didn't even blink at. Another female voice in the kitchen asked Jenny what was going on and Jenny replied loudly, "Angelo's doctor's here to fix him up."

A sliding door off to one side jerked open and she stared into the eyes of a man even bigger than Jake, though there was the hint of a paunch around his waist. She stopped her hand moving to her own spare tire with an inner curse.

"Yes?" he said. His tone was not unfriendly, but he gave her the once-over of a man ready to protect his property.

She swallowed. "I'm here about Jake Brennan."

He stared unblinking for a full five seconds - she counted, refusing to make the next move - then he jerked his head sideways. "Follow me."

His office was so crowded there was little space to sit. Decorations were sparse but for a number of photographs of the manager as a younger man: standing in front of karate studios shaking hands with men in suits; wearing a white *gi* and punching through wood; instructing a class of children.

"Thanks for your time," she offered and lowered herself carefully onto a camp chair.

"Time, I have. Jake Brennan, I don't. What's your interest in him?"

"I've treated him a couple of times," she said. "Also treated a girl he brought in with an anaphylactic reaction."

Angelo thawed a little. His chair groaned as he leaned back and put his hands behind his head. The man must have been pushing fifty, but the bunching of his biceps and triceps were thick as softballs. "I heard about that."

"*I* heard he was in trouble down this way yesterday. We treated him for a gunshot wound shortly after."

Angelo winced and swore quietly. "You understand in my line of work—" he squinted at her name badge "—Doctor, that I see all kinds of strangeness. I mean, I'm inured to it like you're inured to the sight of blood. But Jake Brennan..." He blew out his cheeks and shook his head.

He leaned forward so suddenly it seemed his chair would pitch him on the desk, but he caught himself with one hand expertly. "He was here two nights ago after ditching a day's work, begging to be locked up for the night. Locked up. I sent him away, thinking he was paranoid or something. The next day he gets chased by a couple of carloads of crazies - drug dealers, probably - who shoot at him by the disused rail spur behind here. That's where the bullet would've come from. Cops have been by twice since then, but didn't bother telling me he was in hospital. I would have visited." The lower half of his face disappeared behind one hand, lines creasing his brow. "I should have realized there'd be people after him. I should have found him a place to stay."

Gwen recognized professional guilt when she saw it. "Working with needy people, *woulda shoulda coulda* becomes a bit of a mantra. A frickin' unhelpful one."

He made eye contact, thawed. "Angelo Genero."

"Gwen Cheevey." They shook hands. "I thought he was in less trouble than he indicated, too. I need to find him and fix that."

"Isn't he in the hospital now? I thought you said..."

"Left this morning before dawn. Stole some clothes."

"With a bullet wound?"

"Bullet lodged in muscle wall of his abdomen. He'd lost some blood but he was basically okay. The more dangerous thing is his anaphylactic reaction and I'm worried it might happen again."

"He didn't come here. Not today."

"Can you help me find him? Where does he live?"

"The homeless don't *live* anywhere. They *stay*. For as long as it works for them, or as long as it's safe." Angelo moved some papers around his desk with one hand. "Sometimes long after it becomes unsafe. Parks, bridges, cars, railway sidings, storage sheds. Around Detroit, we have so many abandoned buildings. In some ways this downturn has been a boon for the homeless. That's where Jake would be, in one of them. But which one? Hundreds to choose from."

She indicated at the photo of him instructing the class of children. "You taught karate?"

He followed her gaze, looked wistful for a moment. "Owned three dojos."

"Do you still teach? Or compete?"

"I train myself to stay fit along with a small group of clients for self-defense. But I don't have much time for it these days. Had to sell two of the dojos. My wife and son manage the other one."

"What brought you here?" The question sounded awkward as she asked it. She wondered if he had founded the mission or managed it for someone else? Did he even get paid?

"Without meaning to be rude, you don't have time to listen to it and I'm sick of telling it. Unless I'm asking businesses for money." He flashed a smile and the hand shuffling papers joined the other behind his head as he leaned back again. "Plus I'm going to be serving breakfast to about sixty people in half an hour. So. How do we find Jake? That's the question, huh?"

"I have an idea."

"You do?" Angelo appeared skeptical.

"The girl with the nut allergy. Sophie Wallace. He seemed friendly with her mom."

Angelo's nod was slow and he leaned forward to boot up an aging PC with a monitor almost as deep as the desk. "Sounds possible. I might have her address here."

Gwen pulled the slip of paper from a pocket. "It's okay, I have it." She pursed her lips then, curious. "They're - they use the mission, too?"

He moved the keyboard aside and leaned on an elbow. "Not all marginalized people are homeless. Sophie's mom has a job. She works part time, cleaning. That address in your pocket a trailer park? Thought so. I remember her telling me all of her money goes in rent, and I believe it. She maybe moonlights as a working girl, but most of that is probably just to support a drug or alcohol habit. So they come here for the other essentials, like many other working poor. The girls don't go to school as far as I know, and that's another thing that pisses me off. But you don't need a sermon."

Gwen was impressed that Angelo had such knowledge when he probably saw dozens of people a month in here. "How many clients do you have?"

"Thank you for calling them that," he said. "Most middle class call them *bums* or *winos* or such. I don't know how many, Doctor Gwen.

Depends how you score it. If I counted through my files, my team and I - which is me and a few part-time volunteers - probably saw five or six hundred different people this year alone. Not all of them come in regularly. Some do. Some come once and move on."

He tapped one finger on his cheek. "We could always use the services of a good doctor round here. Say two or three hours a week. I can throw in a free breakfast." He laughed good-naturedly at what must have been consternation on her face. "If you know of anyone looking for pro bono work, that is."

She swallowed and tried to look less embarrassed. "I'll ask around."

It was a lie. He knew it, too, gaze slipping away to the monitor as he tapped in a password. She caught a flash of Windows 98 logo as she stood. Was everything around here so outdated?

"Well, thanks for your time. I'll go visit the trailer park, see if I can find them."

Angelo stood too and held out a hand. She took it. His skin was much colder than she expected.

"Are you okay?"

Angelo flinched, dropped his hand. "Pardon?"

"The girl in the kitchen. Jenny. She thought I was coming to check on your health."

"Oh. Jenny is sweet. But she makes assumptions. No, I'm fit as an ox, Doctor Gwen, fit as an ox."

And just as big.

"It was nice meeting you." She stepped into the hallway. Boards creaked beneath the threadbare carpet.

He'd followed her to his door. "Go see Jenny again and ask for a food parcel for Sophie's family. She'll remember them. Jenny's great with kids. It's a shame I can't give you some clothes for Jake so you can return the ones he stole."

"You have nothing in his size, I guess. He's a big guy."

"We don't have any clothes. I didn't tell you the weirdest thing that happened yesterday morning, shortly before Jake got chased."

"The weirdest...?" She had a moment of *déjà vu*, like she was back talking with Gabby.

"Some kind of animal spent the night in our clothing container out back - tore everything to shreds. Crapped and peed everywhere. Helluva mess. And weirder still, just after we found that mess, Jake Brennan was spotted running up the street here—"

"Let me guess. In a purple dress."

Angelo scratched the back of his head and returned to his desk. "Jake Brennan and weird stuff, huh? You watch yourself, Doc."

CHAPTER TWENTY-EIGHT

The wool pants were uncomfortable. Jake's crotch and thighs itched almost as bad as the gut wound beneath his bandages. That's what he got for stealing some old man's trousers without grabbing undies. But wearing someone else's pants was one thing; wearing someone else's shorts was something else entirely.

He shifted position on Gail's kitchen chair, reached down and adjusted the crotch. The brown slacks were wide on him, cinched tight with a frayed leather belt, but the legs finished above his ankles. The man's short-sleeve shirt was large, easily buttoning across his chest with room to spare. Hell, the clothes might be uncomfortable and looked awful on him, but at least they weren't a purple dress.

More importantly, he was free. Alive, free, safe. He'd been shocked to wake up in the hospital. Realizing the time, he'd lain there wondering how he'd avoided Changing on this last night of the Big Moon, before the bandages and sutures made him realize the anesthetic had done it.

He'd been given another chance.

Gail put another cup of weak coffee on the table in front of him and he thanked her, pushed his soup bowl away.

"You want more, darlin?" She indicated the pot on the trailer's small stove.

Her cupboards contained so little food - and the girls Melly and Sophie were so skinny - Jake felt guilty just eating the one bowl of the tinned broth. He shook his head, smiled his thanks. There was a yawning gulf inside him: he hadn't eaten since the food Eddie had bought him. But he'd been hungry before and he would be again. Hunger didn't kill a man, not quickly. Safety was more important than food. He touched the bandages over his gut gingerly. He was already healing fast. And his ankle didn't hurt at all where he'd twisted it.

Fast healing. Courtesy of a family curse. The words sounded like a cinema advertisement in his head.

The family curse, he thought with a grimace.

He'd had some close calls these past few days. Way too close. He should've fled Detroit the moment that skateboarder recognized him. As soon as he healed up, he could hitchhike out, start over somewhere else. He had twenty-something days until next Moon. Helping Gwen had been a mistake - the kind of thing that might be enough to outdo his evil deeds and get him into Heaven, he hoped, but the kind of thing that had got him noticed.

Gail was scraping the leftover soup into a bowl, putting it in the small fridge. She'd been surprised but happy to see him. Even now she kept throwing him coy glances, smiling when he returned them. He was keeping his own smiles polite, but distant. He really didn't want anything to do with them, not long term. But he still needed something from her, more than just a hiding place. The Animal rumbled something about just taking it. He scolded both It and himself. He needed the EpiPen. Sophie had *two* injectors plus a prescription for more. But he couldn't give in to the wolf.

Halfway through his second cup, while the two girls were distracted watching *Sesame Street* in the bedroom, Jake broached the subject.

"Gail, you been good to me..."

"It's only right. You helped my girl. Saved her life." Gail sat across from him. Her hand crept towards his as if she meant to pet him. He pulled his away.

"See, I used my only injector on her. I... I nearly died yesterday coz I didn't have one." She made a sympathetic noise, but her eyes narrowed. Yeah, she knew what was coming. "I'm wondering if I could have one of yours. You got a spare and that doctor - Gwen - she'd give you another prescription. Angelo'll help you find money for more. Only..."

Gail shot to her feet and fussed with dishes. "My baby girl needs that pen. Why can't you get one yourself? Thought you just came from the hospital."

He waited until she peeped back at him, then raised his shirt to show his bandages. "I got shot, Gail. There's people looking for me. I had to get away."

"People? You didn't tell me!"

"I didn't coz they won't come here. And I wanna leave soon as I can. Tonight, I promise, after it's dark. If I had any money I'd give you that too, but you can see I got nuthin." He wriggled one trouser leg. "I'm in some old guy's clothes, for Chrissake."

"Well." She folded her arms across her skinny ribs, leaned against the bench. "We got nuthin neither."

Anger welled within him like liquid fire. Muscles along his neck and jaw tightened. It was all he could do not to scream at her. "I saved your baby girl's life, you said. You can't repay me for that?"

"Watcha think I been tryin to do? But you keep pullin away. Changin the subject." She scrunched up her face. "You gay or somethin? They shoot your pecker off?"

The Animal surged momentarily, wanting blood. His hand clenched the mug so hard, he was surprised it didn't shatter. "You give me that goddam injector, woman," he said in a low voice.

Gail held up her hands to calm him, then mimed smoking. "Look, I got some crack. A little weed. You can share that. But I ain't giving you my girl's medicine."

"Crack?" His jaw worked as he struggled for control. So they'd had bad men in their lives, huh? Well, how about a mom who wasted her precious little cash on drugs? It wasn't like she needed them, not like he did.

"Oh, you don't use? Where'd those marks on your arms come from then?" She stabbed the inside of her elbow with her index finger.

He started to rise, caught himself when a pang of pain above his hip snapped him out of it. The moon might be shrinking again, but he could feel it out there, gnawing at his control. "I walk out that door and even touch the thing I'm allergic to, I'm dead. You get me? You want that on your conscience?"

She spun away and fussed with the dishes some more.

There was a squeak of brakes outside and Jake was at the window a second later, pain or no pain. A familiar green Lexus came to rest unevenly in the space between this cabin and the next. The hand brake came on with a *crrrk*. Gwen got out the driver's door and some of the tension bled from his shoulders. She was in hospital clothes, like the first time he'd met her. Was she here to check up on Sophie? Or was she looking for him?

"Who is it, darlin?" Gail asked. Suddenly, she was all friendly again, as if the last thirty seconds never happened.

"Speak of the devil," he murmured and stepped aside for her to look.

"Oh. Wow. Maybe problem solved, huh?" She rubbed his arm with her knuckles as she stepped past him to throw open the screen door. "Hi, Doctor! How're you today?"

Gwen made polite conversation with Gail and checked on Sophie, then asked Jake to step outside for a "chat". The request had drawn daggers from Gail, but Jake had preceded her with no more than a grunt.

Terrific. We're back to caveman talk again.

"Show me your dressing," she demanded as soon as the screen door shut behind her. Gail was a hot presence at her back. His ridiculous stolen outfit would have been funny if things weren't so messed up. When she was satisfied the dressing and sutures were intact, she shepherded him toward the car, out of Gail's hearing.

Her foot slipped in a patch of mud caused by runoff from another trailer's unsealed kitchen pipe. She'd never set foot in a trailer park before, but it was exactly what she'd expected from movies: a partially paved property with rusting trailers and pre-fab cabins scattered around it. Long grass, dandelions, old TVs and discarded car parts made up for the lack of garden beds. A round and wrinkled face appeared in the window above the opposite cabin's gurgling kitchen pipe, then disappeared again. People a few trailers over argued loudly; something cracked loudly, a pot or plate hitting a wall perhaps. A dog barked.

I hate this frickin' city.

"Who are these people who shot you?" she asked. "What the hell's going on?"

"Doesn't matter."

"It matters, Jake. You got…" She dropped her voice to a whisper, leaned close enough to smell his sweat. "You were chased around a neighborhood wearing a dress. Some psycho shot you with a silver bullet. You had a life-threatening allergic reaction to it - something unheard of. You almost died, Jake, and you say it doesn't matter?"

He lifted his gaze to hers. "Why's it matter to you?"

She blinked at that, then studied Gail's reflection in the car window. "This family - all these people here - they live in squalor. You live - sorry, *stay* - wherever you can find a dry patch of ground. This is America - *America*, Jake. I … I became a doctor to help people. I've spent years learning and working to do that. But nothing I do makes a difference. The bodies keep coming into the ER, they keep going out. Some of them - a lot of them - reappear a few weeks later. Another bullet wound. Another overdose. Another broken bone from brawling, or riding on the outside of a train, or having the *shit* kicked out of them by their mother's latest boyfriend.

"I can help little Sophie recover from anaphylactic shock, but I can't stop her mom hooking up with a pedophile. I can't stop cars crashing or unsupervised toddlers swallowing their father's sleeping pills or gangs fighting or …" Her voice caught. She coughed it clear, swallowed. "But I can help you. I can help one person. And I want to try. Please let me try, Jake."

He was frowning, but he was listening. And - against type - he was looking at her, right at her, right into her eyes.

The windows of the soul. See me. Let me see you. Please.

"What do you want me to do?" he asked.

Gail had moved out of sight; whether it was this that relaxed Jake or whether he was acquiescing to her concern, Gwen didn't know. She wondered at his and Gail's relationship for a moment - surely he wasn't sleeping with this shrew? - before pushing the concerns away.

She unlocked the Lexus and grabbed the white business shirt from the backseat, Barry's spare. She tossed it to him and he caught it. "First, put that on. The old man's shirt looks ridiculous. Second, come with me. This gut wound needs to heal. You need to get straight and get safe." When his gaze dropped, she dipped her head to catch it. "I'm going to get you help, whatever help you need. You're a good guy. I'm not having you running for your life from crazy people with silver bullets. I'm not having you ruining yourself on drugs."

"I'm not having"? Just who do you think you are, lady?

She was a doctor, that's who. Doctors helped people. Doctors fixed people. She would get Jake on his feet, set him up for a happy life, heal him. It was selfish. It was narcissistic. It sat perfectly fine with her.

Jake's attention flicked up at an idling engine noise behind her. A yellow van was crawling along the weedy lane that Sophie lived on, as if the driver was reading lot numbers. It stopped six homes away. A delivery, then, and not more kidnappers.

"So what's it to be?" she asked.

Jake also lost interest in the vehicle. "Can you help me get outta Detroit?"

Uncle Richard's face came into her mind, followed by an image of her old family home. She needed time to reassess her career. And time to recover - from a personal crisis and from an abduction attempt whose perpetrators the cops still hadn't caught. And she could think of no better place to rest up than Carrington, Michigan, working with the kindest man she'd ever met. Maybe he'd even be kind enough to find Jake a job and help him with his detox.

"I can," she said.

He gave another grunt and headed back to the trailer. "Let me change shirts. And say goodbye to Sophie."

Sophie leapt off the bed and crashed into his stomach, pinning her arms around him and causing pain to spike straight through his middle.

"Easy, easy," he groaned and pried her off as gently as he could. "I gotta go."

"No, you don't."

"I gotta." He didn't know if he was doing the right thing or not, trusting Gwen. She'd rejected him once before. But then this wasn't about that - this was about getting away. Getting safe. There were lots of ways she could help him. He crouched down. "Listen. You girls and your Mom, you've helped me out this mornin. I appreciate that. But the doctor's gonna take me somewhere safe. Somewhere I can heal up good."

"You can heal up here." Sophie wiped tears from her cheeks with the back of one hand.

She reached for him again. Leaning against the small bedroom window, Gail watched jealously as if to say, *You wouldn't let me touch ya.*

Why this girl cared for him so much, he couldn't say. Sure, he'd saved her life, but this was only the second time he'd ever seen her. Lack of a dad in the home? If his had been anything to go by, she was better off without one.

"I'll come back and visit if I can," he said.

She picked the lie immediately, pushing back and launching herself to land face down on the bed. "You won't!" she screamed into the mattress. He glanced behind him and along the short hallway to where Melly looked on impassively from the kitchen. Gail had her arms folded, shaking her head like Jake was some kind of monster.

Well, he was.

He stood, was about to say a simple good bye when there was a sharp cry from outside the cabin.

"Get off me!"

Gwen!

He careened off the bedroom doorway in his haste to get to her while avoiding Melly, wrong-footed as he entered the cabin's living area. He was bracing himself on the sink when the screen door yanked open. A muscular arm shoved Gwen inside so hard, she sprawled across the table, knocking over Jake's cold coffee. Melly retreated against the chairs at the far end of the living area. Gwen rolled along the table and found her balance beside Melly; she reached out to cover her. The trailer rocked as a heavy body stepped inside.

"Well, well," Eddie said. "Looks like you got us all set up, Jakey boy."

CHAPTER TWENTY-NINE

Jake's mouth went dry. Eddie's frame filled the doorway, blocking out the daylight. There was no point asking why he was here.

"Get out," Jake growled.

"That ain't nice. You don't want me around your harem, is that it?" There was more than mere lust in his eyes as he scanned Gwen up and down. Gwen scurried sideways, covering Melly with her body.

"Get out!" Jake shouted, one hand sliding along the benchtop. His fingers brushed the soup pot.

"You ran away from me, Jake. Your own flesh and blood. Pretty damn impolite. You don't want to know how I found you? Oh, your scent is strong the morning after a waning moon."

Gwen frowned at Jake. He wondered fleetingly if she'd worked it out yet. That would be the end of any help from her. He had to get Eddie out of here.

"Outside," he said. "We'll talk out there."

Eddie pressed his lips together and cocked his head, attention shifting from Gwen at one end of the room to Gail and Sophie crowding the stunted hallway leading to bedrooms and bathroom. He huffed dismissively and looked back toward Gwen. "Mmm, no. Not while there's fun to be had here."

Jake's jaw worked as he struggled for control, bracing himself. The fire was back in his chest, his shoulders, his arms.

Eddie took another step inside, intent on the hallway, but still preventing Gwen from slipping past him. "This could be our den, Jake. The beginning of a whole new life." He rolled his head, neck joints cracking, nostrils flaring, and settled on Gwen. "Mm-mm. Smells like violence, this one. She's capable of anything. You can have your crackhead and her spawn. I think I'll start with this. Better breeding."

Jake flung the pot with everything he had, then vaulted across the table. Eddie swiped the pot away. Jake's feet hit him hard in the ribs, smashing him into the wall. Jake got his balance and rammed his left shoulder into Eddie, pressing him hard against the wall while thumping him in the guts with his right hand. The guy was hard; it was like hitting a leather car seat.

Eddie took four blows before Jake's wound twinged and made him falter. Eddie regained his balance and pushed back. Jake's next punch glanced off Eddie's ribs. Eddie grabbed Jake's shirt and pivoted, propelling Jake out of the cabin door.

Jake sprawled on the ground. Something gave in his left wrist. Pain flashed like a bullet wound, then the hand went numb. He sprang up, ready for Eddie's charge. But there wasn't one.

Eddie snarled, "My bitches, then," and pulled the screen door shut.

A flurry of movement in the doorway, even as Jake surged forward: a flash of light blue scrubs. Gwen! Eddie's hand whipped up and Jake heard the slap and Gwen's gasp. The moment's delay was enough for Jake to reach them. He wrenched the door open. Eddie jerked toward him, fists raised. Injured hand pressed against the dressing on his belly, Jake dived shoulder first at Eddie's knees, catching the man against the table. With nowhere to move but backwards, the man's right knee didn't stand a chance.

The knee made a short, sharp sound like crackling kindling as Jake rolled aside. He came to his feet as Eddie went down, screaming and cussing and clutching the leg. Jake dropped his own knee on Eddie's ribs, then punched him in the cheek. Another to the jaw. When the man raised an arm to protect himself, Jake moved his knee to his cousin's injured leg, then grabbed the screaming man's hair and smacked his head into the floor once, twice, three times.

Eddie went slack like a bag of laundry. Blood welled from a cut below his eye. His mouth gaped, spittle collecting inside his ballooning cheek. Jake wanted to reach into Eddie's mouth and rip out his tongue, for making him do this, for forcing him to violence. But it had been the right thing to do. The good thing. He'd protected the innocents. They were staring at him, terror in their eyes. As if he'd had a choice.

"Out," he rasped.

Gail and her girls didn't need to be told twice, circling him, familiar with the drill. Gwen took longer, pausing to hold the screen open for him. "C'mon." Her voice was either gentle or shocked. He couldn't tell. "My cell's in the car. I'll call 911."

He rose unsteadily, shallow-breathing to control the pain. His voice rebelled when he tried to respond. He grit his teeth and preceded her outside.

Gail stood by another trailer where a small knot of gawkers had gathered, her girls hugged to her thin frame, her mouth tight, hatred blazing in her eyes. He shook his head, moved to the car and leaned there. She needed to get her girls away from Eddie.

The Lexus unlocked with a double-pip that startled him. Gwen shoved the key remote back in a pocket and reached for the door handle. He placed his hand on it just long enough to stop her before pulling back.

"Let them call the cops." He flicked his head at the onlookers. "Tell Gail to take the kids away from here. Angelo could find them another place to stay. He could come with her tomorrow and get her stuff for her."

Gwen studied him. "I'll save questions for later. But you better listen. That man in there is hurt bad." She lifted a hand to forestall him. "I'm grateful you stopped him hurting us. God knows what he…" Words jammed in her throat. For the first time, he noticed the discoloration on her cheek beneath her left eye. To her credit, Gwen wasn't even touching it the way other people would. She swallowed, collecting herself. She seemed resolute, focused, strong. And that made sense: she was used to emergencies. "He needs an ambulance. The Wallaces need the cops. If that *freak* recovers, the whole frickin city needs him behind bars." She ripped open the driver's door and rummaged in her bag. "I'm calling 911."

He slumped against the car, cradled his injured wrist and thought that maybe just this once, he should listen to someone else. Ambulances had pain killers.

The paramedic closed the rear doors tight and tossed Gwen a sympathetic glance.

Eddie was strapped to a cart inside, still unconscious. Part of her hoped he'd stay that way. That was one dangerous psychopath right there. But then, the side she'd seen of Jake again - wasn't that equally dangerous? So far it had been turned in the right direction, namely her defense. But what if she angered him? What if this wasn't his last resort in a conflict, but his first?

Two squad cars had turned up. The crowd of rubberneckers had vanished at the sight of them. One of the cars took off trailing after the ambulance. The other remained while an officer, notebook in hand, chatted with Gail.

Gail didn't look like she was giving a statement anymore; more likely complaining about how close they'd come to death and why didn't the police department do something about it.

As if Gwen's day hadn't dealt her enough crap already, the other officer was the one who'd come on to her in the ER the day Ormond had killed Willie Anderson: Officer Creep. He strutted over, hitching his belt, puffing out his chest.

"Thanks for your assistance, Doctor." He peered at Jake over his shades. "So neither of you know this guy well? That's your statement?"

Jake shrugged. "Like I told you." Standing on the far side of the Lexus, he turned his back, adjusting his sling and worrying at the tight bandaging on his left forearm. He'd told the police - three times by Gwen's count - that Eddie's van looked like one of the cars that had chased him around the mission neighborhood yesterday, only a different color.

Shifting her handbag on her shoulder, Gwen added, "I've never seen the bastard before. Did you find anything out about him?"

"You could say that. Edward Barrow is a serial rapist. He's already done time. Now he's wanted by the FBI, believed involved in a murder-robbery in Dayton, Ohio, and a rape-homicide in Chicago."

Gwen put her hand to her mouth, blood turning to ice. *That could have been me. Twice in a month.*

Jake still had his back turned, but he'd settled, listening.

A serial murderer and rapist armed with silver bullets had been hunting down a homeless man? No, that wasn't it. Barrow had been talking about dens and full moons and *smelling* Jake. He'd said he was Jake's flesh-and-blood. Jake had a lot of explaining to do.

"And you have no idea why this guy has been chasing you?" The cop's question was directed at Jake, mirroring her own wondering.

Jake half-turned, gave another of his trademark shrugs. "The hell would I know? You just said dude's crazy."

The cop grunted unhappily. He focused his mirror shades on Gwen, jerked a thumb at Jake. "Sure you're okay here?"

"Fine, thank you."

"He told me he's going with you?"

"*Thank* you."

Creep scowled. He huffed and tugged at his belt. His partner was too busy to give him moral support, enduring the endless stream of verbal diarrhea from Gail. Creep murmured something derisive about women as he moved off.

Melly and Sophie played Go Fish in the shade of the trailer, their tone hollow, their movements jerky. Jake had tried to tell them to leave; it had been good advice and Gail would surely ignore it. The mom was picking at the skin of her arm while she babbled. Jake never scratched, Gwen realized, never picked, never looked pale - in fact the faint needle tracks on his arms were the only giveaway that he had ever used heroin. Perhaps he wasn't an addict then. Perhaps he self-medicated when overly stressed. There were professional people who did that: lawyers, detectives … doctors. By contrast with him, Gail had cracked lips, a filthy home, barely any food in the cupboard, burst blood vessels in her eyes. She picked at her skin, and her teeth were on their way to brown-tinted rubble. She smoked something regularly, probably meth. Gwen watched the dull-eyed marionettes playing cards for a moment. Gail's life wasn't going anywhere good and her kids would get pulled down with her. It wasn't fair, and there wasn't one thing Gwen could do about it.

That's me, the helpful doctor who can't help anyone.

"How's the arm?" she asked Jake.

"Better, with the meds," he mumbled. "I can move."

"Good. Get in. I'm sick of this place."

After parking Barry's pride-and-joy in the space she'd borrowed it from, Gwen retrieved her handbag from the back seat. Jake was a dull presence in the passenger seat. For once he was completely chilled, pupils dilated from the morphine the paramedics had given him.

Just what I needed, a junkie with more junk in him.

But was he truly a junkie? Again, the doubts. He'd had access to things in her home to steal, to sell for his next hit. He hadn't done that. He was big, plenty of meat on his bones and in good shape - young and fit enough to recover from his drug use and manage his mental illness. If she and Uncle Richard could help him now, they could spare him further decline. Richard was friends with a great psych near Carrington. Between the three of them, they could handle Jake's issues. He could find work, get a foundation, start rebuilding. He could live a normal life.

And I'll be Little Miss Savior, Doctor of the Year, the Michigan Messiah.

I'll actually have helped someone get better.

She pulled the keys from the ignition. "Jake?"

"Hm?" His eyelids levered upward. He'd been napping.

"I need you to hop out of the car. You can sit against the door if you want."

He wiped at a thin shine of drool beneath his lip. "Sure." Fingers fumbling, it took him a moment to get the door open. He half climbed, half rolled out of the car.

She got out, locked the car and rounded it. Jake sat propped against the car, his chin on his chest, hair like the branches of a willow.

Shit. Please, God, don't let security see this.

"You be okay here? I won't be too long."

He stirred. "Oh. Sure. Where you goin'?"

"To take Barry's keys back. Get my stuff. Ask for leave." *Demand leave, you mean, Michigan Messiah. Got good deeds to do and no bureaucracy shall stand in thy way.* "I'll get an EpiPen too."

"Cool."

More gripping conversation. The car trip should be a hoot.

"Jake?"

He raised his head a quarter inch. "Mm?"

"Stay. Here."

He shifted on his haunches, drawing his knees up.

She crossed the parking lot in a forced march. Inside, the corridors were full of a busyness that seemed suddenly pointless. How many of those they cared for wouldn't make it through the week, the night, the hour? The upwardly mobile doctors, interns desperate to impress and prove their brilliance - all meaningless. Avoiding the ER, she also avoided her closest coworkers, those who would be compelled to ask her about the burgeoning contusion beneath her eye. As it was, a few people stared at her or did double-takes, but broke eye contact quickly when she held it in silent challenge. Maybe they were starting to think weird and Gwen Cheevey went together like weird and Jake Brennan.

Her first stop was her locker where she used a discarded plastic grocery bag from a nearby bench to scoop up chip packets, spare undies and socks. She hesitated over her coffee mug, coffee bags and a dog-eared novel. Was she coming back for them?

The door on the far side of the room opened, but the bank of lockers meant she couldn't see who entered. The person stayed on their side, settling onto a bench with an exaggerated male groan. She decided the coffee paraphernalia and the book could stay. There was a slim chance she might be back one day. It'd be nice to have something to come back *to*.

So what now, girl?

A trip to the pharmacy where she'd fill in a prescription for an EpiPen and buy it herself. Hailing a cab to go around and pick up Jake. Back to her apartment to plan the trip home. Tomorrow she'd be in Carrington, and then...

Then, she'd make it up as she went along.

She locked the door, knotted the plastic bag's handles and rounded the locker bay headed for Barry's - the one he never locked, arrogantly expecting no ill to befall the great doctor, especially not theft.

*The un*locker*, he should call it.*

She came to an abrupt halt, one shoe skipping on the polished floor with an ungodly squeak. Barry sat astride the central bench running down the aisle, turning his pager over and over in his hands. He favored her with a bright smile and a wink. "Heard you'd come back. They my keys?"

She blushed, lifted her chin. "Just bringing them back. I needed the car."

Duh.

"It's okay." He swung one leg over to place both on her side of the bench. The pager went into his shirt pocket. "I trust you. No problem. As long as you looked after my baby." He narrowed one eye. "You did look after her? Sure you did, that's what I thought."

She tossed the keys to him and he snatched them from the air without taking his eyes off hers. Sure hands. Safe hands. Trust me, I'm a doctor.

"Well," she said, about to slip past him.

He stood, blocking her way. "What happened to your face?" He made to reach for her, then pulled his hand back.

She held her ground. "Violent patient. Just one of the things I love about the ER."

He made a sympathetic face. "I heard about the Decision." She could hear the capital letter when he said it. Instantly her guard went up. *Here we go.* "I can't believe they'd do that to you. Weng should know better."

"Weng only believes what his trusted sources tell him. *Someone* must have said I'd be a poor choice."

He pulled back, distancing himself from her opinion. "You can't think I'd do that."

But there was no question in Gwen's mind. And no patience to play this game. "I'm not interested, Barry. I have things to do."

"Wait." He put out an arm to stop her. He hadn't touched her, wasn't threatening - especially after the truly threatening behavior she'd so recently witnessed - but she backed up a step anyway. "I've been thinking, Gwen. Seeing you again, spending so much time together lately. It's been kind of … nice. I realized I miss you. A lot actually."

She forced all emotion from her face, wondered if she looked like Melly and Sophie had once their terror had subsided into shock. He seemed to take it as encouragement to continue, edging closer. She stayed where she was, arms by her sides.

"I can help you, Gwen. You know I always wanted to. I have a friend at the Children's Hospital. I could get you an interview."

She got it then. It was all part of Dr Barry's master plan. Move her to another hospital and he could have her there and another chick here - a ship in both ports, knowing nothing about the other.

"How about I organize dinner with him? Just the three of us. And after dinner, a concert at Orchestra Hall."

"So you had nothing to do with Weng's decision?"

"Of course not. Get that out of your head."

"Those things you said in the car the other night?"

He waved it away. "Heat of the moment. You know I have the highest respect for you, Gwen."

She held his gaze for a long moment. He shifted under her scrutiny, then slipped a little closer. Close enough to kiss. So close, his Acqua Di Parma cologne was strong and his swamp-breath noticeable beneath it. She allowed a little twinkle of mischief to creep into her expression.

"Hold out your hand and close your eyes."

He blinked, wrong-footed. He'd lost control. But he went with it, smiled, plunged one hand into a pocket and held out the other. His eyes closed slowly. She took a pen from his pocket and his smile broadened at the contact. She took his hand in hers, his skin cold. He gave a little tremor at her touch. She placed the pen ball on the furrowed skin of his palm and wrote in big letters: *I QUIT*.

"That's for Weng." She let his hand drop.

His eyes popped open to squint at the message. He reached for her. "Gwen."

She slipped inside his embrace and kneed him in the groin, darted back.

"That's for you."

She left him sucking oxygen on the bench and found it difficult not to skip as she made her way to the pharmacy. She giggled, drawing strange looks from people she passed. That knee in the balls had been the most satisfying physical contact she'd ever had with him.

CHAPTER THIRTY

The trip would have taken a confident driver two hours. It took Gwen three - three long hours of trying to make small talk, station-surfing on the car radio, and wishing she'd thought to pack her CDs.

They had spent the night at her place, he on the couch, she in her bed staring at the ceiling and wondering if it had it really been only a week since they'd met. She'd fallen into a deep sleep about the time the birds started making noise outside her window and the next thing she knew it was noon and he was waking her. It took another hour-and-a-half to freshen up, pack and hire a rental car. When they finally hit the road, it was with relief.

The first view of Carrington was a smudge of gray-brown and primary colors visible from the hills on the very edge of the district where farms supported cows, pigs and horses. The town marker appeared a hundred yards ahead of the first gas station.

Carrington, population 19,590
Sister-Cities:
Weisswald, Germany
Jaworzno, Poland

The town was just as she'd left it - her mom always complained it had barely changed since the Vietnam War. She found herself prattling as they cruised Main Street, telling Jake about the homes clustered around the central strip, the two small lakes, the high school south of the fire station. Carrington also boasted a decent middle school and three elementary schools, one of them belonging to the Catholic Church. The kids from her elementary school had often fought with those from the Catholic one, though she couldn't remember why. Kids being kids, today's crop probably still did it.

"Speaking of churches," she added, putting on her best imitation of a tour guide, "last time I counted, there's one from every major franchise: Lutheran, Baptist, Pentecostal and Catholic - and no one in my family's set foot in any of them."

Jake had been playing with his mother's brooch for the last hour, turning the small piece over and over in his hands, running the chain through his fingers. Now he looked up at her with a quizzical expression; perhaps he'd never seen a tour guide. She pressed on regardless, glad for something to talk about at length. Carrington's population was largely Caucasian still, though she'd noticed a growing Hispanic enclave each time she'd visited over the past ten years; her mother had complained about them, like they were bringing the place down. As if the witch ever spent any time here anymore. Gwen liked the diversity.

She was always glad she had to pass through the township to get out to her family property; downtown always felt more like home than the house had. Perhaps because her mother rarely ventured there or perhaps because the food was better than her mother's cooking. The main strip boasted a steak house at each end, a scattering of mom-and-pop diners, and a Domino's by the post office. There was an excellent Chinese restaurant out by the high school, she told Jake, and a mediocre one in a converted corner store near the Lutheran Church.

Cafes flanked the police station and a Taco Bell sat beside the small cinema. The rest of the downtown strip was composed of book stores, jewelers, a few furniture outlets, law offices, banks. A single bar. And a small mall that punched through into the back street near the hospital.

"See the mall there?" she asked. "The rear part was taken up by a Walmart that forced the two smaller supermarkets we used to have out of business. The hospital's behind there - nowhere near as big as Detroit Receiving - and there's a veterinary clinic, a courthouse and fire brigade kinda nestled around it. Uncle Richard's practice is in the hospital's old admin wing. They added a new admin floor so the old wing's used for clinics and x-rays and so forth."

"He's the guy we're meeting?" Jake asked, speaking for the first time in an hour.

"Richard is the *gentleman* we're meeting," she said with a chuckle. "I don't think he'd like being called a 'guy'."

Conditioned to paying for parking, she was always surprised by the lack of ticket machine and security barrier as she turned into the hospital grounds. The rented hatchback snuggled nicely in the slanted parking spot closest the clinic doors. Here was another thing it would take time to get used to: not having to walk far. For anything. Also, she ruminated, craning her neck toward the back seat full of crap from her apartment, she wouldn't have to worry about people breaking into the car. She reached back while Jake studied some novel detail of the town. She straightened the grocery sack of books she'd brought. She'd only half emptied the apartment: the stuff she'd cry about if the place was robbed in her absence.

And just how long are you planning to stay here, Missy?

Indeed, that was a good question. What she needed now was space. Time and space to make a solid decision about the direction of her life without interference from well-meaning Pam, from Barry, from her mother and sister. Carrington was the place to do it: a secure job with Richard, no stress, clean air. Great Chinese food. The restaurant wasn't that far from her parents' place.

Home. The house. The memories. Her Dad's car left there by her sister Lauren - that would need a new battery by now.

She snagged her handbag from the back seat and turned to Jake. "Okay, buster. Mall first. We get a bite to eat before the food court closes for the evening. We buy you some clothes and a toothbrush. Get some groceries to tide us over until we can do a proper shop." She checked the dash display: 4:29. The flipside of small town living was early closing times for stores.

Richard would be here when they returned. He was a late worker, tireless, often seeing patients well into the night on weekdays. And his '90s model Audi gave testimony to his presence on the far side of the lot, conspicuous beside the Fords and Chevies.

She bumped into three people she knew at the mall, making small talk and introducing Jake as "a friend from Detroit". The interruptions wasted so much time that Varney's Menswear had closed by the time they got food and they had to buy Jake's supplies off the shelf from Walmart. She had money. A lot of it, compared to Jake. Once he started working, he could buy his own clothes, pay her back if he wanted.

They dumped the bags of clothing and groceries in the hatchback and with bellies full of fries and chicken nuggets, waddled to the clinic.

The reception desk was still open, though a sign with a cardboard clock indicated it would close in twelve minutes.

The young receptionist was vaguely familiar in the way people who shared her Detroit neighborhood often were. The girl was catalog-model pretty and her tag read *Hi I'm Cate*. She smiled warmly with perfect teeth.

"Yes?"

"I'm here for Richard Weatherhead. No appointment," she added as the young woman drew breath to ask. "Family friend. He invited me to drop in."

"Your name, ma'am?"

"Gwen Cheevey."

"If you'd like to take a seat, I'll buzz him." *Hi I'm Cate* lifted a white phone and murmured into it as Gwen sat by Jake. She studied Jake's appearance out of the corner of her eye. A woman with kids was doing the same - so was the receptionist until she noticed Gwen's scrutiny. Cate dropped her head, blushing.

Yep, dreadlocks aren't really the southwest Michigan look this year.

"Gwen!" An older man with a thick helmet of white hair marched out of a side door. She met him halfway, where he enveloped her in a hug. She could feel his bones and wondered just when he'd gotten so thin. But then, Richard must have been pushing seventy. The woman with the kids watched them with open animosity, her meaning clear: *I was here first.*

"This is my friend, Jake," she said as Jake ventured closer.

"How'd you get here?" Richard asked, eyes on a price tag swinging from Jake's long-sleeve tee.

"Rental."

"You drove, Gwen?" He held out a hand to Jake, squinted conspiratorially. "And you survived, son?"

Shaking the hand, Jake's gaze flicked to her and back again, unsure. "Yep."

She yanked the tag from his shirt and explained, "We left Detroit in a hurry."

"You got the Mob after you or something?"

If he noticed her flush, he didn't show it. He headed back to his offices. "I'm with a client," he called over his shoulder and twinkled his fingers at the little kid waiting. "This little one's next. After that, I'm all yours."

The door banged shut.

He might have been thinner, but Richard was exactly as she'd always known him: energetic, sharp, warm. The tension in her gut began subsiding.

Things were going to be okay.

CHAPTER THIRTY-ONE

"Okay to go now, boss?" Jake wiped his hands on the dishrag and raised his eyebrows hopefully.

Janey, the hospital kitchen manager, marched over, clipboard in hand, to give the sink and stainless steel counters a once-over. Despite her outward hardness, there was something about her he liked. And trusted. She was round and soft and motherly, and probably about the age Momma was when she'd—

He tossed the dishrag on the counter, concentrated on the here and now. He had nine days until the next Big Moon started. He had work. He had hope. Things were looking up.

Janey's severe expression dissolved into a smile. "Take off that hairnet, honey, and set those ridiculous dreads free."

He did just that, hair tumbling onto his neck and shoulders like a heavy rain. She surprised him by stepping closer - he'd expected her to move on to some other task. She always had something else to do. She pulled an envelope from the clipboard and slapped it into his hand.

"Your first paycheck."

His fingers closed around it gingerly. He'd been paid before. Why did this one feel different? "Thanks."

"Ya got time to make the bank and cash it if you hurry." She turned her attention to a stock list. "Don't spend it all at once."

Checking the figure, Jake realized it would be hard not to. Ten days' work in the hospital kitchen didn't amount to much in dollar terms, especially when on closer inspection the slip said he hadn't been paid the full ten. "Uh, this is for five days."

"Tha's right, hun," Janey said without looking up. "It's just for the first week you worked. Hospital always pays a week behind. Guess the suits figure less people quit without notice if they're a week short. You'll get it eventually. As long as you don't quit without giving notice."

Five days' pay. He sighed. He owed Gwen a lot for clothing and food and board.

He was happy she'd let him stay with her. Not only did it mean he wasn't squatting in some empty building - which he admitted would have been his only choice, given he had no cash - but it meant he was close to her. It was probably a real dumb thing to do, but he *wanted* to see her every day. He was even coming to enjoy her sense of humor, and the way she talked all the time. Even better was the fact she wasn't bugging him about rehab and detox any more. Those early conversations had dwindled away after the first couple of days, and especially after she saw he wasn't hurting without heroin. That proved he wasn't a junkie. Richard had tutted over the fading needle marks on his arm and expressed wonder at how quickly his sprained wrist and wounded gut were healing.

He balled up his apron and dropped in the laundry sack. Drugs was a topic *he* would have to bring up soon as the month turned and day by day the moon out there grew bigger again. That was a conversation he wasn't looking forward to.

The kitchen clock read 4:33 as he headed out the staff door into the car park. Plenty of time to cash the check. After that he'd find a coffee shop to sit and wait. Or just walk around for a while. Most afternoons - the days his work coincided with Gwen's, anyway - he had to wait around a couple hours until her last patient.

Crossing the parking lot, he sucked rural Michigan air deep into his lungs, smelled fresh cut grass from the easement, ripe garbage from the kitchen dumpsters, an overlay of car exhaust and burning fat from the McDonald's the far side of the mall: the smells of civilization.

An elderly couple on their way out of the mall nodded hello to him. He smiled back. People were friendly here, most of them. The unfriendly ones weren't dangerous. That was the difference between most small towns and cities: small towns, people got used to you, they treated you with respect. Cities, everyone thought you might hurt them. Well, he agreed with that. It was safer to be on guard. As he legged it toward the bank, he saw many stupid things: parents leaving babies unattended in unlocked cars while they dashed into a store; schoolgirls maybe eight or nine years old standing on a street corner unattended with bags and milkshakes; cash registers left unattended with workers out of sight. Bad things would come of this behavior if this had been Detroit. Or Birmingham. Or Branson.

Or Rockford.

He hadn't thought about Rockford for over two weeks, not since the last moon cycle. Not since his car trip with Eddie. And he didn't want to think about it now. Whatever had happened to that lady - Elizabeth, her name was Elizabeth - it wasn't his fault. He'd done everything he could to dose himself properly that night, to protect the world from himself as much as to protect himself from them. And yet she'd died.

That made five. Five bodies he was personally responsible for.

Five that I know of.

Jake shuddered, jaw clenching at the rush of unwelcome thoughts. If he'd been a fighter pilot, that'd be five strokes on his fuselage. Two had earned it, maybe three, though he hadn't wished it on them. The others were black marks against him. The kinds of evil deeds that might get him sentenced him to Hell.

He shook his head, dreads swinging so violently they nearly whipped an older lady walking the other way. She scowled and was past him before he could apologize.

Sentenced to Hell. He'd never worked out where those words came from, but he suspected it was something his father had told him rather than Momma, the words scored deep into the fabric of his identity like graffiti carved in a train seat.

"Well, not any more," he muttered.

He'd rescued Gwen from rapists, saved Sophie's life at the risk of his own, protected the four females from Eddie. He was holding down a job now, sharing a house with a Normal woman, living a Normal life. He'd even been to church the past two Sundays: three services in total. The Catholic Mass had been as confusing as the Baptist night service. And all that yelling in the Pentecostal service scared him; he'd left before it was over, seeking Gwen out in her office where she'd gone to catch up on paperwork while he "got religion," as she called it.

She said things like that with a twinkle in her eye. He liked that twinkle, was coming to like it more with each passing day. There'd been no more intimate moments like the one in her Detroit home. But half a dozen times, he'd caught her checking him out. He had been doing the same when she wasn't aware. Hell, he couldn't share a house with a woman and not look.

But he hadn't touched her, no matter how much *It* wanted to, another thing he felt was in his favor.

The Pentecostal preacher had ranted about the stupidity of trying to "score points" with God, the impossibility of it. But Jake didn't see the problem. After all, if those people in the pews with their tidy clothes and short haircuts hadn't been trying to impress God, then why were they there? The Catholics hadn't been nearly so uptight and they certainly believed in "keeping the slate clean" as their priest had called it in his much shorter sermon. The Baptist preacher had made no sense whatsoever, but the people there had been equally as kind as the Catholics, making small talk with him and insisting on a second cup of coffee after the service. A couple of the men had invited him to go fishing with them some time. Surely the more Normal things he started doing, like fishing with the guys, the more good points he'd score...

The bank doors swished open to let him in. The wall clock read 4:42. The cashier cashed his check without small talk. No offer of a coffee here. Her gaze sneaked up to his hair. That happened a lot round here. Maybe he should cut it?

Screw that, he thought. Or maybe the Animal did.

He left the bank, counting his money, and headed toward the clinic where he'd wait in the foyer, slowly picking his way through the magazines piled about the chairs. He'd found one yesterday with an article about coyotes in urban areas. Many of the words were impossible to decipher, but he was getting the idea by the time Gwen had come out. He was looking forward to finishing it, maybe rereading it and then asking Gwen to help him understand it better. He passed the school girls with their shakes and felt a pang of melancholy: if only he'd been able to live their Normal life. There'd been a season when he thought he would. His foster parents had been cold, but they'd provided for him. He was on track for a solid education before puberty and the onset of the problem kicked the shit out of that idea.

The girls caught him looking and he dropped his gaze, as was his habit. He had a cold flush: would they think him a perv? Would they tattle? Would a couple of cops come looking for him at the weekend, march him out of town? It'd happened before. The girls went silent until he'd turned the nearby corner, then tittered. He relaxed, understanding. They'd seen a big guy with funny looking hair, and they'd reacted with pre-teenage silliness.

He envied them their innocence.

The letter lay on the corner of the desk. Cate must have left it there while Gwen had been busy elsewhere. With Jake waiting in the foyer, she would have opened it at home if not for the Detroit Receiving Hospital logo in the top left corner. It had been forwarded from her home address.

Crappy crap crappison. What now?

The *what-now* was a terse letter from the hospital's COO dated a week ago, demanding her presence at a disciplinary hearing for assaulting a fellow doctor. She considered her options. Barry wasn't pressing criminal charges as far as she knew; with no witnesses, how could he? But his pride wouldn't let it go. He wanted to disgrace her.

"Good luck with that, asshole."

She took a new envelope and a Post-it note. She wrote,

What assault?
By the way,
in case you didn't
get the memo,
I quit.

She signed it. She took their letter and tore it into strips, then into postage-stamp-sized pieces. She poured them from her palm into the envelope, slipped the post-it inside, addressed the envelope to their return address and sealed it. She left it on her desk for Monday's mail and reached for her cardigan, keys and bag.

In the foyer, three patients looked up hopefully when she opened her door. She averted her gaze. If Richard wanted to work late, Richard could work late. But he'd agreed that Gwen would always finish at five. And it was already twenty-five after.

Jake put a magazine aside at her approach.

"You're chauffeuring." She tossed him the keys. He might not have a license, but he was a far better driver than she was. She was happy to admit that. An adolescence perfecting the fine art of auto theft had evidently taught Jake one valuable life skill.

So. License. Add that to the To Do list for the recovering drug-user living under my roof.

She put on her cardigan and thought about those living arrangements. Things had worked out better than she'd expected. Lots of permutations had rolled through her mind that first sleepless night in her childhood home, sleeping in her parents' old room while he slept in Lauren's directly above her: he would murder her and steal her car along with cash for dope; he would *rape* and murder and steal the aforementioned things; he would steal the aforementioned things in the night and thoughtfully leave her unmolested. He would live quite peacefully with her, keep the job Richard got him in the hospital kitchen, then after a few days he would self-sabotage and do a runner, drift to Grand Rapids or Toledo, Chicago or back to Detroit. Find a supplier. Shoot up. Get hunted by monster-chasers.

Or. He would turn out just fine and never need her help again.

This last possibility was the best she could hope for and it had made her sadder than the others. She was becoming as crazy as him.

He stood, intent on the keys, forehead creased. She knew what he'd say before it came out of his mouth. "Thought we agreed it's not a good idea. If the cops pull us over…"

Cate looked up at the mention of cops. Gwen made a face at Jake to shut him up. She took his elbow and steered him towards the door. "Let's discuss that outside, shall we?"

He noticed Cate belatedly.

And Cate, the little minx, made *cutesy eyes* at him. Gwen tightened her grip on his elbow then forced herself to let go, feeling stupid.

Why shouldn't Cate make eyes at him? And why shouldn't Jake respond if he wanted to? It was none of her business. Right? They were acquaintances, housemates.

Right?

"Sorry," she mumbled as she led him to her dad's 2004 Taurus. Every car he'd ever owned had been a Ford, much to her mother's disgust. "Just didn't want her calling the cops on us."

"She won't. She's cool."

He got in ahead of her and when she was sitting next to him, she asked, "Cool? You mean you guys…?"

Jake returned her gaze, key in the ignition but not turning it.

She made busy with her handbag, pretended to check for messages on her phone. There were none. "Anyway," she said as he finally started the engine, "today's payday at the hospital, I hear."

Jake would finally have some money of his own. He had done so well, had stabilized, was following through on living a responsible and steady life. Richard - and Jake's boss, Janey, who they'd told quietly of his background - agreed there were no signs of him being a junkie or an unreliable drifter. He was settling into something new and doing it well.

"So, you been to the bank?" she asked.

He grimaced, intent on reversing safely. "I was gonna tell ya. I'll pay you some of what I owe, but they only paid me for one week."

She shook her head. "No, no, no. That's not what I was getting at. Pay me back some other time … or don't; I don't care. It's your first *check* from a *new employer*, dummy. That means you buy the drinks."

God, after the way she'd just reacted to Cate's flirting, she could do with one. Or three.

"Oh." He shifted the automatic into drive and the car glided smoothly out onto the road, joining a light diaspora of departing workers. "You trust me with booze?"

She blinked, then caught his meaning. "Jake, you had needle marks, for God's sake." *Still do, last time Richard looked, but there's no fresh ones. At least not on his arms.* "But I think a drink or two will be okay.

Look, I didn't bring you to Carrington to be your sober companion. Let's not be a doctor and a guy who was kind of her patient once. And let's not be the attempted kidnapping victim and the guy who stepped in to stop it. Let's just be two people, *friends*, celebrating one of the friend's first paycheck. That fair enough?"

"Fair enough," he said after turning right with exaggerated care. His eyes scanned all over, the mirrors, the corners, the peripheries, as if a cop would leap out with a radar gun. But he seemed to have thawed a little. In fact, he'd come down about twenty notches on the Wariness Scale in the past week alone. He seemed to be making progress. There'd been no mention of people chasing him. Of needing to move on. Of the moon.

"Where?" he asked, turning onto Main Street and picking up a little speed, heading towards home.

She pointed to the liquor store a block ahead. "Pull in there." When he'd complied, she held out her hand. "Money. I'll go buy."

He reached into the fleeced reverse jacket she'd bought him now the September nights were hinting at the autumnal chill to come, pulled out a wad of notes and peeled off a twenty.

"That do?"

She nodded. "Beer for you?" He made a face. "Wine? That's what I'm having."

He made the same face. "Something sweet."

"Oh. Okay." She shoved the door open. "I'll surprise you."

Twenty bucks bought her a bottle of Australian moscato, a can of bourbon-and-Coke and a pint bottle of sweet English cider.

The act of purchasing alcohol always made her feel like a teenage girl getting away with something illicit; it was far more exciting than the actual drinking ever was.

She proffered the dime she'd got as change. Jake eyed it carefully.

"What year's on it?" he asked.

She checked the back. "Eighty-seven. You got a problem with that?"

"Nope." He slid it into a pocket. "Anything after 1965's okay."

She frowned, then remembered his allergy, felt her mouth round into a silent *Oh*. "They're not made of silver after '65?"

"Or '64. One of those two."

A silver allergy. She'd found no reference to it. Maybe she hadn't looked hard enough. He had a couple of EpiPens now, so he was safe, but she wondered at it.

"You are one curious creature, Jake Brennan."

He turned the key and they headed back onto the road out of town. In the back, the bottles clinked.

CHAPTER THIRTY-TWO

Jake had come to like Uno. The game was simple, it moved fast and he won as often as he lost. But he mainly liked it because he played it with her.

Crosslegged at the living room coffee table, he played a Blue 3 and said, "Hit me."

Gwen was the first woman he'd come to trust since Donna, his girlfriend at sixteen. Back then, for a couple of months, the world had been her. Donna was the first person since Momma who'd been inside his heart, who'd been gentle and affectionate. - And she'd run like hell when she first caught a glimpse of his problem. But he trusted Gwen: she seemed like someone who deserved the chance if she wanted it.

But did she want it?

She didn't use him like other women wanted, exchanging their sex for his protection, enjoying some weird sense of owning a guy. Gwen gave, and gave again. All she expected in return was respect, the kind of respect she showed him even in the way she'd made him pay for the drinks, treating him by Normal rules like a Normal person.

A thought slipped across his mind before he could shake it off. Eddie could have helped him control It; Eddie could have helped him be Normal. He chased that thought away as she slid catlike from her mother's chair by the window, sprawling sideways across the thick rug in front of the cold fireplace. As she considered her cards, he studied the line of her thigh and willed his thoughts towards her.

You make me feel Normal.

Warmth like spring sunshine swelled in his gut, spread to his chest. The Animal, for once, was dead quiet. All his thoughts were his own.

She pulled herself upright, mimicking his posture and played a Blue 8 and raised her chin in mock challenge. He dropped his gaze, suddenly scared she'd seen the thought in his eyes. He threw out another Blue without thinking and glanced at her. No, her focus was on the game, not him, chewing her lower lip as she shifted cards around, deliberating.

She really was pretty, her sweater swelling pleasantly, hair a little wild, throat graceful beneath her soft chin. Her eyes … he couldn't think of words to describe what he liked about them. Perhaps it was what she broadcast through those eyes, her inner liveliness, what Momma might call her *soul*. Jake had never met anyone like her.

She played a Draw 4 and grinned at him, reached for her wine glass.

He faked a groan and picked them up. "That's just mean."

She sipped and shrugged. "All's fair in cards and war." Her eyes twinkled, but whatever the words meant was lost on him.

He jerked his chin at the coffee table, indicating for her to play on. "Game's not over yet."

"Mm," she said and played her next card.

He rubbed the stubble on his jaw and thought about where this might be going. With the moon swelling again soon, Gwen would have the choice that Donna had. What would her choice be? And would she get hurt helping him?

He wouldn't hurt her. He'd find a way to protect her from *It* the way he'd protected her from others.

"All's fair," he teased, hoping it sounded smart to her, and played a Draw 4.

A flush warmed Gwen's throat and cheeks, and she covered it with another sip of wine. Jake was studying his cards, but his focus was all wrong: he was thinking, not seeing. He ran his tongue over his bottom lip, wetting it. She remembered how good those soft lips tasted, how right his muscles had felt beneath her hands. She could have it again; she could have way more than a kiss.

But…

Lamplight made prisms in her wine and she swished it to clear them. Undoubtedly there was a *but* or two she should be thinking about. Jake had control of his life. He was going to be okay. Her job as a doctor was done. There were probably other reasons to think twice, circling her on orbits so distant she couldn't make them out.

She put down her glass and played another Draw 4 on top of his, giggled at his pained expression. She leaned closer across the coffee table and dropped her voice. "Your move, Mister."

He held her gaze this time, then laid his cards on the floor and shifted onto his knees. He reached for her hand and stroked her knuckles with his thumb. A thrill raced through her.

"I reckon this game's been going on long enough," he said and bent close until his lips brushed hers ever so slightly, then pulled back a half inch. "I win?"

He smelled of apples and musk. His fingers moved up to the inside of her wrist. His dreads felt like tangled wool as she grabbed them with her free hand.

"We both do," she said and kissed him hard.

CHAPTER THIRTY-THREE

Carter Moffat lay in his bed, staring at the street light's glow against his curtain without a hope of sleeping. Tonight - just like every night since leaving Detroit - anxious questions chased each other around his head as he tossed and turned.

Who *had* murdered Tim? It didn't matter except that although Carter hadn't made him out clearly through the windshield, the driver must have gotten a good look at Carter. Would he come for him in the middle of one night? Would the Feds? Had the cops found his prints in Tim's car?

A creak elsewhere in the house, a scrape against the outside wall. Was it him? was it them?

He checked the bedside clock. It was 11:53pm on the nineteenth night since he'd shot Jake Brennan with a silver bullet, and the one-hundred-ninety-first night since Beth had died. And it was damn time he stopped tormenting himself.

He pulled on his dressing gown, padded to the kitchen and made himself a cocoa. Then he took a notepad and wrote:

1. *My prints weren't on the magazine I left in the grass. Tim Darkrider loaded it in before he gave it to me. And I still have the gun. With my prints. The FBI don't have it.*
2. *Yes, I left my DNA in the car, but I torched it.*
3. *If any one goes looking for my fingerprints, they aren't on record any-where because I've been a law-abiding citizen and if I remain one, then I'm perfectly safe from prosecution.*
4. *No matter who was driving that van, he had no idea who I was. He couldn't have. No one is coming for me. I'm safe.*
5. *Yes. I'm safe.*

6. *It's over.*
7. *It's really over. It's finished.*
8. *I'll never get my life back. But I can get half of it back, the 1/2 that contains Elijah.*
9. *That's enough to live for. That's enough for me.*
10. *Everything is actually going to be all right!*

He took the note, read it out loud three times. Then he downed the dregs of his cocoa, tore the note into very small pieces and tossed them in the trash.

Tomorrow he'd seek counseling and look for a job.

Tomorrow he'd start over.

Carter Moffat returned to bed and slept peacefully and dreamlessly for the first time in months.

CHAPTER THIRTY-FOUR

He was older now. No longer thirteen and confused over his sudden violence at the Armstrongs' home. No longer eighteen and reeling from his other self mauling a man to death in the woods. He was twenty-three and he was running.

Three men after him wore leather coats. Two lagged behind, one was faster, but none of them approached Jake's kinda speed.

As Jake neared the top of the hill, something bit into his ankle. Then he heard the gunshot, and he fell. Time slowed, the air thickening like rubber around him. He pitched forward and used the momentum to roll up and over the other side of the hill with poison in his leg and the rubbery air refusing to enter his lungs—

Waking was like surfacing from underwater. He gulped in breaths, sheets clutched in a death grip.

Damnit. His problem was always there lurking and waiting. He could ignore it for a week or two each month, but eventually, the rhythms of earth and moon brought him back to it even if his dreams didn't.

He had waited long enough to prepare for this month; it was almost time. He had to tell her. Over breakfast. He had to make her understand and help him. It had been six nights since he moved to her bed. In three more nights, the moon would be big enough to Change him. He couldn't let another day go by. For both their sakes.

Gwen realized she'd been standing there with her glass of water halfway to her mouth for the entire time the news story had played out. She put the glass carefully on the bench and swore softly. She flicked off the TV, but the news anchor's phrases continued to bounce around inside her head.

Escaped prisoner. Two officers critical. Manhunt.

Her cell rang, startling her. Her breath snagged in her throat. But there was no way Barrow could have her number. No way. She snatched it up.

"Hello?" came a male voice. "Dr Cheevey?"

The familiar voice got her breathing again, though she couldn't place it. "Who's this?"

"This is Officer Holland, Dr Cheevey. From the Detroit P.D."

Officer…? Creep!

Her fingers tightened around the phone. "I remember you. You couldn't have told me before I had to see it on the news?"

"Where are you? We dropped by your home, but no one was there. Hospital said you'd quit."

"I'm … out of town. Staying with a friend."

"Oh." Creep sounded disappointed. "Well that's probably good. But listen. Barrow's no doubt left Detroit. He was from Florida originally, so chances are he's heading back to more familiar places to hide out. Most of these assholes return to what they know or try to skip into Canada from here. But I was you, I'd be vigilant for the next month or so. When are you returning to Detroit?"

That was the big question, wasn't it?

Since the night of their *Uno* game she'd been thinking more and more about Angelo's mission, about Jenny in Angelo's kitchen, about all the little kids in trailer parks like Sophie Wallace. About the cluster of men with hacking coughs milling in front of the mission. About the homeless people who came into her ER, men in their forties who looked older than her grandfather.

About that hospital disciplinary hearing for "assaulting" Barry.

"I don't know when I'm coming back," she told Officer Creep, but she did. She did know. "I'll touch base if I do. Can you keep me in the loop if Barrow reappears? Or if you catch him?"

"You can count on that, Doctor. We catch him, you'll be called as a witness in his trial."

Gee. Thanks for caring.

She hit the end button before he could say more. Or she could.

A moment later she cursed herself for not asking if they'd ever caught the first guys to try and kidnap her.

Goddamned incompetents.

They hadn't caught the first two rapists and then when they caught the third, they let him get away.

Jake's footsteps sounded on the stairs. Heading to the upstairs bathroom. He preferred to leave her the bathroom off her parents' old room they shared. He'd be down for breakfast in twenty minutes. That was his habit: make potty, have a shower, then come down to eat. She had twenty minutes to decide if she should tell him about Eddie. But that decision was a no-brainer.

No, not yet.

It would freak him out, kick in that survival instinct. He might run. After all, Eddie Barrow couldn't know where they were. He didn't even know Gwen's name. Better to let Jake consolidate another month or so before telling him about it. Hopefully Barrow would be back in custody by then.

She made a pot of coffee while he moved about upstairs. She poured them both a cup as the stairs creaked beneath his two hundred pounds. He appeared at the kitchen door just as she added cream to his. He was dressed in a baseball tee and chinos, the pair of hiking boots he'd bought with his own cash still a little muddy from yesterday's fishing trip. Ah well, a bit of dirt wasn't that big a deal, not when he'd been painting and patching drywall, and weeding garden beds, for the past three weeks.

She carried the cups to the table and pushed his across. "Sugar's already in there." He took three, his sweet tooth consistent with that of most recovering drug addicts. "You sit, Mr Fisherman. I'll get you a couple of Pop-Tarts. That okay?"

He smiled, eyes soft. His voice softer. "Awesome."

There was something in his tone. Something hesitant. She wondered if his religious interest was becoming serious. Was he feeling guilty about premarital sex?

Speaking of Sunday...

"You're already late for the morning service. Going tonight?"

"Might skip it."

"Over your God fixation so quickly?"

"The people are nice and all. Just don't think..." He fell silent. She dropped the tarts into the toaster. Whatever he'd been about to say had been sucked inside his head, the conversation continuing there judging from the ripples of emotion crisscrossing his face as he sipped his coffee.

"Don't think what?"

He put his cup down, both hands wrapped around it. "Guess I was looking for an answer. It wasn't there."

"Wow, here I was thinking you'd found religion and all along it was a case of existential angst."

He made the face he made when he didn't understand her but thought her choice of words funny, screwing his mouth up, narrowing one eye at her.

"You wondering where you came from, big guy? Where you're going?"

He held her gaze. "I know where I'm going. At least if it's up to me."

"Heaven, I suppose?"

"I keep goin' the way I am, then yeah." He raised the coffee cup and slurped.

There it was again, that *something* in the set of his jaw. She dropped the teasing, but wasn't willing to drop the subject. "What's going on beneath those dreads of yours, Mister? Spill it."

He shifted on the hard wooden chair. "Just sayin'. My Momma's in Heaven. My Papa's in Hell. I don't wanna spend forever with my dad."

The line came out as rehearsed, probably something he'd thought over and over, a piece of self-talk like computer code, running its routine every day to keep the mind on track.

Daddy must've been a real piece of work.

The toaster popped with such force, both tarts flew out onto the bench. She scooped them up and onto the plate. She slipped into her seat and sipped her coffee while he dragged the plate over and nibbled at a corner of one tart. Her tummy tightened and she imagined cartoon aroma-tendrils slipping their sneaky little hooks into her olfactory cortex. She'd eaten two of the things an hour earlier, plus a bowl of rice bubbles. She was full. But the smell, the goddam evil delicious smell. Her tummy felt like it was reaching towards the plate, like Oliver holding out his bowl. *Please, sir, can I 'ave summore?*

Yeah, like you need more sugar and saturated fats, she told the roll of soft flesh above her jeans.

"You never talk about your family. I mean, I've told you a bit about mine." She'd wondered about who'd raised him to have such clear morals and strong work ethic, and how he'd ended up an itinerant drifter with no birth certificate or social security number. "I know your cousin is a murderer and rapist. What are you saying about your parents?"

For a long second, he covered the struggle within himself by biting into a tart, swigging coffee and chewing on the morass it made. He swallowed and wiped his hands on his pants. "I remember my father bein' a violent man, a frightenin' man. But Momma taught me right from wrong. She was good to me. She was my … my whole world, I guess. And then they both died. When I was small. That's all I need to know about my family. The rest is about me. When you live on the streets, when you have … problems, you make a lot of … You do a lot of bad things. You get a lot of sins against your name. Black marks. I have to get rid of them. Rub them out, one by one. And stop myself getting more."

She narrowed her eyes. "That's why you helped me, helped Sophie? To balance the ledger?"

"I'm tryin' to be good, Gwen. I have to be good."

"You are good, you dope. You don't need to prove that to anyone."

He dropped his head, hid behind his hair. His way of saying *time to change the subject.*

She reached for a segue. "Speaking of deciding where we're going, I'm thinking about returning to Detroit." He gaped at her as if it were she who were mentally ill. "Not to the ER. I want to help Angelo, or someone like him. I know one clinic for less fortunate people in

Midtown. Must be others. I'll work a couple of nights a week in a diner to support myself, if I have to.""But…"

"Go on. Say something."

"We go back there, them Hunters'll be on us like flies on turd."

She pushed back in her chair. "Okay. First, this hunters thing. You're talking about the guys who put a silver bullet in you. Whoever those freaks are, you need to tell the police as much as you can so they can catch them and you can stop worrying about them." He opened his mouth, but she raised two fingers, cutting him off. "Second, you need to be thinking about what's next for you, Jake. I'd love you to come back with me. I would. But you got a job here. You got a life."

And Eddie Barrow could be the one looking for you there.

It was best he stayed here, completely separate from the people who'd endangered him. Her too, for a couple of months at least.

He went blank, drained the rest of his coffee in two long gulps. When he lowered the cup, his head followed it down, dreads falling over his face.

"I'm not breaking up with you, big guy. I'm just saying there's some changes coming for me, but there's no need to destabilize you. We can work it out. Beside, you don't need me around all the time."

"You're wrong," he mumbled.

"No. I'm not. You have friends here now. The men who took you fishing, even if you don't share their faith, they seem like good guys. You're holding down a job. Janey's very happy with your work and she told me she's going to recommend you to the steak house beside the antique store if you want some evening work. You've been working your ass off around here helping get the house back into shape. You haven't hooked up with any undesirables in town." She paused, caught his eye and flashed a stern look. "Have you?"

"No," he snapped, sounding ridiculously like a chastised teenager. She believed him.

"And you have a nice place to live. Not stay: *live*. You can live here while I'm away, look after the place for me. I can visit on weekends. You can pay the bills eventually - that'll keep my bitchy sister off my back. But for now, the work you've been doing about the place is payment enough."

"But Carrington is… This is your home."

"You love it here, but I don't."

"It's quiet. People are nice. It's *safe*."

For you, sure, but me?

"It's a reminder of everything I hate about my life. Barry came from here. Richard's always talking about my mom and my sister. I keep bumping into old school buddies who treat me like I'm a fifteen-year-old nerd who should be grateful they're deigning to speak with her. And the job with Richard has been a nice break, but these people have access to whatever medical care they want. Not everyone is so lucky. You know that. I have to do something worthwhile with my life, help people who need real help. In Haiti, malnutrition contributes to two thirds of all deaths in children and ten per cent of children die before they're five. In Detroit, there's Americans dying on the streets of hypothermia and the flu. Here in small-town USA, all I do is treat measles, menstruation and menopause. Emergency was too fast for me, and I couldn't follow up on people to make sure they made it through their issues. But there was good there too, I can see it now. I think I know what's next for me. I want to try something new."

He stomped into the living room, then back to the door. He gripped the frame as though it were the only thing holding him up and growled, "How long? How long 'til you leave?"

She flinched. He kept up like this, it might be sooner rather than later. "Maybe a month. I'll have to make some inquiries, work out what my next steps are."

She hadn't canceled her lease, so she had a place to move back to. But she mightn't stay there long. If Jake could find her there, then so could Barrow. Or would a month be enough time for Barrow to be caught or be gone?

"Okay, then," he said, and God help her if he wasn't pouting. "You need to help me one more time before you go. You need to help me get through this Big Moon."

"What?" *Oh, geez, not this garbage again.* He was so stable otherwise, why was he fixated on this one thing?

"I need you to - what's that word? - *sedate* me. Three nights in a row: waxing moon, full moon, waning moon. If you don't want me to go back onto heroin. If you want me to stay away from 'undesirables', then you have to find me a way to sedate myself every month. Like I said, I'm gonna stay on the good path. But you gotta help me do it."

Was he making this up, a desperate ploy to show her he couldn't live without her? No, the earnestness in his face was real, to do with his own crap and not with any puppy love.

She almost laughed at that thought: a would-be werewolf with puppy love.

Yup. Hilarious. I'm sure he'd see the funny side of that.

"I'll think about it." He stepped back and she raised a hand to forestall him. "I'll help you. You know I will. Especially if I'm really helping you help yourself. It's just that, full moon, silver bullets? C'mon Jake, you can't really believe this stuff, deep down."

But he was already stalking across the living room. A moment later the front door squeaked open and banged shut. Windows rattled.

Way to go, Doc. There's that killer bedside manner again.

She reached for the Pop-Tarts, then stopped herself and rubbed her eyes. She threw the box back in the cupboard.

"Goddamnit," she muttered. "You want me to help you, then I'll help you all right."

She stomped into the bathroom, twisted the shower taps and tugged at her clothes. If she was staying just a few weeks more, she would help him get through this full moon and set him up for the next. But not the way he wanted. She'd demonstrate that he was not a werewolf, that there was no such thing, that he was and always had been a man. He had to capitalize on his fresh start and leave that delusion behind. When full moon came around - *or Waxing Moon or whatever* - she'd give him some pills all right. Just plain old paracetamol: a placebo. Whether he psychosomatically relaxed himself to sleep or whether he stormed about wondering why he wasn't sleepy - either way, he'd have to face the truth.

And they would face it together. That would be her gift to him. No matter what else happened between them, she was going to fix this about him.

You'll see, she told him silently as she closed the shower door and put her head under the water. *This full moon, you'll finally see. And you can be as free as I feel now.*

CHAPTER THIRTY-FIVE

By eight o'clock the background buzz of the Animal's restlessness pressed heavily enough on Jake's mind to drive him outdoors, while Gwen fussed about the kitchen. For a time he stood and watched the moon rise above the trees, sneaking up on the world from the side, as if it was *intending* to replace the setting sun. He paced the yard next, listening to crickets, listening to cows in the farm behind Gwen's property, waiting. The moon was a near-solid circle now as he had felt it would be. Gwen had a habit of dunking a cookie in coffee and nibbling off the edge; missing *its* edge, the moon looked like one of those cookies.

Jake paced some more, and waited some more. There wasn't much else to do for the next few hours. He would take Gwen's pills at eleven. The Change always came around midnight. He usually shot up earlier than eleven, but Gwen had told him an hour would be safe. Until then, there was nothing else to do.

He flirted with the idea of asking Gwen to play Uno, and that got the Animal talking about using her. He pushed Its voice away.

He was *not* like Eddie.

The pills were in a little bag in his jeans pocket. Maybe he should get Gwen to chain him up in the basement. Just for good measure. He'd suggested it, but she'd refused and said these pills would do the trick. She'd be safe. And so would he.

He had to trust her. It was weird to trust someone else with this. She didn't believe him, of course, and still wouldn't come morning because he would remain a man all night. The only way to prove the truth was to *not* take the pills

good! don't take them!

He closed his fingers around the pills. He was gonna take the damn things. He was! But what to do with all this energy? Usually he did pushups, sit-ups, sometimes went for a jog, just ran and ran and ran until it turned dark and he had to return to his

den

squat.

With the sun below the treeline and the temperature cooling, his thoughts turned to the approaching winter and he went round back of the house to the wood pile. The perfect way to work off some steam. He retrieved the ax from the shed. Gwen was watching him from the kitchen window. Perhaps she suspected he'd murder her.

blood! joy!

He waved with a tight smile and pointed to the woodpile. She vanished.

He doffed his shirt and started chopping. When it got full dark, he went inside and found a flashlight. He put it on the ground with the beam played on the wood. He chopped and chopped, trying to lose himself in the rhythm of the work. But the closer it got to midnight, the harder he had to concentrate on what he was doing, on not screaming and shouting and running around in circles or going into town and looking for a fight. This is why he shot up early most moons, when he couldn't stand the build-up anymore.

Finally, he tossed the ax aside and went inside. The kitchen clock said quarter after ten. He cursed, then took the stairs two at a time, ignoring Gwen's startled questions. He crashed into his room and slammed the door, dropped onto all fours and smashed out a hundred pushups. He switched to sit-ups, got to fifty, then went for a shower, running the water colder than he'd like.

Afterwards, he stood before the mirror naked. Something else lived beneath his skin - though he couldn't see anything, the pressure was building; the *something* strained for release, flexing.

soon

soon

He'd seen It coming once, standing like this before a different mirror, naked and afraid, without drugs or booze to dampen its onset.

In shock and terror, he had watched the transformation snaking beneath his skin, muscles and joints twisting and bulging.

He pulled on shirt, shorts, pants - the rattle of the pills vial made him dig one hand into the pocket. Whether it was eleven o'clock or not, he couldn't wait any longer. He popped the two pills - they were bitter on his tongue - and scooped enough water into his mouth to swallow them. Didn't want them sticking in his throat. Would two be enough? Gwen said she had more.

Once again, there was nothing to do but wait.

Wait and hopefully find himself on the nods very soon.

Gwen forced herself to remain seated as Jake came downstairs. She'd heard the creaking of the floor, the water running. He'd changed into track pants and a long-sleeved tee. The sleeves were down as if he were still self-conscious about his track marks. As if it mattered with her anymore. He was grim-faced and antsy, his stride jerky. When he reached the bottom, he veered off to the kitchen via the hallway and drank two glasses of water. Then he stomped into the living room, avoiding her gaze, pacing again.

Now this was junkie behavior. This was the kind of withdrawal she'd been expecting earlier in the month.

Or it's anxiety.

"Chillax," she said, tossing her novel aside and rising from the couch. She checked the time on the mantelpiece. Just gone eleven. "You took the pills? Both of them? Good. Then all you have to do is sit down and—" she shrugged "—chillax."

"What the hell's chillax? Stop sayin' that."

"Jake. How're you going to fall asleep marching around like that? Come here. Lie down here." She pointed to the rug in front of the fire place. It wasn't yet cold enough to burn anything, but in a month, they'd be glad for all the wood he'd chopped.

No: Jake *will be glad. I'll be in Detroit.*

"What for?" He moved further away from her, over to the window, studying the darkness beyond the glass.

"I'll give you a back rub. Settle you down." He looked at her. God, but his eyes were ablaze! She held an index finger up. "Not coming on to you. This is in my capacity as a medical professional only, Mister."

He slumped his shoulders with a *hmph*. He strode to the rug and dropped, his cheek on his hands.

She placed her feet either side of his hips and sat on his ass. He grunted. She play-slapped his shoulder.

"No getting ideas, okay? You're to go to sleep."

His clothing stuck to him in a few places, glued there with water. He hadn't dried fully after taking the shower. Or he was starting to sweat. She couldn't tell. She reached forward and dug her fingers into each trapezius - or tried to. They were hard as tire rubber. She persisted, moving around to his teres and lats.

After a few minutes, he relaxed a tiny bit. At least he wasn't as stressed as he had been. His breathing slowed. He shifted beneath her ministrations a couple of times in quick succession, and made a noise of pleasure. The metronome of the mantel clock lulled her, doling out the meter of her movements.

At eleven-forty-three, a tremor rippled along Jake's back. His legs jerked and he sucked air hard, as if he'd been pricked with something.

"Wha...?" he cried and bucked her off.

She came up on her haunches, startled. Offended. "What the hell, Jake?"

He pushed up onto hands and knees, shaking his head as if dis-lodging a fly. "No. No, this is wrong." He flipped onto his back, head narrowly missing the brick step of the fireplace. Hand on his belly, knees drawing up - she wondered if he'd done something to strain the gunshot wound.

He was cutting wood pretty hard out there.

Another spasm and he was in the fetal position, gasping for air. She shifted closer, reached for him. His eyes popped open, wild and wide. His lips peeled back from his teeth and a hand whipped out at hers, fingers clamping around her wrist like a vice.

He snarled at her, "What did you do?"

"What did you *do*, Gwen?!"

He screamed it this time and she recoiled, toppling as he released her wrist. He pushed himself to his feet. Seconds earlier, he'd been drifting, relaxing. Then *It* had returned, swimming up from beneath his languid thoughts: the thrumming, the vibration in his blood, the echo of Gwen's heartbeat behind and above him, slightly out of sync with his.

And the first pain had struck.

Another hit him now, merciless as a stab wound, rocking him back against the hearth. One bare sole slipped against the bricks and he almost went down, but he caught himself on the mantel. The clock went flying. A picture frame shattered.

A compost taste punched up out of his throat to sting his tongue and singe his nostrils. He coughed, half choked. "No, no, *no!*"

He lurched toward the door. He had to get *away*. Vivid images sprang up, misting his vision: ripping, breaking; bones and meat and tendons and

blood!

Gwen was a smudge in his peripheral vision, cowering against a bookcase, a hand over her mouth.

And then he was out of the living room and crashing into the front door.

Locked!

He fumbled with the chain, the lock, the chain again. It was too close. His hands began curling arthritically, palms pulsing. He couldn't get a grip on the metal links. He smacked the door with the heels of his hands. Again. Again. Again. The door shuddered. Gwen sobbed his name. Another pain, spiking out from his chest along both arms, tendrils of fire shooting up into the freshly massaged shoulder muscles. He splayed against the door, yowling.

The back door! He hadn't locked it when he'd come inside. He darted that way, but cramps bent his legs. He slipped on the hallway runner, fell, piling into the shelves that lined the wall. Stuff fell on him. His skin boiled, breath keen and scalding like tabasco. He writhed, trying to find his feet, and succeeded only in roping the runner around his knees. He was bigger, shirt seams cutting into his shoulders.

Gwen was framed in the kitchen doorway. Gwen, his lover, his
betrayer!
enemy!
food!
kill!
"No!" He'd meant to shout it but it came out in a huff, like a bark.
Friend! he told the Animal. *Friend!*

He dragged himself along the hall. A nail popped off; he hissed at
the sweetness of it. Gwen's voice cawed tunelessly. She retreated into
the kitchen. His body swelled and stretched. His straining shirt gave.
The very air came alive to him. It carried a world of information: pines
and maples and apple trees. Paint and perfume and soap. Distant cattle
and burned pork chops from dinner and other kinds of
meat!

The agony stopped him an arm's length from the back door as his
pants split down both thighs, and then his face split, his skull. He
threshed about on his back.

"Gwen! Please!" but his words were just noise.

The night curdled. Yellow. Gray.

Then the world was gone.

CHAPTER THIRTY-SIX

It was cold and it was morning, the light soft with the sun a mere hint behind the clouds along the horizon. Jake blinked at the flat gray sky for some time until he realized he was shivering. He was naked, with blood on his hands and mouth, his chin and chest. His skin was stiff and sticky with it. No body lay nearby, but there was flesh between two of his bottom teeth. He picked it free, gagged at the sight. Puked until nothing came out.

He couldn't look at the mess on the grass, in case there was something of Gwen's in it, an earring or a patch of her hair. Like the animal he was, he scrambled away on all fours. He wrenched a clump of grass out by the roots, rubbed it against his chest and throat and chin, then scooped a handful of soil and repeated. But he wouldn't have gotten all of the blood off. It clung to him like shame.

The pile of puke sat in the grass, the stink fit to make him heave again.

Don't look at it.

"Have to," he groaned.

Can't. Don't want to!

But *want* had nothing to do with it. So he did.

No jewelry. Nothing that would indicate … Gwen. Before the tension could drain out of him, a thought hit him: it didn't mean he hadn't done it.

His chest swelled with grief, with terror, forcing a desolate cry from between his lips to scare a couple of crows from a nearby tree. What had she done? Why hadn't the drugs she'd given him worked?

The two questions played over and over like the squeaking of a rusty merry-go-round. She'd known what she'd done; instinctively he believed this. He'd seen a wince in her expression as she'd watched him bring the ax to the woodpile; not fear of him, he understood now, but worry for him, and maybe a little guilt too.

"What now? What now? What now?" He found himself on his feet, moaning, breathing shallow. The shivering had lessened, overwhelmed by adrenaline. There were scratches on his shoulder and his hands. They hadn't been there yesterday, but they had scabbed over, already looking a few days old. The bullet hole in his gut was a pucker of scar.

He tried to get his bearings as the light grew stronger. Around him towered a huddle of jack pines, but fields were visible down the hill. He took a couple of stumbling steps down the slope until he saw a windmill. He knew that windmill. The sun coming up *there*, the windmill was *there* and that line of trees - yeah, that was the road. And over that fence four hundred yards to his left and up the next slope, was the boundary with Gwen's property.

Voices drifted up the other side of the hill - stressed-out male voices calling to each other. The farmer. Maybe one of his sons. Jake thought he understood then, the gristle in his teeth, the blood, their strained shouts: they were looking for the predator that had taken one of their cows. Maybe.

He ran toward her house until the voices fell away, then dropped into a trudge, in no hurry to see what he feared most.

The merry-go-round squeak in his mind started at him again: why had she let him Change? What in hell had gone wrong? As he carefully navigated the barbed wire of the fence, it came to him that he had the question the wrong way round. He should have been asking why *he'd* let it happen. Why he hadn't done what he'd always done? He had money. And there had to be someone in town who'd sell him junk.

Why had she let him Change?

Why had he left it to her?

It seemed like a moment later, he was at another fence. The deep stretch of backyard behind her house was before him. Did he have to go there? Did he want to go there?

Want had nothing to do with it.

Wood chips jabbed his feet as he traversed the litter from last night's frantic chopping. He felt the impacts only distantly. His johnson had shrunk real small, his balls pulled up tight beneath it - whether that was because of the coolness of the wind or the terror in his gut, he wasn't sure. What was left of the back door shifted uneasily in the breeze upon a single intact hinge. He picked his way across broken wood and glass and ventured a step inside.

He heard nothing but the moan of the wind, a distant lowing of cows, the rumble of a tractor farther off. Deep scratches grooved the hallway floor. The dresser had been knocked away from the wall, partially blocking the way, the torn runner scrunched around it. The kitchen looked intact. But the scrapes in the floor led toward the living room.

"God, no," he whispered. "Please."

He took one step and stopped. Six more and he'd be able to see into the living room. A seventh and he'd be in it. Then he'd know; there'd be no more guessing and wondering and fearing, just cold hard reality. Making his way to the living room was like walking through water.

Gwen sat in her mother's chair. She'd been crying, but she didn't look scared, she didn't look sad. If anything, she looked mad.

Her being mad was good. Her not-being-torn-to-bloody-pieces was real good.

The rifle in her hands wasn't so good.

She stared at him, not at his eyes or his face, but at his chest, somewhere near his left nipple. There was dried blood there, a stain his scrubbing hadn't removed. Her mouth worked for a moment, then her lips pressed tight. The rifle shifted, not pointing straight at him, but near enough for her to shift it and shoot him dead if he so much as moved.

Eddie's words came back to him: *You think any one of those "innocent" people wouldn't try'n kill you, Jake? If they saw you as you really are? If they had a gun in their hands?*

With a strange peace washing through him, he sagged against the door frame and wished she would.

He was naked and Gwen marveled obscurely at how quickly perspectives could change. Wearing Barry's shirt open at the front, she'd wanted him. At the end of a night of cards and drinks, she'd wanted him. Now completely nude, he couldn't be less sexy if he tried. Mud and grass seeds stuck to his legs and arms; cuts and scratches marked his inner wrists. The cold wind had given his skin the appearance of a plucked chicken and shrunk his pecker. Blood had dried, rust-colored, around his mouth, throat and upper chest.

He followed her gaze and put a hand over the blood below his collar bone. His voice was hollow, dulled, exhausted. "It was a cow, Gwen. Just a cow."

What amazed her most was how detached she felt right then, as if she were back in middle school theater class, rehearsing a play. From the back of her mind someone fed her a line and she repeated it.

"You were telling the truth."

He cupped his groin. "It's okay."

Did he think she was apologizing? Hell, no. Someone fed her the next line and she delivered it. "It's not okay. It's wrong and insane and it's the morning after the worst moment of my life."

"But I didn't hurt you." His eyes raked up and down, a small crease appearing in his forehead. "Did I?"

Line?

"Depends. Physically? As you can see I'm hale and hearty. Psychologically? When the shock wears off, I'll probably commit myself. Tomorrow, I'll be the one being sedated."

He slid down the doorframe to a crouch. His skin made a kind of fingers-on-blackboard squeal that he didn't seem to notice. His hands hung between his legs, affording him modesty. "Why didn't you?"

"What?"

"Why didn't you sedate me?"

No. He was reading from a different script to hers. She'd done nothing wrong. There was no apology in her version. And she was the one in charge of the conversation, not him.

"So the choices in front of me are pretty simple. I shoot you and call the cops. I call the cops without shooting you. Or I could call Animal Control." The joke had sounded lame when she'd practiced it a few times in the small hours, but she delivered it with aplomb worthy of the finest stand up comedian.

"What'll you tell them when they come? The cops."

Line?

"That you attacked me."

"I … attacked you?" He looked confused and well he might. By all rights, she should be dead. The *thing* that he'd become, the *thing* that had been inside him all these weeks, that thing could have ripped her sixteen ways from Sunday. She'd been without a prayer as it chased her into the living room. It had stood above her as she'd crashed into this very chair and crumpled into a heap. Its warm, rancid breath had clogged her nostrils. She had been moments from death. And then its yellow eyes widened and it snorted like a startled horse, and it clattered back out along the hallway and smashed the back door like a cheap Hollywood prop and left her broken in spirit and wallowing in her own snot and tears and urine.

Her trigger hand dropped to brush her pants. The pee had dried. But her mother's chair was ruined, and the smell remained to remind her it had all been real.

As if the chunks torn from the floor and the shattered door weren't evidence enough.

"Did I attack you?" he asked again.

"Near enough," she whispered.

"I'm a danger to you," he said. "Do it."

She stuck her finger through the trigger guard, curved it around the comforting cool steel. She aimed it at his heart. "I could, you know."

Do no harm.

Shut the hell up.

His shoulders rose and fell in a long, deep breath. "You should. I can go. I've done a lot of good lately. I might have erased my sins. I can go."

The peace in his eyes frightened her. A tiny smile curled his lips. He wanted this?

"You've done good? What good? You almost killed me. You - that thing—"

She choked on fresh emotion and swallowed it hard.

Not in the script.

"But I didn't," he said. "I *knew* you. Didn't I? I couldn't hurt you coz I knew you."

Was that what that widening of the monster's eyes had meant? The snort? That was recognition? She smelled like *friend*? Or *mate*?

More questions strobed through her mind. Did he think at all when he'd turned monster? How much control did he have? Why didn't he remember? What the hell was going on?

Her voice came out in a stage whisper. "Are you a monster or a man?" *Is the man outside the monster or the monster inside the man?*

Misery stole the peace from his eyes, chased the ghostly smile away. "Both. Neither. I don't know. I don't care anymore. I just want to go." He leaned forward and placed a fist on the floor for balance. "If you don't shoot me, even if you get me put in jail, I'll hurt someone tonight. And tomorrow night, too, if they don't kill me tomorrow. If your drugs don't work, there's no way to stop it. You have to shoot me, not just for me, but to protect other folks."

That wouldn't happen, though. She'd tell the police what she'd seen, what he was. They'd lock him up good and tight on his own.

Only they wouldn't. They wouldn't believe her any more than she'd believed him. She'd get referred to therapy or at least asked if she'd been drinking. He'd be on the loose; someone could get killed.

She tightened her grip on the rifle.

Do no harm.

He tensed, preparing to leap at her. To pretend to leap at her.

He's forcing my hand.

"No!" she cried and swept the barrel up toward the ceiling. "I won't!"

He collapsed, face on the floor. And broke into huge, wracking sobs that shook his body like a doll in a dog's mouth.

Gwen watched him stone-faced, eschewing the instinct to comfort. She put the safety on and lowered the rifle and waited. When the sobs subsided, she reached down to the folded blanket by her chair. She used it on nights when she stayed up late reading. She realized she'd shivered through the early hours of this night without giving a thought. She tossed it toward him. He dragged it closer without lifting his head.

"What am I gonna do, Gwen?" he asked, his voice muffled.

Her heart thawed a little at the forlorn note. "What will get you through tonight?"

He gathered the blanket about him as he rolled onto his back, eyes scrunched tight, the filth on his skin streaked by tears.

"Drugs," he said quietly. "Like I said. Anything that'll calm me down, knock me out."

"Booze?"

"I'd need a lot of it and it might not work. Something stronger. That's why I use heroin."

"Morphine." She kneaded the tension from her cheeks, thinking.

He sat up, his back to her. "And you need to lock me in the cellar and leave for the night. Go stay at Richard's or somethin'. Come back after dawn."

"Cellar?"

"In case. You need a thick padlock for the door." His head shifted to acknowledge the dresser just visible in the hall. "And shove that in front of it. Maybe brace it with two-by-four. I'll take everything valuable from down there first. Put some meat in there; it might keep me calm. I don't really know. I ... I black out when I'm ... when I Change."

God, they were discussing werewolf stuff. *She* was discussing werewolf stuff. She felt like an inductee into a different universe. "My cellar?"

"Unless you know somewhere stronger I can't break out of."

"I'll give it some thought." She would give it a *lot* of thought. Right now she was still thinking a police cell would be quite strong enough. "So nothing will happen to you during the day?"

He shook his head, snugged the blanket tighter, stifled a yawn. "Round midnight. Like ... like last night."

"Okay then. You need sleep." So did she, but she wouldn't be able to, would she? He was used to this; she wasn't. "I'll head into town, get the stuff you need." And try to explain to Richard why she couldn't work today.

Sick. I'm sick today, Richard. Sick in the head. I'm convinced my boyfriend's a werewolf.

No, not sick in the head: she had the empirical evidence of a broken door and scratched floors to prove it.

Jake slunk up the stairs. Left Gwen sitting alone in a half-destroyed house, one floor down from a mythical creature that could have killed her.

But he didn't. He didn't kill me.

She didn't know what to make of that.

CHAPTER THIRTY-SEVEN

"And there you have it."

Carter broke off. He had more to say, of course, but he'd been talking for twenty minutes straight according to the clock to the side of the couch - placed there, he was sure, so Pastor Gillis's counseling clients could see how long they were keeping him. Twenty minutes, and the whole *blessed* time, Pastor Gillis had been nodding like one of those bobble head dolls. The man even looked like one: skinny body, pencil neck, head too large. He watched the Adam's apple bob up and down and nearly rupture the throat's taut skin. No wonder that huge head was bobbing so much; it was a wonder he could ever get in balance.

"Well, that's very good," Gillis said, his voice a noncommittal murmur. "I think you're ready for that job I mentioned to you." Slight emphasis on *think*.

"The drugstore. Yes. I am ready for that." He forced enthusiasm into his voice and smile. Anything was better than nothing. An income would mean a further step in the direction of normalcy, allowing for phone contracts, paid utility bills and eventually an access visit to Elijah.

"So let me repeat what I'm hearing to see if I have this right. You no longer believe a werewolf took Beth's life."

Carter bowed his head in contrition. What a silly thing to believe.

"You've forgiven whatever did do it."

"Correct, Pastor. It was just an animal and I've let it go. I'm sleeping better, eating better, thinking better. Wish I'd gotten this straight months ago."

Gillis made a face as if to say *Don't we all?* "I'm certainly hearing peace in your tone of voice. It was good to see you in church last weekend. And it's good to know you're praying again, having morning devotions."

Another little lie. But for a good cause. Another step closer to his son. He forced some piety into his tone. "Beth would have wanted that."

In fact, Beth had been the only one who'd ever gotten him to do it. And Beth was gone.

Gillis scribbled in his notes, sucked the end of his pen and read through what he'd written. Carter endured it with a beatific smile, hands clasped on his lap, the model of sobriety. The clock was one of those 1970s digitals with the number panels that flipped over. As he watched, two flaps clicked over, taking him from 9:29 to 9:30.

Gillis made a satisfied noise. "Well, I have morning service in thirty minutes, so we'd better wrap this up. I'm very happy with your progress, Carter. Let's see how the work goes for a week or two and then we'll catch up again. All going well, I should be able to write a favorable report for the court. Get you on your way to your first access visit." He stood and placed the file face down on his desk. "If you'd like to wait here where it's comfortable, I'll telephone Ron from the other room and tee up that work for you."

Carter offered a thumbs-up, his face serious and grateful until Gillis had left. Why'd the guy have to make the call in another room when there was a perfectly good phone right there on his desk?

Probably has some reservations and warnings he needs to pass on to "Ron" without me hearing.

Whatever. As long as he kept moving in the right direction, he could take as much of this bullshit as Gillis insisted on.

"Just don't expect too big a tithe from me this morning, Pastor," he mumbled.

Bored, cagey, he stood and stretched his back. The bed was uncomfortable without Beth, badly weighted. Lately he'd found himself singing the refrain from an old Police song. *The bed's too big without you.* He hummed it under his breath, bent sideways one way, then the other. There was a newspaper on Gillis's desk, folded neatly and lined up exactly with the desk edge. He unfolded it, intending to flip to the job ads. He'd be damned if he'd work for minimum wage if something better was out there begging for his particular skillset.

He froze at the front page. In the corner was one of those teasers, a headline intended to attract a would-be purchaser.

Wolfman sighting: no bull - full report page 5.

In his haste turning to page 5, he tore a corner. He didn't care. He didn't care if he tore the whole damn paper. He didn't care if Gillis came back in now and saw him standing with one hand tapping his forehead, panting like the very madman he'd been pretending not to be. He didn't care that the words *Holy Shit* kept coming out of his mouth in a church office. Earlier that morning, a dairy farmer in Carrington, Michigan, had seen a creature chowing down on one of his two prize bulls. He'd thought it a bear - maybe an escaped pet or circus animal - and fired a gun to scare it, but when he'd shone a light its way, he'd seen a creature out of a horror movie. The man had shot at it, scaring it off, but the farmer had hightailed it in the other direction, hoping it didn't change its mind. An expert from some "Parisian Werewolf Center" had commented that it was probably wildlife mistaken for a supernatural creature in the predawn light, but there remained the possibility the farmer was right. "These ancient legends were based on something in reality," the expert said. "A bear, or even a cougar if they still existed in Michigan, would need a far greater bite radius and jaw pressure to get past a bull's thick neck." Local parks officers said a pack of wild dogs may have been responsible and laughed off rumors of the Michigan Dogman.

Carter read it a second time. He could hear Gillis negotiating conditions in the other room.

Carrington, Michigan. Couldn't be far from Detroit. Brennan was still alive.

Or not. Tim had said there were many theryons.

Either way, he had to be sure. Because tonight was a full moon, and if Brennan was alive, and Carter still had a pistol with silver bullets, perhaps there was a reason for that. Perhaps God was actually on his side. The town would only be a few hours' drive. But there was little gas in his tank. The Church had been happy to swing him $20 a week plus a big food parcel, but he'd need more. And how the hell was he going to track down Brennan without a Hunter to guide him?

It hit him then: he didn't need help. He knew exactly what to do.

Screw it.

Gillis's jacket was on the back of his office chair. Carter unclipped the cross from the lapel. Gillis's wallet was in the inside pocket. Carter took out sixty dollars and kept rifling until he came upon the chaplain's card. He put the cash, the card and the pin in his shirt pocket and slipped the wallet back in the jacket. He straightened it, folded the newspaper as neatly as he could and went to stand by the door.

When Gillis returned three long minutes later, Carter, sweating with the effort of standing still and looking sane, barely heard a word he said. He took the proffered slip of paper with the drugstore's address and slipped it into his shirt pocket, hoped with a start that Gillis hadn't seen the booty he'd tucked there already.

But Gillis was already moving toward his desk.

"Well, thank you," Carter said. "Thank you again, Pastor." He fought to keep his speech normal. He stuck out a hand and Gillis gripped it limply. "Eight a.m. Monday, you said."

"Eight a.m." Gillis raised a finger like a parent. "Don't be late."

Condescending little rat.

Carter laughed politely. "No sirree."

He couldn't get out of there quick enough. He needed to dig up the pistol he'd buried beside the garage. After that, he'd fill up the tank, check the map and head off to Carrington, Michigan. To unfinished business.

CHAPTER THIRTY-EIGHT

At eleven o'clock, with her bladder fit to burst, Gwen decided she should move. Leaving the chair was like leaving the womb: moving meant entering a new world, a new reality. She took a change of clothes into her bathroom, locked the door and shoved a towel rail and an oil heater in front of it. She relieved herself, then ran the shower hot and slumped against the tiles, weeping silently on and off for a long time. Afterwards, she brushed some life back into her hair, scrubbed her teeth, applied makeup and assessed the affect.

Good enough.

Her outfit was casual, comfortable, neat: her oldest jeans, a light knit sweater, bobby socks.

Swallowing the lump in her throat, breathing through her mouth, Gwen forced back panic. It had been real. This was all real.

The upper floor creaked above her, the noise cutting through the silence. Walking fast, she grabbed keys, purse and phone, then raced to the car, gripped by an irrational terror that he would come roaring outside and try to stop her.

She pulled the door shut and drove the lock down with her elbow, sat sucking in air as she watched the porch. There was no sign of him. When he'd been that *thing* last night, he hadn't hurt her. Why did she expect him to now?

She started the car and put it in gear.

Gwen drove around the outskirts of town and then out again, lost in a gray malaise. She drove so slowly that a hay baler had to pass her. The dash clock told her she'd been out of the house for two hours. She could barely remember anything of that, apart from the phone ringing a couple of times and buzzing with SMS alerts.

Her knuckles were white on the steering wheel. Her life, her reality, had been turned upside down. Turned upside down, but not like a picture that if you turned it around twice it would be back the way it started. No, this was more like a carton of eggs that if turned over once got cracked a little then got turned again and *slammed hard onto the bench so that they CRACKED AND SMASHED AND YOLK RAN OUT AND THERE WAS NO WAY TO UNSMASH THEM...*

A flash of hair, teeth, muzzle. Fetid breath. The growl rumbling in its throat. Saliva dripping from its muzzle. The widening of its eyes as it leaned in for the kill - *it knew me!* - and the clatter of its - *his* - claws as it scrabbled across the timber floor before smashing through the back door.

She shook herself, clamping down on the panic.

There were werewolves.

Maybe other crazy things existed also, fictional things, mythical things.

Maybe the girl who jumped off that roof really was a superhero. Maybe she died fighting her arch nemesis in defense of the city.

Maybe those kids sleeping in coffins really were Dracula's spawn.

Maybe there really was a heaven and a hell, like Jake believed.

Her vision misted but she blinked the tears away. She pushed terror and grief and despair down inside and kept on pushing, deeper and deeper until she could cover them with sheer perverse doggedness.

She had a decision to make. She had to face it, and make it.

Should she give him up, turn him in?

Hi, Officers. My boyfriend gets a little violent around full moon. Perhaps you could lock him up for the night?

It seemed like the smart thing to do, but it also seemed like betrayal. He trusted her. In reality, Jake was the victim of a *condition*.

What's that oath I took about doing no harm?

So was turning Jake in doing him harm, or was it doing the world good?

Another car came up behind her fast, swerving around her at the last second, a couple of kids broadcasting hostility as if she had ruined their day.

Do no harm, Doctor.

Never had she felt so alone and powerless.

And then it came to her that, yes, she had felt exactly this powerless before, the memory exploding from the deep waters of her past like a shark attack. She was nine years old, back at her grandpop's house in Grand Rapids. Her parents weren't around, just her and Lauren. The old man lay in the hallway, clutching at his sternum and gasping for breath. She had no idea what to do. While Lauren rang 911 and ran outside to wait for the ambulance, Gwen knelt at her pop's side, watching as he fell quiet, turned blue. Powerless Gwen - ignorant, *stupid, weak Gwen!*

She pulled over, threw the car into park and stared into her psyche, allowing the revelations to wash over her. At the sixth anniversary of the old man's death, a week before her sixteenth birthday, she'd vowed to find ways to help people. She was going to be a doctor. But it had never really dawned on her how *bad* she had felt at the time - not the grief, not the fear, they were no-brainers. It was the impotence, the feeling of being just plain dumb - these things had been buried beneath the more immediate roil of emotion and had never been put into words, had never been allowed into the light.

Until now.

Gwen Cheevey was a doctor because she couldn't stand not knowing What To Do. She had studied and practiced to become an expert on What To Do. She had embraced the ER, a constant barrage of new and novel and sometimes terrifying emergencies so she could prove over and over that she was up to the challenge, that she was *enough.*

The death of little Willie Anderson had shaken that, she saw now. But Jake had immediately presented her with an opportunity to redeem herself. And redeem herself she had: he'd been doing fine until she outsmarted herself with that placebo.

And now?

Now, you have to admit you've done all you can for him and that it's not enough, it won't cure him. You have to accept that's okay. His ... condition... is beyond you. That doesn't make you less a doctor. It just makes him more needy.

She pressed her thumbs to her swollen eyes. "That poor bastard."

A monster he might be, deep within, below his humanity. On nights where the big moon took him. But she couldn't imagine his pain. His loneliness.

His helplessness.

She left her bag in the car, taking just keys and cell with her. She checked her messages as she walked to the clinic. Seven *Where are you*s from Richard and Cate. One from Janey about Jake. Richard and Cate had sounded concerned. Janey sounded pissed.

Cate looked up as Gwen breached the clinic doors. The seats were about half full, which was busy for a Sunday.

What, is there a full moon or some—?

She made herself look as apologetic as possible as she veered off to her office.

She called Janey and launched into an elaborate lie about Jake being ill and her phone being disconnected for some reason and all the troubles she'd had with the phone company all morning. Cate slipped in towards the end of the call, while Gwen weathered a torrent of invective about Jake losing his job if he couldn't be more responsible than this. Gwen held the receiver away from her ear and made a face. Cate didn't smile. When Janey paused for breath, Gwen said, "Once again, I apologize on his behalf, and I have to go. Very busy over here. Thanks, Janey."

She put the phone down before Janey could reply and put on the apologetic face again.

"Where've you been, Doctor?"

"Very sick today."

Cate's eyes narrowed. "You *and* Jake?"

Too exhausted for diplomacy, Gwen said, "We live in the same house, Cate. Not in the same bedroom."

Cate flinched.

"Anyway, I'm sorry about all the patients. Richard must be really peeved."

"Peeved's not the half of it," Cate muttered. She didn't seem at all interested in Gwen's apparent lack of symptoms.

"I just have to get a prescription pad and some other stuff, then I'm off home again." She slid open a drawer while she spoke. She hadn't been in since Thursday and there were three letters on the desk - one from Detroit Receiving.

Oh, God, that's all I need.

"Doctor. Listen, it's weird. I just had a pastor here looking for Jake. And—"

"A pastor? From the Baptist church?"

"Er, no, he wasn't from here. He was from Rockford near Chicago. His name was Gillies, something like that."

Illinois? What did that mean?

She pocketed the prescription pad. "What did he want?"

"He said Jake's mom died."

Gwen gripped the back of her chair and tried to keep her expression neutral. Both Jake's parents were dead - wasn't that what he'd said? It had sounded like they'd died when he was little. And his accent definitely wasn't Chicago. "What did you tell this guy? What did he look like?"

Cate wrapped her cardigan around herself. "I didn't tell him anything. But he had a photo. It ... It was you and Jake on a street somewhere. Looked like you just kissed him. Or something."

"Cate! What. Did. He. Look. Like."

Cate folded her arms tighter as she described a thin guy in his late thirties.

The vague description was meaningless to Gwen, which was a relief: it wasn't Barrow. But who the hell was it? What other religious people did Jake know? Had he lied about his mother? Her head ached with the pressure of it all.

"I'll tell Jake tonight. Did the pastor say where he was staying?"

"No, but—"

"Doesn't matter. We'll look into it. Thanks, Cate." She picked up her mail and feigned interest in hopes Cate would take the hint and get out of her way.

"There's something else. There was this *other* guy came in about an hour before the pastor."

Gwen froze. "*Other* guy?"

"When I was coming on duty he was asking Margaret about Jake and showing her the same photo. He was…" She shivered. "I dunno. Creepy."

"Was he about this tall, in his forties, green eyes?"

"That's the guy. You know him?"

Gwen shouldered past her, a ringing like tinnitus building in her ears as she ran for her car.

CHAPTER THIRTY-NINE

Carter arrived in Carrington just after two. He started asking questions with the photo in his hand at one end of Main Street. At the third store, a teenage employee said he knew both Brennan *and* the lady in the photo: a doctor at the clinic behind the hospital. Brennan, he said, worked in the hospital kitchen.

"Nice guy," said the shop assistant. "That sucks about his mom."

Carter followed the guy's directions and drove around to the hospital. He tried the clinic on the off chance it was open Sundays. It was, but the female doctor, Gwen Cheevey, wasn't in - though she should have been, the receptionist said.

His chaplain ID card gained him access to the kitchen manager, happy for the opportunity to complain about Brennan's tardiness she emptied scraps. He thanked her, ignoring her perfunctory "God bless" as he stepped into the service corridor. He wandered, finally locating the admin area. Possibly Brennan and Cheevey taking the same day off meant they lived together. Maybe they were both at home right now. The doctor would be a problem: he didn't want to hurt her.

But she wasn't going to stop him.

With most admin staff away for the weekend, he was able to search several offices unmolested until he found the personnel files, grateful they still kept hard copies in a filing cabinet. Brennan's manila folder was in his hands two minutes later, the home address staring from the page like a challenge.

And now, like Elvis, I leave the building. The thought had him chuckling all the way back to his car. He was unlocking the door when a comradely shout made him stiffen.

"Hey, buddy! Don't I know you?"

The voice was friendly enough, and Carter relaxed a notch as he turned. A middle-aged man was approaching fast, his face split in a big smile. He was broad-shouldered and muscular beneath his dress shirt and chinos, but he wasn't Brennan.

Carter returned the smile quizzically. "I don't think so."

The guy stopped less than an arm's length away. He rubbed his stubbly chin as he squinted at Carter, then snapped his fingers. "I remember now. You're the guy who shot up my ride."

Shot up—?

The punch slammed into Carter's gut like a hammer. His breath fled in a whoosh and the world turned a bright white.

His attacker lowered him into a squat against the car and said, "The woman in the kitchen said you were looking for Jake Brennan. What's your interest in him?"

Carter's lungs refused to let air in. Tears misted his vision. But he gave the man the best *screw you* face he could muster. A hand clamped around his throat and squeezed. Carter clawed at the iron fingers and they did release, but only long enough to reattach to his shirt. The man lifted him to his feet, shook him like a throw rug and threw him chest-first into the car. Another punch battered his lowest right rib. In blessed relief, his breath came back in a rush. He pushed off the car and turned on wobbly legs, his arms up like a boxer. The guy had backed just out of reach, his arms hanging loosely, hands open. Blood pounded in Carter's temples and his stomach spasmed again, sucking him in on himself until he had to place his hands on knees to stay upright.

"I'll ask again," the man said. "What's your interest in Jake Brennan?"

"What's yours?" Carter got out.

The man backhanded him, the crack of the blow like a bowl breaking on tiles. Next Carter knew, his legs were sideways and he was trying to hold his face out of the dirt with both hands while his vision speckled. He now understood where the expression *seeing stars* came from.

"Next smartass answer gets you a boot in the ear. One after that, I take you for a joyride and apply some pliers to your nuts. You want that?"

This guy had killed Tim. But why? Who was he? Why was he protecting Brennan?

"He killed my wife!" Bile came up with the words. Carter spat it at the man's boots.

His attacker didn't flinch. But he straightened. Carter craned his neck up at him, expecting the boot to come anyway, trying to get in a position to anticipate and dodge. But the man was eyeing him speculatively.

"Your wife was that little church do-gooder. In Rockford." The man laughed and dropped onto one knee. "You been chasing him over that?"

That laugh again: mocking, inhuman. Carter wanted to thrust a hand in the man's gut and rip out his intestines.

"You been chasing the wrong man, Einstein. Yeah, gape like a fish at me all you like, but it's the truth. Wasn't Jake who killed your do-gooder wife." He winked. "Guess who?"

Rage boiled up out of the maw in his soul left by Beth's death. Hot bloodlust lit him up, flooded his limbs. "You!"

Carter made it halfway up before a punch sent him spinning into the car door. His teeth clacked together and stars flared in his vision again. He tried to catch himself against the metal and failed, ended up where he'd started on the ground. Except now the ground was tilting slowly to the right and it was all he could do to throw out a hand and stop it from engulfing him.

"You wanna try me? C'mon, then, try me now." His attacker was so close, spittle hit Carter in the eye.

The bloodlust still burned bright but no matter how he tried, Carter couldn't find his feet, couldn't stop the world from sliding, couldn't even get a decent breath.

"All you Hunters are the same up close and personal: slack-muscled, wet-eyed pussies. What are you without your little pop-guns?"

That confirmed it. This guy was … was a …

"What's that, pussy? You want your little silver spitwads? Well, lemme help you out. Lemme find your bang-bang for you."

Carter found himself face down on the ground with a knee in his back while his attacker frisked him. The man was strong, an irrepressible force. When he found no gun, the weight in Carter's back lifted. It was all Carter could do to lift his head and suck oxygen. His rage bled away as he tried to get his lungs working properly.

"Must be in the car, huh? Well, here's how it's gonna go: you catch your breath—" he slapped Carter lightly on the back of the head "—I'll search your car. Then I'm gonna take it and drop it off a bridge somewhere it'll get nice and wet and rusty. Meantime, I'll leave you something to worry about." Horrifically, the man's face began to stretch and tremble. His jaw thickened and his teeth elongated. Carter barely kept control of his bladder as he jerked his head away and tried to rise.

The knee returned to his back. The man - *the wolf!* - wrapped vice-like fingers around one arm and sank his teeth into Carter's wrist. Carter cried out. The man-wolf spat in the wound and suddenly the pressure was gone. Carter scrabbled away, injured hand clutched to his chest.

The man's face was perfectly normal again, as if it had been a nightmare, a drug trip. He opened the car door. "You know the way it works," he said. "Now you're one of the club. Or one of the cubs. In about nine hours, we'll see how you like it on the other side of the—"

"Hey! What's going on there?"

The shout came from the far end of the laneway toward Main Street. Six farmers and a couple of teenage boys were approaching. Carter's attacker cursed, then started backstepping. He winked again at Carter. "Be seeing you again," he said, and bolted.

Three men helped Carter to his feet while the others jogged after the wolf-in-man's-clothing. "You all right, bud?" asked one.

Carter couldn't answer. The bite hurt worse than his gut, but the physical pain was nothing compared to the terror engulfing him.

Full moon tonight. In about nine hours…

"Hey, he's a pastor," one of the men said, pointing at the cross in Carter's lapel. "That sumbitch was beating up a pastor."

"We should find him," said another.

"Jay, go get the cops."

Carter shook them off, waved away their concern and weaved through them. He slumped into the driver's seat and fumbled the keys into the ignition.

"Where ya going, padre?"

"Yeah, we should get you to the clinic, make sure you're okay."

"Fine. I'm fine." He wasn't sure if they heard the words. They came out like air from a seat-cushion. He shut the door, banishing their concern to the outside world, started the car and lurched it away.

He pulled the car out of the lot and around a corner, bumped the curb as he braked hard. He stumbled from the car and got the spare gas can from the trunk, yanked back his sleeve and doused the bite. He screamed and dropped the can. It felt as if a dozen burning cigarettes had been stabbed into the wound, but perhaps—

Please God!

—the fuel would disinfect it. Or had he waited too long? Or was theryonism non-biological, but, rather, something supernatural?

He collapsed, weeping. A car passed him at a crawl, but it didn't stop, and sped up once it got past. A few days ago, he'd been ready to get on with his life; now, because he couldn't let go of his goddamn vendetta, he would lose everything.

Come midnight, Carter Moffat would become that which he most hated.

Carrington Police Station was a single-floor administration-type building with a small parking lot. A couple of conifers either side of the entryway were its sole salute to landscaping. Gwen shoved open the single glass door to find a shallow waiting area like she might find in a mechanic's. A counter ran the width of the room, blocking access to the rest of the open-plan station. A pudgy, prematurely balding officer was hunched over paperwork on the counter. He jerked his head up as she burst in.

"Help you?"

"I need to speak—" She saw him then, the one police officer she knew, at the back of the office. Sonny Garner was short and slight and bespectacled, but he had a reputation as a savvy cop, one you didn't mess with.

"Sonny!" she called.

He turned from the coffee pot.

"There's a man you need to catch. He's been down at the hospital. Please."

The desk cop backed off, presumably to let Sonny take over the talking. Or maybe he thought Gwen mad.

Well, maybe I am.

"Woah, woah, Gwen. Slow down." Sonny walked over with his thumbs tucked into his belt. "What man? What's going on?" He leaned on the counter, the pudgy cop at his shoulder.

She pulled out her cell and checked the call registry. Officer Creep's number was easy to find. She held it out to Sonny. "Ring this police officer in Detroit. Ask him about Eddie Barrow. He's wanted for assaulting a family and for assaulting officers. He assaulted *me*. He's escaped custody. And he's here."

Sonny frowned, but punched the number into a phone. Gwen sucked oxygen while Sonny traded cop-speak. He moved to a computer and clacked away at it, the phone nestled between cheek and shoulder.

The other cop's gaze kept swinging from the screen to her with the rhythm of someone watching a tennis match. She glanced at his name tag. Pierce. *Like what teeth and claws do to flesh*, she thought.

Garner hung up and swung the screen around to show Barrow's mugshot. "That him? What's he wearing?"

"I didn't see him. But," she added hastily, "Cate at the clinic did. She could tell you. And I know it's him. He's here for … me." He was here for *Jake*, but why? And how had he found them?

Sonny turned to his colleague. "Get Tom. Check in with the receptionist at the clinic and lemme know what this guy's wearing. I'll rouse Jerry and Paul and we'll get a grid happening." Pierce scooped up a hat from his desk and trudged off toward the rear of the station. Sonny patted Gwen's hand in a brotherly fashion. "Gwen, it's good you came straight here. If we don't catch him, we'll have someone out at your house tonight. Or if you'd like to stay in town, that'd be easier for us."

"He doesn't know where I live. I'll be safer out of town."

He chewed his lip for a moment, then slid a business card from his pocket. "You drive straight home and call my cell if anything - *anything* - happens."

She squeezed his hand in thanks. Sonny Garner had been one of the few good guys in high school. A good man, a reliable man. She hoped, as she hurried out into the lot, half expecting to be ambushed at any moment, that she wouldn't need to call him. She hoped they'd catch Barrow in the next five minutes.

And if the suspicion that was currently sneaking around the back of her mind was correct, she hoped they'd put a bullet in his head and end this well before midnight.

The shadows of nearby trees were touching Carter's shoulders when he finally ran out of tears. He brushed himself off and came to a decision. There was still one thing he could do. Perhaps Beth was up there bending God's ear and the two of them had given Carter a gift, a way to make it right. A way that wouldn't need silver bullets.

He was behind the wheel of his car and had it started when he realized the thug at the hospital had taken Brennan's file.

CHAPTER FORTY

"He's here? In Carrington?" Jake sank into the kitchen chair and put his head in his hands while Gwen paced. This couldn't be happening.

"I just said that. Didn't I just say that? Yes, he's here. Now answer the goddamn questions! He's family right? So why's he looking for you?"

He avoided her gaze. This morning she'd been frozen in terror, a mess. Now she vibrated with fury, looking fit to murder someone. Her anger baited the Animal; it turned and twisted within him. He took three deeps to quell it and focused on her question.

What Eddie was doing here was obvious. And it was just as clear what Jake would have to do. What he always did: run. But this time, Gwen would have to run with him. Strong as she was, she sure as hell couldn't fight something like that.

"Eddie's my cousin." He'd told her this once before. What he hadn't told her was… "My problem kinda runs in the family."

"Your…?" She leaned against the fridge, arms wrapped around her. "He's one of you? A werewolf?"

"Long story and I'm not sure how much of it's true. All I know is, yeah, it runs in the family. The men, that is. It's why I can't have kids. I can never pass this on."

"I don't care about that. Why are you telling me that? What are we going to do about Eddie?"

"We're leavin, that's what."

"No we're not. If the cops don't catch him, they'll have someone here to guard us tonight."

"That's stupid. Listen. This morning you said you're movin to Detroit. So let's do it." A better idea hit him and he raised a hand to forestall her next interruption. "Okay, let the cops come over. But *you* go back to Detroit like you said. I'll stay here and help them stop him."

The hell he would. The cops weren't going to get a glimpse of what Eddie and Jake were, not if Jake could help it. Coiled within his chest and spoiling for a fight, It rumbled agreement.

"No, Jake. Please. Let the police handle it. Can you even remember what you do when you've turned?"

"Changed," he corrected her.

"What-the-hell-ever. You can't control it, can you? Can you? And you think you'll be able to cooperate with the police? What if you do *change* and you run into town and slaughter all your church buddies?"

It wouldn't happen like that. Jake wouldn't let it. Eddie was injured. Even with a month to heal, that knee had to be a weakness. Jake was as fit as he'd ever been. His gut wound had healed. And he hadn't used drugs for eight weeks. He would send the cops away for safety's sake and find a way to draw Eddie out into the wild - piss on the ground every half a mile or something - face him out there where only the two of them could get hurt. One or both of them wouldn't be returning, and with youth on his side, Jake was sure he'd be the one to win.

yes, It purred. *take him. kill him.*

Gwen was rocking on the balls of her feet, eying him hard. She was scared of him. And she was scared *for* him. She didn't hate him completely, then. She knew what he was, but she hadn't run like Donna had. There was still a chance.

He leaned back and closed his eyes, trying to block out impossible dreams of a Normal life, to block out the hum of the Moon, the pressure building within him. He tried to concentrate and think this through as a man, not a beast. Fighting with teeth and claws was one answer, but there were others. There was Gwen's rifle, for starters. Maybe he could track down Eddie and shoot him dead. He might end up on a murder charge. But he'd disappeared before. He could do it again. And Gwen would be safe.

His fingers curled in frustration. It was so crazy: if he hadn't saved her ass in that alley, he wouldn't have put her in danger from Eddie. Was this the way it would always be for him? Trying to do the right thing and making things worse? Erase one black mark and score two more?

"Hello! Are you hearing me?"

"I gave you an answer," he growled. "You go, get safe. I'll take care of it." She drew breath to object but he shot to his feet. The chair tipped over, startling her. He stomped to the window, hands in his pockets. "This is between him and me."

Outside, the light had turned that particular golden shade he'd come to love this time of year, as the world turned its thoughts from summer to fall. Robins fussed in the gutters above the window and pecked in the yard for worms. A dog barked at a car down the road. Animals. They were animals. And so was he. He had no right thinking he could love a woman like Gwen. He had no right thinking he could escape Hell and make it to Heaven. There was only one end possible for a monster.

But it didn't have to be that way for Gwen.

"Pack your stuff and get back to the city. I'll call you when this is done."

Or, more likely, someone else would.

The front porch creaked and Jake's head whipped up. Gwen pressed back into the fridge as he launched himself toward the hallway. He froze, off balance and exposed. A man stood in the doorway, a pistol aimed at Jake's head. It was the same pistol that had shot him in Detroit. And the man holding it was the guy who'd pulled the trigger.

The last time Carter had seen him, Brennan had been wearing a dress; now he wore a long-sleeved cotton tee and blue jeans. Far more becoming.

"Yeah, you're not going anywhere," Carter said. He took a step inside and let the screen door slap against his butt. The harder he clenched his fist around the pistol grip, the harder his wrist throbbed from the bite wound. But dropping the gun could be fatal. Who knew what Brennan would do? As it was, the man-wolf couldn't move before the first bullet would hit.

There was a scrape of feet in the room beside Brennan. Of course, the doctor was home; nothing could ever be simple. Carter stayed where he was, unwilling to move past the living room doorway and allow her to get behind him. "I think I'd be happier if the lady came out here. And if you got on your knees, Brennan."

When neither immediately complied, he had an urge to fire a warning shot into the ceiling. That's what they did in the movies. Dumb thing to do, wasting a bullet like that.

"Please," he said.

Glowering like the cornered beast he was, Brennan lowered himself onto one knee. Carter waved the pistol at his other leg and after a beat, Brennan obeyed.

"Dr Cheevey, I've got nothing to lose by shooting him if you don't come out here. But I mean you no harm. I have something to tell you both. It'd be easier if you weren't back calling the cops."

"Gwen, don't," Brennan warned her, then his shoulders slumped as she appeared around the bookcases in the living room, palms up.

Carter pulled out his wallet, letting it fall open to expose the photo of Elizabeth. He held it toward Brennan. "Remember her?"

Brennan's eyes widened.

"My wife," Carter said.

Brennan's face fell, his tension draining away. "Do it. Just do it, if you have to. But leave Gwen out of it. She's like your wife was - a real good person. She helps people, like your wife did."

"I'm not doing anything to you, Brennan," Carter said, his throat clogging with emotion. His left cheek where his attacker had punched him throbbed with every heartbeat. "Not if I don't have to. It was some other guy who hurt Beth, not you. The same guy who did this." He dropped his wallet and pulled back his sleeve, rotating his gun hand to reveal the wound on his wrist.

"Is that a *bite*?" the doctor asked. "Did Eddie Barrow *bite* you?"

Brennan's eyes had grown large again. Carter steadied his aim at him.

"Whatever his name, he wants to find you. I'm guessing he's the guy that killed my ... partner, too. When we were ... after you." How was he to know it hadn't been Brennan? That there were two of them?

"What did you say about Beth?" Brennan murmured.

Sounding more angry than scared, the woman spoke over him. "Who the hell are you?"

Carter waved the question away. The real issue wasn't who he was now, but what. He told Brennan, "I don't get why he protected you back in Detroit, not if he's chasing you now. Are you two in a pack or something? You have an argument?"

"A pack?" Brennan seemed stunned.

"Jake's not the bad guy here," the doctor said, taking a step closer. "You said yourself, it's Eddie Barrow who hurt you and your wife. Can't you put the gun down?"

"You know what he is?" He waved the gun at Brennan while images of Barrow's bizarrely elongated face surged up from his memory. Dull pain throbbed along his arm at the thought. "I put this gun down, how do I know he won't tear out my throat?"

"Are you sayin' I didn't kill Beth?" Brennan asked, his tone child-like.

Carter met his stare for the longest time. He'd labored under a falsehood for so many months. He'd hunted this guy, shot him. He could easily have killed him. Tim had died trying to catch him. But the villain had been someone else all along. He didn't know who else Brennan might have hurt in his life - he was still certainly a monster - but he hadn't hurt Beth.

"No, you didn't."

Brennan collapsed forward onto his hands, bowing so low, his head touched the floor. Carter wondered fleetingly where the scratches in the timber had come from. Brennan's shoulders shook and Carter tensed. Was he turning theryon? Then a great sob erupted from the man and Carter sagged against the wall, his gun arm drooping. It seemed Brennan had been laboring under a misconception too The man's palpable relief made him more human.

In the living room, the doctor ventured closer. "What's happening?"

"Come see."

She edged past him, her gaze on the pistol, then crouched by Brennan and rubbed his shoulder. "What is it? Jake, what it is it?"

Brennan squeezed her hand, grated, "One less black mark, Gwen. One big one gone." He raised his head. His eyes were moist, red, as he regarded Carter. "So what are you doing here?"

"I had nowhere else to go. I've joined the fallen, Brennan. I'm one of you." Carter waggled his wounded arm. "Judge not lest ye be judged." He sank to the floor. The pistol clattered onto the floorboards.

"Once the moon is full and its light touches me, I become one of those things. That's how it works, right?"

Jake ignored the guy's question. He had questions of his own. "What's your name?"

They were at the kitchen table. Gwen had helped the Hunter to a seat, handed him an icepack for his face and was busy making tea. Jake had placed himself at the opposite end of the table. The gun lay on the bench near the sink where Gwen had put it. This little prick had shot him. *Shot* him. For a moment, he was sorely tempted to take the gun and pop the guy in the gut, see how he liked it. *It* rumbled agreement, urging him to rip the thin triangles of muscle from the top of the Hunter's shoulders.

"Carter. Carter Moffat. This is so weird. So freaking surreal. I'm here. With you. About to have tea. In a few hours we'll both be—" He swallowed loudly. He lifted the icepack from his cheek and laid it on the table.

Gwen poured water into three mugs. "I'm Gwen. And he's Jake. Not Brennan - Jake."

Carter wiped his nose on his sleeve then glanced at Gwen to check if she'd seen. She hadn't, fixated on the curls of steam rising from the cups. "So, this Eddie guy is after you? Then we can put an end to this, together. Two versus one. We both want him gone, right?"

kill them. kill them all. all threats. carter. eddie.

Gwen?

Jake went to one of the windows and moved the scrim. It was almost dark. With the lights on inside the house, the yard was indistinct. That made him vulnerable - *them* vulnerable. If Eddie was out there… "Does he know where I am?"

"I had your personnel file from the hospital. That's where I got your address." Carter swallowed again. "He took it."

"Shit." Jake let the curtain fall and moved to the wall between the window and bench.

There was a long silence, while Gwen stirred in cream and sugar. Ever the good host, she brought Carter's over first. The Hunter caught her eye and pointed to the pistol. "That's yours. If I attack you, if I ever look like I'll hurt anyone - anyone human - I want you to shoot me."

"Sure." She turned back for Jake's tea.

Carter snorted. "You don't have to be so keen about it."

Her hand stopped inches from the mug, then dipped to grasp the benchtop. Her hair hung down across her face. It had gotten longer in the past few weeks. She looked prettier with longer hair, Jake thought.

good enough to eat.

"A couple of days ago, Carter, I didn't believe in werewolves. Now I have not one but two in my kitchen. Drinking my tea." She held out a mug to Jake. He took it, enjoying its warmth. She picked up her cup and studied its contents as if it held the answers. "And there's a third one on the way, apparently. The world's changed, so I'm changing too. You better damn well believe I'll shoot you if I have to."

Her eyes flicked across to Jake's chest and back to her cup. Obviously "you" meant the both of them. That was good, Jake thought. She needed to be tough. But it still hurt.

Carter was about to say something but Gwen's short laugh interrupted him. "I wouldn't be surprised if UFOs landed in Main Street tonight."

Another long silence stretched between them. They sipped tea without enthusiasm and Jake took occasional glances out the window to check the yard. It was pointless really; he'd hear a car a long way down the road if Eddie was coming. Maybe this Carter had a point; maybe they should take Eddie two-versus-one. There were lots of problems with that, of course: the two of them might not be strong or savvy enough to defeat Eddie even with his injured knee; Eddie might get around them somehow and hurt Gwen anyway; Carter might have no control over his actions and attack him instead of Eddie.

And that brought up a weird point, that last problem. At the hamburger place, Eddie had told him he was born a wolf. Wolves came from a long line of wolves, a single family. But he'd told Carter the bite would Change him. Like in all the movies. Had Eddie lied to Jake or to Carter? Or were both things true?

Or had Jake's daddy bitten him when he was a kid, before he could remember? He'd done enough other crap to him and his momma, that was for damn sure. There were at least a half dozen scars on Jake's back and legs that could be bite marks, remnants of wounds he had no memory of getting.

He shook off his doubts. None of this was helping. He had to find a way to survive. That's what it always came back to: surviving. Only this time, he had Gwen to think about, too.

no. kill them. move on.

"I think we should lock you up," he said. He swirled the liquid in his mug. Tea really wasn't his thing. His thing was—

blood. meat.

He put the cup down on the table with a bang, sloshing some over the sides.

Carter started and a splash of tea jumped from his cup to stain his jeans. His eyes darted to the pistol and back. He put the mug down. "Bullshit you'll lock me up."

"I've done it to myself a million times. When I couldn't trust myself. When I could hurt people. I know you're worried about hurtin Normal folks and you should be. We should tie you up and lock you in the cellar for the night. Shit, even my Papa did that for us."

Carter stood. He was a head shorter than Jake and not at all scary. Matter of fact, he looked like an office worker, soft in places and skinny in others. But right then, there was iron in his eyes and Jake tensed, spreading his legs, putting his weight on the balls of his feet. The moon tugged at him, lending the Animal strength, making him aware of Carter's pulse, of hot blood just beneath the thin veneer of all that pale skin. Carter must've been feeling it, too, must've wanted to sink his teeth into Jake's throat and *squeeze and tear!*

"Boys," Gwen warned, a hand on the pistol. "There won't be any werewolf pissing matches in my kitchen."

"I'm not going in any cellar," Carter said.

"Then maybe she should shoot you now and get it over with," Jake said.

"I didn't come here to get locked up."

"You got no idea what it's like!"

"Then tell me. Teach me." Carter stabbed a finger at the window. "The moon's already up out there, so I know it's not moonlight that transforms us. When does it happen? At midnight?"

Jake moved back to the wall. He'd have to wait until the guy wasn't expecting it, then get him on the floor while Gwen hunted round for rope or tape. "Round midnight, yeah."

"Really? Seriously?" Carter ran a hand through his hair, muttering. "Midnight. Makes no sense when you think about it."

"What sense? Just the way it is."

Carter lowered himself to the edge of his chair. "But you can transform on your own? Once you're used to it?"

"What d'you mean?"

"Well, Eddie - he transformed a little. Before he bit me, his face, his shoulders, got bigger. His teeth too. Then he changed right back again. So quickly, I could've imagined it, except..." His fingers brushed his sleeve over the bite.

Jake exchanged a glance with Gwen. Her hand still rested on the gun. "I can't do that."

Carter asked, "Why not?"

"He can control it a little, somehow. I can't. I don't know how he does that."

After a long moment, Carter put his face in his hands. "Great. Just great. You have zero control. Which means I'll have even less. But this Eddie guy does." He peeked between his fingers just as Jake was thinking about taking him down. "So he's more powerful than you?"

Jake sure hoped not.

"No," he said, more for Gwen's benefit. He hadn't hurt her last night, so even as a wolf he had some kind of self-control, maybe the way sleepwalkers did. He just couldn't Change at will like Eddie. "I can take him."

The Animal stirred in approval.

Carter straightened. "How? What's the plan?"

Jake raised a hand, cocked an ear. Tires on asphalt. A transmission downshifting.

"Shit."

He darted across the kitchen and slapped at the light switch. Luckily it was the only light they'd turned on.

"Car," Carter murmured and went to the window.

Gwen had ducked down beside the counter. By the sound of her curses, she'd probably spilled her tea.

Jake ran in a crouch to the living room and pried the Roman blinds apart. A Crown Vic crept into view from behind the pines screening the road and turned into the drive with the exaggerated care that drunk drivers took, as if moving between the gateposts was like threading a needle.

"A cop," he called.

The car pulled up close to the house and a fat deputy levered himself out of the driver's side. There was no one with him.

Gwen, patting at a wet patch on her sweater, joined him by the window. She smelled good, like life. Her pulse was drumming in time with his. He took a slight step away from her.

"Pierce," she said. "I'll go talk to him."

Jake followed her out onto the porch. Pierce squinted up at them from the yard, hat in hand. Light from his patrol car reflected in patches off his bald head. "Evening. Chief Garner says to keep an eye on you folks tonight. Couldn't find that Barrow guy."

"We're grateful for your help, but we'll be fine here," Gwen said.

Pierce adjusted his stance, lifted his chin. His hat turned a full circle. "It was you said there was a person-of-interest. We been out looking for…"

"There's two of us here. I can lock the doors for the night, stay upstairs. I'll check in with the chief in the morning."

Pierce fidgeted some more. The man was weak. He would be easy to take down. Jake could attack him front on and the idiot wouldn't come close to even fumbling for his gun—

Jake dug his nails into his palms to stem the flood of thoughts.

Pierce said, "Chief says to stay, I stay. Your choice is if you want me in the house or in the car." Despite the tough words, the look he threw the house was desperate. Deputy Pierce sure didn't want to spend a night sitting in his Crown Vic.

Jake couldn't help but smile when Gwen folded her arms and said, "Car will be fine. Thank you."

"There's another car down the road a couple hundred yards back. You know whose it is?"

Gwen took a breath and Jake stepped in before she could lie. Lying was bad with cops. You had to act like nothing was too much trouble, like everything was cool.

"Friend of ours." He jerked his head at the window. "In the kitchen."

"Kitchen, huh? You always eat in the dark?"

Gwen opened her mouth but Jake cut her off again. "Heard your car. Was checkin if you was Eddie."

"Eddie?"

Jake paused. What did the cop know?

It was Gwen's turn to step in. "Edward Barrow. Weren't you listening to what I said in your office? Now we'd like to get back to our evening."

"You said there were two of you."

"Huh?"

"A moment ago, you said there were two. Now there's three."

Gwen heaved a dramatic sigh. "What, did you take a suspicion pill with dinner? I'm not the bad guy here. Now if you want to protect us from the bad guy, go sit in your car and keep watch."

Pierce pressed his lips together and placed the hat on his head, tweaked it 'til the insignia sat exactly center of his skull. He waddled back to his car and took a full minute turning the car about and easing it out on to the road. He turned left, away from town, drove thirty yards and U-turned before parking.

"Dick," Gwen said.

Jake put a hand lightly on her elbow and was glad when she didn't flinch.

take her, It told him.

"I'll keep Carter talking," he said. "Get me some electrical tape or cable or something." He let her arm go and she faced him with a blank expression. He lowered his voice further. "I want him in the basement."

She leaned in close, so close it felt like her pulse was drumming against his chest. "Or I slip him a sedative. I picked some up before I went to my office." She tapped his chest with a fingernail. "And then you and I are figuring out how to put an end to Eddie Barrow."

Jake made a mental note not to eat or drink anything Gwen prepared for the rest of the night. He went back into the kitchen and poured his tea down the sink.

CHAPTER FORTY-ONE

The sedatives were a damn good idea, Jake thought, watching as Carter went on the nods. The guy had been sitting there for twenty minutes cross-legged on a darkened living room floor, head to chest, a Gideon's Bible on his lap despite the fact there wasn't light to read it. Abruptly, he seemed to become aware of what was happening, swearing up a blue streak and getting halfway to his feet before collapsing. He got two fingers deep into his mouth and vomited up some of the canned soup Gwen had served him - and then Jake got to him, holding him down until he stopped writhing and cussing.

"He puked it up, damnit," he said, nose wrinkling at the wet patch on his knee where he'd slid in it.

Gwen stood above him with hands on hips and shook her head a little. "And now my living room smells like my piss and his vomit."

"Will he stay out?"

She ran a hand through her hair."Should do. Maybe."

They trussed him up while Jake fought to keep from sinking his teeth into the man's neck. Father Dominados's magic was well and truly at work these hundreds of years later, the damn moon trying its best to pull him inside out: drag the animal out and push the man inside.

close. so close.

Jake slung Carter over his shoulder and took the cellar stairs carefully in the sputtering light of the bulb. He only banged the guy's head once on the way down, eliciting a mild moan.

"Recovery position," Gwen called down to him.

Jake knew the position: put the user on their side in case they puked and choked. He turned the unconscious man, wedging him between some old suitcases and the wall. Jake wondered again if he shouldn't just kill the guy. He shook himself violently to end that line of thinking - it was just the Animal talking. Maybe.

In the doorway above, Gwen looked guilty as sin, giving him a wide berth as he reached the top of the stairs. She swung the door shut and locked it, then Jake shouldered a heavy dresser in front of it. She waited 'til the screech of wood on wood ended before asking, "That hold him?"

"Sure. Maybe. I didn't Change fully my first six or seven shifts. Got worse as the months went by. I dunno if that's coz I was a teenager, or if it comes on that way no matter what your age." His shoulders slumped. "There's so much I don't know."

Her hand brushed his hair aside from his cheek and a moment later her lips brushed the bristles of his beard.

The Animal howled, *take her!*

Through clenched teeth, Jake said, "Get to the bathroom. Safe there."

She flinched, then took off upstairs without another word, Carter's gun jammed in the back of her jeans.

Jake was still thinking about the movement of her jeans long after the bathroom door slammed. He deadbolted the front door and retreated along the hall. Wind moaned softly through the gap in the back door. He'd spent an hour in the afternoon trying to fix it, but carpentry wasn't his thing. The best he'd been able to do was to remove both hinges and shove the door into the jam, then brace it there with a couple of big flower pots he'd found in the shed outside. No one was going through that door, neither in or out, not without making a helluva noise.

The lower floor was lit only by moonlight streaming through the windows, but he could see clearly. All of his senses were electrified: the scents of the other people in the house; the draw of his untouched soup bowl almost irresistible; the pain of the splinters in his feet nettling him. His entire body was thrumming with the rush of power through his blood, the singing of his muscles, the crowded world's scents and odors assailing him. He hated it. He loved it.

He checked the microwave clock. 10:56. In an hour, Jake wouldn't be Jake anymore. What the hell was he going to do if Eddie didn't show? What the hell would he do if he did?

In the bathroom above, Gwen was completely quiet. At least she had the gun.

Bit by bit, Carter became aware of pain.

At first he felt it only distantly, the throb in his head, the strain in his shoulders, the reflux burn in the center of his chest, the stabbing in his knees. It frittered around the edges of his attention while he watched Elijah playing stickball in the street with the other kids. Carter was sitting on the porch with his feet up on the rail and Beth was bending low over him, placing fresh lemonade by his rocking chair, brushing his ear with her lips. His head swam with happiness and with the heat of the summer afternoon. He wanted that lemonade, so bad. He wanted to grab Beth and pull her down on his lap, make her laugh. But he couldn't. His arms and legs wouldn't move. He…

… was on his side in a mildew-smelling room with a single yellow bulb flickering like a dying candle above the staircase. He hurt, shoulders and hips cramping, pins and needles prickling along his limbs. Someone had hogtied him of sorts, using what felt like duct tape around his wrists and again around his ankles. The makeshift shackles had been connected with more tape, making it impossible for him to straighten. His throat was raw, burning - he tasted vomit. They'd drugged him, damnit, but he must have gotten at least some of it up. But how long had he been out?

Can't've been too long. I'm still me.

He strained against his bonds, then gave it up as senseless. They had blindsided him. He'd come here for help - and to help them - and they'd done this. He could cry out, risk drawing Jake's attention, in hope the cop would hear him. Sure, and explain this how? Through the mound of suitcases holding him in place, he glimpsed a tower of small packing crates. Maybe there was something in there he could use. Shuffling and wriggling, he worked his way across three or four feet of floor before he had to stop, drenched in sweat, joints burning.

God, if you're there, you gotta help me. I haven't asked for much since Beth
went. But I'm asking you for this. If you're there, you gotta help me. Now!
He sucked in a breath and tried again.

Gwen stood in the bath and raised herself on tiptoes to peek out the
high window overlooking the backyard. The full moon painted the
ground in gray light. Fluffy blurs along on the hill on the far side of the
fence were bushes and trees. Not werewolves. Not monsters.

Had Jake left already? Was he out beyond that hill, trying to draw
Eddie? Would she see any of it happen or would they meet in the
woods beyond the farmland, duke it out where there were no
witnesses? She had a horrible thought as she lowered herself to sit on
the bath's edge. What if the family who owned the farm, the Johnstons,
were out there, patrolling their grounds after last night's "animal
attack"? What if Jake and Eddie—

A thump and a shout startled her. She slipped, fell flat on her back
on the tiled floor. She cracked her head, saw stars, then thanked them
that the pistol in her hand hadn't fired. There was a commotion
downstairs - footsteps, banging, cursing. She raised herself into a tight
squat against the cabinet, pointed the gun at the door and waited.

11.37.

Jake paced the hallway, fingers curled into his palms as if that
simple pain could stave off the Change. If that back door was more
secure, he would have already left. He should have left. Gwen had the
gun. She was tough. She could defend herself. Whatever happened with
Carter, Jake had to get away now, take his wolf with him and hope that
if Eddie was around, he'd follow him.

Something slammed into the kitchen window. He smelled the
blood before he saw it, a coppery sweetness leaching through the gaps
in the window frame, buoyed on the breeze. Human blood. A dark
hand print silhouetted on glass against the moonlight, the fingers
elongated with a partial change into something not -human.

"Catch me if you can!" The shout came from the rear of the
property: Eddie moving fast.

Jake charged the back door, shouldering it again and again until the planter boxes moved enough for him to squeeze through. What the hell had he been thinking, putting them there? They'd slowed him down as a human, but they wouldn't stop a werewolf. The only thing stopping a werewolf was gonna be a silver bullet.

Or another werewolf.

Carter had made it to the crates just as the commotion started upstairs. Swearing, he wedged his toes between the base of the stack of crates and the wall. There was no way in hell he was missing this. With the little leverage he had, he worried at the small tower until it toppled, spilling crockery and knickknacks over the floor. Carter wormed his way into the mess. A broken bread plate looked like his best bet. Frustration banished the last of the drug haze as he worked the plate into his fingers, pushed past the pain in his wrists as he cut at the tape. It gave way suddenly. The piece of plate went flying.

He massaged his joints, circulation returning to his limbs like someone forcing hot needles down his veins. All was silent above him. The door at the top of the stairs was bound to be locked, maybe even barricaded. He decided to try the exterior one - what his dad would have called a storm cellar door. It was held shut with a short chain and padlock - the key was in the lock. Jake and Gwen had either forgotten to check it or hadn't expected a werewolf to turn a key, even if he'd been able to tear through his restraints. The key took a bit of jiggling, but eventually the lock gave and Carter pushed the door open, holding the handle carefully as he followed it up the short set of steps and out into the cool night air. Still getting the knots out of his muscles, he trotted around to the rear of the house. The back door lay on the landing. He held his breath, long enough to confirm there was no noise from within the house. Eddie hadn't ripped the door off to get in; Jake had pushed it outward in pursuit.

But where? Which way?

Camping trips with his grandfather had taught him to listen to nature, to use ears as much as eyes in the wild. Carter listened to the night.

Cattle.

An annoyed robin.

The squawk of the cop car's radio.

Wait.

The *PEEP-PEEP-tut-tut-tut-tut* call of the robin was one his grand-pa said they made when warning others of a potential predator. He jogged to the fence and scanned the hill that ran up behind the house. There. The robin fell silent, but its call had come from a line of baby pines near the top.

Shit. If the two theryons were headed that way, they had a big headstart and Carter wasn't anywhere near as fit. He struck his skinny thighs in frustration; when was the damned transformation going to kick in and lend him strength? He dug a thumb into the wound on his wrist and gasped as the flood of pain sobered him, driving away the last of the woolliness left by whatever mickey Gwen had served him.

Gwen. Her car was out front - perhaps her keys were inside. He unhitched the gate at the back fence - dragged it through the weeds and soil built up over years of disuse. He jogged around the house. The car was unlocked but there were no keys in the ignition. Light from the road and a spike in radio transmissions made him freeze mid-swearword. That cop's radio was awful loud and the cop hadn't answered it once since Carter had left the cellar. Ice water trickled along his spine.

He ran out onto the road. The trees along the verge clicked and cricked with insect life. No robins over here. The patrol car sat in a pool of its own internal light, the driver's door wide open. A dark mass had spilled out onto the ground.

The cop's throat had been torn out - a ragged cavity, slick in the light. Carter's fists clenched at the senselessness of it.

The patrol car would make a better cross-terrain vehicle than Gwen's Taurus and every second he delayed took him closer to midnight, letting his wife's killer get further away. Carter dragged the policeman out of the cabin. The cop's head nearly fell off, lolling at an angle that leaked more gore onto the asphalt. Carter's gorge rose. He dropped the body and turned away, hands on knees, shallow breathing to keep from vomiting. He focused on the sweet night air singing in his nostrils and the bright moonlight. How far away was midnight?

He climbed inside the car. Blood had spattered on the seats and floor, the ceiling and steering column - a sticky warmth soaked through his pants as he swung the door closed - but he was going to get a lot messier before the night was over.

The dashboard clock said 11.43. Damn, it was close.

The cop's revolver had fallen near the gas pedal. Carter had no idea what caliber it was, but it was way bigger than his .32. He shoved it barrel-down between the passenger seat and the console. The inside of the car was cluttered with a mounted laptop, a shotgun in its rack, and radio. The key was in the ignition. He backed up, careful to avoid the body, and swung into Gwen's driveway. Irritated by the radio chatter - a dispatcher and cop discussing cocktail recipes, for God's sake - he found the volume control and turned it down to zero.

Past the rear gate, it was a bumpy ride, the car bouncing and lurching, but he made it to the top of the hill without puncturing a tire. He flicked off the headlights to get a better sense of his surrounds, had to blink hard to get his night eyes back. Before him lay a broad gully, split along the center by waist-high wire fencing. A quarter mile to his right, the gully vanished into heavy vegetation. Half that distance to his left, a hill rose to block out whatever was beyond. The slope opposite was dotted with trees and a couple of hay bales. No sign of Eddie Barrow. No sign of Jake Brennan.

The dash clock read 11.46

What now, genius?

Jake was panting but not hard. Running felt *good*. Action felt *good*. His body buzzed, bursting with energy. He made the top of the hill and slid a few yards over it to crouch and study the gully.

He raised his nose, smelling the air, then crept a few more feet down the slope until he found a sticky patch on the grass. Blood. But not Eddie's. It smelled like...

...like that cop. Pierce.

Visions of meat flashed through his mind. Abruptly ravenous, his overloaded senses swam. The fields around him were dense with the aromas of life, of birds and rabbits, a family of foxes, cows, and…

Eddie.

He bounded down the hill and sprinted to the fence. The wind shifted and he lost the scent. He jogged up and down until he caught it again. He vaulted the fence, landing in a crouch. The mob of cattle was crowding up along the slope to his left, putting distance between them and him. That was smart, since they were nothing more than *prey!*

Tremors rippled through the muscles of his back and thighs. Claws itched and ached beneath the pads of his fingers.

Halfway between him and the cattle, near the top of the hill, grew a forty-foot willow. A man stood beneath it, pale in the bright moonlight. On seeing Jake, he withdrew behind the screen of drooping foliage. Jake headed for the tree. A cramp in his gut drove him to a stop twenty or thirty paces from the closest branches. Another spasm almost doubled him over.

Eddie stepped out from behind the branches. He was naked, a slab of muscle and bad attitude. "Welcome, cuz. Good to see you can follow a trail." His voice thickened as he spoke. Or maybe that was the roaring distortion in Jake's ears as if someone was pumping water into them.

Eddie's nakedness set Jake back: he looked powerful, confident.

"You've come so far. But I think there's only one end to this, Jake. You or me."

"What's wrong with you?" Jake snarled. "Why couldn't you leave us alone? All I ever wanted…"

His swelling jaw cut him off. Words would be near impossible within seconds.

kill kill kill kill kill!

"What? What did you want? To be a good citizen? To be a good *man?*" Eddie slipped closer. "We're not men."

Jake's ears burned. His eyes were contracting, twitching. Someone was driving railway spikes up through his bowels. His back, his hips, every joint strained as if inflating. The air pulsed with pain, with power, with the promise of death.

"Why you doin this?" he moaned.

"What else is there?" Eddie said, and leapt.

Jake caught Eddie's outstretched arms and twisted, flinging him aside. Eddie rolled down the slope a good twenty feet before righting himself onto all fours.

Jake steeled himself for the next attack. Burning lines ran down his spine, sliced into his skull, his fingertips, his jaw. His vision smeared. In it, Eddie crept closer, doglike, shoulders hunching, limbs lengthening, fur sprouting, head swelling.

Across the valley, headlights flared then flicked off. A transmission shifted down. The car paused on the opposite hill then headed straight down it. Eddie - or whatever he was becoming - swung around to study it.

A new cramp threw Jake onto his back. There was no more time to think. Clothing tore as Jake swelled to bursting point. Claws shredded the skin from his fingers. His throat clenched, expanded, clenched again. He roared in agony as his vision turned yellow and gray - his roar was the cry of the Animal.

Then Eddie was upon him.

Over to the left of the far meadow, cattle pressed together against a fence. Their terrified lowing carried across the valley above the rumble of the car engine. Carter scanned the slope again. And there they were. Two figures by a large tree. One on all fours, one hunched and ready for combat. Lights still off, he turned the wheel and headed down the slope, gunning the car at the bottom to crash through the fence. Wire squealed against steel. He drove along the flat of the gully floor before cranking the wheel to head straight up the slope toward the tree.

The men were rolling on the ground, locked in battle.

Ten yards from them, he hit a stump or rock and came to a hard stop. His head cracked against the sun visor. The engine stalled. Carter flicked on the full beams and cried out, pushing as far back into his seat as he could. Caught in the lights were two shapes that should not have existed: vicious brown-gray hulks encased in thick shaggy fur. The two figures separated, yellow eyes reflecting back at him. The mouths reminded him of sharks: row upon row of huge and deadly teeth…

Brennan and Barrow had already metamorphosed, no longer men but creatures of nightmare. Carter's own nightmare.

They had changed. But Carter had not.

Carter was still a man.

CHAPTER FORTY-TWO

One beast braced to leap at the car, but the other leaped on its back, biting at the neck. Blood spurted black in the moonlight. The first slammed his head back into his attacker's snout, shrugged him off. There was a moment's pause while each took stock, and then they went at each other, snarling and snapping, swinging long muscular arms tipped with razor-sharp talons.

Carter wrestled the door open and pulled himself outside, turned his face to the moon. "C'mon!" he screamed, ripping his shirt open, buttons flying.

Nothing happened. Nothing. He rubbed at his wounded wrist in wonder.

"He lied to me. He fucking *lied*!"

He was not going to become a theryon. He was not going to lose control. He was not a monster. He was …

Defenseless!

Fear pooled in his gut. He scrambled back into the car and yanked the door closed. He had to get back to the house, get the Glock from Gwen. He thanked God as the car started first time. Hands shaking, it took him three attempts to get the shifter into reverse. But the car wouldn't budge. He slammed it into first and tried again. Wheels spun, kicking up dirt. It was wedged tight on whatever he'd hit.

The two werewolves, locked together, rolled down the hill. Carter coughed against the stink of torn flesh and wet fur. He fumbled the revolver free from where he'd jammed it and wrenched around in his seat - just as a mass of fur smashed into the side of the car. The rear passenger window cracked and the vehicle rocked sideways. The pistol jolted from his hand and fell into the passenger footwell. Carter's foot came off the clutch and the engine stalled. The creature pushed away from the car just as its opponent crashed into it, throwing them both against the vehicle with enough force to shatter the window. The car bounced, tilted crazily as they grappled. Carter had a moment of panic that it would roll but it rocked to a stop upright. When the wolves moved away, Carter realized the car was free of its obstruction. He stamped a foot down on the clutch, turned the key. The motor stuttered to life and he cranked the wheel until the hood pointed downhill.

The two theryons circled each other at the bottom of the gully by the gap in the fence. He maneuvered the car until the lights shone directly on them. And gasped. The bigger wolf wore a silver-gray stripe on his shoulder - the same marking as the creature that had killed his wife.

He grit his teeth hard and accelerated, adjusted his aim as they moved out of his trajectory, a red mist settling over his eyes. There was the chance he could hit Jake, kill them both, but he didn't care.

"For you, Beth!"

He stamped the accelerator to the floor. The V8 roared and the car slammed down onto the gully floor with a sickening lurch. Ten yards and closing fast.

The larger wolf dived aside. The car caught its leg - the wolf bounced off the front guard and spun off out of sight - and then he slammed into the one he thought was Jake. Carter had the impression of gaping wounds and blood-matted fur before the car took Jake in the torso and flipped him headfirst into the windscreen. The glass starred around the impact and the body careened over the roof to land behind him somewhere. The car hit a fencepost and came to a sudden stop. With a pop, the airbage slammed into Carter's face and chest, shoving him back.

Winded, he felt around for the revolver. He clutched it as he pushed the door open and fell outside. He forced himself upright, sweeping the gun around, looking for Eddie. He pulled the hammer back like he'd been shown with his .32. A blur of movement in his peripheral vision - he swung and fired. The recoil was harsh, worse than the Glock. His arm kicked back, nearly overbalancing him. Wolf-

Eddie dropped into a crouch. He was twenty feet away and Carter had missed. He braced his forearms against the patrol car roof as he took aim. Damned if he was going to miss this time.

The shot took the theryon high in the chest. Eddie stumbled, then raced away on all fours. His speed made Carter gasp. He squeezed off two more shots but hadn't a hope of hitting it. He tossed the pistol and dived back into the car, wrestled the shotgun free of its mount. He cocked the slide and set off. Around the back of the car, the other theryon lay unmoving on ground.

So maybe you don't need silver bullets after all.

He regretted Jake's death, but this was about Beth. And not just her now. The direction of Barrow's escape was clear. If Carter didn't stop him, another innocent woman was dead.

She couldn't sit up here in the bathroom all night.

She couldn't not know.

Gwen checked her cell phone: had it only been two minutes since Jake's banging and cursing, and the cop car speeding up the hill? It had been silent since. Jake and Officer Pierce had chased Eddie off the reservation; that's what had happened. Wherever the battle was, it wasn't on her property.

And yet: leaving the room? Going downstairs? What was she, an air-headed blonde in a teen slasher movie? Carter was in the cellar; he could be one of them now. A...

"Say it, girl. Get used to saying it. Carter could be a werewolf." She sighed and got to her feet, put the cell on the vanity and probed the contusion on the back of her head. "A werewolf."

She leaned her head against the door, turned her ear to it. Nothing. She slid the lock slowly and softly, pointed the pistol muzzle into the crack of the door as she teased it open an inch, two inches, three. Without any windows to let in moonlight, the hall was pitch dark. She panicked and shut the door, bolted it, backed away. Anything could be out there. Anything.

She pressed up against the vanity until the edge was hurting her hip, then grunted in frustration, got control of her breathing. The plan was stay here all night until someone - someone human, someone human and rational and safe - came to tell her it was all over.

Stick to the plan, Gwen.

But it wasn't exactly a well-thought-out plan. Sitting in a cold tiled bathroom? All night? It was so frickin' uncomfortable. And she was a doctor, an *ER* doctor, for God's sake. Crises came to her and she dealt with them. She didn't hide. She didn't dodge and duck and weave.

And she had a gun.

"Okay. Stick with the plan. But I need a chair. Or a beanbag."

Really? Downstairs?

"Just a chair then. Jake has one in his room. And blankets. Ten paces there. Ten back." She scrunched up her face.

Maybe twelve. I have a gun with silver bullets. I'm a country girl. I know how to use guns. I've checked the magazine for bullets. Twice. The safety is off.

She debated it for a few more seconds, just standing there murmuring nonsense, then moved to the door. She leaned her head against it again, fingers on the lock. "Nothing's out there. Nothing is out there. Twelve paces there. Twelve back."

It took her thirteen to get there. The last three steps were little skipping things as she lost her self-control. She swung Jake's door closed behind her and backpedaled into her sister's old high-backed chair.

She sat, listening.

Nothing but the occasional creak and pop of a house cooling after a warm day, though even those familiar noises were enough to give her the heebies.

The crack of a gunshot came from out in the farmland. She jumped to her feet. Another shot. The curtains were drawn over the bay window overlooking the backyard; silver light leaked through where they parted. She peeked through the gap without touching them, saw nothing. Two more shots came in rapid succession. Then nothing for a minute or so. What the hell was going on out there? Officer Pierce? A farmer? She prayed to God one of her neighbors wasn't caught up in it, wasn't being eaten right now while she stood safe and sound in her own house with the only weapon that could actually kill a...

Something big and hairy rocketed down the far slope and through the half-open gate at her back fence, galloping at close to a horse's full speed. Its head swung toward the window. She jerked away, then, hunched lower, stared out again. It was gone. She clamped down on a whimper and returned to the chair, gun pointed at the bedroom door, and wondered how she'd hit anything, shaking the way she was.

It was okay. The thing hadn't come in the house. It had run toward the front yard, the road.

It might have been Jake.

Or Eddie. Jake might be dead for all she knew.

She was a sitting duck up here if it came looking for her. What the hell was she thinking, hiding in a bedroom - or the bathroom for that matter? How were they going to protect her if something came crashing through the door or wall? How much time would she actually have to squeeze off a couple of shots? How much time until the silver took effect? She should have made Jake lock Carter up here and hidden herself in the cellar. Or better yet...

Goddamnit.

Why the hell hadn't she thought of it earlier? There was a drop-down ladder for the attic at the far end of the hall; she could pull it up behind her. She got her breathing under control, forced herself to go to the door and ease it open.

The dark hall mocked her. Another stupid thing: leaving the house in darkness when those things could undoubtedly see better in the dark than she could. The pull-rope for the ladder was a few steps past the bathroom door. It would be easy to find. There'd be noise, bringing down the ladder, but if she was fast, it wouldn't matter. She'd be safe before anything could enter the house, get up the stairs and get her.

She had taken one careful step into the hall when she smelled it. The rangy smell of an animal. Wet fur mixed with sour masculinity. Reflected moonlight picked out the stairwell archway. It dimmed suddenly as something blocked it. Something was down there. A stair riser creaked in confirmation.

Gwen slipped back into the bedroom, closed the door silently.

What do I do what do I do?

She ran on tiptoes to the window, stuck her free hand between the curtains while angling the pistol at the door. She unhooked the window clasp and nudged. The left-hand pane swung outward, a little stiffly. Cool air soaked into the room and she sucked in a lungful while climbing out, holding onto the fixed half of the two window panes. She stood on the shingles directly above the kitchen. Obscurely she remembered her father complaining about the low pitch of the roof, the easy angle that left it more affected by Michigan weather and in need of more frequent repair. She pressed her stomach to the wall and shuffled to her right, grateful for the occasional patch of sticky repair-gunk assisting her footing. The tiles were worn and shaky, but if they were bad for a woman in sneakers, they'd be worse for a two-hundred-and-fifty-pound werewolf. She was at the corner when the beast broke through the bedroom door. A snarl rolled out the open window, thunder announcing an oncoming storm. She could have sworn it said her name. Gwen couldn't keep the whimper from slipping through her lips.

A shaggy head and neck emerged from the window. A dripping muzzle turned her way. A long forearm reached out and a football-sized paw tested the roof. It wasn't Jake: the ears tapered more bluntly, the fur was grayer where his was more brown. This was either Carter, escaped from the cellar, or Eddie had returned to finish her.

The pistol was in her right hand, the creature to her left. Gwen took a tentative step back, trying to bring the gun to bear. Unbalanced, she began to topple. She reached for the wall but failed to find a hold. She landed heavily on her left side. Pain flared. The gun flew from her hand. Sliding, she rolled onto her front and grabbed at the tiles. The tiles rasped against her ribcage and hips, snagged against the wool of her pullover. The toe of her right sneaker dropped into the gutter and jammed there, arresting her fall.

The creature snorted as if laughing and put its other forearm out onto the tiles, uncertain of its footing. The damn thing was ten feet away, its vicious stink rolling over her. As one back leg came out, she could see it more clearly. It definitely wasn't Jake, she was sure of that now. It had a light streak of fur over one shoulder and its head was bigger. Dark patches around its muzzle may have been drool or blood.

Patches of fur and flesh hung on bloody tendrils from numerous wounds. A guttural drone came out on each breath as it brought its last leg out onto the roof, reminding her of the satisfied purr of a house cat. A two-hundred-and-fifty-pound house cat that was actually a wolf that wanted to eat her. Where was that goddamned gun?

The wolf raised its head, focusing past her, deepset eyes widening, ears flattening. Gunfire boomed and chunks flew from the wall and tiles near it. Flecks of fur and skin sprayed from its left shoulder. It pushed upright on back legs. Another shotgun blast grazed its chest, spinning it sideways. It rolled and bounced past her, dropping off the roof, a small avalanche of tiles tumbling in its wake.

She twisted around to see the shooter drop down on one knee twenty feet inside the gate and brace the stock against his shoulder.

Carter?

He shucked the slide, aimed and fired, but the wolf kept coming. He had only time to moan "Oh, God" before it was on him. Jaws and claws flashed like a thresher amidst the screams. She turned away, scanned the roof around her.

Where's the gun? Where is it!

Carter's screams choked off and the growling abated. In the silence, Gwen looked down, directly into the yellow eyes of Eddie Barrow. The message was clear. She was next. A gust of wind blew the road kill reek of Carter's remains her way and she gagged.

She pushed herself up the roof in a reverse crab walk, left arm numb and trembling from her fall. Wolf-Eddie stood fully upright, eyes gleaming, tongue lolling, shoulders heaving. He seemed unaffected by his gunshot injuries. Another whiff of death blew her way. She had to get in that window. Get into the attic. She tried to go faster.

Eddie lifted his muzzle and sniffed at the wind. Growling, he whipped around towards the paddock. He dropped to all fours and backed up, as if coiling the tension on a spring. Gwen followed his gaze and saw another shape running down the hill toward the gate. Not as fast as Eddie had, but unmistakably another wolf.

Hope swelled inside her, fixing her in place, until the new arrival made it to the gate and she saw the way he limped. One back leg wasn't working as well as the other. He, too, was matted and frayed as if he'd been torn to pieces and sown back together. Eddie, by comparison, seemed unhampered. Her heart sank. There could be no running away. She had to find that gun.

She clambered up to where the roof met the wall and pushed herself upright.

Snarling, the two monsters circled each other on hind legs, shoulders high, heads down, ears flat. She went to the corner where she'd slipped and peered around, in case the gun had fallen that way. No sign. It must have gone onto the ground.

The last fricking place she wanted to be.

The drop was about twelve feet if she let herself over the edge. Survivable. She scooted on her ass down to the guttering and sucked in a breath. The gun was sticking out of the corner downpipe inches to her left. She reached for it as the two wolves collided like stags, locked together, jaws clamped on each other's shoulders. She nearly lost her balance when she tugged on the pistol. It was stuck.

She jiggled and twisted and it came loose with a jolt. She jammed both feet against the gutter and sighted, then dropped her weak left arm. Its trembling was throwing her aim. The two werewolves still grappled, twisting and turning like grotesque dance partners, vying for better purchase. In the flurry of movement she couldn't tell them apart. But she'd seen the gray stripe on the one hunting her. Up close, it would be easier. There was only one thing she could do. Injured, Jake could well lose this battle anyway.

She fired. Missed. Swore lavishly and lined up again. Fired. Fired again.

Again and again and again.

The two monsters flew away from each other, skidding in the dirt. Writhing. Convulsing. She'd hit them both. They whined in unison and their whines turned to gurgles.

Anaphylaxis. Airways swelling. Hearts racing. Finally something familiar.

She scrambled back to the window without slipping and falling to her death. Inside Jake's room, she ripped the six drawers out of the dresser and wrenched open the cupboard. All were empty. Where the hell was his stuff? On intuition, she dived for the bed and plunged her hands beneath it, felt the soft crinkle of department store plastic bags and the corrugations of his back pack. The habits of a lifetime died hard. She yanked out the pack and felt around for what seemed an eternity before she found the three cylinders. She fled the room, praying she had time.

CHAPTER FORTY-THREE

Jake came to himself in a terror of choking and searing pain. The thickness inside his throat was as familiar as the creeping cold prickling all over his body. He'd been shot with silver.

He felt with unwieldy fingers for the puncture wound. Shoulder. Could've been worse. He pulled his bloodied fingers back and studied them in the moonlight. They were fat and tipped with the remains of claws, though it looked like the skin was rapidly healing over. He was naked, covered in blood and grass, his body cut and bruised. Gwen's backyard. Two other bodies lay nearby - Eddie, naked and twitching, and the mutilated corpse of Carter. The silver poured molten pain through him and he fell back. Through half-shut eyes, he saw Gwen running from the house, arms full of stuff, gabbling into a cordless phone clamped between her jaw and shoulder.

He tried to ask for help, but couldn't make the word form.

"Easy," she said, falling beside him on her knees. "Ambulance is on the way." She dumped her cargo and began rummaging through it.

The welcome prick of an EpiPen against his thigh brought relief to his breathing seconds later. She held up a couple of other too-familiar items - a syringe and an ampule, of morphine, she said.

She filled the syringe with practiced speed and jabbed it into his bicep. When the syringe was empty, she shoved him on his side, lifted his left arm and took hold of the muscles over his ribs.

"This is gonna hurt, Jake, but I gotta get the bullet out," she said. "With luck, the bullet's still in there somewhere, not deep."

The drug hit his bloodstream like treacle, like a mother's caress. It might even be enough to stop him turning wolf again once she had the silver out. Maybe she'd thought of that too; maybe that's why she'd given it to him.

He grunted when the knife went in.

"Sorry," she said. "Gotta get this out."

He groaned again as the knife probed within the wound, causing his stomach to lurch and spots to swim in his vision. His flailing right hand hit a stick and he latched onto it, stuck it in his mouth and bit down hard. His fingers clutched at the dirt as the white-hot pain shot through his back.

"Yes!" she said and dipped her fingers into the wound.

He whimpered and wondered what the hell she was so happy about. A moment later, she showed him a bullet, coated in gore, between her finger and thumb. He pulled his head away from it and spat out the stick. "Poison," he mumbled thickly, but his breathing was better and his throat felt more ... human. The swelling around his eyes and mouth was going down.

She placed the slug aside and marked the spot with the empty syringe, then pressed a dressing to the wound. The one wound of many. He vaguely remembered Eddie coming at him, the collision of bodies, the agony of a Change...

Grating breaths and the *shoosh* of limbs on grass drew his attention. Eddie lay on his back near the fence. Blood seeped from wounds on his chest, arms and shoulders - his jaw and upper chest was spattered with it - and he was convulsing, gulping air, arms and legs spasming as if drowning.

The moonlight was strong enough for Gwen to follow Jake's gaze and scowl at what she saw.

Jake's emergency was over. Eddie, however, was near death. In a triage situation, he was due the last EpiPen to keep him alive until the paramedics arrived.

You can't save everyone, Gwenny-bear, you remember that. But you do your best.

This is *my best, Daddy*, she thought, and turned away to let Eddie die.

Jake kept his focus on Eddie's body while Gwen applied surgical tape to hold his dressing in place then searched his body for more bullet wounds. It had only been a few seconds since it stopped writhing.

"You shot him?" Jake asked, still having trouble getting his tongue to form sounds properly.

"Both of you," she said. "Sorry." She sat back on her heels with a huff of breath. "You're a mess, Jake Brennan. But you might just live. Here, take this, in case." She pressed a second EpiPen into his hands.

He propped himself up on his elbows, then caught sight of a bloody mess on the ground by the open gate and knew instinctively what it was.

Meat!

How had Carter gotten free?

"What happened with him?" he asked.

"He saved my life."

"Did he ... Change?"

"Only from your enemy into our friend."

So it wasn't passed on through a bite, only by birth.

She put her fingers against his throat and he panicked, feeling threatened. His hand jerked up to pull hers away, but he forced his fingers to touch hers softly. He should thank her. She slipped her hand from beneath his and lurched away toward Eddie. He saw now that she carried a filleting knife, the knife dark with Jake's blood. The gun was in the waist band of her jeans, poking over her sweater. She bent over Eddie and prodded him gingerly while holding the knife near his throat.

"Still alive?" Jake called.

"Barely," she replied. "He'll be dead before help arrives. They won't revive him." She walked back to Jake.

"You sure of that?" he asked.

She frowned, eyes narrowing.

Jake opened his palm. "Gimme the gun."

She recoiled. "What?"

"No chances, Gwen. Where'd you shoot him?"

"What!"

"Where'd you hit him?"

She paused. Eddie's breath wheezed. "Cheek, shoulder, thigh."

Jake shook his head. "See? That's a problem. When they find him they'll be askin what killed him."

She squatted beside him, grinding her teeth while she thought.

"Gwen. I have to."

She swore and handed over the gun, put her fist in her mouth and kept her back turned as Jake pushed himself to his feet. He winced as he shuffled over.

"Oh, God," she moaned.

He fell back to his knees by his cousin. The guy was in worse shape than Jake, that was for damn sure, even not accounting for the ragged gouges in skin and muscle. His face was puffed up beyond recognition and there was blood everywhere. Those silver bullet holes weren't healing, not with the poison still inside. Despite his desire to be a better man, despite what his momma had taught him about love and forgiveness, Jake was glad Eddie had suffered. The bastard had come to turn Jake back into a monster. And he'd almost killed Gwen.

He ground the muzzle against his cousin's sternum. Eddie's left eye opened; he took a long, wheezy inhalation. His lip curled up, either in snarl or smile. He said, "Atta boy. Thass what I'm talking abou—"

The gun jumped as Jake pulled the trigger. Hot blood sprayed his hand and chest. Eddie spasmed once, blood spilling from his mouth, then lay still. The heady reek of a slaughterhouse surrounded Jake. It made him sick. It made him

hungry.

"Jake. Jake, come away from him. Jake! It's over."

He rotated on his heels, sank onto his butt and closed his eyes. An ambulance siren sounded in the distance. Three minutes away, maybe. He'd made a good choice.

"Not yet it's not," he said. "We still have to come up with one hell of a story to explain all this."

CHAPTER FORTY-FOUR

No news crews had turned up. Yet. If Gwen was lucky, it would stay that way. She knew Sonny Garner was no fan of the press, but some dumb cop was bound to share the wrong thing over the radio where it'd get picked up on a reporter's scanner. Then it would be "Michigan Dogman Strikes Again."

The only vehicles currently choking her front gateway were an ambulance with its light still flashing and two cop cars. Richard had parked down the road and walked the final few hundred yards to keep out of the cops' way. Garner and a couple of other officers kept circling the dark yard with flashlights, dropping markers and swearing. Sitting in the kitchen, with a paramedic attending to Jake and Richard attending to her, Gwen caught occasional snatches of conversation from outside.

"Careful, dufus, it's a crime scene, ya know."

"State Police here in twenty, Sonny."

"D'ya see what the dog did to that Moffat fella?"

"Forget Moffat. Poor Pierce. What the hell kind of dog does that?"

She exchanged a glance with Jake and colored when Richard caught it. He raised an eyebrow and went back to applying butterfly stitches above her hip where a roof tile had slit her.

The story she'd told Garner - the one she and Jake would stick to, come hell or high water - was simple. Eddie Barrow had some crazy obsession with her and had tried to abduct her. Carter was a guy who'd been hunting Barrow for years because he believed him responsible for the death of his wife - which was true in its own way. Barrow had kept some kind of mastiff with him that had killed Pierce and Carter. In all the hullaballoo and in the dark, they hadn't gotten a good look at the breed and it had fled when the shooting started. But she and Jake had "decided" it may have been a wolf crossbreed, and perhaps the dog had killed Carter's wife, causing him to think that Barrow was a werewolf. This, they hoped, explained the silver bullets in the gun she'd killed Barrow with.

Sonny had looked dubious, but Gwen told herself that cops were paid to look dubious. If they stuck to it, the story would work. It would have to. Garner had mumbled phrases like "under investigation" and "self-defense" and made her promise to speak to a lawyer ASAP and work out a strategy in case she was charged with anything. He'd do what he could to help her, he promised.

A lawyer, she thought. She could always call her mom.

Stranger things had happened.

When the paramedic was called away to consult with Garner over something, Richard leaned in close and lifted a bandage to take a good look at a deep gash in Jake's side.

"Mastiff, huh?"

Jake shrugged. "The thing was a monster."

Gwen had to bite down hard to keep from snickering at his sudden wryness.

Richard considered the wound some more. "And you got this last night? Just a few hours ago?" He settled the bandage back in place and raised his eyebrows at Gwen. "Looks awful neat for a fresh wound. Already some granulation tissue here."

Gwen placed a hand over her lower face to cover the new flush. She was terrible at lying. She'd have to become better at it. Like Jake was. "We told you what happened," she said. It wasn't hard to force some weariness into her tone. "Besides, the light's bad in here."

Richard watched Jake putting on a shirt. "Lot of scars there, son. Fight huge dogs often, do you?"

Jake winced as he struggled to get his left arm into the shirt. He turned his back, buttoning. "You grow up on the streets, you fight a lot of things."

Richard huffed and began packing up his gear. "Well. I was going to recommend a trip to hospital, Jake - and I still do, as a professional -

but I'd say you'll be fine on your own. Get your doctor here to prescribe some antibiotics and run a blood test, make sure you didn't catch anything from the *dog*." He clipped his bag shut and shook his head. "You know, if you really do heal this quickly, there'll be some labs who'd love to take a blood sample and millions of people around the world who'd like to have what you have."

Gwen thought: *No they wouldn't. No no no.*

"Thanks, Uncle Richard," she said. "We'll be in town later today. Get proper once-overs at the hospital."

"I told you, it's just Richard." He placed a hand on her shoulder, his eyes clouding. "Glad you're in one piece." He peered through the window to where a paramedic picked up bits of Carter Moffat and put them in a body bag, looked about to say something else, then set off for the front door.

When he'd closed it behind him, Gwen said, "Jake. I've never needed a coffee more in my life."

He looked up from the hoodie he was contemplating wearing. As stiff and sore as he was, it had to be too much effort to get it on. "My turn to make it."

She nodded, then jerked her chin at the hoodie and stood. "First, let me help you with that."

Later, after the cops had finally gone and with dawn a glow in the east, Gwen slumped across the kitchen table, hands wrapped around her second cup of instant. When Jake had gone upstairs to use the bathroom, she had tossed the one he'd made and started over. Jake made terrible coffee.

She listened to him stomping around in his room above the living room, allowed flashes of memory to pepper her awareness: standing up there, hearing the gunshots that must have been Carter shooting at Eddie, peeking through the window to see a monster racing into her yard, climbing out the window. Carter drawing Eddie away from her.

I don't know who you were, Carter Moffat, but I hope you find peace.

The floor above creaked.

"What are you doing up there?" she called. The footsteps stopped for almost a full minute then moved into the hallway. The stairs squeaked as he came down. Seconds later, he limped along the hallway and leaned against the door jamb.

"A fair few scratches up there. In the carpet and the walls. And the door's smashed in."

"I know. I was there, remember?"

He came over and slipped the EpiPen from the table into his hoodie pocket. Then let something drop onto the table.

She recoiled from the clump of gray fur.

"Another souvenir from Eddie. Was on the window sill. Not sure how we're gonna explain things like that when the cops find them. Or the doors." He took the fur and dumped it in the trash can, shoving it down deep, and washed his hands in the sink. She'd buried the bullet she'd dug out of Jake in a compost bin in the backyard.

"We stick to the story," she said.

He dried his hands on a tea towel. A spot of blood showed through his hoodie where she'd dug the slug out. Richard was right: Jake needed a trip to hospital to get a proper job done, if only to minimize scarring. He had enough scars as it was.

"Jake. You need to know you're a good man."

He dropped his head. "Not enough. Not nearly good enough."

"Yes, good enough."

She drained her coffee and joined him at the sink, reaching across him to rinse the mug. He didn't withdraw. He smelled of sweat and blood and antiseptic.

"When you were a wolf that first time, you didn't hurt me," she said. "Last night, you did everything you could to protect me from Eddie. You could have left me and risked him coming here to get me. But you didn't. You helped that little girl Sophie. You shoot up every month just to protect the world around you from your curse." She turned about, butt against the bench, and stared hard into his eyes. Those beautiful, haunted, honey-caramel eyes. "If that's not a good man, I don't know what is."

He blinked back at her, skeptical.

She placed a hand on his arm. "As many black marks as you think there are against your name, you erase them as soon as they appear by the good that you do. The good that you *are*. Your momma would be proud of you."

He embraced her, pulling her head to his chest. She felt something under his shirt. Was that his Momma's brooch? Why was he wearing that?

"We both want the same thing, it seems, Mr Brennan. To make the world a better place. We must be crazy."

His chuckle was a deep rumble in his chest. "Two normal people like us, believin' in werewolves? We're crazy as hell, Dr Cheevey."

She snorted and pushed him away, batting him gently in his uninjured arm.

"Instant coffee sucks," Jake said. "We need tea."

"I'll do it. The English way, like Grandfather did it."

He stepped away as she dug the teapot out of a cupboard and grabbed a canister of loose leaf. She rinsed the pot and scooped tea into it, pondering her future.

What now?

She couldn't stay here. She'd have to sell this place. Maybe two days a week in Carrington working with Richard, and two in Detroit? Two days in private practice would provide a simple income, allowing her to do something good with her life the rest of the time. If Jake had opened her eyes to anything - anything apart from the existence of ancient curses and such - it was the needs of the homeless. Amidst that crowd were human beings, many of them kids, disadvantaged people who couldn't pay for the medical attention they had a right to.

Do no harm.

One could harm people as much by neglect as by malice. One could harm people by doing nothing.

The idea popped into her head fully formed and obvious and just plain *right*.

"I've made a decision," she told him, pouring hot water into the pot. "Angelo needs help with his mission." She placed the lid on so the tea could draw. "What, no comment?"

She turned. Jake wasn't there. She went into the living room, but he wasn't there either.

What ... the ... hell?

She trawled through her short-term memory. Had the stairs creaked? Had he returned upstairs? Had the front screen door opened and closed while she'd fiddled with the tea or was she imagining that? She'd been lost in her thoughts.

No, the stairs hadn't creaked, he hadn't gone up there. But now she thought hard, the screen door might have opened and closed.

She knew suddenly and clearly what he was doing.

She had the front door half-open before she stopped herself. Sure, she could run outside, try to catch him on the road. She *could* do that. Instead, she returned to the kitchen, gave the pot a turn to stir the brew and put one of the mugs back in the cupboard. She swallowed to clear the sudden lump in her throat, drove her hands deep in her pockets and leaned her ass on the bench. It was never going to be a hollywood ending, and Gwen Cheevey would survive without one.

"Tea for one, then," she said.

EPILOGUE:
January 22nd — Waxing Moon

Night's shadow had slipped across the world, erasing the narrow valley's features. The white of snow drifts and powder-coated bushes had long since faded to gray blurs, visible only because Jake's night sight was kicking in. He pressed his cheek against the chilled glass of the shack's single window and tried to make out the waxing moon through the clouds.

He wondered where Gwen was, what she was doing, who she was with - and he sighed, letting it go.

She had her life.

He had his.

She was safe now. He could only hope she was happy, too.

Tiny heartbeats pulsed from inside the cabin ceiling. Hibernating bats, he knew now, from his couple of months working in animal control. They preferred the warmth of a human habitat to that of a cave, snuggling up in the insulation and foraging out every two or three weeks to eat before the cold and the dearth of insect life drove them back.

He felt sorry for them.

i want to eat them!

He grunted in shock as the first tremor kicked him in the gut. The familiar burn started in his arms, pain gnawing his joints with blunted jaws.

He pressed his head harder against the glass. He couldn't see the moon, but he knew exactly where it was. And what it wanted for him. The Animal rose to meet its god, its lover. Images flooded his mind, impressions of running and hunting and slashing and ripping...

free me!

"Not this time, you sonofabitch."

He took the deepest breath he could and held it.

free me!

This time he would control it. He would bring the Animal to heel. He would find a way to be free.

free me!

Another tremor shook him and Jake clamped down hard.

ACKNOWLEDGEMENTS & NOTES

Some errors or untruths in this novel represent an author taking liberties, bending the truth to serve the story. Others, I'm sure, are simply errors.

That said, I owe profound thanks to several people who generously offered their expertise and experience to ground this novel and its characters in the real world.

A big shout out to Jonathan Pippenger, a good friend since our "daddy bloggers" days. Jonathan's patience with my frequent question-bombardments were crucial for my story building, as were his careful perusal of my first crappy draft, and his assistance in understanding Detroit and creating "Carrington".

Traci McKinley, Danielle Friedman, Jo Prentice and author DP Lyle taught me about the worlds of the Doctor, of the Nurse and of the Emergency Department. Ladies and gentleman, your help has been insightful, liberal and has enhanced my understanding of the world. One of the benefits of being a writer is the invitation into the "different" worlds of professionals like you.

Thanks to my novel buddies, EJ McLaughlin, Ian Welke (to whom I owe one of Gwen's lines) and Kevin Ikenberry. They read whole drafts and kicked my butt hard on several issues. They are wonderful authors in their own rights and I'm privileged to call them friends and colleagues. Similarly, I'm grateful to: authors Michel and Peter Cooper for late read-throughs of long passages; Dy Loveday, Aly Ware and Beth Cato for early comments on plotting; and a special *gracias* to Joseph D'Lacey, horror author extraordinaire, who mentored me through the early stage of this project and helped it see the light of day. I recommend googling these people and seeing what they've written…

To Jason Nahrung, whose editing polished the hell out of a rough diamond, a huge thank you for taking me and my work seriously.

My wonderful wife: thank you for not one but two "final" proofreads. And for partnering in my writing. I love you. I couldn't have asked God for better support and encouragement that you give me.

ABOUT THE AUTHOR

PETE ALDIN is an Australian-based writer and a member of the Australian Horror Writers Association.

His professional life has included empowering people with "disabilities", helping professionals shape their career and work-life balance, working with migrants and with youth, as well as designing courses and courseware for training companies.

He follows Chelsea FC in the English Premier League. He watches Breaking Bad over and over and over, plays FIFA games on xBox, and reads way too much when he should be writing. He owns a sonic screwdriver and a TARDIS.

His short fiction has found a home at publications including *Andromeda Spaceways Inflight Magazine*, Orson Scott Card's *Intergalactic Medicine Show*, *Niteblade* and Poise & Pen's *ABC Anthologies*. He has written for several parenting magazines including Kindred and Natural Parenting. He is the author of Doomsday's Child (a novel) and Illegal (a Kindle Short Story cowritten with Kevin Ikenberry).

Connect with Pete at www.facebook.com/PeteAldinAuthor and www.petealdin.com.

ONE LAST THING...

If you enjoyed this book, I'd be very grateful if you'd post a short review on Amazon and on Goodreads.

Your word-of-mouth support really makes a difference and your feedback helps make the next book even better.

Thanks again for your support!

Made in the USA
San Bernardino, CA
22 September 2018